The King's Mystic

Randi-Anne Dey

The King's Mystic
Copyright © 2023 by Randi-Anne Dey

Cover Design - R Dey
Original Mystic portrait - C Biagi
(With permission, modified by R Dey)
Beta readers - M Verronneau, M Harris, T Street
Editors - B Whittome, T Street
Portrait of Author - G Woodward

Disclaimer

This is a work of fiction. Unless otherwise indicated, all the names, characters, businesses, places, events, and incidents in this book are either the product of the author's imagination or used in a fictitious manner and bear no meaning to where they were placed within the book. Any resemblance to actual persons, living or dead, or actual events is purely coincidental.

The only exception is the guild and raiders of Honors Light, which was a friend's dying request that I place them in my book, to which I have honored. Where they are placed has no meaning, other than she wanted her guild written into my world and so I have done so.

This book contains sensitive or potentially triggering content involving violence and tastefully done romantic interactions. Reader discretion is advised for the chapters 'A Costly Mistake' (violence) and from 'Enchanted Beginnings.' (romance)

Tellwell Talent
www.tellwell.ca

ISBN
978-1-77941-236-2 (Hardcover)
978-1-77941-166-2 (Paperback)
978-1-77941-237-9 (eBook)

Dedication

This book is dedicated to those that have entered into my life, be they still in my life, passed through my life, or have crossed over to the other side. Thank you for enriching my world and making me who I am today.

Special Dedication to Loni Rose Jones – Gwynevere – Guild Master of Honors Light. May your sweet soul rest in peace. I am sorry I did not get this done in time for you to have a book in your hands. Gwynevere's motto – 'Everyone is welcome, no matter their skill. We turn no one away...Oh crumb.'

Table of Contents

Thanks

Thanks to my parents, Dia and Rob, for supporting me in all my crazy endeavors!

Thanks to my pups, Azlyn and Sandor, for putting up with hours at the computer writing.

Thanks to my neighbor Roger, for all the help he has given me while I was distracted with writing.

Thanks to all those that added to the process and creation of this book.

Ferfolk Ocean

Hontby

Slario

Oxfrost

Oblait

Sroni

The V

Westshore

Thetis

Teshem

Nantou

Pleta

Vline

Terrenwood Heights

Mala

The Heartless Sea

Grim Tun

Vidip

Rumtia

Roburg
Bay

Terreview

Lamador

Ewhela

Rixlen

Khotin

Introduction

K ING'S SEER.
  She can barely remember what her true name is, as that's all she has been called since she was nine years old when her parents sold her to the king to be his seer and left her there. Some days she wonders if they think about her, other days, she wonders what she did to deserve being sold to the king. Then there are days when she doesn't even remember they exist. She is the King's seer, and this is her tale.

Her parents told her they were going on a trip, one that would take several days, but it would be worth it in the end. You see, they were going to meet with the king, a real live king. They had a lavender dress made, with black embroidery and royal purple ribbon adorning it in all the right places. The dress only enhanced the pale lavender of her eyes, pale skin, framed with long straight black hair, making her look like the princess she should be. Little did she know, they had already made arrangements with the king for her to stay, for she is special. She could see snippets of the future, and the king's past seer had died. The winning applicant will be compensated handsomely should the seer prove her worth. The child was excited to see the castle, finding herself wondering what the king would be like as the stories of princes and knights that saved the princess from dragons had always excited her.

A Royal Encounter

"**I**S THERE A prince, Mama?"

"No, dear, I don't believe there is."

The child nods, growing thoughtful again. "What about knights? Are there knights that save the maidens from dragons?"

"There are knights, dear, but I doubt they fight the dragons. They just protect the king. Dragons, you see, live deep in the woods and mountains and don't come into the cities."

"Oh. I see."

"Don't you worry about it, dear. Just give the king a glimpse of the future when you see him and show him what gifts you were given."

"But what if he doesn't like what I see?"

"Try to see the nice stuff, dear."

"Yes, Mama."

"Read your book, dear. We will be there before you know it."

The child nods and curls up in the back of the wagon. She pulls a book of stories out of her bag and she sets about reading as they travel. On the third day of travel, the family arrives at the city gate of Teshem. The guards stop them, asking them to state their business.

"We are here to see His Majesty, King Zane."

The guards look them over before glancing at the child reading in the wagon. "Straight down the main road; wagon and horses at the stables on the left. The king's chamberlain sits near the front of the castle. He's the one you want to talk to if you have business with the king."

"Thank you very much."

The child tucks her book away, peering over the wagon's edge as it meanders through the streets, her eyes wide with awe at all the people moving around the streets. She has never seen more than a few people in one place at a time. She gazes at the dresses the ladies wear and tugs on her mother's skirts. "Can I wear pretty dresses like those, Mama?"

"Of course, dear. I am sure the king will provide you with fancy dresses."

She smiles, her eyes shifting from the dresses to the merchants selling their wares before drifting to the fighting rings they passed. She moves in the back of the wagon to keep her eyes on the rings for as long as she can. "Are those knights, Mama?"

"I don't think so, dear. I believe the knights remain in the castle, but I can't be certain. Come, let me fix your dress. We will be at the castle soon."

The child nods and moves to stand before her mother in the back of the wagon. Her mother adjusts her dress back into place, re-ties the bows, and tightens the lacings. She runs a few fingers through the child's hair, pulling a few strands off her face and tying them in a ribbon.

"There are so many people, Mama. It is hard to tell what I see."

"Yes, dear, though I do believe the castle will be quieter."

"Will I get to live in the castle?"

"It is part of the deal we made if you secure the hand of the seer."

"I hope I do well, Mama."

"I know you will, child. There are many out there that are frauds, but you are not one of them, and the king will see that."

"I love you, Mama."

"I love you too, dear, but this is for the family. When you finish your duties, you will return home to us."

"How long are my duties, Mama?"

"I believe they will be for a few years, five at the most, dear."

The child nods and turns as the wagon pulls up to the stables. She watches a young man run out of the barn and grab the reins. Her father jumps off the wagon, giving a nod to the stable hand before turning to assist his wife and her out of the wagon. Each parent takes one of her hands as they walk to the castle, her mother going over how to behave in front of the king.

The child struggles to listen to her mother as she looks up at the castle walls, noting the guards patrolling behind the crenellations and watching the sun glint off the armor. She turns forward as she feels a tug on her hand, stepping in beside her father as they move indoors. She looks around in wonder at all the decorations, the ivory floors with flowers inlaid in the corners, to the elaborate metal holders hanging on the walls with candles burning even in the middle of the day.

The child drops her gaze to the feet of the man leading them, hearing his plate sabatons clicking on the floor beneath him before she studies the back of his armor. She watches as it moves slightly, the plates like feathers on a bird, shifting when he shifts. She glances up at her parents, noting their stoic expressions as they step into the grand hall, and her hands tighten on theirs for a moment. She looks around, from the benches on the side walls to the tall ivory pillars that reach the ceiling, before her sight settles on the king sitting on a throne at the end of the room.

King Zane is tall, his long blonde hair pulled back in two braids and pinned behind him. Piercing green eyes stare at them, enhanced by black and green robes with gems sewn into the edges and the cuffs. A crown with matching jewels adorns his head and glints in the light as he turns his head. The throne is hand carved into a dragon; the head looms over the back and stares them down as the king does. Claws curl and provide the king's hands with places to rest, just as the feet frame the king.

King Zane

The child stares at the king before backing up a step. "I don't want to stay, Mama. I want to go home."

Her mother kneels down before her. "You can do this for us."

"Please don't make me stay."

"Enough." Her mother straightens her dress a bit. "It's only for a few years, sweetie. Just help the King see bad people."

She whispers softly. "But he is a bad people, Mama."

"Shh, none of that child. Now, let's go meet him and tell him what you see." Her mother takes her hand, and they approach the king, bowing as they stop. "Greetings, Your Majesty."

"Greetings Madam Boxxe. This is the child that has visions?"

"Yes, Sire. This is her."

He lifts his hand, gesturing her forward. "Come here, child."

She looks up at her mother, who gives her a nod and pushes her forward. She stumbles a bit as she approaches him cautiously, fear embedded deep in her pale lavender eyes as she stands before him.

Zane studies the child for a moment, noting the shake to her body and the nervousness in her eyes as she stares at him. He leans forward and speaks to her softly. "What do you see, child?"

"Lots, Mister King."

"Tell me one thing."

"You don't like dragons."

He sighs, disappointment in his expression as he leans back on the throne. His eyes drift to the guard that led them in, gesturing for him to approach and remove the child and her parents. "Yes, everyone knows that."

"A dragon ate your mama, and your papa was mad at you."

Zane holds his hand up, stopping the guard, before he leans in again. "What did you say?"

"That the dragon ate your mama…"

"How do you know that, child? No one knows that."

"I see it. The dragon, he bit you on the leg, and your mama saved you, but then the dragon, he bit her. Your papa was mad cause you hid under the wagon. The dragon got away, but your papa killed him later and keeps him in the castle."

"There is no dragon in this castle."

"Yes, there is, with your mama."

"My mother is buried in the graveyard out back."

"No Mister King. Her maid is. She's downstairs with the dragon."

He narrows his eyes on her for arguing with him. "Only the dungeons are downstairs."

"No, they are in a special room your papa had built."

"Where is this special room?"

"In the bedroom."

Zane laughs at the audacity of the child. "I sleep in the bedroom; I think I would know if a dragon is there."

The child's eyes glow ever so softly. "It is. The third book, the third shelf; you will see. It's full of magic lights but different than the magic flames on the way in."

The Sight Tested

ZANE RISES FROM his throne, glancing at her parents before he takes her hand. "Come, let's see if what you speak of is true."

The child flinches slightly at his firm grip, her eyes pleading with her parents to stop him while she is pulled from the grand hall. "Mister King, I walk slow, please."

He pauses a moment to look her over, noticing just how short she is. He gives a nod and slows his pace as he winds through the castle passages, up a grand set of stairs to a long hallway. Exquisite paintings hang on the walls, and ivory pedestals line the hall, each holding some object of value. He pushes open double doors at the end of the hall and steps in as she pulls back on his grip. She whispers softly as she stares at the king-size bed in the center of the room. "Mama says I am not allowed in anyone's bedroom but my own."

"Do you promise to stay here and not run back to your parents?"

"Yes, Mister King."

Zane nods and releases her, moving to the bookshelf that he has never had time for. He studies the book covers, running his fingers over their spines as he touches the third book on the third shelf. He looks around, half expecting something to happen, then sighs as he pulls the book off the shelf. He hears a soft grinding as the wall next to him shifts, shock filling him as an entrance opens into a passage that descends downward. He places the book on a nearby table as he looks in, lights flickering along the ceiling, floating around like fireflies. He steps into the narrow corridor, following its long spiral down, well below the castle.

At the bottom, the passage widens to a set of double doors, which are carved with an image of his mother and an inscription; *Here lies Rimorhia and the death that took her from me too soon.* Zane pauses, glancing back up the passage, before he pushes the doors open and steps into the room. He gasps in fear as the nightmare from his youth stares back at him, feeling a shake to his body as he approaches it. He runs his fingers over the orange scales before turning to the coffin in the center of the room and seeing his mother's name upon it. He stares at the casket, placing both his hands on it as he kneels beside it, resting his forehead on the cool wood while he ponders the child upstairs. After a few minutes, he rises and makes his way back up the passage, his thoughts in turmoil as he steps back into the bedroom. His eyes land on the book. He picks it up, and places it back on the shelf, watching as the door closes after him as if it was never there. Zane turns to the child, sitting in the hallway and playing with the ribbons on her dress.

"Child."

She looks up, "Yes, Mister King?"

"How old are you?"

"Nine, Mister King."

"Hmm, come, let's return to your parents." He leads the child back through the winding passages in silence. They enter the grand hall, and he lets her go, watching as she runs off to hug her mother. "I will take her. Randolph, inform Kivu to bring the agreed-upon gold for her."

She clings to her mother, whispering softly. "Please, Mama, I want to go home with you."

Her mother shakes her head, moving to detangle her daughter from her legs. "NO, sweetie, you are to stay here with the king and make us proud."

Tears spring to the child's eyes as she struggles to maintain her grip. "But Mama, I don't want to."

Her father narrows his eyes on his daughter. "Enough of this! Now behave!"

She nods and looks down for a moment, struggling with her fears versus her father's anger before turning back to face the king. Another guard walks in with Randolph, carrying a silver tray with an embroidered sack sitting upon it. The child's eyes stare in horror at the sack as she backs up a step. "NO! YOU can't kill them. I won't stay if you do. I will run away!"

Zane's eyes widen ever so briefly before narrowing at her. "What makes you say I will kill them?"

"I see it in my story. When they are on their way home, just past the bridge. You will make them look like bandits and take your gold back."

"Interesting. I won't kill them, child. I promise."

She narrows her eyes, a soft glow flickering in them for a moment. "Yes, you will."

"Come here, child."

She shakes her head and wraps her arms around her mother's leg. "No, I don't want to."

Her mother gives a worried glance to her husband before pulling her daughter off and kneeling down at the child's level. "Go talk to the King, sweetie."

The child catches the stern look in her mother's eyes that does not match the softness of her voice. She looks down to the ground as she turns before raising her gaze to the king, and walking hesitantly back to the throne.

Zane motions her closer until she is standing a foot from him. "Tell me how your sight works."

The child glances back to her parents, who both nod before returning her attention to the king. "Sometimes, when I see someone or something, I get stories in my head that tell me things. Sometimes the stories are just them making food or walking. Other times, the stories are like I told you, where you was bitten by a dragon and that the dragon is downstairs. Sometimes I don't see stories 'cause themes are hidden, and I have to search for them, but it doesn't always work. Sometimes they just have no stories, and sometimes there is more than one story, like with you." She lowers her gaze as a blush crosses her cheeks.

"More than one? As in, you saw other stories for me?"

She keeps her eyes focused on his boots. "Yes, Mister King."

"What was the other story you saw?"

"Something Mama said I was not allowed to do, or I would lose my powers like you were doing with the church lady."

Zane has the grace to blush, giving a nod. He looks to the other guard standing nearby, who suddenly avoids his gaze. "And my Chamberlain, Kivu, has a story to tell?"

"No, Mister King. The bag does. It will return here, and my parents will be dead."

"Can these stories ever be changed?"

"I don't know, Mister King."

He gestures for Kivu to put the bag down before her, watching as she avoids looking at it. "Look at the bag again, child; tell me what you see."

"I don't want to."

"Trust me, child."

She avoids the bag, looking instead into the king's eyes as hers glow a moment. She glances down at the bag, seeing the story shift before her eyes and her parents making it home with the bag of gold.

"What do you see, child?"

The child frowns slightly, staring at the bag and searching for the old story but not finding it. "I see my parents on their farm."

"Good. Now take it back to your parents and say your goodbyes."

She nods, picks up the bag carefully, and moves back to her parents. She hands it over to her father before hugging her mother tight. "I love you, Mama. You will come to visit, right?"

Her mother hugs her back. "Of course we will, dear."

The child backs up a step and gives her father a quick hug, tears slipping from her eyes as she knows she will never see her parents again.

A New Step

ZANE WATCHES THE farewells, seeing the glisten of tears on her face while her parents are led out of the main hall by Kivu, another guard replacing him next to Randolph. "Alright child, let's find you a maid and a place to stay, shall we?"

She looks up, tears shining in her eyes. "Yes, Mister King."

He moves forward and drops down on one knee before her. "You will see your parents again, child."

"No, Mister King, they will stay on their farm and forget about me."

"I am certain they won't forget about you."

"They will. They did not want me. That is why they sold me to you."

Zane ponders her for a moment, thinking her wise beyond her years but understanding she is a nine-year-old child and not an adult that is seeking some measure of approval. "Well, you are wanted here. Now come, this is a new step in your life. Let's make the most of it, shall we?"

She uses her sleeve to dry her eyes, nodding at him as he rises, and follows him out of the main room, her eyes glancing back to the two guards that follow them this time. He leads her up two sets of stairs, through more winding passages, before stopping at a door and opening it. She looks up at the king as he gestures for her to step inside, hesitating as she stares at the room.

"It's your room, go ahead, child."

"My room?"

"Yes, this is where you will stay while you live at the castle."

She steps into the room and looks around in wonder. "It's as big as our whole house."

He chuckles as he steps in after her, offering a hand. "Come, this door leads out to the gardens, and the other door is your own private bathing chamber that you can look at after."

She takes his hand and follows him down the stairs behind the door, out to a high walled garden with a locked gate inset in one wall. A winding path circles around it with a few benches that sit as places to rest. "This is yours as well."

"Mine?"

"Yes, the gardener Patrycia tends to it, so you just need to enjoy it."

"I can come here any time?"

"Almost. In the morning, I hold council with my men and my people for about four hours. I expect you to be there with me, standing behind my throne."

"Four hours? That's a long time. Do I tell you if I see a story?"

"Yes, and I understand that you are nine, so you will have your own chair for a few years until you can stand for that long. If you see a story, you are to place your hand on the throne, and I will address it when I am done speaking."

"Yes, Mister King."

"Tomorrow, I will have maids brought forth that you may look at to choose from. I will also have a tailor measure you for outfits, as I understand this is your only good dress."

"Yes Mister King."

"For now, Martha will attend to you. You will take meals either with me, or in your room. For my court, you will have your maid ready you, and a guard will knock on your door to retrieve you. You are not to leave your chambers unless you are with a guard of my choosing to ensure that you stay safe. There will be the odd day I will require you for the afternoon as well but those are not often."

She nods, following him back up the stairs to her room. "Yes Mister King."

"You have already proven you have the gift; now, let's make this kingdom great again."

"Yes, Mister King," offering a hesitant smile up at him.

"Good. I will leave you to get settled as I have things to do. Breakfast will arrive at seven in the morning, lunch at high noon after court, and dinner in the evening. If there is anything you don't like, please let the maid know so the cook can avoid plating it for you."

"I have only had our farm's food, and I liked all that except the trees."

"The trees?"

She holds her hands together and measures about an inch apart. "Yes, they are white and green trees. They taste bad."

He laughs as he heads to the door. "Ah, broccoli and cauliflower. I will let them know; no trees on your plate."

"Thank you, Mister King." She relaxes at his laughter, watching as some of the darkness that she has seen from him fade away.

"I will see you in the morning, child." He smiles her way, giving her a nod as he closes the door behind him. He stops to speak to the two guards following him. "I want a guard at this door at all times, as well as two patrolling the outside walls of her garden. This child is valuable, not only in the fact it cost me a thousand gold but that she truly has the gift of sight, and I don't want her stolen." He chuckles, one that would have chilled a person to the core of who they are. "Her parents have no idea of what this child is really worth. I would have paid ten times their request to get her power."

"You don't want us to retrieve that gold, Sire?"

He looks at the closed door, where he knows his asset is exploring her room. "No, I suspect she will see it as she did in the main hall and shut down. I need her power to grow and for her to trust me enough that she is willing to share all the stories that come to her. Part of ensuring that happens is for her to see her parents return home with the gold. She is young enough to shape, and with her behind us, we will go far in securing a legacy the other kingdoms will fear, as well as eradicating all the dragons from the lands. Now, what I do want is for her parents to have guards on their journey home, to ensure that actually happens so she knows they are safe and stays happy here. We need to make her believe this place is where she belongs. Is that understood?"

Randolph's eyes widen in shock. "Yes, Sire, I believe they are staying at the Red Boar for the night, as it's a three-day journey back to their farm."

"Good. Send a few guards to patrol the inn and six to travel with them. That should deter any bandits from thinking they are an easy mark."

"Right away, Sire." He bows and heads off in another direction.

Zane turns. "Alvero, you find guards to protect her. I want the same ones on her at all times. Pick eight of your best men and rotate them on watches. If someone is sick for the day, the replacement is one of the ones chosen. No one but you and your men are to watch this child. Is that understood?"

Alvero bows. "Yes, Sire, shall I stay here for now?"

"No, no one knows she is here, so she should be safe for the night, but people will. When her power grows, they will seek her out. At that point, we can re-evaluate how many people watch her rooms. Send messages out that we require a maid for a child. On duty at all times to start and will stay in the adjoining room as I suspect the child will suffer homesickness in the coming months, and I want that dealt with efficiently. Perhaps a motherly type of maid that will replace the one she lost. Now, send Martha to me; I wish to speak with her."

"Yes, Sire, I will relay the messages and come back to stand guard."

He pauses. "Oh, and find her some toys or books or whatever children of her age do." He strides away from the door, heading to his own chamber to ponder how he can use her gift to his own advantage.

She watches the door close behind him, hearing the soft murmur of conversation behind the door, but ignores it as she looks around the room. She moves to the dressers, opening the drawers, finding them empty, before peering into the armoire. A few books line the bookshelves next to a desk and she picks them up, looking them over, unable to read any of them. She places them back before heading to the bathing chamber, pushing the door open as her eyes widen on the tub in the center of the room. She stands on her tiptoes to peer into it, before moving to the tray nearby, smelling all the pretty soaps. In the corner behind the screen is her privy, surprised that it is indoors as the one at the farm was in its own building. She squishes the fluffy towels down, having never seen such a thick one, before moving to the washing bowl. A small bucket of water sits nearby, and she dips her hands in, washing up, before drying off with the towel, giggling at the plushness. She moves back to the bed and crawls up onto it, jumping a few times at its softness before curling up in the multitude of pillows, already missing her parents as she drifts off to sleep.

A few hours later, she is startled awake by a knock on the door. She glances around the room in confusion before recalling that her parents had left her there. A few tears creep from her eyes as she looks at the door. "Who is it?"

"It's Martha, dear. The King sent me; may I come in?"

"Yes, if you want."

The door opens, and an older lady stands there, a slight scattering of wrinkles lining her pale blue eyes and lips. Strands of soft gray mingle with the light brown hair. She is dressed in a simple gown of pale green, with a bit of embroidery around the neck and sleeves. "It's your room, child. It's only if you wish them to enter. You have the right to say no, be they guards, maids, or guests of the castle. Remember that. If you don't want them in the room, they don't come in. If they press the issue, you let the King know, and he will deal with them." She steps into the room with a hint of a limp as a younger servant carries a tray of food in and sets it on the table before bowing and leaving, closing the door behind her. Martha moves to sit on the chair at the table, "Now come, let me take a look at the King's seer."

Miss Martha

"Yes, Ma'am." She slides off the bed and approaches the lady, pulling at her dress a moment to straighten it, knowing if her mama was here, she would get scolded for sleeping in it.

Martha reaches out, placing a hand under her chin, looking into her eyes a moment, before turning her around to look her over. "Well, you are a pretty little thing. When you are older, the boys will be falling all over you. The King is going to have his hands full."

She shakes her head. "Mama said I am not allowed to see boys."

Martha chuckles. "Oh my dear, in this castle, you will see many, but yes, no boys are to enter this room unless it's the King himself, and even then, your maid should be here with you. It is not proper for any man to be in a lady's chamber without a chaperone unless she is married to that man. I have already scolded the King for showing you this room without one present."

Her eyes widen slightly. "You scolded him? Are you allowed to do that?"

"No child, I am not, but I do it anyhow. I am probably the only one who can get away with it because I was his maid when he was a boy."

She nods, smiling up at the woman before her, hugging her tightly. "I like you. Can you be my maid?"

Martha pulls her close, patting her back gently, waiting until she steps back in her own time. "I run the castle servants now, child, but we will find you a maid you like. Does that work?"

"Yes, Ma'am."

"Good. The King tells me you see stories, so if you see any bad stories from the maids I show you, you just let me know."

"Yes, Ma'am."

"Now, eat your dinner; I will return later to draw you a bath and get you a sleeper so that you may sleep properly. Tomorrow will be a busy day for you. I will be here to prepare you for court in the morning. Then you can eat lunch with the King in the dining chamber. After that, we will bring maids for you to look at. Once that is done, we will return to your room and have a tailor measure you so that you have some casual dresses and court dresses. Does that sound good?"

"Yes, Ma'am. I hope I do good."

"You already have, child. Now, this old lady needs to get the castle organized. I will return in a couple of hours." Martha pats her head gently and leaves her to eat in peace.

She clambers up onto the chair and looks at the stacks of food on her plate, having never seen so much at a time. She tastes a bit of it, thinking whoever cooked this is far better than her parents. She happily eats most of it, feeling content and full as she swivels in the chair. Her eyes land on the door to the gardens, deciding she wants a closer look. She pushes the door open and runs down the stairs out into the evening sun. She flits between all the flowers and the trees, noticing that she could climb one as she clambered up into its branches to sit, peering over the wall into the city beyond, watching the people move about.

The Castle Adapts

MARTHA MOVES BACK to the King's chamber, knocking lightly on the door, before entering at his command. Her eyes find him standing on the balcony, and she moves up to stand next to him. "Your Majesty."

"Martha, so what do you think?"

"She seems sweet enough." Martha's eyes glance to the gardens below as she follows his gaze to the child exploring the plants, smiling as she climbs the arbutus tree in the center. "I suspect she will be a handful when she comes of age."

"Yes, she is quite exquisite even now with her light skin, lavender eyes, and black hair. I have never seen anyone quite like it. She certainly does not look like her parents, who pale in comparison, so I have to wonder where she got her looks from."

"If she has mystic blood, that will explain the lavender eyes, and that can skip generations. As her power grows, her eyes will grow more vibrant purple. Mystics were long thought extinct. How did you find her?"

"Her parents. I guess they heard I lost a seer, sent a letter via carrier, describing their daughter and her sight, asking for a thousand gold and they would bring her to me. As soon as I heard she had lavender eyes, I knew I had to meet her. Her stories, as she calls them, are accurate." He shifts his gaze back to the wall behind him before returning to the child swinging her legs while in the tree, peering over the wall. "We might need to take that tree out."

"Sire, she's a child, and a farm girl. She grew up climbing trees and will be rough around the edges for a while. Leave her that joy while you can, and we will train her to be a lady that does not climb trees."

"I suppose. I am more worried that if she can see out, assassins can see in."

"You have guards patrolling; she will be fine. In a few years, if she's still climbing that tree, then either raise the height of the wall or cut it down. Right now is the age she needs to be happy with you, to give you what you want. If you go cutting the tree down, you will push her away, and you don't want a mystic angry with you, no matter their age. A lot of their powers are tied to emotions."

"Yes, I could see the fear in her eyes as she looked at me, so I know she saw more than she told me."

Martha nods. "I suspect she did, and while I disagree with most of your practices, I made my promise to your father to always be here for you and speak honestly. A true mystic will have seen your jaded past, so you need to show her that you are worth supporting. Can you be good for a few years?"

He narrows his eyes on his maid. "Of course, I can be good. I am the King; I can portray anything I want my populace to see."

Martha smiles. "You don't need to convince me; I know who you are, and so does that child. The populace already believes you to be good. What you need to do is convince her you have changed from the dark past we both know she saw."

"Did you convince her to like you?"

"Of course, she showed no fear of me. She even hugged me and held me close for a few minutes asking me to be her maid, but I don't have the same past as you."

Zane's eyes flare as he turns, grabbing her by the throat and lifting her off the ground, glaring at her, angry at her words but knowing she is correct and not wanting to admit it. He stares into her blue eyes as her hands come up to his, studying them for a moment before releasing her. "Yes, I had to forgo taking my gold back just to keep her happy enough to stay as she saw me kill her parents."

Martha rubs her throat with a sigh. "She will be worth more than the gold you spent. Your worry should be that word will spread, and her parents will want her back, selling her stories to whoever will pay once they figure out what they lost. They could have made thousands by exploiting her gift, just as I am sure you will."

Zane shakes his head, looking back out over the garden. "The child stated she would never see them again as they would stay on the farm and forget about her."

"Interesting."

"When they were in the grand hall, the only emotion shown was from the child herself. Her parents seemed only interested in the gold they requested for me to take her off their hands. Even their farewell was a quick hug."

Martha ponders it for a moment. "Perhaps they did not know how to deal with a mystic. A lot of people believe those magical in nature are aberrations, so they could be that way of thinking. Either way, I suggest you check in every so often, perhaps someone visits the farm to ask questions about their family. See if they mention having a daughter as the King's seer. It would better prepare you if they do decide to come back for her."

Zane nods. "Thank you, Martha. You are my sane right hand as always."

Martha chuckles. "Of course, and if the child asks, I scolded you for being in her room without a chaperone. Make sure next time you bring a maid; we don't need her learning men can come freely into her room."

He chuckles. "Oh, she already knows to stay away from boys because, apparently, she saw one of my dalliances. She stated quite clearly she wasn't allowed to do what I was doing or she would lose her powers."

Martha's eyes widen, appalled. "She saw that?"

"She did."

Martha shakes her head. "Yes, I foresee that you are going to have a handful with that child, Sire."

He smiles. "Are you a seer now, Martha? Could I have saved a thousand gold and have you standing behind my throne?"

She gives a bow, teasing him gently. "Only when I need to be, and that would not work. I mean, however would I keep this castle running if I had to stare at your back all morning? Now, on that note, if you are done with me, I need to go set up schedules and get back to the child to prepare her for bed. You know, you could have picked a less busy maid to deal with her."

Zane reaches up to touch her cheek. "You are the only one I would trust with her, Martha. Find one that is like you to look after her. Make sure there are no stories about her from either the populace or the child."

"I will, Sire." She gives another bow before turning and heading from the room.

He turns his attention to the child, watching her remain in the tree before clambering down to chase the butterflies that flitted about the garden, making a mental note to have the tailor make some play clothes; something he was never afforded. After an hour, his gaze follows the child heading indoors, wondering how in less than a day, a child could drastically change his life, grumbling a bit as he turns back into his room.

After about thirty minutes of pacing, he leaves his room, striding to the dungeons below, into the room that he kept there as part of his daily joys. His gaze lands on the prisoners that are strapped to the torture devices, the moans of pain filling his heart with delight. He growls in frustration as he stalks forward and unleashes the first one, dragging the prisoner to a cell and throwing him into it.

The guard on duty stares at him in shock. "Sire? They have not done their punishment yet."

Zane snarls at the guard, causing him to back up a step. "I realize that, but upstairs is a child-seer that I need to trust me, so things will have to change for a short time. Included in that is no torture simply because I feel like it, as I am quite certain she saw it."

The guard stammers, "Yes, Sire, would you like help to unstrap them then?"

"Yes, the faster we get them into cells, the better. Also, send a runner to fetch a healer, just enough so that they don't die."

"Are you certain the child can see this, Sire?"

"No, but Martha suspects she's a mystic. So she will, if not today, then tomorrow, or the next day; it's only a matter of time. She saw something that scared her, and I can't have that yet. Not while she's young enough to be influenced."

The guard stops unstrapping the victim to stare at the king before bowing his head, "Like a REAL Mystic, Sire?"

"Yes." He assists the guard in releasing the other four and moving them back to their cells, locking them in. Once they are done, he turns to the guard. "Send Dunivan to my war room when he returns this evening. I will need to speak with him. And close this room up... for now."

"Yes, Sire, as you wish, Sire. I will let him know as soon as he returns, Sire."

Zane leaves the dungeons, winding his way down the halls, pausing at the child's door for a moment before continuing to the war room. He looks over the maps he laid out there with his spies in the places they need to be. He moves to the table nearby, pouring out a whiskey, and downs it fast, refilling it as he turns back to his table, feeling the warmth fill his belly. He narrows his eyes, as he sweeps all the figures off and onto the floor in anger, glaring at them scattered around his feet.

"Sire?"

He turns, his eyes full of fury. "Dunivan, you are back earlier than expected."

"Yes, Sire, we did not find who we were looking for. We will resume the hunt in the morning." His eyes stray to the figures on the floor.

"When you find them, place them in the cells to rot."

"Not the room, Sire?"

"No, apparently, that needs to stop for a time."

"Stop? I don't understand, Sire."

He shakes his head as he downs the whiskey in his hand, sinking into the chair behind him. "Martha thinks I need to be good for a few years."

"Good, Sire?"

"Yes, good. As in no torture, behave, that sort of thing. The stuff I present to the kingdom. Good."

"Pardon me for saying so, but what does Martha know? She's not King and does not rule the kingdom. You do, Sire."

Zane rolls his eyes. "Yes, and ruling the kingdom is different from who I am. I bought a seer this morning. One that can see one's nature, and in order for her to trust me, I need to be good."

Dunivan frowns. "Bought? I thought your last seer was on the payroll as I am Sire."

He chuckles. "Indeed, this one is only nine years old, Dunivan. I bought her from her parents."

His eyes widened in disbelief. "Nine? Are you certain her parents were telling you the truth that she's a seer?"

He looks at his empty glass. "Quite, she has already given two accurate predictions."

"Her parents could have done the research, Sire, and told her what to say just to get the gold." He moves to the whiskey bottle, taking it back to refill the king's glass.

"No, the stories, as she calls them, were ones no one knew, including myself. Secrets that died with my father." He takes a drink of whiskey.

"I don't understand Sire; if they died with your father, how can the sights be proven?"

"Apparently, there is a secret room in this castle, and she knew about what was in said room."

Dunivan arches his eyebrows skeptically. "And she is nine and saw this?"

"Yes, Martha believes she's a mystic as she has lavender eyes. It would explain her power, even at the age she is."

"I see. So what are you going to do, Sire?"

He looks up at the captain of his guards. "I pretend to be good and slow down my plans to take over and rule all the kingdoms."

"Will she see through it?"

"Let's hope not, Dunivan. I would hate to have her killed because she doesn't comply with my *requests*."

"She's nine, Sire; just make her comply."

"If only it were that simple. She has power, a power I want. If I force her, she will shut that power down. If I kill her, I won't have that power, and chances of finding another mystic are rare, especially when they are thought to be extinct. No, I NEED her to trust me, to follow me blindly, without a hand of force, until it's too late for her to turn back. In order for that to happen, I must portray myself as someone she wants to trust, and thus, as Martha so kindly put it, be good."

"Well, Sire, if anyone can do it, you can."

Zane rises, placing his glass down and giving a nod to Dunivan. "Continue your hunt; the thief should still be caught. Leave your spies in place. I still want information as to what's happening in the other kingdoms. I will speak with you again tomorrow night."

A New Life Begins

MARTHA KNOCKS ON the door softly and enters the room, carrying a small, covered basket. She looks over the child sitting on the bed, a small pillow in her hand as she rolls it around in her lap. "Is everything alright, child?"

"Yes, I just have nothing to do. Mama kept my book about knights and dragons, and I can't read the books on the shelf 'cause they have strange writings, and there is nothing in the dressers to play with. Though I played in the garden for a bit. There are lots of butterflies out there to chase. I even sat in a tree and could see some people moving outside the wall."

Martha places the basket on the table next to the door. "I will have some books you can read and toys to play with brought up in the morning while you are at court. Now, come, let's get you out of this fancy dress, bathed, and into the sleeper I borrowed from a maid's daughter."

She nods, placing the pillow aside as she follows Martha into the bathing chamber. She stands still as Martha undoes her lacings and slips the dress off, folding it and placing it on the table next to her. "Don't we need buckets of water? Mama always had Papa bring in buckets."

"No child, the King had magics placed in here, along with a few other rooms in the castle." Martha moves to a small silver circle at the edge of the tub, hovering a hand over it for a moment as it starts to glow. She runs her finger along the outer ring as different colors appear. "Each one of these colors does something. Blue fills the tub." Martha holds a finger on blue until she feels the tub is full enough for the child.

"Now, that is cold water; to heat it, you want red, but we need to be very careful as it can get hot fast." Martha places a hand in the water while the other touches red, ensuring the temperature does not get too hot. "If it gets too hot for you, yellow will empty it, and just re-add some blue. But you won't have to worry about it for a few years, as you will have a maid drawing a bath for you."

She gasps softly as she watches the tub magically fill with water, giving a nod at Martha's words, bouncing between watching the glowing circle and the water. "I like this better than carrying buckets."

Martha laughs. "As do I, child. I wish all the rooms had this. Now, let's get you into that water. Did you want to pick a scented soap?"

She nods, pulling her chemise off, waiting as Martha lifts her over the edge of the tub and settles her in, laughing as she splashes at the water. "I smelled them earlier. I like the blue one best."

"Blue one it is."

Martha hands the bar of soap to her, picking the chemise and undergarments off the floor where she dropped them, and carries them back to the bedroom, placing them on the dresser. Martha moves over and locks the garden door, continuing to the balcony doors and closing them as well, knowing it would do no good for her to catch a chill. She returns to the basket she brought and carries it to the bed, pulling the warm nightgown out and laying it on the bed before tucking the heated stones that were rolled in it under the covers. Once she is done setting the room up, Martha returns to the child, smiling at her delight in the bubbles the soap created in the water. "Alright, child, let's get you rinsed and into bed; you have a busy day tomorrow."

"Yes, Ma'am." She stands up carefully in the tub as Martha pours lukewarm rinse water over her. She lifts her out, and dries her off with a towel, then leads her into the bed chamber. She dresses her in the sleeper and lifts her into the bed, tucking her in. "Now, if you need me, ring the bell by the door. I will be right next door tonight."

"Yes, Ma'am. Thank you."

"You're welcome; sleep tight." Martha watches the child pull the tiny pillow into her arms, curling up with the covers tightly clutched in her hands. She sighs inwardly, hoping that she doesn't lose the innocence and sweetness that she has, but also knowing a court life and the king's life is likely to taint her. Martha slips silently from the room and heads to the adjoining room, settling in for the night herself. She wakes the next morning, feeling a measure of surprise that she did not disturb her, knowing most children staying in a new place away from their parents would have. She rises and does her morning routine, setting the room up for the new maid that will be moving in this afternoon. Once she is certain the room is ready, she leaves, heading to the child's room. She knocks softly, hearing the soft "*come in*," and opens the door. Her eyes move to the bed, seeing it already made, albeit not well, but made nonetheless, finding the child sitting at the table, pillow in her hand, dressed in her purple dress. "Child, you did not need to do that."

"Mama made me every morning before I was allowed food. Will I get food this morning?"

Martha frowns slightly. "Of course, you will get food. Did the King not tell you when breakfast is?"

"He said seven, but he didn't say whether I had to make my bed or not, so I did. And I don't know when seven is exactly, so I woke up with the light like I had to with Mama to get food."

"You've been sitting here since dawn?"

"I guess so, Ma'am."

She moves over to the child, gesturing for her to stand up as she kneels before her, straightening her dress and retying the ribbons into perfect bows. "You are the King's seer, child. You don't have to make your bed. The maid will do it for you, and you will get fed every morning, whether you do or not. Is that understood?"

"Yes, Ma'am."

"As well, you may sleep past dawn. When the maid arrives, she will wake you up with enough time to get ready and eat before the King requires you."

"Yes, Ma'am."

Martha touches her cheek gently, seeing the conflict in her eyes at the new rules, wondering just what her parents were like. She gently takes the pillow out of her hands and places it on the table. "I know this is a lot to handle, but I will be here if you need help. You will also have a personal maid you can talk with. Now, since you are already dressed, you may come with me to the kitchens and eat there while I set about scheduling staff." She rises to her feet, takes the child's hand, and leads her out of the room. The guard sitting at the door stands, following along behind them as they wind their way down through the castle. The kitchen is bustling with activity as people move about it, all turning to give a curious stare at the child as she is placed at the table. "Here, I will get you some juice to start."

"Thank you, Ma'am."

The guard moves to the wall and leans up against it, out of the way of the workers, keeping his eye on any that get too close to the girl.

Martha places a freshly squeezed orange juice in front of her, sitting next to her with her parchments as she outlines to those in the kitchen what they need to do.

The child stares at the juice, pulling it close to look at it, before glancing at Martha, who gives her a smile, tasting a tiny bit before returning her smile and taking a bigger drink. One of the servants places a plate of food in front of her, bacon and eggs like she saw on the farm but rarely had. She looks up. "For me? But that's Mama and Papa's food. I am supposed to have oatmeal and bread."

The servant pauses, glancing at Martha, catching the slight shake of her head before giving a slight bow and returning to her work.

Martha smiles at the child, reaching out to pat her hand gently. "Remember, child, you are the King's seer. You are in better standing than your parents and can eat what you want. If you want bacon and eggs, then eat it. If you want oatmeal, I am certain we can have some made."

She leans over and whispers. "I have never had it. What if I don't like it?"

Martha chuckles. "I am certain you will, but if you don't, we will make you what you like."

She looks down at the food, picking up the bacon with her fingers, causing a few in the kitchen to gasp in shock, her gaze lifting to them before moving to Martha.

"It's alright dear, but next time use the fork that's there."

She looks down at the silverware and picks up a fork. "Yes, Ma'am. Mama and Papa always picked up meat strips."

"Most do, but there are standards here in the castle. Gossip will spread if you use your fingers."

"Yes, Ma'am." She takes a bite of the bacon, her eyes widening in delight at the taste, bringing a round of giggles from the kitchen staff, who earn a stern look from Martha as they quickly resume their duties.

Martha watches the child for a moment as she samples everything on her plate, each one earning its own expression, before returning to her reading and scheduling. Partway through the meal, a guard comes running into the kitchen, scattering the servants there. "Miss Martha, the King would like to see you; apparently, the seer is … Not missing?"

"Of course, she's not missing Trevyr."

"What is she doing here?"

Martha looks up from her papers with a sigh. "Eating breakfast, of course. I have work to do, and she's under my care until we find her a maid. Here I can do my work and watch her. Now, what is the King doing at her door at this time of the morning?"

Trevyr shakes his head. "He was walking the halls and noticed the guard missing from his post and her door open. He saw the garden door still locked, but she was not in the room. He is not happy."

The kitchen staff turn at the clattering of a fork on a porcelain plate as the child starts to slip off the chair. Martha grabs her hand, stopping her. "He is not mad at you, child. The King will be mad at me; sit, eat."

She whispers softly. "He's mad; he broke my room."

Martha reads the fear in the child's expression, turning to the guard. "Does she speak the truth?"

Trevyr looks at the child, shaking his head, "How does she know?"

Martha snaps, anger in her voice. "She's the King's seer. What did he do to her room?"

Trevyr pauses, backing away from Martha's anger. "I am not at liberty to say; you have to ask him."

Martha rises, slapping her papers down on the table. "I intend to. You stay here, child; finish your breakfast." Her eyes shift to the guard standing nearby. "Alvero, watch over the child. Make sure she finishes breakfast and try NOT to scare her. Where is he?"

"I left him in her room, Miss Martha."

"Fine, like I don't already have enough on my plate today." Martha leaves the kitchen at a pace far faster than she should be moving at her age.

She stalks to the seer's room, her eyes blazing as she enters, seeing the mess he created. The broken chairs, the toppled dresser with a few drawers splintered nearby. "Have you any idea what you have done, Your Majesty?"

Zane turns in anger, "Where is she?"

"In the kitchens, and she's seen your temper. YOU MUST keep it in check!"

He stalks toward her, grabbing her and slamming her into a wall, flinching slightly. "YOU have no right to talk to me like that!"

She grimaces in pain as she hits the wall, her eyes narrowing in anger as she slaps him across the face, feeling the sting as she did. "I HAVE every right to if you want the child to like and trust you. Now, as I have a castle to run to YOUR demands, I took her to the kitchen with me. She is NOT a prisoner to be locked and kept in her room."

He stares at his maid in shock that she would dare, his fist clenched at his side. "I bought her!"

Martha matches his stare, shaking her head, "DO IT, and I will take the child away right here, right now, and you will not see either of us again, oath be damned. I will risk the consequences. That child SAW you destroy her room Zane, and tried to run away from the kitchen. All because you didn't take the time to think or ask where she is."

He glares at her, his thoughts processing her threat, before storming out of the room. "Make sure she's at court on time."

Martha follows him out, glaring at his retreating back. "Make sure someone deals with this room while you're at court. She cannot come back to your destruction!" She spins, heading back to the kitchens and the chaos that awaits her there. She sees the child looking down at her untouched plate and the two guards standing nearby in the quiet kitchen. She moves to sit next to her. "You should eat, child. The King will fix your room while you are at court."

The child looks up. "He didn't say he would."

"He will."

She whispers ever so softly. "You slapped him."

"Yes, and I would do so again. He is wrong, now please, eat your breakfast."

"I didn't think anyone was allowed to do that."

"They aren't. It usually means their death."

Tears well in the child's eyes. "I don't want you to die. You are nice to me."

Martha frowns. "Have you seen my death then, child?"

"No, Ma'am, you just said it, though."

She smiles, patting her hand gently. "Yes, but he wouldn't dare to kill me, and nor can he. We are both bound by a magic oath made to his father, one we cannot break."

"I see."

Martha smiles. "Come, let's see that smile again. Shall I have the cooks warm the food up for you?"

She smiles hesitantly. "No, it's alright, I can eat it cold. I am used to it."

"You eat your food cold?"

"Yes. Sometimes I don't get my chores done on time, so I have to wait until I do. Then I get my food."

She narrows her eyes ever so slightly, gesturing to the maids to bring her a fresh plate. "Well, you do not have to eat cold food here, and the only chore you have will be to serve the King and tell him your stories. Do you understand?"

"Yes, Ma'am."

"Good, now eat your new breakfast."

She nods and returns to her food, eating quietly as she watches Martha work on her papers. Her eyes drift around the kitchen, looking at all the helpers going about their business, noting how different it was from home. Once she finishes, she places her fork down and moves her hands to her lap, playing with the ribbons on her dress.

"Don't touch those, dear."

She looks up at Martha in surprise, not even aware she was watching as she continues to look at her papers.

Martha places the papers down, smiling at the child. "I have raised a lot of children, little one. I have eyes in the back of my head."

"Truly?"

"Truly. Come, we should get you to the grand hall." Martha rises, leading her out of the kitchen, catching the child's quick peaks at the back of her head, knowing it distracted her from the incident this morning. She leads her through a side door behind the throne, where a smaller chair sat, mouthing the word *smile* as she felt the child's hand tighten on hers when they enter.

Zane's eyes narrow on Martha before smiling at the child, gesturing to the chair beside him. "King's seer, I hope you slept well."

"Yes, Mister King. The bed is very soft. Thank you."

"That's good. Have a seat; we will start shortly."

"Yes, Mister King." She moves forward to sit in the chair as she glances around the room, seeing her guard following her in before returning her attention back to the king.

"Have you seen any stories, King's seer?"

"Yes, Mister King."

"And what did you see?"

Her gaze shifts to Martha a moment, looking down at her lap. "You broke my room."

He reaches out to pat her knee, causing her to jump in the chair. "I am sorry about that, little one. I will do better to keep my temper in check. Your room is getting fixed right now with better things."

"Yes, Mister King. Papa had a temper too, but he never broke my room." She looks up at him, studying him for a moment, giving a slight nod, returning her gaze to her lap. "I didn't mean to make you mad, Mister King."

He frowns at the child, his gaze moving to Martha, who shakes her head at him before addressing the child gently. "You did not make me mad, little one. I, as King, need to know what's happening in the kingdom and my castle, and this morning you were missing when I did not expect it. As I said last night, you are part of this castle now, and I was mad at the fact that I didn't know where you were and was concerned you were gone. I should have trusted that Martha and Alvero would keep you safe. I didn't. The fault lies with me."

She nods, keeping her eyes in her lap.

Martha sighs inwardly, thinking the next few months will be a bit more chaos than she needs in her life. "It will take time for you both to adjust to this new situation. The King has never had a child like you in his castle, and for you, going from farm life to castle life will take you time to learn. Most little ones I know could not leave their parents at such a young age."

"Yes, Ma'am." Her eyes catch Martha's smile, offering a hesitant one back.

"Now, put a brave smile on, and after court, we will have more bacon for you while we look over maids you might like. How does that sound?"

She nods, a smile lighting her face at the thought. "That sounds good. I like the meat sticks."

"Good." Martha turns to the king, offering a bow, before turning and leaving the hall, knowing she has a list of duties to do.

Zane goes through court business, introducing the child to the people in court. He pauses at each one to ask the child if she sees anything, sometimes earning a shake of her head, other times telling the story she sees to the amazement of those in the room at her predictions. He brings forward the eight guards that Alvero chose to work with, introducing them to her. "These are to be your guards King's seer. Alvero you have met. The others are Cedrik, Xyl, Tai, Deryn, Drue, Krim, Jesper and Luis." He carefully watches her expression as she studies them. "Do you like them, King's seer?"

She looks to the king a moment before looking back at the guards before her. "They seem nice, Mister King."

"Do you see any stories about them?"

"No, Mister King."

"Good. They will be the ones that will watch over your safety."

She frowns slightly at him. "But Mama said I would be safe here."

He chuckles at her innocence. "You are safe, child, for now. That will likely change as you become more known for what you can do. Some will not like you for it, and that is why I am picking your guards now, so that you can get to know them."

"Yes, Mister King."

"Now, if you see any stories with them or a new guard appears for some reason, I want you to let either myself or these men know. Is that understood?"

She nods, turning her eyes back to the men before her. "Yes, Mister King."

Zane dismisses them, nodding to Randolph to let in the city folk, hating this part of the day with a passion, listening to their gripes and complaints, wishing he could be anywhere by here. He focuses on paying attention, noting some of their eyes wandering to the child, wanting to reach out and strangle them for daring to look her way before squashing the rage. He hears her shift in the chair and turns to her, seeing her pale face looking his way, her eyes wide, wondering if she could read his thoughts. "Did you see something, King's seer?"

She answers quietly. "No, Mister King. What if I don't see anything? I know I am supposed to, for you."

He sighs inwardly, finding himself wondering just what he bought, chuckling at the thought that he considered her a mind reader when it is just insecurities. "King's seer. You are not obligated to see anything, but if you do, I would like to know. I am certain in some sessions, you will see nothing, whereas in others, you might see a lot. How about we call it a day and get an early lunch? I, for one, am starving for those meat sticks you like so much."

"Are you allowed to do that, Mister King?"

"Of course. Randolph, close the doors for the day; we are going for food." He stands up, stretching slightly, offering her a hand. "Come, King's seer."

"Yes, Mister King." She nods, rising when he offers a hand and takes it, following him quietly to the dining area.

A few of the servants rush in, shocked at seeing the king enter, pulling a chair out for him as another leads the child to a chair of her own. "What can we get you, Your Majesty?"

"Lunch, of course, and some of the meat sticks this little one likes. Lots of them." He winks her way, earning a smile and a giggle.

"Of course, Your Majesty, coming right up." The maid rushes from the room.

Once she is gone, Zane turns to the child. "So, now be honest, what did you think of the court?"

She looks up at him, chewing on her lip. "It's alright."

He chuckles. "Admit it; it's boring. Even I find it boring."

She giggles. "But why do you do it if it's boring?"

"Because a King must listen to his people to keep the kingdom happy."

She ponders it for a moment. "Perhaps if you had toys to play with when they talked, it wouldn't be so boring."

He bursts out laughing. "Now that would be a thing, wouldn't it? King of Oblait plays with toys during court sessions. I am certain people from all over the realm would come to see that."

"Miss Martha said I was getting toys. I can give you one of mine if you like."

"That is very kind of you, but I will buy my toys, and perhaps we can play together."

"I would like that, Mister King."

The maid pauses at the king's laughter, a rare thing in the castle, before stepping in and offering a bow. "Lunch is served, Your Majesty." She places her plate down as the others file in with theirs, one being an entire plate of bacon.

"Thank you." Zane smiles before returning his gaze to the youngster at his table. "Dig in, little one. There are plenty of meat sticks by the look of it."

The two of them eat their food, most of the plates remaining untouched, but the bacon is devoured as they get to know each other on a more personable level.

Pippa

THE MAIDS RETURN to the kitchen with haste, the whispers spreading fast about the king smiling their way. The laughter they heard before entering and allowing a child to eat before him, which breaks a protocol he had set years ago. Martha lifts her eyes from the papers she is reading. "Shush, you don't want him to hear you whispering like that. I think it is good the child is turning over a new leaf in the King. Perhaps she will bring more light to this castle. Now, as they are eating early, I need to up some of my scheduling, like bringing the new maids around for the pair to see when they are done."

She rises and heads out of the kitchens, pausing at the doors to the dining room. She hears the light-hearted chatter inside and finds herself hoping that this child could change him. She remains there a few minutes, catching them arguing over who got most of the bacon, with the king teasing the seer and saying she had an unfair advantage, causing her to giggle. She smiles as she continues on her journey to where the new maids are waiting, hoping that one of them will work for the child. She had specifically reached outside the castle so there would be no stories attached to them.

Martha pushes the door open and studies the five applicants sitting there, each one with an expression of hope that they will be chosen to work in the castle. Little do they know what it is really like to work here, but she is not going to be the one to tell them that the castle is not all that picturesque. "It seems the King has called court today, and so you will be presented earlier than I planned. Now, remember, you are here for the child, not the King. If any of you have designs on the King, leave now." She watches as they look at each other, none of them rising. "Alright then, follow me."

Martha leads them back down the hallways, hearing their gasps of awe at the wealth on display, and mentally shakes her head. She understands the palace is opulent and that one item is worth more than any have seen in their lifetime. She stops at the dining hall, tapping lightly on the door before stepping in and bowing to the king. "Your Majesty, the maids are here for your approval."

Zane reaches slowly for the last bacon strip as the child steals it before him. He laughs at her, trying to snatch it from her hand playfully, before turning to Martha. "Alright, send them in. This child needs someone who can stop her from being a bacon thief. I am certain she ate most of it!"

The King's seer giggles. "Oh no, Mister King. I think you got most of it; I just got the last one."

Zane chuckles. "I will have Martha bring me a piece, and then I will have the last piece."

Martha teases him gently. "Perhaps I will give it to the child, Your Majesty."

Zane grabs his chest, pretending to be in pain and dying. "Ouch, stabbed in the chest and betrayed by my maid! The only way I can survive is with bacon."

The King's seer hops out of the chair and moves to his side, holding the last piece of bacon up to him, her eyes growing serious for a moment. "Here, Mister King, I will be like the knights in my book and save you."

He takes it, stuffs it into his mouth, and eats it, leaning over the side of his chair. "Oohh, I feel it working already, Thank you, King's seer. You are a good knight."

Martha smiles at the pair, feeling a lightness in her heart at how well they are getting along. "Alright, you two, now that the bacon has healed the King, what do you say we see the prospective maids?"

Zane looks up at Martha and sighs. "Fine, bring them in."

Martha bows and steps back outside the room, seeing the nervousness, the excitement, the anxiety all within their eyes as she gestures them forward to stand against the wall in the room. Zane eyes them all carefully before turning his gaze to the child who watched them enter. "What are their names, Martha?"

"Belinda, Clover, Pippa, Nessa, and Lena, Your Majesty."

"And they come from good backgrounds?"

"Of course, Your Majesty."

"Well, King's seer, do you see any stories?"

The King's seer moves to stand in front of Belinda, noticing that she is shorter than Martha and has long brown hair, tan skin, and green eyes. Belinda's blue clothing has more flow than the others, bringing a smile to her face as she admires it, watching to reach out to touch it but knowing she shouldn't. She gives a nod Belinda's way before moving to Clover, studying her with the same intensity. She looks up into Clover's hazel eyes, her light brown hair that is almost blonde but not quite, framing her oval face, noticing her clothing is more subdued in style and color.

The King's seer shakes her head as she moves to Pippa, a shock of red curls falling around green eyes, a smattering of freckles, and lines that crinkled around Pippa's eyes as she smiles down at her. The King's seer looks down at the green dress Pippa is wearing, noticing the skirt is full, and the white top has a few light stains that look as though they were scrubbed to remove them. She stops, taking Pippa's hand in hers, and looks it over, playing with her fingers a moment before turning to the king. "Pippa will be my maid."

Pippa

"How can you be sure, child? There are two more to look at."

The King's seer shakes her head, still holding Pippa's hand. "I see it. She is the one tying me into another pretty purple dress."

Zane nods. "Pippa it is. The rest of you are dismissed. Martha, take them away. I will walk the child and the maid Pippa back to their rooms."

"Yes, Your Majesty." Martha starts to gather the other four when the King's seer stops her, her eyes glowing ever so softly on Lena, meeting her brown eyes, noticing she is short like Belinda but has auburn hair. "They are unhappy with him. They will find him and make him pay."

Martha stops them, looking at the maid she is talking to. "Who will Child?"

"I don't know. I just know they will."

"Interesting. Alright, let's go." Martha looks at the woman, who pales considerably at the child's words, seeing they clearly have meaning for Lena. Martha guides the maids out of the room, closing the door behind her, leading them to the front doors of the castle, thanking them all for coming, and wishing them luck on their journeys.

Meanwhile, Zane rises, giving a quick nod to Pippa, and holds a hand out for the child. "Welcome to the castle. I will show you ladies back to your rooms."

The King's seer smiles up at Pippa. She releases her hand and moves over to the king's side, walking with him back to her rooms. She glances back at Pippa every so often, noticing that along the way, they picked up guards that had not been present in the dining room. A few minutes later, they are at her door; Pippa bows and moves forward to open the door as Zane steps into the room, inspecting what has been done to restore it.

The King's seer looks around, seeing the new furniture briefly, distracted by a box of toys and books, and runs over to it immediately. She pulls out a stuffed bear, hugging it close as she turns to the king with a smile. "Thank you, Mister King."

"You're welcome, King's seer. I will see you tomorrow for court."

"Yes, Mister King."

"Good, then I shall leave you two to get to know each other until Martha returns."

Pippa bows, "Yes, Your Majesty. Thank you for hiring me."

"It was not me that hired you. It was the child and her visions."

Pippa's eyes move over to the child standing there, stuffed bear in her arms, then bows her head again. "Understood, Your Majesty."

He nods, barely registering the maid, his eyes on the child hugging the bear, happiness in her eyes at the toy. He turns and leaves the room, closing the door behind them, and turns to the guards who remained outside. "Xyl, are there guards patrolling outside?"

"Yes, Your Majesty, Drue, and Jesper are."

"Good. The maids that were rejected will start to talk about her gift as well as those in court today. I expect word will spread soon of those wanting to meet her, and I want her protected at all costs."

"Yes, Your Majesty."

He looks at the door for a moment before turning and heading to the war room to speak with his guards. "Trevyr, find Dunivan and bring him to the war room. Benson, with me. I want protections put up around this castle."

The King's seer looks up at Pippa and smiles her way. "Do you like my room, it's pretty now. The King fixed it up, and he brought me toys."

Pippa glances around, moving to kneel next to the child standing at the toy box. "Thank you, Miss, for hiring me."

The King's seer smiles, her fingers reaching out to touch the stain on the shirt. "I saw it in my stories, and you need it to pay for the healer from when your Mama was sick."

Pippa's eyes widen. "How could you know that? I haven't told anyone that."

"Cause I am the King's Seer."

"But you didn't tell the King."

"No. My mama didn't like my stories, so I don't tell very many. Only some of them."

"How many stories do you see, little one?"

She hugs the bear tightly, looking down at it like it is a lifeline for her, feeling panicked that Pippa will change her mind and not be her maid. Her voice barely whispers. "I see them all the time, Miss Pippa."

"Oh child, come here," Pippa pulls her in for a hug. "Where are your parents?"

"They didn't want me. They sold me to the King."

A soft gasp escapes Pippa as she tightens her hold on the wee child. "When?"

"Yesterday."

"Oh, little one, I am here for you, no matter what."

She nods against Pippa, one arm tight on the teddy, the other wrapping around her, leaning against her as she responds to the soft knock at her door. "Come in."

Martha steps in, a gentleman standing behind her holding a soft satchel of belongings. She looks over the pair, arching a slight brow as Pippa releases the child. "The tailor Habo is here, child; come, stand over here so he can measure you."

She hands Pippa her teddy as she moves to stand by Martha, her eyes studying the tailor as he approaches. Habo is an older man with brown eyes, wearing soft leather in shades of brown, a few gray strands peeking through dark brown hair that is pulled back into a ponytail. He opens his bag and pulls out a measuring tape, moving over to her and kneeling down. He takes a variety of measurements, murmuring to himself about her age and growth spurts, knowing that some of the skirts will need to have a way to be lengthened. "How many dresses are we talking about, Martha, and what style?"

"A few to play outside in, a court dress for each day of the week, some sleepers, and some to just hang around the room in. As for style, she is a child and a seer, flowing, silk, lace, gems perhaps, but covered. NOT revealing."

Habo nods, taking a few more measurements. "And when would you like these ready?"

"As soon as possible, the only dress she has is the one she is wearing."

He looks up sharply. "She is in the King's castle with only ONE dress?"

Martha frowns at his look. "That is correct. Her parents did not deem it necessary to bring anything with her. That is why you are here."

He nods, looking at the young girl standing there. "I will build her dresses in layers, with several shades of purple, perhaps greens, to accent the eyes; this way, you can change the colors of the dress with the layers. Light silks, long sleeves, some embroidery or gems lined into them. It will go further that way, especially as she will be growing."

"That sounds lovely."

He lifts the child's arms gently, taking another round of measurements, his brown eyes meeting her lavender ones.

"You are going to make me some very pretty dresses, Mister Dressmaker. I like the ones that jingle."

"Jingle?"

"Yes, some will have pretty belts with dangling chains and beads that sparkle. I like them."

"It is a new style, child. I have not perfected it yet."

"You will, Mister Dressmaker. Lots of ladies will like it."

His eyes find Martha, who nods and smiles at him. "So far, all her stories are true, so I am certain you will find a way. Apparently, when you do, we will need to buy some of those."

He chuckles, patting the child's head gently. "Good to know. I will work on it specifically for you."

"Thank you, Mister Dressmaker."

"You are welcome, little one. Alright, Martha, I have what I need. I will send a few over later this afternoon and more by the end of the week."

"Thank you, Habo." The pair leave the room, closing the door behind them as Martha leads Habo out of the castle, returning about twenty minutes later to go over what is needed with Pippa.

Whispers on the Wind

MARTHA LEADS PIPPA to the room next door, leaving the child to explore her toy box and the new toys inside it. "This is where you will stay. I expect there might be a few nightmares when the child realizes her parents left her, though she did sleep straight through last night, which is surprising. Court is at eight every morning except Sundays, so you are responsible for ensuring she is fed, bathed, and dressed for that. Breakfast is ready in the kitchen at seven every morning. She will remain in court until noon, at which point she will either eat with the King or be led back to her rooms, where you will bring her food. For the most part, you both have the afternoons off, but you are at her beck and call, so you are not to leave the castle for now. Once we are certain she is comfortable and does not need you, we can revisit this as these first few months are crucial to ensuring she feels safe."

"Cleaning can be done while she is in court, and no matter what anyone says, you are not required to clean anything but these two rooms. If someone does, let me know. You are strictly the child's maid. What she needs, you will grant her. If she does not need you, you may rest. Dinner is at six in the evening and can be taken where she chooses unless the King requests to dine with her. So far, we have discovered she likes bacon and eggs and does not like broccoli or cauliflower. The rest will be a learning curve, as it seems her parents were cold and strict with her. The only thing we will be strict on is she is NOT to leave these rooms unattended. She must be either accompanied by the guard at her door or you. Is that understood?"

Pippa nods, "Yes, Ma'am."

"You will report anything and everything to me. We can set a time once you develop a routine with the child."

"Yes, Ma'am."

"Now, I understand you will need to retrieve your belongings, so I will watch over the child this afternoon while you move and settle in."

Pippa bows, "Thank you, Ma'am."

Days pass into weeks, and weeks into months, with Pippa arriving every morning to feed and ready the child, dressing her in Habo's designs and sending her to court with the guard on duty. She then sets about cleaning her room, smiling each morning at the child's attempt at making her bed before moving to her own, settling into a routine. Once she is done, she returns to the kitchens to give Martha her daily report, taking a moment to chat before delivering her lunch to her rooms and enjoying an afternoon of rest or play with the child.

The King's seer arrives every morning for court at eight sharp, watching as her guard moves to stand behind her chair while the king's guard stands to the right of him. She studies all that come into the court, giving the king stories she figures he or they would be interested in. In a matter of weeks, word spread like wildfire about her stories as more flock to the castle doors, all wanting an audience with the king and his seer.

Six months later, as the seer is entering the hall, Zane smiles her way. "We have some diplomats arriving today, King's seer, from the kingdom of Lamadow. I think you will like them. Hopefully, you will see good stories about them."

"Yes, Mister King."

He winks at her, giving a nod to Randolph as he starts to let people in, listening to their requests and grievances, going through what needs to be done to fix things, pausing when the seer has a story. An hour into the court, Kivu steps out from where he sits at the audience table, leading a pair of elves to stand before the king. "Dawnelda and Nelowyna, Your Majesty, on behalf of Queen Diadradey of the kingdom of Lamadow."

The King's seer gasps, earning a chuckle from Zane and causing the guards to snap their eyes to him that he would allow such an interruption. She looks to the king, whispering softly, "Are they real?"

"Yes, King's seer, they are real. The kingdom of Lamadow is mostly elves. Do you like them?"

"They are sooo pretty."

"Would you like to meet them?"

"Can I?"

"Of course."

She smiles his way, rising from her seat, her pale lavender dress floating about her as she moves closer to the elves, who bowed to King Zane. She stops in front of Dawnelda, looking up at the blue eyes, pale face, the long straight blonde hair braided with thin braids and set back with golden leaves to expose pointed ears. She walks around her, noting the intricacies in the dress, wanting to feel it but knowing better, keeping her hands clenched in her skirts. She smiles in awe as she circles back around before shifting her gaze to Nelowyna, who looks similar but with long red hair, dressed in the same colors of pale green and blue. "You are so beautiful."

"Thank you, Child." They both smile, giving a bow to her, before returning their gaze to the king. "King Zane. Always a pleasure to be here in your court. I gather this child is your seer."

"Indeed, she is."

"And is she accurate in her sights?"

Zane narrows his eyes momentarily at having his seer questioned before smiling. "Of course she is. You have heard word of her visions. It is why you are here, is it not?"

They both look down at the lavender-eyed child staring at them in wonder. Nelowyna drops to one knee to be closer to the level of the child, looking her over as Dawnelda answers. "It is. How much?"

"She's not for sale."

Dawnelda laughs, switching to elven. "I'd be surprised if she was. How much for a vision, as I am quite certain you are profiting off her?"

Zane answers in Elven. "Indeed I am. Depends on what she grants you."

"And if she doesn't?"

"You pay nothing, but she will."

"How can you be sure?"

"It's her gift, and she does it well."

Dawnelda looks down at the child running her fingers lightly over Nelowyna's hand. "Then we accept whatever charges, within reason, of course, to receive a vision from her. We have an object for her to look at."

He nods, switching back to the common tongue. "King's seer, they have something they want you to look at, and tell them a story about it."

The King's seer turns her gaze to the king for a moment. "They have lots of stories, Mister King. Even their Queen has a story. I can see it."

The pair of elves gasp in shock. "How can you know that child? We haven't shown you the object yet."

"Her husband, Mister Robertts, he's in trouble and missing. You have one of his crowns and want me to find him for you." She holds her hands out, waiting for the object to be placed in her hand.

Dawnelda and Nelowyna look at each other before pulling the crown out and placing it in her hand.

The King's seer accepts the crown, looking it over as she studies it carefully, touching each of the gems gently before handing it back to them. "It is very pretty. I like the purple gems. Mister Robertts was in a carriage with two shiny white horses, and they were crossing the sands. Then a big brown dragon appeared, and the carriage went right when it should have gone left. The horses, they ran as fast as they could but the elf driver, he couldn't stop them. The dragon chased them off the cliff." Her eyes well up with tears as she looks at them. "He ate the horses and the elf and then went back to his cave. It's dark by the rocks that stick out. Mister Robertts is still in the broken carriage by the water. His leg hurts too much for him to move."

Dawnelda shifts her gaze to Nelowyna, still kneeling at the child's height. "There is water all around our lands, Child."

Her eyes glow ever so softly as she looks up at her. "He is against the cliff, next to the mountains, by the waters where the ladies with the fishtails live. There is one watching him right now."

"You mean the mermaids of Roburg Bay?"

She looks up at the elf, pondering it a moment, "I am sorry he ate your horses and your friend."

Nelowyna takes the child's hand gently. "Thank you, little one; we will start searching the western side. We assumed he would be near the east side as that's the way into our lands."

The King's seer smiles. "We have pretty horses in the stable, but not as pretty as yours. One day I will get one of my own, and it will be polka dotted."

Zane arches a brow at the child's words, suspecting he is going to have to start looking at horses that a child can ride, especially if she saw herself receiving one. He smiles, his eyes returning to the Elves. "I do hope that her words are enough to find King Robertts."

They each bow towards the king, switching back to Elven. "I am certain it will. It is far more than we had. How much for her vision?"

"Fifty gold and an additional fifty when it proves true."

"You have yourself a deal, King Zane." The elves pull out a sack of coins, sort through it, and hand it to the guard that approaches. They offer another bow to the child before turning and leaving the grand hall. The King's seer watches them leave, moving back to her chair. "Thank you, Mister King, for letting me see the elves."

"You're welcome, King's seer. You will see more of them as time passes, as well as other races such as dwarves and gnomes, to name a few."

"Thank you. I can't wait till I get my polka-dot horse and we go for rides together."

He chuckles. "You are still a bit young, King's seer."

"Yes. I know I am older when I get it, but it's still very pretty. You will give it to me for my fourteenth birthday."

Zane frowns slightly, realizing he has no idea when her birthday is. "When is your birthday, child?"

"I don't know, Mister King. I just know I am nine 'cause my mama told me."

"What do you say we pick the day you arrived as your birthday."

She looks at him, nodding. "Yes, I like that."

"Right then, I will confer with Martha, but I suspect you will be ten soon. Lunch today, King's seer?"

"If you want, Mister King."

"Good, now let's finish the court and get us some bacon."

She nods, the remaining hours passing in a blur as her thoughts drift between the pretty elves and the people brought before her, offering a few of her stories. The court ends, and Zane takes her hand, leading her to the dining hall as they take their places at the table. "You will see more elves, King's seer, don't worry. Now, what I am interested in is how you knew where the dragon was."

She looks up. "I didn't until I held the crown, Mister King. I just saw that the queen and the elves were sad."

"Are you saying if you touch an object that's tied to a dragon attack, you can see them?"

She looks confused. "I don't know."

"It's alright, child. Here, eat your lunch." He calls out to the guard outside the dining hall. "Randolph, I want you to go to the war room and bring me the broken goblet on the sideboard."

"Yes, Your Majesty." He returns ten minutes later with the goblet in question.

"Thank you, Randolph." Zane takes the goblet from him and places it on the table before his seer. "Do you see any stories tied to this goblet child?"

She looks up from her lunch, eyeing the goblet, shaking her head. "No, Mister King."

"Try picking it up, King's seer."

She nods, placing her fork down and picking up the broken goblet. She runs her fingers over it carefully before placing it down. "A blue dragon broke it. He was near the lake, and there were people there. They killed him, but he ate two of them first."

Zane grins in delight, his thoughts whirling on how he is going to hunt dragons better from this day forward, and pats her hand lightly. "Thank you, King's seer. I must go; there are things I need to do." He collects the goblet, striding from the dining hall, heading to his war chamber. "Randolph. Find me Dunivan, and place a call on the info board that we are seeking two things, first groups of dragon hunters and second, objects that were in a dragon fight or attack of some kind."

"As you wish, Your Majesty," Randolph bows and leaves the king.

Dragon Hunters

A FEW WEEKS LATER, Dawnelda and Nelowyna return, thanking the king and the seer for what she had seen.

"Sire, our Queen offers her thanks to you and your seer for returning King Robertts to her. We would not likely have found him in time if not for your help. She said if there is anything you need, just let her know."

He nods. "You are welcome. In fact, I do believe there is. You have a court mage, yes?"

"Indeed we do, Sire. Her name is Ini."

"Can she make talking stones?"

"Yes, Sire, the Queen uses them all the time."

"I wish for some to be made, perhaps about ten or fifteen."

"Of course, Sire. We will have them made and sent over as soon as we can."

"Thank you."

Over time, people come forward, each with a tale of how they survived a dragon attack, seeking to get paid gold for their items. However, each item receives a shake of her head by the King's seer, indicating that the object has not, in fact, seen a dragon. Frustration grows as weeks turn into months; Zane's dreams are dashed as this new way of tracking fails. He watches the seer study the most recent object, a glimmer of hope in his eyes that perhaps this holds a story since all of the other items took only a few seconds for her to say no.

The King's seer lifts her gaze to the king. "It is not a dragon Sire, similar but almost as if it is crossed with another creature. The trees are strange, with large pointy leaves and one trunk all the way up. There is a cave in the mountains nearby, where he lives, but it is deep and the entrance small. I do see some gold in the cave, but it is dark, so it's hard to see."

Zane smiles. "That will do, King's seer. Thank you. Now we just need groups to hunt it."

She smiles, handing the goblet back to the people that brought it. "You will have two that will answer the call you placed. One called the Rug Rattens, there will be four within that group, and while young, can hold their own. Another is the Belhain Protectors, six within their group, who are much stronger, but neither will arrive for several months, one being closer to the end of the year."

"WHAT!"

She flinches slightly. "Your courier did not make it, Sire, so the missive hasn't traveled past this kingdom. It seems he was ambushed by bandits."

"And you are just telling me this now?"

"I am sorry, Your Majesty, it just showed up with the goblet. I had not seen it before."

He growls at her, "RANDOLPH!"

Randolph moves forward, bowing before the king. "Yes, Sire?"

"After court, send more missives out that I am looking for dragon hunters. Apparently, our courier did not complete his duty."

"Forgive me, Sire, but it's far too soon to know that. It's only been a few months."

"I was just informed by the seer that he was ambushed."

Randolph bows again. "Understood. I will send several this time to ensure they get to the other kingdoms."

Zane turns back to the person with the goblet. "Now, please tell me where you were when this happened."

"On the way to Vidip in Ewhela, Your Majesty. Our caravan was attacked on the way through the jungle. Some did not make it as the dragon surprised us, but the guards chased it off."

"Yes, that would make sense. Palm trees have pointed leaves. How close to Vidip were you?"

"We were about halfway there, Your Majesty."

"Thank you. You may collect your reward from Kivu."

Zane looks at his seer. "Do you know why the vision of the courier's death is tied to the goblet?"

"No, Sire, I picked it up and got the vision of the creature, then it moved to the cave, where I could see the gold. Then from the gold, it went to the courier, the missive on the ground beside him, struggling against a group of bandits. Perhaps some of the gold he carried is in the pile, and it drifted to him or something else I did not see. Possibly the creature ate one of the bandits. Somehow they are tied together, but I can't see how."

"And the groups that you saw?"

"They each held a missive in their hand. It did not show me how they got it, just that both were heading this way."

He nods. "Not as fast as I would have liked, but having two groups hunting is better than none. Thank you, King's seer."

"You welcome, Your Majesty. I wish it was clearer, but this one jumped around a lot."

He ponders it for a moment. "Randolph, I will need tokens to mark locations until the dragon hunters get here."

"Yes, Your Majesty."

"King's seer, if you saw a map with the object in question, could you pinpoint it?"

"I am not sure, Your Majesty, but I am willing to try."

"Good; after lunch, I will take you to the war room."

"As you wish, Your Majesty."

After court, Zane leads the King's seer to the dining hall, asking her further questions as they enjoy their lunch along with the usual plate of bacon. Afterward, he leads her to the war room, where a large map sits on a table. Small miniatures rest upon it in various places, most in Oblait but some in other kingdoms. She moves to the side of the map, wandering around the edge, reaching out to touch one of his statues, knocking it over. "There is no spy here, Sire; they have been removed from the board."

A wicked smile crosses Zane's lips as he watches her work her way around the map.

Her gaze moves to the small triangular flags, noticing a few spread out across the map. She picks one up to look it over before collecting a second piece. "These are markers for your troops?"

"Yes, King's seer, and where they are heading."

She nods, turning them over in her hand carefully as she studies the map, her eyes drifting to the goblet that sat on a shelf nearby. "The blue dragon that was killed is here." She places the marker at the base of the lake near Pleta. Her gaze shifts to the south, dropping the second marker on the mountain range between Oblait and Ewhela. "And the creature is here, under this peak, feeding off the caravans that pass through." She runs her fingers along the edges, pausing at troops heading into Spokane, her eyes saddening as she picks up the markers, taking them off the map. "These will not make it; the mountains will break apart, crushing them before they get there."

"King's seer! Do you know what this means?"

"No, Sire, it is just what I see."

"Endless possibilities. Thank you, King's seer; you may return to your rooms." His eyes study the changes made on his map in delight, ideas racing through his head at what he could use her powers for.

She bows. "Thank you, Sire. I thought perhaps to visit Martha in the kitchens first."

"Of course, do whatever you want, King's seer."

She turns to leave, an ever so slight smile gracing her lips, walking away from the war room with her familiar shadows following her, knowing by granting him that hint of power, things are going to change. She slips into the kitchens, spending an hour with Martha, before returning to her room to relax and ponder her own possibilities.

Another few months pass, a visit to the war room is added a few times a week to the King's seer's routine, giving her both a chance to see what Zane is up to and what is in play. During that time, a few more dragon artifacts come in and she is able to pinpoint their hunting grounds, now identified with a purple marker, bringing a smile to her lips each time she picks one up. One morning, as she stands in the court, she feels their presence, placing her hand on his chair before Randolph lets anyone in.

Zane lifts his gaze to her, "King's seer?"

"The Rug Rattens are here Sire. They wait in line outside."

"Randolph! Find the group called the Rug Rattens. I want them here first!"

"Yes, Sire."

In a few minutes, Randolph leads a group of four before the king and bows. "The Rug Rattans Sire."

The King's seer looks over the group; two humans and two gnomes, the latter being the most adorable of all the races she has seen in the court. Her gaze shifts to the king momentarily, seeing the delight in his features that a group of hunters is here, returning her attention back to the human that speaks.

He has hazel eyes and brown hair, kept relatively short, taller, and leaner than most humans. He is dressed in blue robes with white and silver trim, white boots peeking out from beneath as he steps forward. "My name is Decklane, Sire, wizard extraordinaire; we are here about the job offer. With me are Liaam, a mighty barbarian, Aeryen, master of locks and opening them, and Eastonator, our tracker and hunter."

The King's seer's eyes shift to the others. Long blonde hair flows on the human barbarian, wild and free, matching the slightly edged look in his blue eyes that gives the indication you don't want to press him. He is dressed in leathers and furs, much like the little gnome tracker. She meets tracker's dark brown eyes, long hair that hangs over one eye, and a bow slung to his back, smiling at his skill she can see in her vision. She studies the locksmith, knowing there is more beneath the dark cloak than just the hazel eyes that met her gaze.

Zane shifts his gaze, eyeing his seer, who is studying them intently. "King's seer. Do you see anything?"

She nods, her violet eyes returning to him. "Yes, Sire, they will bring you many dragons, including the one in the mountains that's not really a dragon. They fight together well, though they do tend to take more time than necessary to make plans and need to trust their instincts more than they do."

"Good. Rug Rattens, welcome to Oblait. Kivu will discuss the particulars with you regarding payment. He will also give you a pearl that will allow messages between us. When my seer sees a dragon, I will send a message via it, allowing you to answer if you are not within a day's journey of the castle."

They all bow. "Thank you, Your Majesty."

"Randolph, please take them to see Kivu and set them up. King's seer, when is the next group arriving?"

Her eyes glow softly. "Six months, Sire. They have a quest to finish in the North and then will head here."

He leans back in his chair, delighted at the thought that dead dragons are going to start pouring in now that he has one set of hunters and even more when the second group arrives.

Weeks become months, each day drawing them closer to when the second group is due to arrive. Each morning, excitement fills Zane as he questions the seer as to whether today is the day, only to be deflated when she shakes her head.

Nearing the six-month mark though, she smiles as she enters the court to stand behind him. "The Belhain protectors will be here today, Sire. They have already slain a green dragon and a black dragon of another realm."

"Are they bringing their heads, King's seer?"

"No, Sire. It was several years ago, before you put a call out. One of the little gnomes, her name is Shamil, is known as a dragon slayer amongst them as she often has the killing blow."

He nods at her, "And when are they due to arrive?"

"We will be in court late today, Sire, as they will arrive just before noon."

He frowns at that. "Can they not get here any faster?"

"Sire, they ride as fast as they can, but the guards will stop them at the gates, causing a delay."

Zane holds a hand up for a moment. "Randolph, tell the guards NOT to stop the Belhain protectors and to guide them directly to the castle."

"Yes, Sire."

Zane taps his fingers on the chair, feeling court drag as he waits, muttering under his breath about the speed at which time passes. He straightens in his chair when he hears the pounding of horses' hooves in the courtyard outside. Several guards file in, surrounding a group of six adventurers. "Sire, these are the ones that you have requested we bring straight to you."

"Indeed, please, step forward, Belhain Protectors."

A few of them glance at each other, wondering how the king knows their name already.

The King's seer smiles at their entrance, resting her hand on the king's throne.

"You may speak, King's seer.

She nods. "I know all your names, Belhain protectors, and that you own a mansion in the town you saved from a green dragon. Your coming was foreseen nearly a year ago."

The tall human steps forward. He has long brown hair, brown eyes and is dressed in robes. "Your Majesty, King's seer. We have heard tales of your skill in the gift of vision."

She smiles gently. "All good, I would hope, Jaxon of Belhain."

"Of course." He bows to her, turning back to the king. "Now, may I present our group?"

Zane nods. "Indeed, I have been waiting for you to arrive, especially as my seer has seen you kill not one, but two dragons already."

Jaxon grins. "Indeed we have; both were a challenge in their own right, but both were defeated." He turns, waving his group forward one at a time. The first to step forward is a gnome, well-dressed in dark colors, and who bows at his name. "Sir Perry of Belhain." The second, a female gnome with bright purple hair, dressed in colors to match. "Lady Shamil, our jokester."

The King's seer smiles, "And the dragon killer."

Jaxon arches a brow. "Indeed, her arrow was the last to sink into them, thus killing them." Jaxon turns back to the group as an elf steps forward, dressed in greens to match his green eyes and compliment his brown hair. "Jyrine, ranger, and tracker." Another tiny folk steps forward, his face hidden under an oversized cloak, shorter than the gnomes, "Koralyck, our boomkin."

"Gütel."

"Yes, astute seer, I am impressed; not many recognize his race. And last but not least, our very own Leeroy, defender of the faith."

"Yes, he charges into battle before the others are ready for it. That will get him into trouble when you face the purple dragon." The King's seer catches Zane's look, gives a bow, and steps back to where she belongs.

Zane returns his attention back to the group at hand. "And you wish to hunt dragons for me?"

"Of course, sire, who wouldn't with the gold you are offering? If only we had had a seer of our own to tell us that we needed to keep the heads of those we fought. We would be two thousand gold richer."

He chuckles. "Indeed you would; so be it. Randolph will take you to Kivu at the door. He will give you the details and set you up. Welcome to Oblait, Belhain protectors."

They all bow, following Randolph out the door.

Zane turns to his seer and studies her for a moment, seeing her standing back in her place. "So King's seer. What do you think?"

"I think they will bring you many dragons, Sire."

"You seemed to have overstepped slightly today."

"I am sorry, Your Majesty." She offers him a bow of respect. "It is a delight to see you so happy with the hunters that I forgot myself. I will take care not to do so in the future."

Zane slaps his hand on the chair. "I am happy, King's seer, and I will overlook it today. Thank you for bringing these groups to me."

"I didn't, Sire; they came because of your summons."

"You did. You noticed our first courier was killed. If we had not sent out others, they would have not received my call; thus, this is on you. You may take a day off tomorrow. We are closing the court down for the day."

Her eyes snap to his eyes in shock. "Yes, Your Majesty. You are most welcome. Perhaps Martha can take me shopping? I have never been and only read stories about it. I would like to try it."

"Of course, but I will ensure you have double your guards if you do. I want to make sure you are safe."

"Thank you, Sire."

The next morning, the King's seer rises early, moving out to the balcony, and watches the sunrise as she waits for her maid. Her eyes drift to the city below her, knowing that within a few hours, she is going to be down there, looking at wares, and shopping with the small pouch of gold the king had given her. She moves to the bathing chamber, draws a bath, and soaks in it, closing her eyes as she ponders her day of freedom. After a half hour, she scrubs herself down, rinses, and dries herself off as she pads back to her main room. She pulls out a pale green underdress, slips it on, and ties it up. She rifles through the wardrobe, deciding on a dark green and violet overdress, pulling it on just as Pippa knocks on the door. "Come in, Pippa."

Pippa enters, closing the door behind her and giving a shake of her head. "Miss, that's my job, what are you doing up so early?"

"I get to go shopping with Miss Martha today. Did you need anything while I am there?"

"No, Miss. The King is allowing this, I assume."

"Yes, in thanks for bringing him two dragon hunting groups. There will be double the guards surrounding me, but I don't care. It will be the first time I have left the castle since I got here."

Pippa expertly adjusts the dress, fixing the ties and guiding her to sit as she sets about drying her hair and styling it. "That is exciting, Miss; you be careful out there. Make sure you wear a cloak. Shall I fetch your breakfast?"

"I will eat it in the kitchens with Miss Martha."

"Alright, Miss. Have a good day."

"I will, Pippa, Thank you." The King's seer rises, heading to the dresser, and pulls the drawer open, lifting the small sack of gold out of it. She tucks it in the pockets of her skirts and grabs a matching cloak, practically running down the stairs and through the hallways to the kitchen. Her silent guards are not so silent as they run to keep up with her. She smiles at Martha as she slides into the chair at the table next to her.

"Your early King's seer. Have you eaten?"

"I know Miss Martha, and not yet."

She arches her brow. "Pippa didn't bring you breakfast?"

"She offered. I said I would eat it here with you."

Martha laughs. "This wouldn't have anything to do with the fact that you get to go shopping with me today, does it?"

The King's seer smiles, watching as a plate of food is placed before her. "Of course not."

"If you are going to learn to lie, my dear, you have to do better than that."

She laughs, picking up a fork and eating her breakfast. "Ok, perhaps you are right."

"I know I am Dear. We will leave within the hour. Is that soon enough for you?"

"Whenever you like Miss Martha."

Martha shakes her head, feeling the excitement emanating from the seer. She makes a mental note to speak with the king about the seer partaking in more days out of the castle. Martha turns her attention back to her papers, sets the schedules, and looks at the lists of what is needed and what can wait till her next trip into the city. An hour later, she makes a few notes on her parchment and rises, watching as the King's seer jumps up with her. "Alright, King's seer, let's go shopping."

Martha leads the King's seer to the main doors, where they pick up her entourage of nine guards, who move to surround the two ladies as they leave the castle. The King's seer practically skips as they leave the castle, looking around everywhere and seeing everything as if for the first time. Martha smiles, watching her childlike wonder, realizing in that moment, the King's seer is only twelve, which is still a child in most people's eyes and one that has grown up far too quickly being in the castle.

They move through the market, looking at all the wares. The King's seer buys a few soaps that she likes, berries rather than the florals that are in her room. She stops at a jeweler, spotting a few hairpins that would match some of her dresses, only to have four necklaces draw her attention, each one of a dragon with gemmed eyes. She picks them up carefully, noticing just how well-made there are, before adding them to her to purchase. She follows Martha to the clothing district, seeing Habo's stall with him sitting behind a table sewing a dress. "Mister Habo!"

"King's seer! What brings you to the market?"

"I get to shop today with Miss Martha. It's my first time ever."

His gaze moves to Martha and the guards that surround his booth. "And are you having fun, King's seer?"

"Oh yes! I've bought lots of stuff."

He chuckles. "Well, the market vendors will love you for that. Are you here to buy dresses?"

She turns to Martha, who shakes her head.

"No, Habo, We will call you when she needs more. I just thought I would show her the clothing district, and she spotted you."

"Alright, Miss Martha." He turns back to the seer, eyeing the skirts she is wearing and the way her dress fits. "I expect she will be outgrowing the last batch in the next six months. I will start now."

"She is growing like a weed."

The King's seer looks between them. "Is that good?"

"It is for me, child, perhaps not for the King's purses, but he hasn't complained yet."

She pulls her pouch out and opens it. "I have a few gold coins left. I could pay for it."

He places a hand on the pouch, catching the guards stiffening around him. "Keep your gold, child. The King has already agreed to cover all expenses regarding your wardrobe."

She smiles, tucking her gold away again. "Thank you, Mister Habo. I think Miss Martha needs to get food now."

"Yes, King's seer, if you want to eat, then we need to hit the food district next." Martha leads her away, heading to the food district, working her way through the stalls, picking out items, and placing them in the cart behind her.

The King's seer wanders along behind Martha, looking over the food and watching Martha for a while, realizing she has no clue as to how or what Martha is doing. She turns her attention to those in the market, her gaze drifting over the people, seeing stories on some of them but mostly daily activities. She stills as her eyes land on a tall woman standing a ways off dressed all in black, long dark hair, and brown eyes that watch them a touch too intently. She can see a jagged scar running along one cheek. The King's seer frowns, realizing that the woman has something on her blocking her vision, causing a shiver to run through her as she steps backward into Xyl.

Xyl catches her, steadying her, concern in his eyes. "King's seer, are you alright?"

The King's seer looks up at Xyl for a moment, turning her gaze back to the woman only to find her gone. "Yes… There was just a strange woman watching us, but she's gone now."

"Did you see any stories about her?"

"No, nothing."

"Then I wouldn't worry about it. You are rather striking, King's seer. Many will be curious about who you are and why you have an entourage of the King's guards."

She turns back to Xyl, studying him carefully. She gives a slight nod as she turns her gaze to scan the marketplace around them, pulling her cloak tighter around her as a chill fills her. "Perhaps." She pushes the woman out of her thoughts and returns her attention to Martha, following her along for the rest of the shopping trip and enjoying the time away from the castle.

Marked for Death

ANOTHER YEAR PASSES, the court sessions remain the same length of time, but the lines grow outside the castle as more people wait, some even spending the night in order to be first in line. The King's seer is granted one day a week to enter the market, each Saturday, for an hour with Martha and an entourage of guards. The guards pay close attention to anyone the seer's eyes land on for too long or anyone that pays too much attention to her, bringing them before the king.

One day, in midsummer, as she stands in court, she feels a shiver of fear creep through her. Her eyes scan the hall as she tries to determine what is setting her on edge. Zane, noticing her attention is elsewhere, pauses the court. "Is everything alright, King's seer?"

"Yes… No… I feel there is someone watching us, Sire, but I can't determine who or where they are. It makes me nervous as I sense they are angry, but I am seeing no vision tied to it."

"Has this happened before, King's seer?"

"No, Your Majesty. I always see my visions. That's what's making this so strange. It's like this one is being blocked somehow, and I have never had that before."

He studies her expression, noticing a very real fear in her eyes. He lifts a hand to Randolph. "Randolph, bring in more guards to stand around the room and protect the King's seer."

"As you wish, Sire."

"I'm sorry, Your Majesty. I do not wish to trouble you."

"Quite alright, King's seer, perhaps your gifts are growing, and they haven't quite settled in. That's why you are feeling uneasy. Either way, more guards for the day won't hurt."

"Perhaps." She frowns slightly in confusion as she glances around the grand hall again, watching the extra guards filter in at the edges. "Thank you, Your Majesty."

The rest of the court passes uneventfully; Zane leads her to the dining hall, where they enjoy their usual plate of bacon with their lunch. After lunch, he rises from the table. "I will see you tomorrow, King's seer."

"Of course, Your Majesty."

He starts to head out of the room, pausing to look back at her as she picks at her food, having never seen her so uncertain of herself in the past four years as she is now. "King's seer."

She lifts her gaze to his, placing her fork down. "Yes, Your Majesty?"

"We have always known your powers will grow, but as there are no other mystics to ask. We will have to accept there are times you will not understand your gift. This is one of those times, and I am confident you will figure it out."

"Thank you, Your Majesty." She nods, watching him leave the dining hall. Her gaze drifts back to the food, moving it around the plate until a maid startles her out of her thoughts. "Miss, your food is cold. Would you like me to bring you some more?"

"No, Elo, it's alright. Thank you. I'm not really hungry today. Tell the cooks it was lovely."

"Yes, Miss."

The King's seer rises and moves to the kitchen, her guards following like the silent shadow they are. She sits down at the table with Martha, who looks up at her. Martha studies her for a moment, noting the seer's full plate of food going past her. "Are you feeling alright, King's seer?"

"Yes, Miss Martha."

Martha arches a brow at her lie. "It seems your lunch is barely touched."

"Yes, sorry, it was good. I was not hungry."

"Is there something going on?"

The King's seer shakes her head, a shiver running through her as she looks around the kitchen. "I just feel as if someone is watching me."

"We are all watching you m'dear. You are still a child to many of us, even if the King sees you as older than you are."

"It's not that…" She glances around the kitchen again, her eyes moving to the windows. "It's like someone bad is watching."

"Does the King know?"

The King's seer looks back at her entourage, doubled for the day. "Yes, he knows; he called in extra guards."

Martha smiles, patting her hand gently, "Then I am certain it will be fine."

"Yes, Miss Martha. Thank you." The King's seer rises from her seat, gives Martha a bow, and heads back to her room. She closes the door behind her, moving straight to the garden door and shifting the latch to lock it closed. She peeks into her bathing chamber, seeing it empty, before heading out to the balcony. The light curtains flutter in the wind as she scans the city before her, knowing whoever it is, is out there. She allows her gaze to wander to her gardens, suspecting she is being foolish, but she isn't going down there today. She pulls the light glass doors closed as she backs into her room, wishing there is a lock on these doors as well. She collects the book Martha gave her for her thirteenth birthday from the table, crawls into the pillows on the bed, and reads as the hours pass. A knock startles her out of the book, noticing that the sun has shifted across the sky. "Who is it?"

"It's Pippa, Miss; it's always me."

"Sorry, come in, Pippa."

Pippa enters the room, carrying a dinner tray and placing it on the table. She looks at the seer sitting in the bed, a teddy in one arm and a book in the other. "Dinner's here; I will set the bathing chamber up for you, Miss."

The King's seer slides from the bed, leaving her book and teddy behind as she pads to the table and eats her dinner, watching Pippa move about the room. "Thank you, Pippa."

Once Pippa has set things up, she returns to sit at the table, talking as they always do. Pippa gathers the empty plates, giving her a bow. "Thank you, Miss. I will see you in the morning then."

The King's seer nods, watching Pippa leave the room and close the door behind her. She resists calling Pippa back as a slight uneasiness creeps in while she moves toward the bathing chamber. She closes the door behind her, strips out of her clothes, and steps into the tub, sinking into the water to soak. After a while, she scrubs herself clean and rinses off. She steps out of the tub to grab one of the fluffy towels she loves so much, pressing her face into it before drying herself off and slipping on her lavender sleepers. She crawls into bed to read again, eventually drifting off to a restless sleep with darkness creeping into her dreams.

She feels a warning within the shadows but is unable to determine its source, shifting restlessly as the darkness grows. She wakes suddenly in pain as a blade descends into her shoulder, crying out in agony. She struggles against the man who has her pinned in the bed, feeling the blade slice through her arm. Her hands glow softly as motes of purple light surround her, slamming into her attacker and knocking him backward off the bed. She rolls over and falls off the other side, rising to her feet, and runs for the door, feeling the blade sink into her side as her attacker drags her to the ground. "Xyl! Help me!"

Her door swings open at her cry. Xyl immediately notices the seer pinned to the ground, covered in blood, and struggling against a man twice her size, dagger in hand. He draws his blade and charges into the fray, driving his sword into the man, who suddenly realizes he is outnumbered as the four guards race into the room. The attacker rolls off the seer and away from the guards, running for the balcony and jumping off as the guards watch in shock. Xyl moves to the seer, drawing her into his arms as she curls up into a ball and cries. "King's seer! We need a healer."

Her voice is barely a whisper as her body shakes against him. "NO, get to the King. There are two on his wall right now."

Xyl pales. "I will stay with the seer. Drue, you wake Pippa. Cedrik, Luis, go to the King. Sound the alarms that we have intruders."

"No alarms; they will run. Please hurry." The King's seer closes her eyes, her breathing growing shallow as the darkness creeps in.

Drue races to Pippa's room, banging on the door. "The King's seer needs you now!" He follows Cedrik and Luis to the king's rooms.

Xyl shakes her slightly. "Don't you go there, Miss Seer; you stay awake, you hear me?"

"It hurts so much…" She cracks open her violet eyes, finding him for a moment, and struggles against the shadows, but fails and slips into oblivion.

Pippa runs into the room, seeing her mistress on the floor in Xyl's arms and blood everywhere. "No, Miss. What happened?"

"She was attacked, Pippa; we need to stop the bleeding and get a healer immediately."

Pippa pales, moving swiftly to the dresser, pulls out an undergarment, and tosses it his way. "Bind her wounds to slow the bleeding. I will wake Miss Martha. She will know where the healer is." Pippa turns and runs through the hallways to Martha's room, banging on the door. "Miss Martha, We need help."

A minute later, a half-asleep Martha stands facing a panicked Pippa. "Do you have any idea how late it is, Pippa?"

"The King's Seer was stabbed; We need a healer!"

Martha's eyes widen, breaking into a run for the seer's room, her eyes landing on the child lying on the carpet as Xyl cuts up strips of undergarment, trying to stem the bleeding. "Pippa, go to the kitchens. Fetch me a mortar and pestle, cloves, calendula, turmeric, lard, and flour. Xyl, in the gardens, you will find yarrow and the flowers of spilanthes. I need those now."

The pair nod, one running for the kitchens, the other running to the gardens to get the ingredients Martha requested.

Martha lifts the child carefully, moving her to the bed, and brushes her hair aside. "Oh, child. We should have listened to your feelings. You might be young still, but we should know better."

Meanwhile, Drue, Cedrik, and Luis run through the corridors, stopping at the king's door to inform Benson what is happening. They open the door, slip into the room, and see the king sleeping peacefully. Within the shadow, they could see a pair of assassins moving cautiously towards the king. As the intruders reach the edge of the bed, Luis creeps behind them towards the balcony to block any escape, while Drue and Cedrik draw their blades and move to attack one shadowed form. Benson slips to the side and takes the other on by himself. Swords clash with daggers as the assassins realize the guards have seen them, each struggling to win the fight. Drue and Cedrik take down their assassin quickly, but not before Drue is struck by a blade to his midsection. Drue sinks to his knees as the poison on the blade weakens him while he tries to stop the flow of his blood. Cedrik glances at Benson, moving to help as the other assassin turns to run, taking a blade to the heart from Luis, who stood in the shadows of the balcony. "Is that it?"

Luis nods. "I saw no more on the wall. The King's seer said there were two."

Benson moves over to wake the king, who has slept blissfully through it all, shaking his shoulder and earning a glare from Zane as he wakes up. His eyes take in the four guards in his room. "WHAT! And what in the bloody hell are the seer's guards doing in my room."

Benson bows. "Your Majesty. The King's seer has been stabbed. Xyl remained with her. She said, as they rescued her, that two intruders were on your walls, intending to kill you. Her guards helped dispatch the assassins, but not before Drue was stabbed with a poisoned blade."

"Did she survive?"

"As far as we know. She was bleeding heavily when we left her with Xyl."

Fear fills Zane as he jumps out of bed and grabs a robe. He pulls it on as he runs to the seer's room and arrives just as Xyl and Pippa do with the ingredients. Benson follows right behind him. "Martha?"

Martha glances his way while grinding the items she requested and quickly making a paste out of them. "King Zane."

"Will she live?"

"I don't know, Your Majesty. Near as I can see, she has been stabbed three times. I can't ask her what happened as she was unconscious when I arrived. I am trying to stop the bleeding and quell the pain, but she will need a healer." Martha pulls away the seer's sleepers, spreading the paste on her wounds, before wrapping them as best as she possibly can.

"Where is her assassin?"

Xyl points to the balcony. "He jumped before I could kill him, your Majesty. I figured the King's seer is more important, so stayed with her in case there was another attacker."

Zane walks over to the balcony, seeing the dead man on the ground two stories below. His gaze moves to the locked garden door. "How did he get in?"

Cedrik and Luis arrive, carrying Drue, his arms draped over their shoulders. "Our guess is the same way they were in your room. Through the balcony, but there are no ropes or indication as to how they got up."

"It's TWO floors up!"

"Yes, Your Majesty. The seer said they were ON the wall and not to sound the alarm as that would chase them away."

"So, what you are saying is, if it was not for this child, I would be dead."

"Yes, Your Majesty. We didn't hear them at all, even as we watched them cross the room in your chamber."

Zane moves to the seer laying on the bed, rage in his eyes as he stares down at the child fighting for her life. "Cedrik, go and get that body, find the blade, and bring it to the war room. I want to know if it is poisoned as well. Luis, get the blades from my room, so we can ensure they match. In the morning, I want locks on her balcony, ones that lock on the inside, like the garden door."

"Yes, Sire." Cedrik and Luis move Drue to one of the chairs before leaving the room to retrieve what is required.

"Xyl, Who was patrolling outside?"

"No one while she sleeps, Sire; she's never in the garden at night after Pippa's last call."

He turns to Pippa, "Is this true?"

Pippa bows, "Yes, sire, she doesn't like it outside after dark. It scares her, so I lock the door at dinner."

Zane nods, "Benson, who's on castle duty patrol."

"I'm not sure Sire, Dunivan appoints them. I will find out."

"Tell him I will meet him in the war room shortly."

"Yes, Sire." Benson bows and leaves the room.

"Martha, once you're done, I want the best healer gold can buy here within the hour. I will pay double their fees to get them here in half that time." His eyes move to Drue slumped over; his eyes glaze slightly as he listens to the conversation. "Treat them both."

Martha nods, "Yes, Sire, I will fetch them right away. I am done applying the paste. Pippa can reapply if any blood seeps through it."

"Make it quick, Martha."

Martha bows. "Yes, Sire."

Zane turns, slamming his hand against the wall and causing all of them to jump. "Dammit, she knew too. She felt someone watching her, and I brushed it off."

Martha pales, "You didn't, Sire. You doubled her guard. She said as much when she came to me in the kitchen."

"But it wasn't enough, was it? I understand why people wish to see a King dead, but she is still a child!"

"There are people that believe those with the gift of sight are the work of demons, Your Majesty. Perhaps that is it?"

"No, there is more going on here, and I'm going to find out what it is. She felt as if her vision was blocked in some way. She is NOT to be alone until there is a lock on that balcony. Is that understood?"

"Yes, Sire." Martha grabs one of the seer's cloaks and races from the room. Zane follows but instead heads to the war room.

Xyl and Drue look at each other, their gaze drifting to Pippa, who hovers over the seer, each knowing that had they been seconds longer, there would be no seer to speak of.

Zane arrives at the war room just as Dunivan does, looking half asleep. "Sire? Benson filled me in. I sent him to retrieve the patrols and find out how the assassins made it past them. I am sorry; I figured we had enough around the castle. Will she live?"

"Let's hope so. Martha is running for the healer as we speak. There were three assassins, but I have the feeling there is someone waiting to see if they would succeed. Since they didn't, another wave could arrive. The seer herself said earlier she felt as though someone was watching, but she couldn't see it clearly as she felt her vision was blocked. This was a planned attack by someone with power behind them. I should have listened to her; she has always been accurate in every story she has given."

"You couldn't have known, Sire."

"But she did. In the morning, find us a mage, and do a search of the castle, as magic would be the only thing I can think of that would affect the seer's powers."

"Yes, Sire. King Ludy has the two most powerful mages in the realm, Runestone and Antimagic. We could request an audience with them."

"Antimagic? Strange name."

Dunivan nods. "It's a nickname that kind of stuck, Sire, a long-standing joke between them. Runestone is a creator of magic, and Myke undoes magic, hence Antimagic. The only thing is, they are across the water, so it will take at least two to three weeks as we have to ride down to Westshore for the ship passage."

"Do it. Send our diplomats David and Charles out with a message immediately."

Luis returns with the two blades, laying them on the table before the king. "I have searched the bodies and found nothing on them, Sire. For the time being, I have placed them in the cells downstairs until you decide what you want done with them. I have also woken a few maids to clean your rooms, but you might need to replace those rugs."

Zane moves to the blades, seeing the green glisten of poison on each of them, knowing that if one took Drue out of the fight, two were intended to kill. "Where is Cedrik? He should have been back with the blade by now. Benson is not back either. What the hell is going on?"

Luis shakes his head. "Want me to go look, Sire?"

"Yes, find them."

Luis nods, running from the room. He returns several minutes later with another blade, covered in poison as well. "We have four guards down, Iyan and Bert are in rough shape. Both Benson and Cedrik are trying to help with tying their wounds closed, but they also keep bleeding. All the guards patrolling the seer's side of the castle are dead."

"Damn, whoever attacked the castle meant business. In the morning, put a call out for more guards. Have Iyan and Bert moved to the infirmary where they can be treated. Get a guard on Martha immediately. She left the castle for a healer, and whoever is watching may target her."

"Yes Sire, I saw her; I will run after her." Luis sprints to catch up to Martha

"Dunivan, go to Cedrik and Benson, and help them get the injured into the castle."

"Yes, Sire," Dunivan bows, running out of the war room.

Zane growls under his breath at the losses he has suffered, his rage directed at whoever would dare to target the castle. He narrows his eyes at the tokens on his map, knowing whichever country did this is going to go down first when he makes his move. He makes his way back to the seer's room; his rage continues to grow as he struggles to contain the desire to kill or destroy something. Upon arriving, his eyes land on Drue, who is barely conscious as he sways in the chair. "Xyl, take him to the infirmary; we have guards down outside that need healing; the healer will see them all there."

"Yes, Your Majesty." Xyl tucks himself under Drue's arm and lifts him to his feet, staggering out of the room to the infirmary.

Zane drags a chair over to the side of the seer's bed, sitting next to it. His eyes take in the amount of blood on the seer, the bed, and the floor. "So much blood loss for a child."

"Yes, Sire, but the paste is slowing it down. Hopefully, the healer can stop the bleeding completely, and we can save her."

"They will, Pippa. Martha will bring the best as she knows where to find them all."

Pippa looks up at him, fear and concern laced in her eyes. "Why would they attack her, Your Majesty? She hasn't done anything but help people."

Zane narrows his eyes, his barely contained rage edging out into his voice. "I don't know, Pippa, but I aim to find out. No one attacks my seer and gets away with it."

"I hope you do, Sire. They deserve it for what they have done to her."

"We will find them; I promise you that."

Within the half-hour, Martha and Luis enter the room. Accompanying them is a cloaked lady with gentle brown eyes and long dark brown hair, carrying a heavy black bag. "Sire, the healer Irma is here."

Zane looks the lady over, watching as she approaches the bed. "Is she good, Martha?"

"Yes, Sire, one of the best."

"Good."

The healer bows to the king. "Sire. Martha said the child has been stabbed, possibly with poison. Do you have the blade?"

"Yes, downstairs. Luis, please retrieve them."

She nods and moves to the side of the bed, placing her bag nearby as she looks over the child. Irma pulls the lavender sleeper aside, studying each wound, a slight frown on her face as she notes the seer's pale features. She tests the seer's temperature, fingers resting on her neck and feeling an ever-so-slight pulse. She turns as Luis returns; he holds the blade out as she inspects it. "Interesting. This is Dragonfire poison; it is called a slow death. That is why her wounds continue to bleed. What poultice have you applied to her wounds, Martha?"

"Cloves, calendula, turmeric, yarrow, and the flowers of spilanthes, mixed with lard and flour to stop the bleeding."

Irma arches her brow. "Impressive; that probably saved her life, but she will be on limited activity and bed rest for a while." She opens her bag and pulls out four rose quartz, placing them around the seer and chanting a few words. A pale green magic springs from her fingers, spreading out to the crystals and creating a blanket of magic over the seer. "The magic will last an hour or so, depending on how long it takes to draw the poison from her system and heal her wounds. Once the poison is removed, the shield will shift to a pale blue, and the stones can be removed. She will be weak and sore for another week or two from the effects. I understand there are others that are injured?"

"Yes, in the infirmary."

"I will see them next?"

"Of course, Luis, take her there." Zane waves them away as he watches the child beneath the magical blanket, seeing hints of dark green magic in her wounds, pulling the poison from her body.

Irma grabs her bag, heading back down the stairs with Luis. At the infirmary, she notes that all three guards are in the same condition as the seer. "What happened here?"

"We had an attack on the King and the seer; four guards did not make it."

"Right, we need to lay them together. The magic will take longer as I don't have that many stones." She assists in moving them all together, placing her remaining four stones down. She chants a few words as the green blanket spreads, covering all three of them with one cast. "While the child's healing will take about an hour or so, these three will take about eight to twelve. They really should each have a shield of their own, but I was not prepared to be treating four poisoned victims."

Luis bows, "Thank you, Healer Irma."

"You're welcome. Martha can return these stones to me in the morning. All of them should survive and be fine in a few weeks. If anything should happen and they take a downhill turn, send a messenger right away."

Luis nods, escorting her back to the chapel where Martha had found her before making his way back.

Hours pass. The King, Pippa, and Martha sit in the seer's room, the shield fading as they wait for her to wake up. The silence in the room is deafening; each of them sits lost in their thoughts, rage emanating out from Zane while worry and concern from Pippa and Martha.

Just before sunrise, the King's seer shifts in the bed, opening her eyes to see three people staring down at her, each one breathing a sigh of relief. A few tears creep from the seer's eyes as she looks up into their gazes. "I'm sorry. I didn't mean to…"

Zane takes her hand. "Shh, it's not your fault, King's seer. You warned us; we didn't listen. Next time we will."

She shakes her head, "I should have seen better."

Martha takes her other hand, speaking softly. "Child. You can't be expected to see everything."

She shifts her gaze to Martha. "But I am the King's seer; I should see it."

Zane scowls slightly at her words, earning a stern look from Martha, and softens his voice. "King's seer. You see more than any other seer in the realm, with an accuracy that none can even come close to competing with. This is NOT your fault. This is our fault for not protecting you properly."

"Yes, Mister King," her voice is barely a whisper.

He pats the top of her hand gently. "I will send Xyl back up to stay in the room with you and Pippa. Until we get a lock on your balcony doors, you are not to be alone until we find out who did this. Understood."

"Yes, Mister King."

"Good, Now I need to go check on my men that were injured as well. Thank you, King's seer, for mentioning the ones in my room."

"I didn't see them till I saw the man in here. I tried, but I couldn't see; I just felt it." She closes her eyes, a few tears creeping down her face. "I will do better."

"You did well, King's seer. Remember that." He reaches out to brush her tears away, watching sleep pull her away from them again. He rises and works his way down to the infirmary, knowing as soon as she is able, he will be training her to defend herself against further attacks. He glances at the wounded guards under the same healing magic, his eyes shifting to Dunivan, Xyl, and Luis. "Dunivan, you watch these three. Xyl, Luis, I want you back in the seer's room until your shift ends, then switch with Krim and Jesper. Put Tai on her balcony and have Alvero find a locksmith."

Dunivan, Xyl, and Luis nod, "Right away, Sire."

Luis and Xyl make their way back to the seer's room, noticing the door is still open. Xyl moves to stand near the entrance of the balcony while Luis remains in the hallway just outside her room.

The King's seer sleeps through the morning, missing breakfast, missing the king coming in to stand watch for a few hours, even missing the locksmith that installs better locks on all her doors. She opens her eyes to a room full of people around lunchtime, noticing the concern in their eyes as she reaches up gingerly to touch her shoulder.

"Miss, don't touch that; there are poultices on your wounds to help them mend."

The King's seer nods, her eyes drifting to Pippa. "It hurts Pippa. Everywhere hurts."

"I know, Miss, it's probably gonna hurt for a few days."

"Were you here all night, Pippa? You should get some sleep."

"We all were, Miss. The castle's pretty much on shutdown for the day."

"I didn't mean to cause so much trouble."

Zane rises from his chair, moving to sit on the edge of her bed. "You didn't, King's seer. I am just glad you made it through. Now, you are not to get out of this bed for at least two weeks while you heal."

Her brow furrows; her eyes dart to Pippa and Martha before looking back to the king. "But what if I need to?"

"There is nothing that you need to do, King's seer. The court can live without you for a few weeks."

She nods, struggling to sit up as Pippa helps her. She glances at the other guards in the room, then whispers to the king. "But I need to use the girl's room."

Zane blushes, giving a short nod of understanding. "Right, well yes, you are allowed to leave if you have Pippa assisting you. Understood. Then right back to this bed until you are healed."

She nods, "Yes, Mister King."

"And once you are better, I want you to be trained to defend yourself. This was too close; clearly, someone wanted both of us dead. Dunivan will assist you with that, and perhaps some of the guards who are on duty."

She nods, shifting in bed a touch. "Yes, Mister King. Can I leave the bed now?"

He rises from the bed as it dawns on him that she meant right now, ushering everyone out of the room. "Of course. Guards, out. The King's seer needs time to herself."

The King's seer watches them leave before sliding out of the bed with Pippa and Martha's help. She staggers to the bathroom as best as she can to do what she needs to do. Once she is done, she washes up a bit before heading back to the room and crawling back into bed with their help.

"Are you hungry, Miss? I can go get some food while Miss Martha watches you."

"Yes, a bit. Thank you."

"Anytime, Miss."

The King's seer watches Pippa leave, her eyes drifting to Martha as she pulls her bear into her lap, playing with its ears. "I didn't mean to keep everyone up all night, Miss Martha."

"It's quite alright, King's seer."

The King's seer nods, looking down at her bear, making a silent promise to herself to do better.

Blades of Prophecy

DAYS PASS AS the King's seer rests, her wounds healing faster than expected but not fast enough for her liking. Pippa attends to her as the seer stays in bed, reading books that Martha brought her to keep her entertained. The king stops in several times a day to check on her. At the end of the week, she feels well enough to leave her bed and heads down to the dining chamber to have lunch with the king. He narrows his eyes slightly as she steps into the room. "Should you be out of bed, King's seer?"

She nods, sliding her dress off her shoulder to show him one of the stab marks. "They are all better. I only feel a little bit tired, Your Majesty."

Zane's eyes follow her as she moves to sit in her designated chair. Her guards disperse but remain close enough to react if needed. Zane lifts his hand, indicating another plate needs to be brought in for the seer. "The usual, King's seer?"

"Yes, Your Majesty."

He calls out to the maids, "The usual." Zane turns his attention back to the seer, who sits before him, having disobeyed his order to stay in bed for two weeks. "Is everything alright, King's seer?"

"Yes, Your Majesty."

"Then why are you really here when I gave the direct order to stay in bed for two weeks?"

She studies him for a moment before looking at her lap. "I didn't mean to. I am better and feel like I should be doing something rather than sitting in my room reading. I am not used to not being in court, Sire."

He arches a brow and chuckles. "Are you saying you are bored?"

The King's seer starts to open her mouth in denial but closes it as she tries to decide the best way to answer the question.

Zane watches her carefully, knowing she isn't going to dare confess boredom to him, and leans back in his chair as his fingers drum the table lightly, waiting for her reply.

She lifts her gaze to his. "No, Sire. Pippa talks a lot, and Miss Martha brings me lots of books to read. I just…"

"It's quite alright, King's seer. I will make you a deal. You may return to court this week, but only for two hours a day. I still do not think you are ready to be up, especially as none of the guards are even moving. Will that work?"

She smiles. "Yes, Your Majesty. Thank you."

"You're welcome. Now, eat your lunch, then I will take you back to your rooms. Next week, we will head to the training compound, and you will learn how to defend yourself."

"Yes, Your Majesty."

After lunch, Zane returns her to her room, waiting until she crawls into the bed and closes the door. He sends a dark look at her two guards. "She was to remain in this room for two weeks. You did understand that, correct?"

They both nod, bowing their heads. "Yes, Sire. She insisted, Sire."

"If she relapses, it's on you." Zane turns and strides away, leaving them looking at each other nervously.

The week passes; the King's seer attends two hours of court a day. She finds herself exhausted the first morning and sleeps through the afternoon, but gains strength with each day that passes thereafter. At the end of the week, Zane escorts her to the dining hall and sits her down before settling himself into his own chair. "Well, King's seer. I must say, I am impressed. I didn't think you could do it."

"Thank you, Your Majesty."

"After lunch, I will take you to see the training area. You can start training on Monday, after court."

"Yes, Your Majesty."

Once they finish lunch, Zane leads her to a section of the castle that she has never been to. The hallway is adorned with weapons of all types hanging in racks and on the walls. He feels her hand tighten on his arm and pauses as she backs up a step, fear clearly written all over her expression. "Are you alright, King's seer?"

Her free hand moves to her shoulder as her gaze locks onto a dagger hanging on the wall, her voice becoming quiet. "Yes, Mister King."

Zane follows her line of sight to the dagger. "Are you seeing things on the weapons, King's seer?"

"Some things, Mister King. Mostly I see that man's dagger that stabbed me. I see that a lot."

"I suspect you would. I can imagine those thoughts will not leave you anytime soon. As for these weapons, many of them have been in battles defending this kingdom. The one we had made for you is new and has not seen a fight, so you should be alright handling it."

"Thank you, Mister King." She averts her gaze, keeping it pinned to the floor as she is led to an open area, the clang of steel rings through the air drawing her gaze up. She can see training dummies positioned along one wall, traveling to the guards fighting against each other in the center space, and the one commanding them. She watches blades strike each other, the formation of the guards' steps, and the way their armor moves with them. She lifts her gaze to the king for a moment, then turns it to the one that he watches approach them. "Sire, King's seer. Is she here to train Sire?"

"Not today Dunivan. I am just bringing her to show her where the training grounds are and what is required."

Dunivan bows. "Yes, Your Majesty. Welcome to the training barracks, King's seer. We will start you on learning how to handle your sword, then move to the dummies over there. After that, perhaps you can practice with your guards."

She nods, her eyes drift to the pairs fighting each other. "Will I be as good as they are?"

Dunivan shakes his head; his eyes move to the king's. "You could, I suppose, if you put enough work into it, but I am under the impression we are just training you to defend yourself."

"That is correct, Dunivan. King's seer, in order to be that good, you would need to train twelve hours a day, and you have other duties to attend to."

She looks up at the king, determination in her gaze as they drift back to the guards. "I will learn fast then."

Both Dunivan and Zane chuckle. "Alright, King's seer, your afternoons are yours. If you wish to spend them all here, then you may do so. But the mornings are mine, you hear me?"

"Yes, Sire."

"Are you staying then, or shall I escort you back?"

"I shall stay if I may?"

"As you wish, King's seer, just don't overdo it."

"I won't, Your Majesty."

"Dunivan, I leave her in your hands then. Xyl, Alvero, please ensure she returns to her room in time for dinner."

"Yes, Your Majesty."

The King's seer watches the king leave, then turns her attention back to the fighters as Dunivan leads her away. He places some armor on her arms and hands her a sword.

"This one is yours, King's seer."

She inspects the sword carefully, noticing "KS" engraved on the hilt. Purple leather wraps the pommel, and the silver blade glints in the light. "It's heavy."

"Yes, I suspect it is. It will become lighter as you learn to use it."

The King's seer frowns, "I don't understand. How can it become lighter?"

Dunivan chuckles, reaching out to her upper arms and wrapping his hands around them. She watches in shock that he would dare touch her. "You have no muscles there, King's seer. As they grow, your power with the blade will too. Now first, we teach you the basics of holding the blade and the movements needed."

She nods, paying attention to what he says, practicing what she learns on the dummies, feeling her energy ebbing after an hour and a half. She lowers her blade and stares at the dummy in dismay, turning to watch the guards who are still sparring.

Xyl comes over to her, seeing the defeat in her eyes. "King's seer, we have been training all our lives. This is your first day. I admit, you lasted an hour longer than we expected you to, but you should return to your room and rest. There will be more days to train, and you will get it, I promise."

The King's seer hands her blade over to Xyl, who in turn passes it to Dunivan. "Do you think so?"

"I know so, King's seer. Now come, let's get you back, shall we?"

She glances at the fighters once more before following Xyl and Alvero back to her rooms. Her thoughts drift back to the training rings, resulting in her missing the glances Xyl sends her way. She thanks them both as she enters her room and closes the door behind her, moving to the bathing chamber to do what she needs to do. She returns to her room and crawls into the bed, suddenly feeling very exhausted.

The King's seer wakes several hours later to Pippa's concerned voice. "Miss, are you alright? You didn't answer the door."

She blinks a few times, feeling a stiffness in her body as she rolls over. She catches Xyl watching her with concern in his eyes. "Yes, Pippa. I'm sorry, I didn't hear you knock."

"You always do. Should I get Miss Martha?"

She pushes herself up, flinching at the pain in her arms, and rubs them gingerly. "No, it's fine."

"Miss, I can see you're in pain. What happened?"

Xyl smiles at Pippa, a touch of pride in his voice. "She was practicing with the sword today, Pippa. I think her arms will be sore for a few days."

"What! Why would you do that, Miss?"

"The King wishes for her to learn to defend herself, but instead of taking things slow, she swung her blade at the training dummy for over an hour and a half."

"Oh, Miss, I will draw a bath for you right after you eat your dinner!" Pippa assists her from her bed to the table as Xyl and Alvero back out of the room and close the door.

"Thank you, Pippa."

The King's seer eats her dinner quietly. She hears Pippa move around in the bathing chamber, setting things up for the evening. Once the seer is finished eating, she moves to the bathing room, strips down with Pippa's help, and steps into the water. The warmth eases away some of her aches. After an hour of soaking, she dries herself off, pulls on her sleepers, and crawls back into bed, sleeping straight through until morning.

Xyl and Alvero remain on watch until the shift changes when they are unexpectedly called down to the king's war room, where Dunivan stands waiting for them. The seer's guards bow upon entering the chamber, "Sire."

"Xyl. Alvero. Dunivan informed me that the seer practiced for an hour and a half today while you watched over her."

"Yes, Sire, an hour longer than we expected."

"And how do you think she did?"

"She swung pretty wildly, but perhaps with time, she will adapt. She seems quite determined to learn, Sire."

"She does. It makes me wonder why."

"I would think getting stabbed three times would make anyone want to learn, Sire."

"I suppose you have a point. She did state that the images of being stabbed have not left her yet, which is not surprising. Thank you. You are dismissed."

Xyl and Alvero bow and back out of the chamber as Zane turns to Dunivan. "What do you think, Dunivan?"

"They speak the truth, Sire. I suspect that the child will be sore for a few days with the way she was handling her blade."

"Did she overdo it, Dunivan?"

"Perhaps, but as they said, she is determined. And when she lowered her blade in defeat, Xyl stepped in immediately and returned her to her room."

Zane drums his fingers on the table lightly as he looks over the markers that haven't moved in over two weeks. "Have we heard anything from our diplomats about Ludy's mages?"

"Not yet, Sire, but all's going well. The boat should arrive in Hontby today or tomorrow. We should hear soon."

"Good. I still want a search of the whole castle done. We are no closer to discovering who sent those assassins than we were two weeks ago."

"Yes, Sire. We have eyes out everywhere, but every lead we get comes to a dead end. Whoever did this is extremely skilled at what they do, and I am concerned that they will attempt another strike."

"I agree, Dunivan. I don't like it. I don't like that the seer is learning to fight, but if her guards had not been there, she would have died. We both would have, and that's not an option either."

"I understand, Sire. I will focus on defensive training."

"Thank you."

In the morning, the King's seer wakes up and groans in pain at the thought that she has shopping and four hours of court today. She crawls from her bed, feeling aches all over, wishing it was tomorrow and her day of rest as she pads to the bathing chamber, running another bath. She sinks in the water, feeling the heat take away some of the pain when she hears Pippa's morning knock. "Come in, Pippa."

The door opens; Pippa glances around and closes the door behind her, "Where are you, Miss?"

"In here, Pippa."

The maid heads into the bathing chamber and spots the seer soaking in the bath. She laughs softly. "Still sore, I see. Once you are out, I will apply the cream Miss Martha made to help with that. *'Would do no good to let the King know you are sore,'* she said."

"Thank you, Pippa." The King's seer remains in the tub as Pippa lays out her dress on the bed, then leaves. The maid returns twenty minutes later with breakfast. "Miss, you better get out, or you're gonna be late. Miss Martha is already waiting."

"I know, Pippa, I'm sorry." She rises from the tub and grabs a towel, wrapping it around herself as she heads back to the bedroom. She stands still as Pippa applies the cream to her shoulders and arms before she gets dressed in a light violet and white gown. The seer moves to the table and eats her breakfast as Pippa sets her hair in several braids. Pippa twists them into a bun at the crown of her head and drives hairpins through the braids to hold them in place. Once Pippa is finished, the King's seer rises, feeling the slight warmth on her skin from the cream as it eases the pain in her muscles. "Thank you, Pippa."

"Thank Miss Martha, Miss"

"I will." The King's seer heads out of the rooms, her entourage of guards remaining close as she makes her way to where Martha waits.

Martha studies her, seeing the stiffness in her frame as she approaches. "King's seer, are you feeling alright?"

"I am Miss Martha. Thank you."

"You're welcome. Come, we should get our shopping done, so we can get you back here on time for court." The pair travels through town as the King's seer enjoys her first outing since the assassination. She notices that her guards have tripled for the excursion. The hour passes far too quickly, and she finds herself back behind the throne of the king, watching as he enters the hall.

Zane studies his seer, looking for signs that she is suffering from yesterday and seeing none. "King's seer. How are you feeling this morning?"

"My arms feel a little bit stiff, Sire."

"That's understandable. Are you ready for court?"

"Yes, Sire."

A few days later, Zane watches the seer practicing with Dunivan, amazed at how fast she has progressed in such a short time, putting some of his fighters to shame. He turns as Randolph runs over to him. "Sire, the mages are here. King Ludy sent them both for you. They wait in the grand hall."

He nods and gives a final glance towards the seer as she stabs the dummy while Dunivan shifts her arms slightly to brace her for the impact.

"Thank you, Randolph." Zane heads to the grand hall, his eyes alighting on the two casters as he steps into the room. The human woman, with long white hair and ice-blue eyes, is dressed in a dark blue gown with a pattern of ice crystals embroidered on it, a slight chill surrounding her. The human man is taller than her by a foot. He is bald and has white bushy eyebrows, a salt and pepper goatee, with a gold hoop clinging to one ear. He is dressed in dark green robes, which match his deep green eyes. "Welcome to Oblait. I thank your King and you for coming to our aid."

The mages both bow. "You are most welcome, King Zane; I am Runestone, and this here is Myke, or Antimagic as I like to tease him with. Your diplomats were not exactly clear as to what is needed, just that a child was injured, and you wish to protect her."

"Yes, the child in question is my seer. We had assassins attack the castle two weeks ago, and she barely survived. She felt her sight was being blocked that day. So I am willing to make a sizable donation to your kingdom if you can search this castle and figure out how it was possible."

"It is strange for a seer's sight to be blocked. Is she certain?"

"Yes, she felt as if someone was watching her during the day, then that night, we were both attacked. We lost four guards in the strike; another three were injured and have been on bed rest for over two weeks. She was certain; we just didn't listen to her."

Runestone smiles gently, "I will help find the cause, but undoing magic is Myke's department. Where would you like us to start?"

Zane smiles in delight. "Great, start here in the hall, and then Randolph will walk you through the castle. I will leave you to it then."

Runestone watches the king leave the hall. She glances at Myke, feeling a slight uneasiness inside as she looks around the main hall. "Seems strange someone would want to block a seer's sight." She chants a few words, her eyes glowing a light blue as her fingertips weave a blanket of pale blue light through the room, intertwining it through the air.

Myke watches the spell work its way around and settle on a vase near the back corner. "Well, that looks like my department, Rune." He moves over to the vase, casting his own spell, disenchanting the vase as a backlash knocks him across the room, each mage hearing a scream of anger. Myke rises to his feet, brushing his robes off. "Damn, whoever enchanted that is strong. If there are any more of those, we might want to retrieve Gro to heal us."

"Wise plan, you go get him. I will keep scanning."

"I will be right back." He teleports out, returning shortly with another human, who is dressed in white robes, has gentle brown eyes, light brown hair, a mustache, and a beard.

"Runestone. I gather you requested a healer."

She laughs, keeping her focus on the spell, "Antimagic thinks we do, simply because his last spell sent him flying across the room."

Gronkus chuckles. "Well, he needs to learn to cast things better."

"That's what I keep saying... Now, we should finish the scan." Runestone slowly works her way through the castle, finding four other objects that are enchanted the same way. Myke disenchants them, with Gronkus healing him between each one as it knocks him off his feet and sends him backwards. Randolph accompanies them along their path. Eventually, Runestone finds herself standing in front of a door with three guards hovering nearby. "There is strong magic behind this door."

"This is the King's seer's room."

Runestone stops. "May we enter?"

"Of course." Randolph starts to knock, but the door opens, finding themselves face to face with the King's seer herself. Runestone gasps at the power emanating from the child while hearing a telepathic message almost immediately and feeling a very real fear in her mind. *'Please don't tell them it's me. Tell them it's something else.'*

Randolph glances at Runestone. "Is something wrong?"

"No, sorry, just her eyes are amazing; I have never seen violet eyes before."

"Yes, she's a mystic, as well as a seer."

"No wonder the King wants her protected. I sense magic in the room; may we enter, Child?"

The King's seer nods and steps aside, twisting her hands in front of her.

Runestone wanders around the room, her magic weaving through the air, forcing it to land on one of the toys in the toy bin. "There's the last one; disenchant it."

Myke moves forward, chanting a few words. He frowns slightly as he glances back at Runestone, catching the ever so slight shake of her head. "This one doesn't seem to be as strong, but it's been disenchanted as well. It's almost as if there hasn't been time for it to collect the power the others have. Child, have you had this toy for long?"

The King's seer shakes her head. "No, it's not one of my toys."

He hands it to Randolph, "I am assuming all the other objects we disenchanted have been here longer than the seer has."

"That is correct."

"Then whoever made this toy might have an idea of who bought it and placed it in your castle. Someone has a long-standing vendetta against your King. They will be angry now that we have dispelled all their spying devices."

"Thank you, I will let the King know right away."

Runestone watches the child, standing near the door, catching the soft *thank you* in her mind. She pulls a handful of gems out of her pocket, weaving her magic into them, then she kneels before the child and takes her hands. She places the gems in them gently. "These will stop anyone from watching you as long as you keep them near. Place one in every room that you frequent regularly." Runestone glances around. "So three will go in here, and perhaps one in the grand hall where you stand with the King. The rest can go to him to decide where he wants them."

The King's seer takes the gems, looking them over. "They are very pretty. Thank you, Miss Rune, Mister Mykes, and Mister Gro."

Runestone glances at the others, catching the use of their names when they were not introduced. "You take care, little one."

"I will. Thank you."

The group follows Randolph back to Kivu, who has the gold waiting and hands it over to the trio. "Thank you for all your assistance."

Runestone and Myke look at each other, accepting the large bag of coins. "The King is most generous; the pleasure is all ours. Call us anytime you need us to scan your castle."

Randolph nods. "Would you like an escort back?"

"Oh no, we can portal home. Thank you." Runestone lifts her hands, creating a ring of ice that shimmers in the center. She watches Gronkus and Myke step through it, following once she is certain they have arrived on the other side.

Myke stops, waiting for her to appear and the portal to close. "Alright, are you going to tell me why you had me disenchant a toy that wasn't enchanted?"

"Because the child asked me to."

He frowns. "Wait, I didn't hear her ask."

"She spoke telepathically, asking me not to let them know that the power I felt in the room was hers. I sensed a lot of fear, Myke. There is more going on in that kingdom than meets the eye, and we need to let Ludy know."

"Agreed. That magic is strong, almost as strong as ours, and that's a concern itself."

"Perhaps he can send Niceasilla and Chainz out to scout and learn more about this child."

"Good plan; let's go speak with him."

Back in Oblait, Randolph looks down at the toy in his hands before turning and striding to the king's chamber. He knocks on the door. "Sire, it's Randolph."

"Enter."

Randolph opens the door, giving Benson a nod as he steps inside the room. "And?"

"They found five objects of power and this." He places the toy in Zane's hand.

"What's so special about this?"

"That's the thing, Sire. Five of the objects knocked Antimagic off his feet, requiring him to be healed each time. This one did not, and yet the mage Runestone said there was strong magic in the seer's room."

"Interesting."

"I figured you should know. They did have a valid point that all the other objects were here before the seer. This is the only one to come after, and perhaps it hasn't had the time to collect power like the others."

"We need to find ourselves a mage we can have here at the castle, Randolph. I don't like relying on others."

"Yes, Sire. Runestone also gave the seer anti-scrying gems, some of which should make it to you after the child stops admiring them. One per room that the seer frequents, she said."

"Then I suppose one in the dining hall, the kitchen, as she spends time there with Martha and the fighting rings. How many did she get?"

"A handful Sire. I did not count them, but she did state the seer would need three for her chambers."

"Then we should have enough. Perhaps we have one that just travels with her guards."

"That might be an idea, Sire. I will retrieve them from the seer."

"Let her play with them tonight. I will get them in the morning."

"Yes, Sire." Randolph bows, leaving.

Zane sits in his room, turning the toy over in his hands as he ponders Randolph's words. In the morning, the King's seer hands the gems over to the king, informing him that she has hidden one in her garden, one in her bathing chamber, and one in the bedroom. Zane looks over the gems in his hands, seeing there is more than enough to cover the dining room, the kitchen, the training grounds, and then some. "Thank you, King's seer."

Time passes quickly for the seer. Memories of the attempted assassination fade to the back of her mind, and she adjusts to changes in her schedule. A few times a week after court, the king brings her to the war room to go over his map and identify where dragons may be. Dunivan trains her with the blade in the afternoons for two to three hours, doing his best to keep to defensive training but finding her skill growing rapidly. She finds time to squeeze in a daily visit with Martha, enjoying her time in the kitchen with the head housekeeper, along with the Saturday shopping trip with her before court. On Sundays, she adds horseback riding with the king on the Appaloosa she received for her fourteenth birthday, seeing the wonder of the countryside with him. In the evenings, she takes her dinner with Pippa in her room before settling in to read or play with some of the toys she still has.

Honors Light

THE KING'S SEER wakes up to her maid moving around her room. She stretches as she slips from the bed, moving to the bathing chamber, going through her morning routine before returning to be dressed. She stands still as Pippa slips her chemise on before sliding the skirt over her head and fastening the lacings snugly at her back. Pippa picks up the beaded belt and fastens it over the ties. She secures the ribbons in place, leaving the ends to flow with the silk skirts. The King's seer runs her hands gently over the dangling beads, noticing her dresses are getting more and more elaborate with each passing year. She studies the dress in the mirror, lifting her arms to look at the long sleeves that blend with her skirts when her arms are down. She is ever grateful that the king keeps her covered as she has heard of stories of other seers being scantily clad in hopes of distracting those that hired them.

Once Pippa dresses her, she moves to the chair to sit down to have her hair done. She knows there will be matching ribbons and beads set within it. She lifts her gaze to Pippa in the mirror, feeling the brush run through her hair and the gentle tugs as she braids it. She watches as Pippa places the adornments in her hair: metal flowers linked with chains to the metal butterfly that wraps around the two braids tied in a ponytail. Once Pippa is done, the seer rises to inspect herself in the full-length mirror. Her fingers touch the gems sewn into her dress, the light lavender enhancing the violet of her eyes. She feels her cloak settling over her shoulders as she absently reaches up to fasten it before her maid can. Pippa's sigh draws the seer's attention back to her.

"Pippa, you know I can do this stuff."

"Yes, Miss, but it's my job."

The King's seer turns to face her. "You do know I would never tell the King whether you did your job or whether I did."

Pippa smiles. "I know, Miss, but I like it."

The King's seer smiles, hugs her best friend for the past six years, and heads to the door where her guards await.

"When will you be back, Miss?"

"Hopefully, after lunch. I aim to visit Martha in the kitchens for a short time after the King."

"Yes, Miss. I will be waiting."

"Thank you, Pippa."

She steps out of her room, giving a nod to her guards. She heads to the grand hall, then steps into place behind the king as her guards settle behind her. "Good morning, Your Majesty."

"Good morning, King's seer; are you ready for the day?"

"Always, Your Majesty."

Zane nods, gesturing to Randolph to let the lines in. He watches as each person comes forward individually, casually listening to their requests, complaints, or demands, wishing he can be anywhere but here, getting tired of the facade he is putting on. Near the end of the session, an adventuring group dressed in thin blue tabards embroidered with a small white cross fleury steps into the hall. He watches as the group bows before them, only addressing them after they all show the proper respect. "I am King Zane; who are you, and what brings you to my court?"

The King's seer studies the group as they stand before the throne, drifting to each of the members as visions fill her mind. She determines rather quickly who the leader is and places a hand on the King's shoulder to pause him.

Zanes gaze lands on her hand, narrowing slightly at her daring to rest it upon him as, for all other visions, she has simply touched the chair. "What is it, King's seer?"

"It's amazing, Your Majesty." She steps down to the group, her skirts floating around her as she moves with grace. She stands before the priestess as Zane rises from his seat in shock. The King's seer lifts a hand to him to wait a moment as she studies the human before her. The priestess has blue eyes and long blonde hair that frame a heart-shaped face. The King's seer's eyes drift to the golden pendant of the sun, lying against the priestess' neck and matching the golden embroidery along the edges of her white robes. "Gwynevere, priestess of the Sun Goddess Raya, leader and commander of Honors Light."

The group's eyes widen at the seer's prediction. The seer moves to stand in front of the blue-eyed, bald dwarf with a long white braided beard. She studies his pale green armor, lighter in weight than her guards, suspecting that his skill with the bow and arrow needs the movement it offers. She lowers her gaze to the spotted cat that stands perfectly still beside him. "Ridgestalker of Honors Light, hunter, archer, commander of the bow. His cat Loque."

The guards behind her start to move forward at her brazen action, but Zane shakes his head. He watches the interactions intently, suspecting there is more to this group if his seer is willing to break protocol and approach them without his expressed command.

She glances between the dwarf and the human, a soft smile crossing her lips as she catches the slight nuances between them, let alone the other stuff that filters through her mind. She drifts gracefully past the dwarf to the two elves in the group, a race she has adored ever since she saw her first one at ten years old. Each one of the Honors Light elves is tall, both blue eyes and pointed ears, but that is where the resemblance fades.

The King's seer stands before the first elf, who has long purple hair braided from each side and pulled back into beads. She sees a few feathers dangling down the elf's back as she circles around her. The elf's leather clothing is well made, dyed a purple to match her hair, and there is a silver sash around her waist with a few gemstones embroidered into it. The seer stands in front of the elf again, studying blue eyes and a jagged scar that runs down one side of her face. While the elf sports no weapons, she has the stance of a fighter. Visions flicker in the seer's mind of a purple bear stepping into combat and taking the brunt of attacks as her companions assist. "Solilque, guardian, bear, and protector of Honors Light."

She continues on and pauses at the second elf. Her eyes drift up and down him, then she realizes that while he looks like an elf, he is not something she recognizes nor has seen in the King's Court. He has cloven hooves, pointed ears, white hair, and blue eyes that glow ever so slightly, dressed in light chain mail. She sees images of others like him, but very few exist since many of them died at the hands of magical ogres. She frowns at these images as she pushes them away, not wanting to see the darkness that shifts at their edges. "Myrlani of Honors Light, high shamen and invoker of the elements."

She shifts over crouches before the tiny gnome, another race that she loves, who is dressed in blue and gold robes. He has piercing blue eyes with thick black bushy brows over them, and his long black hair is slicked at the sides, then tied in the back with a leather casing. He carries a staff that is far too tall for his short frame; wisps of fire flicker around it. She rises, brushing her skirts off, smiling at him. "Cecil, mage of Honors Light and master of fire."

She moves to the last member of the group, a human with pale blue eyes and auburn hair that peeks out from beneath a hooded cloak. This woman is dressed in black and red leather, clothing that is full of pockets in which to hide things. The seer rises to her tiptoes and slides the hood off, needing to get a clearer view. She walks around, seeing that she walks easily in darkness and shadow. She smiles at the rogue "Aleandi, of Honors Light, master of the shadows."

She turns to the king, feeling the anger in his eyes as she gives him a slight curtsy, and she glides gracefully back to her spot before addressing him softly. "This group hails from Thermia, within the country of Spokane, and has seen many things in their adventures, including a dragon. They have faced monsters together, slayed threats that others would run from, and have come close to dying in their endeavors. But each time, they have persevered and survived. Unfortunately, I have foreseen a failure that will cause the loss of some of them, one that I am willing to share if the King desires, but for now, they have a gift for you."

Zane settles in his chair, his interest overriding the anger he feels for his seer. He knows if the adventurers are as good as she indicates, they will be an asset in ridding the world of dragons. "A dragon, you say."

"Yes, Your Majesty. A yellow one."

Gwynevere motions slightly with her hand as Solilque steps forward and places a bag at Zane's feet. She pulls out a dragon's head, which is just a touch smaller than the cat that stood within the group. Gwynevere's voice is soft as she addresses the king. "We heard you pay well for dragons, and as we just faced this one, we thought perhaps you would be interested in it."

Delight crosses Zane's features as he moves forward to the dragon's head, running his fingers along its scales. "It is magnificent, and you six, you took this down?"

"Yes, Your Majesty. It was a group effort, as it always is."

"I will have Randolph fetch you gold for this. Thank you. Would you like a job?"

Gwynevere smiles, "Well now, that depends on what you are offering, Your Majesty. We will be happy to hunt monsters for the right price."

"Dragons, my dear Priestess, I only care about dragons."

Gwynevere nods, "Of course, we heard that rumor as we passed through the Grim Tundra. What price are you offering, and will you give us the evening to discuss it back at the inn?"

"A thousand gold per head, and take as much time as you need." His eyes remain on the dragon's head before him, knowing he will add it to the collection on spikes around the castle walls. "King's seer, tell them what you see. They deserve it for a gift such as this."

"Of course, Your Majesty." The King's seer glances at the guards behind her, noting they were all watching Zane and the dragon. Her eyes glow softly, and she shifts her fingers around in a slight pattern as her thoughts touch the party, allowing only them to hear. *Do not fight the red that comes bearing the white flag at Omens Lake.'* Her eyes meet each and every one of them, ensuring they remain silent on the thoughts she placed in their mind before addressing them for all to hear. "You will face a Lernaean Hydra with six heads. Each head will breathe poisonous gas at those that are close. Two of you will be caught in this gas, and it will take you down before the priestess can save you, for you will already have damage from the many bites it will inflict upon your party. You will aim to remove the heads from the creature, thinking this will stop it, but it will only cause more heads to spawn. Do not do this."

Her eyes glow softly as she pauses to search her vision for a way to succeed. A slight smile crosses her lips at what needs to be done. "Now, to combat this monster… Your guardian will be fine; she can take the gas and the attacks, for she has the endurance to deal with it. Your caster will stand in the way of a breath as he cannot move fast enough with his short legs to avoid it. Your shamen will also fall to the breath trying to place a healing totem near the bear; do not. You need to strike at his legs first. Hunter, you stand back and distract him with your arrows, aim for his eyes, blind him if you can. Shamen, place a binding totem at his feet behind him; the less he can move, the less he can bite and breathe on people. Priestess, you are going to want to heal your Guardian, but do not. Have faith in Raya that she will survive; instead, heal your mage. He will need it, for the creature will be most angry at the fire he is casting at him and will strike over your bear at him. Shaman, once your binding is secure, and only after that, place a healing totem at the back side of the monster. Your guardian need not be in them, whereas the rest of you should be. Again, Priestess, even if your bear looks like she's about to go down, do as I say. She will survive; the others will not. If you follow this, then you will survive the encounter; otherwise, only a few of you will."

Zane's gaze shifts from the dragon head to his seer, this being the most he has ever heard his seer speak about a vision. He gestures to Randolph to deliver the gold to the priestess as he moves back to his throne, settling himself and speaking quietly to his seer. "You *will* join me for lunch today, King's seer."

"Of course, Your Majesty."

He turns his attention back to Honors Light. "Priestess, I hope to hear from you tomorrow then."

"You will, Sire." Gwynevere bows, the rest of the group following suit, then turn as they are escorted out of the main hall.

Zane watches the group leave. His attention shifts to the seer, who also watches them leave, curious to know what else she sees. He suffers through another few people before instructing Randolph to close the doors early. He pauses, adrift in thought, before rising. He watches as his seer offers him her usual bow. "Seer, I will see you in the lunch hall in ten minutes."

"Yes, Your Majesty." Her eyes follow him as he strides from the hall before she takes her own leave. Her guards step in behind her as she heads to her rooms at a brisk pace. She enters her room and closes the door behind her, resting against it as Pippa approaches her. She holds her hand up to stop her. "I am not staying today, Pippa. I have been requested to have lunch with the King for daring to overstep my boundaries with a group of power. I need to refresh myself before I head back down."

"Yes, miss, Shall I wait for you?"

"It's alright, Pippa. Go do what you need to do. I do not know how long it will be." She strides to the bathing chamber and closes the door, taking a moment alone with her thoughts and all that she saw. She refreshes herself quickly, knowing the king's temper at being kept waiting, and pauses to straighten her dress as she stares at it in the mirror. She sighs inwardly, knowing her few years of service should be finished, but understanding that the king is never going to let her go; for as she's aged, her powers have grown. She just hopes he will never find out to what extent. She pushes the door to her chambers open, gives a nod to her guards, then she makes her way down to the dining hall. She steps inside, breathing a sigh of relief as she sees it empty, and moves to stand behind her chair, waiting for the king to arrive.

Before long, he strides into the room, his eyes landing on the seer standing behind her chair, and makes his way to the head of the table as a servant rushes to pull his chair out. Once he is settled, he waves the maid away before addressing his seer. "King's seer, you may sit."

"Yes, Your Majesty." She sits at his command and remains silent until addressed.

They sit in silence as they wait for lunch to be served. Zane watches the seer intently, her gaze remaining on the table, her head bowed in respect. Once the food is on the table, he gestures to the seer that she is to start eating as he takes his first bite. "So, King's seer. Tell me why you broke protocol today to step forward to that adventuring group, Honors Light as you called them."

She keeps her hands in her lap as she lifts her gaze to him for a moment before bowing her head again. "I apologize, Your Majesty. I didn't mean to offend or overstep your rules. I was just overwhelmed with all the visions coming from that group that I needed to get closer to them. They have seen so much, and it is the first time that I was able to rewrite a vision to change what I saw. It will not happen again."

Zane studies her for a moment. He knows she is already powerful in her own right, probably one of the most powerful in the land, and she is here at his side, granting him access to that power. He senses she still holds back complete acceptance of him and that despite the act he has put on the past six years, she can see through it but has never dared to mention it. "I will admit, I was less than pleased with your actions. However, if your powers have grown, then I will forgive it this time. Rewriting what you see is impressive. I have to wonder if you will be able to do it again."

"I do not know, my King. I will not step over the boundaries again, as I am here to serve you."

"Indeed, now tell me, what did you see?"

The King's seer nods, eating her lunch with him. She explains some of the battles and creatures that she saw Honors Light face, telling him just enough to have him believe that was all she had seen. After lunch, the king seems appeased and leaves the dining hall. The seer waits just long enough to ensure he doesn't return before heading to the kitchens to visit Martha, then returns to her rooms.

Masquerade of Secrets

A FEW MONTHS BEFORE her sixteenth birthday, the King's seer sits in the kitchen, helping the chefs cut vegetables for the evening dinner while she talks with Martha. Her guards stand watching her work, remaining the ever-silent shadows she had grown accustomed to. She hears a gasp and turns to see the king standing in the kitchen, his eyes narrowing at the knife in her hand.

"King's seer, what are you doing?"

"Cutting vegetables, Sire."

Martha looks up, sighing softly. "What brings you to the kitchen, Sire?"

"I came to find the seer. I did not expect her to be doing the servant's job."

The King's seer places the knife down, rises, and offers a bow. "Your Majesty, I am not doing their job. I just figured if I am invading their space to talk to Miss Martha, then perhaps I should help utilize the space that I was using for them and so I assisted in cutting a few vegetables in exchange for borrowing their space."

He frowns at her words, wrapping his head around the whole space concept. "As long as this is not a daily occurrence."

"No, Sire. Not at all. May I ask why you tracked me down to the kitchen? I do not believe we had an afternoon meeting."

"No, King's seer, we did not, but I was thinking. It's your sixteenth birthday in a few months, yes?"

"Yes, Sire."

"And most young courtiers have a coming-out ball, I imagine, around then. Now, of course, you are different, and many already know that you are my seer, but I thought perhaps you would like to have a ball. A well-known bard has arrived in Teshem, and I will have someone teach you how to dance. Perhaps a gown could be made?" Zane turns to his housekeeper. "Martha, make it happen."

Martha spins around in shock that Zane would even suggest such a thing as her papers drop to the table suddenly. "Do you know how much work that is, Sire?"

"Of course I do; that's why I am giving you a few months' notice."

Martha scowls slightly. "Of course, Sire. I will see it done."

The King's seer smiles, feeling Martha's shock and annoyance. "That would be lovely, Sire. I look forward to my very first ball."

"Good, now don't stay too long here. I don't want the maids thinking they have you to do their job."

"I won't, Sire." She watches the king leave, hearing the immediate chatter and excitement that the castle will see its first ball since the last king reigned.

Martha rises and mutters under her breath. "Did you see this coming, King's seer?"

"Of course."

"And you didn't think to tell me?"

The King's seer places a hand on Martha's arms. "It will be fine, Miss Martha. You will do it with ease. Pippa will assist you with anything you need."

Martha laughs, giving a hug to the seer. "You still could have told me, you know."

"What, and miss the parchment slapping to the table as you spun around in shock?"

"You are evil, King's seer. I will remember this!"

"I know you will, Miss Martha. Now, I need to tell Pippa the good news." She offers a bow to Martha before running from the kitchen, feeling a potato bouncing off her shoulder, causing her laughter to echo in the hallway.

Martha shakes her head, watching the back of the seer as she runs away; a smile spreads across Martha's lips at the imp that she is. "Elo, you work directly under me now. I will appoint another person to cover your duties here. You are to find Habo in town. Tell him he is to focus solely on making a ball gown for the seer. Violet and white, with diamonds and lots of them. Spare no expense. If the King is going to throw a ball on such short notice, he's gonna pay for it."

Elo bows. "Yes, Miss Martha."

"Secondly, there is a dance instructor in town. Miranda is her name. I believe she teaches all the debutantes, so that is the one we want. Again, whatever the cost is to have her solely dedicated to the seer, we will pay for it. Afternoons will be best; the seer will need to forgo her swordplay to learn dance over the next few months."

"Yes, Miss Martha."

"Also, find out what bard is around right now. Once that is done, we will discuss decorations for the grand hall, as well as setting up rooms in the castle for the out-of-town royalty. I will be placing you in charge of a team of maids responsible for ensuring those rooms are cleaned and ready to go. Now go." Martha mutters under her breath as she stalks to the scribe's quarters, knocking lightly as she pushes the door open upon a soft call to enter. Martha looks upon the older gentlemen therein, soft gray eyes, his fingers black with ink, smiling as he looks up from the parchment.

"Miss Martha?"

"Herman."

"To what do I owe the honor of your visit?"

"Apparently, we are having a ball."

"We are?"

"Yes, in a few months, I will need invites sent out."

"Do you have a date?" His quill scribbles notes.

"Yes, April 25th."

"And the occasion?"

"The Seer's sixteenth birthday."

"And who are we sending this to?"

"Let's see. I suspect all the other kingdom leaders, their diplomats, and the nobles, as I am certain the King will wish to meet with them all the next day. Perhaps the adventuring parties and whoever else you think."

"They usually do at events like these. Do you have a list of names, or should I do it?"

"I will work up the kingdom royals and nobles list and leave the rest to you, Herman."

"Indeed, with this many invites going out, I might need an assistant. Perhaps I will bring my son Erik in."

"Of course, do what you need to do. I will have that list within the hour, Herman. Clearly, I don't have to point out there is a rush on this."

"I understand, Miss Martha."

"Thank you." She turns, striding back to her chambers, sitting at her desk as she makes notes of all the things that are needed for the ball.

Dress - Habo - ✓
Dance instructor - Miranda ✓
Bard - ✓
Decorations - purple of some kind
Gifts - discuss with King
Chambers - Elo, Cyndie, Jynn, Abye
Cooks - Ray, Gerrey,
Assistants to cooks - Fil, Anne,
Servers - Dianne, Denise, Liz, Dee, Cyan, Susyn, Edna, Silver, Star, Vycky
Sideboard Feast -
Roast Pig and Beef
Carrots
Parsnips
Potatoes
Pies - Rhubarb, Strawberry
Cake - Vanilla, Carrot

Martha taps her fingers lightly, pulls another piece of parchment forward, and begins writing the names of those who should attend the ball. Once Martha is certain she is done with the list, she heads back to the scribe's office and hands it over. "Impressive. I will get right to this, Miss Martha. Did you want the lesser Nobles as well?"

"Whoever you think, Herman. It needs to be a grand event!"

"Understood."

Martha leaves the scribe's quarters and heads back to the kitchens. She looks through the pantries to determine what they need to stock up on in the coming months as Elo enters the kitchen. "Miss Martha. I found Habo and Lady Miranda. They both agreed to your requests. The bard is known as Cathel Sean. I took the liberty of asking him to meet you, and he agreed."

"Thank you, Elo. I am appointing you, Cyndie, Jynn, and Abye to set up the rooms. Until we get definite responses back, we will need twelve rooms prepared for the royals and their entourage. Six for the three adventuring groups, perhaps more, as I am not certain what their sleeping arrangements are."

"Yes, Ma'am."

"Now go; I have other things I need to get done."

Days pass as the castle's life speeds up, preparing for the grand event, each servant racing around with added duties while trying to keep some semblance of order to the running of the castle. The King's seer continues attending court in the morning, arranging her afternoon and evening schedules to accommodate her added lessons and duties. Miranda teaches her the basic steps of formal dance in the grand hall while Cathel Sean plays his lute for them. Habo works diligently on her gown, bringing it over for fittings a week before the ball.

The day before the ball, Zane watches the seer walk into court. He catches the slight bounce in her step and the clear excitement radiating off her. "King's seer."

"Your Majesty."

"Are you ready for court?"

"Yes, Your Majesty."

"You seem excited."

"Yes, Your Majesty."

"Is that because there is a ball in your honor tomorrow?"

"Yes, Your Majesty. I have learned all the steps. Thank you for doing this for me, I really appreciate it."

He studies her for a moment, breaking into a smile at her enthusiasm. "Alright, King's seer. Keep it together for another few hours, and then you can dance in your rooms for the rest of the day."

Her eyes snap to him in shock. "How did you know?"

He chuckles, "Because I remember my first ball. It's something you never forget."

"I hope not, Your Majesty." She stands, watching the people come and go through court, the hours passing slowly until noon.

Finally, Zane rises. "I will not bore you by forcing you to have lunch with me today, King's seer."

"You are not a bore, Your Majesty. I enjoy lunch with you."

He smiles. "You may run to your chambers. I need to meet with the royals who will be arriving this afternoon and have them settled into their rooms."

"Thank you, Your Majesty." The seer bows then leaves the grand hall. She hikes up her skirts once she is out of sight and races all the way to her rooms. As she pushes the door open, her eyes land on Pippa, who is placing her food on the table, before moving to the exquisite dress that hangs on the wardrobe. It is a dark royal purple with white insets and overlays; diamonds and amethysts are sewn at the neckline, along the sleeves, and layered along the hem of the skirts. The seer picks up the hemline, watching as it drops and a myriad of sparkling lights dancing about, thinking this dress is the most beautiful thing she had ever seen.

"Miss, leave it alone. Come eat."

The King's seer laughs, "I am not hungry, Pippa."

"Eat anyway, Miss."

The King's seer sits at the table and eats her lunch, her mind wandering to what the ball will really be like compared to what she read when she was a child. She rises and runs down to the gardens, dancing and spinning through the trails, pausing at the hint of power outside her walls, feeling it call to her even in her excitement. She moves over to her arbutus tree and pulls herself up, glancing around the city, but sees nothing out there. She catches a flicker of movement on the king's balcony and slides out of the tree and back to the ground, recalling Martha's lectures that she is a lady and ladies don't climb trees. She skips over to the grass and lies in the sun, watching as clouds float past her, hints of red along their edges, willing the day to go faster.

Morning arrives, and the King's seer rises and runs to the bathing chamber to do what she needs to do. She fills the tub with water, pulls her sleepers off, and jumps in, splashing the water between her hands as excitement fills her. She lifts her head at the knock on the door, recognizing it as her maids. "Come in Pippa!"

Pippa enters, bringing in breakfast. "Miss! The ball doesn't start until late afternoon; why are you in a bath already? You are supposed to be resting."

"I am excited, Pippa! When I was nine, I had a book my Mama gave me. It was about kings and knights and maidens, and they had balls, and I always wanted to go to a ball. When Mama said I was coming to stay with a king, I thought they had balls all the time, but there haven't been any. And now I get to have my first one ever!"

"Alright, Miss, but you are not putting on that dress yet. You can relax in sleepers as I understand people are still arriving."

"I won't Pippa."

Pippa moves into the bathing chamber, putting a few drops of oil into the water as the air fills with the soft scents of strawberry. "Miss Martha will be up in an hour too. We have a birthday surprise for you."

"For me? But I have a ball."

"Yes, well, this is from the two of us. The ball is from the King."

"What is it?"

Pippa laughs. "If you haven't seen it, then I am not telling you. So don't go looking too closely, you hear."

The King's seer giggles, "I try not to, with you and Martha, Pippa."

An hour later, the King's seer sits at the table, teddy in one arm and book in the other hand. She lifts her gaze at the knock on the door as Pippa moves to open the door. Martha enters, and smiles at the seer sitting in sleepers, noting her hair is half styled. "Looks like you are getting ready early, King's seer. Perhaps I should wait for our gift until your hair is done."

The Seer's eyes shift to the basket in Martha's hands. "Ooh, what's his name?"

Martha sighs, "Damn, I knew the basket wouldn't work, Pippa."

"She didn't know until now, Miss Martha, and she will stay put until her hair is done."

The King's seer scowls playfully at Pippa. She places her book aside and holds out her hands for the basket. "I don't have to move; he can come to me."

Martha mutters good-naturedly under her breath about trying to surprise a seer as she places the basket down. She lifts the lid and pulls out a tiny black puppy, with white slippers, muzzle and tiny blaze that runs over his forehead and places it on the seer's lap. The King's seer looks down at the pup, feeling an annoyed tug on her hair by Pippa, laughing as she picks the pup up to look at him. "He is adorable!"

"He's yours to name. Now sit still for Pippa."

"Yes, Miss Martha. Does the King know?"

"Of course, he approved it."

"His name is Spider." She hugs the puppy close, placing him gently in her lap and willing Pippa to move faster.

"I know where your thoughts are, Miss. I am *Not* moving any faster than what it takes to get your hair perfect, and if you keep moving, it *Will* take longer. You're the one that decided to have your bath already."

Martha laughs. "Perfect, now that you have her tied down, Pippa, I can go over the protocols for the ball that she's so aptly avoided all week."

"Great, you both planned this, I know it."

"Of course we did, you might be the seer; but we are older and wiser. Now pay attention. You are to enter with the King as you always do. The Royals will be presented to you both first, then the nobles of Oblait. The King will ask you to dance, and you will accept. He will lead you onto the floor alone, where he will present you as the seer and the ball debutant. After the first dance, the King will hand you off to the Royals of the other countries. You are to make sure you return to the King at least every ten dances to show that you stand in his court. At midnight, there will be toasts in your honor. You stay for these, then retire to your rooms. Court is happening tomorrow but in the afternoon after lunch and it is only with the Royals, their diplomats, as well as the head of the noble houses. If you see ANY visions at the ball, they are to be discussed tomorrow during this time."

"I got it."

"Repeat it back to me."

"Martha!"

Martha laughs, "Alright then, don't; it's your hide. Now, I need to get things organized for your ball, my dear. Have fun today."

The King's seer smiles up at her, "Thank you, Miss Martha. For everything."

"You're welcome, King's seer."

Several hours later, after wearing herself out with a puppy, Pippa helps the seer dress in her ball gown, fastening all the laces and adding jewelry to accompany the dress. Pippa returns the seer to the table, fixing her hair slightly, and places matching hair pins with strings of diamonds that dangle down and glint in the light. "Alright, Miss. I think you are ready, and it's near time for the ball to start."

The King's seer stands in front of the mirror, spins a little, and watches the dress come alive with tiny lights, thinking that this is the most beautiful dress she has ever seen. "Thank you, Pippa."

"You're welcome, Miss. Enjoy yourself."

As the King's seer goes through the door, the guards gasp in shock upon seeing her. She smiles their way, a blush crossing her cheeks as she heads to the main hall, the guards close on her heels. The seer stands at the door to the hall, waiting on the king to accompany her and looking around nervously as Xyl steps forward. "You look beautiful, King's seer. He will be pleased."

"Thank you, Xyl."

Just then, the door beside her opens, and her gaze moves to Randolph, noticing that even his clothing has changed from his normal court attire. She places her hand on the one Randolph offers, following his lead to where the king stands by his throne. She studies the king's robes, dark green, and gold, embellished with emeralds entwined with gold threading along the sleeves and over the shoulders, drawing the green out of his eyes.

"King's seer!" Zane turns to stare at her in amazement before moving to stop a few feet in front of her. Zane takes her hand and kisses the back of it. "Happy sweet sixteen. Habo outdid himself with that dress. It's perfect for you."

She blushes softly at his look, giving him a curtsy and bowing her head. "Thank you, Your Majesty."

"You are welcome. Come, Let's get this ball started, shall we?"

"Yes, Your Majesty" Her eyes move around the hall as she follows him, noticing the decorations of violet and white fabric along the ceiling and matching colored carpets on the floor. Small silver coins reflect the light from extra wall sconces, causing them to dance like tiny fireflies as they spin. Tapestries adorn walls that are usually bare; there are a variety of scenes, all of them having some measure of purple within them.

Zane leads the seer to stand beside the throne, thinking she looks every bit the mystic standing there. The diamonds only add to the effect by creating tiny motes of purple lights around her as her dress moves. He smiles, liking the fact that everyone in this room is going to be envious that this seer is his. "Randolph, let's get this ball started."

"Yes, Sire." Randolph moves to the back of the hall and opens the grand doors, where a gathering of people wait in a long line. He presents the Royals to the king and seer, one at a time, each one wearing their own style of finery to represent their kingdom. They first meet King Zane's gaze, then the seer's.

"Queen Naanci of Sibath, her personal guard Brennte, with her diplomats: Kareyn, Jeaniee, and Feryn."

"King Hallihan of Ewhela with his diplomats: Akrinar and Vincent."

"Queen Diadradey and King Robertts of Lamadow, with their diplomats: Dawnelda and Nelowyna."

"King Gordyn and Queen Bobbye of Spokane with their diplomats: Anume and Neico."

"King Ludy of Hontby with his diplomats: Chainz and Niceasilla."

"The council of Lochyae, Your Majesty. Auggie, Keandre, Kittymoo, Treefeared, Yuui and their diplomats: Jeodina and Vynloren."

Randolph bows. "Thus concludes the Royals of the realm."

Zane gives a nod, feeling ever so slightly bored with this aspect of the ball and wanting to get to the drinking aspect of it.

The King's seer, on the other hand, watches the presentations in awe, seeing scatterings of visions for them all. She smiles at the four poodles that normally surrounded Queen Naanci. She sees King Hallihan visiting the dwarves in the kingdom of Ewhela and the gems that they mined from the mountains surrounding their land. The Elves of Lamadow, who fashioned the finest jewelry in the realm from the gems they bought from the dwarves. King Gordyn and Queen Bobbye, who keeps her weaving passion hidden from the world but sells out completely when she slips them into the market to be sold under another. Recognition upon seeing King Ludy, Paladin protector of his lands, with the two most powerful mages in the realm, Rune and Myke, at his side. And lastly, the Council that all turn into bears as Solilque does, each one of them very different from the other. Her eyes pause and linger on the two diplomats with them, knowing they were not from this realm.

Randolph moves back to the main doors, leading a line of well-dressed nobles, their clothes well-made and expensive but nothing compared to the finery the royals are wearing.

"Sire, may I present the Nobles of Oblait."

"You may"

"Thank you." He leads them forward one at a time, announcing each of their names as they appear. "Beatrixe Wythymms, Crimson Warlord, Magnolia Cyrlsen and her Daughter Scarlyt." Randolph pauses to allow the first nobles through the entrance, then continues, "Elder Snow and his sons, Khora Aryann, Zaemar Bachstaub, Ela Shrodyner, Flavvie Henwaryer, Michaella Hayryss, KR, and Kryesta Deight."

The King's seer smiles at each one, knowing these are the pillars of the kingdom outside the king. Each one of them has a story of their own that she keeps to herself.

Randolph moves to assist the other guards in opening the side doors to the courtyard, allowing more space for people to mingle as the rest of the gentry and distinguished guests are allowed into the hall. Zane turns to his seer and leads her down to the ballroom floor. She offers a curtsy to his slight bow, both stepping into proper dance position as the bard Cathel Sean starts to play the first song of the night, joined by other bards he has brought with him. Zane and the King's seer dance the first dance together, each one of them moving in perfect time and harmony to the other. Zane passes her along to the next Royal in line before moving to find a drink and watch her from afar.

The afternoon passes swiftly; the seer moves through the dance floor, talking with everyone she dances with before they pass her to the next partner waiting. She makes certain she stays hydrated, avoiding the alcohol until Zane places a glass of wine in her hand. They stand together off to the side, the seer taking a much-needed breather.

"Are you enjoying yourself, King's seer?"

"Yes, Your Majesty! It is just like I imagined from my books."

"I am glad."

She turns, her eyes glistening ever so slightly, "Thank you for this."

"You are welcome, now go dance."

"I do believe this one is yours."

He rolls his eyes. "DID Martha tell you that you have to dance with me every tenth dance or some bullshit like that?"

"Yes, Sire, she stated it is protocol."

He mutters softly. "Of course she did. Well, here is the NEW protocol. You don't need to. I only expect the first and last dance. Is that understood? If I want more, I will come and get you."

"Yes, Sire. Understood."

He takes the near-empty wine glass from her hand and places it on a server's tray. "Now, go dance; it's your night, after all."

"Thank you, my King." She smiles, turning back to the floor as someone pulls her into a dance. Another few hours pass, before she pleads respite, moving to the courtyard and mingling with the others seeking cooler air and rest. She finds a corner to lean against a wall and watches the moon, thinking the night is the most magical she has ever had. Her eyes shift to the side, feeling the king's presence as he steps in beside her, handing her another glass of wine. "King's seer."

"Your Majesty." She takes a drink, enjoying the taste of this strange concoction.

Zane studies the beautiful woman standing beside him, recalling the day she was nine and had just arrived in the castle to now and how much she has changed and also how much she has changed him. He reaches out to touch her cheek lightly, knowing if she wasn't a seer, he would be escorting her up to his rooms this very evening after the ball. His eyes darken with desire at the thought of having her beneath him, her violet eyes seeking his approval, before he squashes such thoughts since bedding her will never happen, for he values her power more than her body. "It's nearing Midnight. I do believe the last dance is owed to me."

She blushes softly, averting her eyes to the wine, taking another sip to quell the images he just placed in her mind with his thoughts and the direction they took. "Yes, my King."

"I will find you when it is called."

"Yes, my King."

Zane nods and walks away from her, knowing that if he stays in the dark corner with her, he is likely to kiss those soft pink lips, and that would be the end of him.

A half-hour later and another glass of wine, the last dance is called. The seer wanders through the crowds, scanning the ballroom and looking for the king. She feels his touch on her elbow as she looks up, wondering where he came from. "Sire."

"I believe this one is mine."

She smiles, feeling the soft warmth of his touch blending with the wine that she is unaccustomed to. "It is, my King."

He leads her onto the dance floor. The song is slow and sweet as the two dance together, swaying to the music. In that moment of happiness, she forgets who she is dancing with and where she is as time seems to stand still for her and the king. As the dance comes to an end, she reaches out to touch his cheek tenderly, completely oblivious to the gasps of shock from the onlookers, who are astonished by her familiarity with the king. Her eyes glisten with tears of joy as she looks up at him, her voice soft and gentle. "Thank you for this night, my King."

Zane looks down at her, his eyes widening in shock, not because of her gentle caress or that she dares to touch him, but instead from the flickering of an image entering his mind. That of a gold dragon in this hall, breathing flames upon him and his throne, causing him to step back slightly in pain. He nearly drops her as he stares at her in anger before composing himself quickly. "King's seer. I do believe there are toasts to be made."

The King's seer staggers back, confusion within her gaze at what just happened, feeling his hand tighten on her in anger and seeing stiffness in his frame. "Yes, Sire."

He takes her hand, leads her back to the throne, and spins her to face the crowd as a glass of wine ends up in each of their hands. "I extend my heartfelt gratitude to all of you who have gathered here tonight to celebrate the sixteenth birthday of my seer. I can clearly see the joy on her face, and it warms my heart. Now, I invite each one of you to raise your glass in honor of this remarkable young lady, who first arrived at this castle when she was merely nine years old and has since been a constant pillar of support in all my endeavors. To the King's seer. May we cherish many more years together, and may her visions always ring true."

An echo among the crowd answers. "To the King's seer."

Once the toasts are done, Zane turns to Randolph. "Please escort the seer to her room and place guards at the door."

"Yes, Sire."

The King's seer follows Randolph back to her room silently, trying to make sense of what she has done wrong.

Pippa rushes forward, seeing her expression. "Miss! Is everything alright?"

The King's seer looks up, a sadness in her eyes. "Yes, Pippa, I just wasn't ready for it to end, but it looks like it has."

"Oh, Miss, there will be other balls, I am sure."

She nods absently, seeing the threads rewrite themselves as she realizes what happened, then sinks to the floor with tears slipping from her eyes.

"Miss, please don't cry. It will be alright."

"It won't, Pippa; it never will be again."

"What does that mean, Miss?"

She shakes her head, "Nevermind. I think I have had too much of that strange drink that makes the mind fuzzy, and I need to sleep."

"Yes, Miss."

The King's seer stands still as Pippa undresses her. She runs her hands over the gown gently, knowing that the memories will always be trapped in the fabric. She gets into her sleeper and visits the bathing room before she crawls into bed with her pup and drifts off to a fitful sleep.

A Costly Mistake.

THE KING'S SEER wakes the next morning to a pounding on her door, a feeling of grogginess clouding her mind as she struggles to realize who is at her door. "Come in." The door opens, and her eyes alight on the king, fear waking her up suddenly as she crawls up the bed away from him, doing her best to hide Spider.

"King's seer. I want to see it."

"See what, Sire?"

He narrows his eyes on her, "I know you saw it. I want to see it again."

She shakes her head, her eyes darting to Deryn and Cedrik, who stand behind the king. "I don't understand, Sire."

Zane grabs her hand, yanks her off the bed, and stands her before him. His stare darkens as he grasps her wrists and lifts her hand to his cheek. "SHOW ME!"

The King's seer tries to pull her hand away. "I don't know what you want, Sire."

His grip tightens on her wrist. "IF you won't show me, I will make you." He hisses quietly in her ear as he pushes her back down to the bed, then storms out of the room. The seer's eyes lift to the guards, tears welling in them as she rubs her wrist, watching the door close behind them.

She huddles back on the bed with Spider, pulling him close, knowing she is safe for as long as the guests are at the castle, but after that, her life as she knows it has ended. Three days later, after dinner, she hands Spider to Pippa. "Can you watch him tonight?"

"Miss, he's your dog. He should stay here."

"Please, Pippa, just for tonight."

"Of course, Miss."

"Thank you. I will see you in the morning."

"Yes, Miss. Is everything alright? You've been out of sorts the past few days."

"Yes, Pippa, you better go."

"Alright, Miss." Pippa leaves the room, glancing back at the seer, who stands, twisting her hands nervously. Pippa glances at the guards standing at the door, feeling as if something is amiss, but heads to her room, placing Spider down to wander around.

The King's seer moves to her wardrobe and sifts through her outfits. She removes the dress she is wearing and pulls on an older gown, knowing shortly there will not be much left of it. She moves to kneel at the edge of the bed, places her hands on the mattress, and rests her head against them. She stays there until she hears the door open and doesn't dare look up at the king and her two guards.

Zane studies her position and how she doesn't move before slamming the door behind him. "King's seer. Were you expecting me?"

"Yes, Sire."

"Deryn, Tai, hold her down."

The seer listens to their approaching footsteps, feeling the two guards seize her hands and pin them down to the bed where she kneels. She flinches slightly as the king uncoils his whip and cracks it in the air above her. "Show me, King's seer, and this won't happen."

"I don't know what you mean, Sire."

"I think you do." He cracks the whip through the air, slicing it in her back.

She stiffens in pain, tears springing to her eyes, but refuses to cry out, knowing that is exactly what he wants. "I don't."

"I saw the look you gave me that night. I felt the power of the vision. You've been holding back on me!" The whip snakes through the air again, crisscrossing the strike he just made.

She tries to pull her hands from the guards, struggling against them. "No, Sire, I haven't."

"You are lying!" Zane rages, striking her again, the whip digging in deeper with each strike.

She feels the pain twice over, once from her visions and once in reality, though the sting of reality is far worse. She keeps her eyes closed, feeling the blood flowing down her back and her body weakening under each blow. She fights against the darkness that threatens to overtake her as two more lashes sink into her back.

Realizing he isn't getting her obedience, Zane moves to the seer. "Stand her up." The guards grab her arms, forcing her to her feet, and spin her to face the king, as she sways before him. Zane reaches out to grab her chin, jerking her face to his. "Look at me, Seer."

She lifts her tear-stained eyes to the king, struggling to keep her gaze on him.

"Good; I want you to know who your master is. YOU will tell me eventually, and the only way this is going to turn out well is if you show me what I want to see."

Her voice is quiet, with an ever so slight hint of defiance. "I don't know what you are talking about... Sire."

He growls, resisting the urge to slap her. "Turn her around. Another three lashes for being spiteful."

The seer feels the lash tear into her, allowing the darkness to take her as she slumps into the guard's arms, not even aware that two more strike her, nor that she is dumped on the bed and left in a heap. She wakes the next morning to Pippa crying over her, pain searing through her back and shoulders, and finding herself unable to move.

"Miss. No, what happened?"

"Pi-pa. He's mad at me." The King's seer's voice is quiet and filled with agony.

"He can't be doing this."

"He can, Pippa. He owns me. He was very clear about that last night."

"I will return."

The King's seer grabs Pippa's hand, stiffening in pain. "No, don't go to him. He will kill you. Go to Martha."

Pippa nods and leaves the chamber. She glares at the two guards standing beyond the door before running for the kitchens. "Miss Martha, please, come quick. We need pain herbs."

"What happened?"

"It's the King's seer; she's hurt badly."

Martha moves to the pantry to grab a few herbs and follows Pippa back to the seer's room. Martha gasps in horror at the sight of the unconscious seer's back. "What the hell happened?"

"I think it was the King, Miss Martha. She said he's mad and owns her, so he can do this."

"We need to pull the fabric out of her wounds. Then get her up and standing. The King will expect her in court. After which, he and I will be having a talk about this."

"Miss Martha, she said no to me, that he would kill me."

"The King likely would, but he can't kill me."

"Why would he do this?"

"Something happened. I am not sure what, but I aim to find out. Did she know?"

"I think so, Miss Martha. She sent Spider to sleep with me last night."

"Then she saw this coming. Next time she does, you come to the kitchen. I'll have a herbal cream to apply to her back that will dull the pain of the lashes."

"Yes, Miss Martha." Pippa carefully pulls the fabric out of the seer's wounds

Martha runs back to the kitchen, knowing she will need more herbs than she had brought to make a paste. She returns to the chamber in a few minutes and sets about grinding herbs into a salve, applying it gently to the wounds that Pippa has cleared.

The King's seer wakes to a stinging in her back, her hands grasping her bedding as she struggles away from the maids. "No, it hurts."

Martha takes her hand, squeezing it gently. "It will stop stinging soon, I promise."

The seer nods, tears creeping from her eyes at the pain. "Thank you, Miss Martha."

"King's seer, why did the King do this?"

"He's mad at me. It's never going to stop 'cause he's always going to be mad at me now."

"Why is he mad at you, Sweetie?"

"I can't say."

"So, you know why he's mad at you?"

"He wants more stories, and I don't have them."

Martha looks at the seer with concern, suspecting there is more going on than meets the eye but isn't going to push further. "Alright, King's seer. This salve will numb your back in about ten minutes; then, we need to dress you and get you down to the court."

"I don't want to go."

"You must, Sweetie. If the King is still mad, then this could happen again if you are late."

"It will. It's going to happen a lot now. I couldn't find a way to make it stop."

"What do you mean you couldn't find a way?"

Her eyes shift to Martha's before finding Pippa's, glancing down to the hands that hold hers. "He's mad now. I can't make him not mad. He is always going to be mad."

Martha looks at Pippa, shakes her head, and rises to pull out a loose dress for the seer. The two maids help the seer to her feet and dress her carefully, ensuring that she eats some food while they style her hair quickly. Martha helps the seer to the door, scowling at the two guards. "Cedrik. Luis. Were you two on watch last night?"

"No, Ma'am, Deryn and Tai were. We took over first thing this morning."

Martha nods; she looks at the seer standing beside her, features pale and swaying slightly. "You can do this, King's seer. I will be back later this afternoon to check on you."

The King's seer nods, walking stiffly to the court and arriving a minute later than normal. She slips into place behind the king.

"You're late, King's seer."

"I'm sorry, Sire. I will do better next time."

"See that you do."

"Yes, Sire."

"You understand why you were punished."

"No, Sire, I cannot give you what I do not have to give."

He narrows his eyes on her. "You will learn why eventually."

"If you say so, Sire." She watches the king signal to Randolph to start court, listening to the people that come into the hall, seeing nothing that she is willing to divulge.

At the end of the court, Zane rises and narrows his eyes on her. "It's unusual for you to see nothing, King's seer. Are you remaining silent because of last night?"

"I wouldn't know what you are talking about, Sire. There was nothing to see today." Her voice is quiet as she addresses him. She is fully aware that the safe path is no longer an option, that the stakes have shifted, and now she must engage in a dangerous game to earn her freedom.

"I don't believe you, King's seer. I think you are asking for another round." He glares at her, knowing she is keeping things from him.

The corners of her lips lift wryly. "It doesn't matter, Sire. The rounds have started, and they will not stop since I cannot give you what you want."

"You will, King's seer. You will." He growls under his breath, striding off to the dining hall and leaving her standing there alone.

She uses the throne to steady herself before staggering back to her room and closing the door. Seeing Spider bounce over to her, she picks him up, tucks him into her arm, and crawls into the bed, slipping into darkness despite the pain.

At noon, Pippa enters the room and spots the seer on the bed. She sets her lunch down, opting to let her sleep and letting Martha in an hour later. "How is she?"

"She's been out since I got in here."

Martha nods, checking the seer's temperature as she rests. "I have brought more salve to apply as I suspect the dose I placed on her this morning will have worn off. She will need it for a few days to dull the pain; after that, we need to watch for infection. I will have batches made in the kitchen for you to pick up with her meals, Pippa."

"Thank you, Miss Martha."

"Right, let's get her up and get some food into her. Then we will reapply and put her into a sleeper."

Pippa moves over to the seer, waking her up gently, seeing the confusion in her eyes for a moment. "I have food for you, Miss. You need to eat. Miss Martha also brought more salve to help with the pain."

She nods, stiffening as she reaches for Pippa, who helps her out of the bed. A wave of dizziness comes over her as she sways on her feet.

Martha moves over to help as both of them lead the seer to the chair and sit her down, ensuring that she eats some food. Once done with her meal, Martha and Pippa strip her down, reapply the salve, and dress her in sleepers before guiding her back to bed. "Alright, Pippa, I will leave her in your care. I will check in with you at dinner."

"Yes, Miss Martha."

Martha leaves the chamber. Rage creeps into her as she moves through the castle to the king's quarters, pounding on the door, causing Benson to jump in shock at the force.

"I know why you are here, Martha; GO away."

"To Hell, I will!" Martha pushes the door open, glaring at the king as she slams the door behind her. "What have you done!?"

"What needed to be done?"

"Bullshit! That girl has given you everything since she was nine years old, even when she didn't want to be here."

Zane rises from his chair and stalks over to Martha, glowering at her. "She's been holding back, Martha."

"If she is, do you blame her?"

Zane slaps Martha across the face, feeling the sting on his own cheek. "You are pushing it, Martha. I will keep you in the dungeons if you continue along this path."

"I warned you, Zane, about pissing off a mystic. This is a sure-fire way to do that."

"If she gives me what I want, the beatings will stop. I am simply teaching her who's boss."

"You are making a mistake, and if you continue to whip her, it will be your end. I don't need to be a seer to see that."

Zane grabs Martha by the throat and slams her into the wall, holding her off the ground. "No, that's the thing. She shared a vision with me, and I SAW my death in the breath of a gold dragon. I KNOW I saw it too. I could see it in her expression, but she refuses to share further. I WILL get it out of her." He releases Martha, feeling a shortness of his own breath as he watches Martha struggle for hers at his feet. "BENSON, Please remove the maid from my chamber."

Benson enters the room, picks Martha up off the ground, and carries her from the room as Martha's eyes narrow coldly. "You will regret this, Zane. One day, she will fight back."

Days pass, shifting into months and then into a year. Zane continues to take his temper out on the seer while her guards hold her down. All except Xyl, who takes a beating himself when he tries to stop the king, nearly costing him his life. Zane does his best to break the seer, knowing she is keeping the vision close to her heart, but she refuses to budge, taking the abuse. Each night that she sees it coming, she hands Spider over to Pippa and takes the pain-numbing herbs Martha has prepared for her. She suffers in silence, only to be treated by both Martha and Pippa the next morning, the process becoming almost routine.

The dragon hunts begin in earnest, the punishments escalating for every month there is no dragon brought before him, forcing the seer to find one to appease the king in order to survive. The rewards double and triple for dragons, which start racking up, their heads on stakes for all to see. All colors but gold, that is, which only angers the king further.

One day, late in her seventeenth year, the King's seer stands on her balcony, feeling a power out there and knowing it is her way out of the castle, a power she has sensed before. She reaches out to it mentally but receives only silence back. Timelines and threads filter through her mind as she stares out over the city. She feels the power wrap around her, soothing and comforting her as she sorts through how to bend that power to her will. An hour later, she smiles and glances at her door, lifting her hands to weave a pattern of purple lights. She twists her hands gently, sending the lights out under the door, and waits until she hears the thump of her two guards falling asleep. She opens her door cautiously, seeing Deryn and Tai on the ground, knowing they will be punished for letting her escape but finds she doesn't care.

The King's seer collects Spider and steps past them, then down the hall to Pippa's quarters, slipping in and placing Spider on the bed. "Be good; I will be back." She grabs one of Pippa's cloaks and pulls it on, shrouding her features as she makes her way to the servant's entrance. Once outside, she creeps along the wall towards the front gate, reaching it just as alarms in the castle sound. She breaks into a run, slipping under the portcullis as it crashes to the ground, pausing to face the guards on the other side. She gives a slight bow before turning and racing straight to the inn district, since that is where she can sense her freedom coming from.

It isn't long before she hears horses behind her, continuing her run until the back of the cloak and her hair are grabbed as she is unceremoniously lifted off the ground, then dropped across the king's lap. Her escape is short-lived but necessary because she knows her power will leave a mark for the one she is seeking.

Zane's hand tightens on her as he swings the horse around; rage vibrates within him as he gallops back to the castle at the fact that she dared to try and escape. He pulls the horse to a stop in the courtyard and dismounts. He drags the seer off with him and watches as she attempts to crawl away from him. He grabs her arm and pulls her to her feet, spinning her around to face him, gritting his teeth to resist beating her right here, right now. "King's seer."

She lifts her gaze to his, her violet eyes flashing dangerously as she pulls away from him. "Zane."

"Where were you going?"

"Anywhere away from you."

He narrows his eyes, backhanding her across the face. "You dare to think you can leave me?"

She can see the slap coming but doesn't expect the power behind it, landing on her hands and knees, tasting the blood in her mouth, and spitting it out. She reaches a hand up to rub the side of her face and brushes her hair aside, feeling her own anger rising to match his. She struggles to her feet to face him again, lifting her chin defiantly and glaring at him. "Now there's the King we all know and love. Do you want to match the other side, Sire?"

Zane growls, obliging her request and taking her off her feet again.

The King's seer nods, laughing softly as she collapses, rolling over to lie on her back, feeling the darkness creep in at the edges of her sight. Her eyes drift over the guards, who do nothing before they return to the king. "Are you gonna take me downstairs, Zane? Or lock me in my rooms? I mean, both are options from what I see right now. But I will say this, if you take me to the room, you will NEVER get another vision from me as long as I reside in this castle. So choose wisely, *My king*... Oh, and know this, Zane, I will escape this hell hole of castle. And next time, you won't catch me." She closes her eyes, succumbing to the darkness that calls to her.

Zane clenches his fists at his side as he stares down at his seer, unconscious at his feet, red welts covering both her cheeks and her lip split in two places. He can see the blackening starting already beneath her eyes, stark against her already pale features. He leans down to lift the seer in his arms and carries her back to her room. He drops her on her bed, frustrated that she has become so defiant lately.

He turns to the guards who follow him. "Find me a locksmith. I want a lock placed on her door. It will only be unlocked when she is led to court or when her maid brings her food. For court, she will be in chains to restrict her movement. After court, she will be returned here and locked in. All extracurricular activities have been banned from this day forward. Is that Understood?"

"Yes, Sire."

He glares at Deryn and Tai, slumped on the ground. "Take them downstairs for sleeping on the job. Get Alvero and Cedrik up here to keep watch. And tell Kenworth I want to see him in the war room right away."

"Yes, Sire."

Zane arrives at the war room, rage boiling within him at the seer, trying to determine how to stop her from escaping.

Kenworth enters, bowing to the king, and watches as he paces in anger. "Sire. You called?"

"Yes, I need a way to keep the seer from running away."

"Did you not call for locks to be placed on her door?"

"Yes, but she's threatened that next time I will not catch her, so she clearly has a plan. You are known for your ways of keeping people contained."

"Perhaps you should place poison in her food randomly, give the antidote just before it kicks in, then repeat the process. You could keep it a secret, but if you tell her, she will know that she needs to stay to get the antidote and won't know which one it is."

"She is a seer; she very likely could see it."

"Test it then. Don't tell her and just poison her food; see if she eats it. If she doesn't, then you will know."

"She would be defiant enough to eat it anyways."

"Most won't willingly eat poison. She will do her best to avoid it if she knows it's there. Especially if it's a poison that can kill."

Zane ponders it for a moment. "Then we try it and go from there."

That evening, Pippa returns to her room, surprised to see Spider on her bed. She looks around and notices her cloak is missing. She pales slightly, suddenly understanding what the alarms were for, and races from her room. She stops at the seer's door, her eyes landing on the brand-new padlock hanging there. "Alvero? What's going on?"

Alvero frowns at Pippa. "The King's seer tried to run away this afternoon. Her freedom has been taken away."

"May I enter?"

"Of course." Alvero pulls a key out from around his neck and unlocks the door, opening it for her. Pippa's gaze lands on the still form of the seer, immediately noticing the bruising on her face. "Oh, Miss, what have you done?" She catches the door locking behind her as she retrieves some cold cloths, placing them on the seer's face to stop the swelling.

An hour later, the seer opens her eyes, the pain in her face echoing throughout her body. She finds Pippa hovering over her, knowing she doesn't understand why she is provoking the king. "Pippa. Is Spider alright?"

"Yes, Miss. He's in my room."

"Thank you, Pippa."

"Why, Miss?"

"Cause it had to happen, Pippa. One day, soon, you will understand."

"Shall I get you some pain herbs?"

"No, Pippa, it's alright. I will have time to heal as the King is not letting me out of this room all week."

"Alright, Miss. Shall I keep Spider tonight?"

"Yes, please."

Pippa nods, squeezing the seer's hand lightly. "I will see you at dinner then."

The King's seer shakes her head. "I believe Cedrik is bringing my dinner up tonight, so you may take the night off."

"Why would they do that?"

"Because I angered him today when I tried to run away."

"Ok, Miss."

That evening, her dinner arrives at the hands of her guards. The King's seer pushes herself off the bed as she watches Cedrik carry the meal to the table and place it down, before moving back to stand at the door. She eyes him carefully. "Is there something I can help you with Cedrik?"

"No, King's seer, I am here to stand guard."

"Then get out!"

Cedrik pales slightly, bows, and leaves the room, closing the door behind him.

The seer moves to the food, scanning it carefully and seeing the tinge of darkness within the food, knowing the poison card has just been played. She sits quietly eating her food, understanding it is risky not to remove it, but also knowing that the game she is now playing requires her to eat it. She pulls a chair out to the balcony and sits in the setting sun. She hears her door open, someone collecting her plate, and the locks click into place after they leave. And so it has started; the dangerous path to her freedom has begun. She will either leave the castle alive as she hopes or be dead at the king's hand.

Another six months pass, the seer remains locked in her room, being bound and chained when she leaves. She gives the king the bare minimum of visions. She eats both the poisoned and antidoted food. All the while, she suffers through the king's torture whenever he deems she has done something wrong.

Silken Threads of Fate

THE KING'S SEER rises, stiffness permeates her entire frame as her back feels as if it is on fire, suspecting the king is doing everything he can to make her feel the after-effects of his abuse. She heads to the bathing chamber, filling the tub with semi-hot water. She grimaces as she gently pulls the torn chemise off her body, the dried blood fusing the fabric to her flesh and re-opening some of the lash wounds as it is pulled away. She fingers the chemise lightly, seeing the rips and stains upon it, and drops it to the floor.

She steps into the water, feeling the sting in her open wounds, resting gingerly in the tub and closing her eyes, thinking how desperately she wants out of the castle. After thirty minutes, she sighs inwardly, then rises from the tub and dries herself off; the blood on the towel hints that she has soaked too long. She pads back to her wardrobe, slips into a clean chemise, and pulls a black underdress on to hide the seepage of blood she can feel occurring. She pulls out a dark-over gown, wondering if anyone has ever noticed the change in hues of her attire once a week. She is tying the ribbons when she hears the lock turn on her door. A gasp from her maid follows shortly as Pippa places Spider on the ground. "Miss, you are not to do that."

She turns and smiles, her hands stilling on her ribbons as her maid takes over. "Pippa, I am perfectly capable of dressing myself."

Pippa places a hand on hers and glances at the door. "I know, Miss, and I know why you are dressed. You don't need to hide it from me."

The seer smiles sadly, patting Pippa's hand gently. "You shouldn't have to deal with it, Pippa; I will be fine."

"He has no right, Miss."

"He has every right to, Pippa. He bought me when I was nine, so I belong to him whether I like it or not. I am one of the lucky ones since I have avoided his tyranny for many years by keeping him happy. But I can no longer do that."

Pippa looks at her, her eyes filled with sadness and concern. "I wish I could help you, Miss."

"I understand, Pippa. Just be careful to stay out of his line of sight. He is not as forgiving of his servants as he is of me. If he kills me, he will have no visions, and he won't risk that."

"Yes, Miss. Shall I go get your breakfast now?"

"That would be lovely. Was Spider fed this morning?"

"Yes, Miss, as always."

"Thank you. When you return, you may let Deryn in." She watches as Pippa moves to the door and taps on it to be let out; it closes promptly after her, the latch sliding into place and locking the seer in. She moves to the balcony, resting her hands on the railing as her eyes lift to the sky. She can see in her visions that one of the next times she is beaten, she is not surviving, but she does not dare to tell her maid. She stands in the rays of the rising sun, looking over the people starting their day and knowing that within the hour, she will be walking among them. Market day used to be a time she loved, but now she avoids the gazes of the people as it is just another way for the king to force his people to pay him gold he needed to fund his dragon hunts. She sighs, then moves and sits at the table just as a knock can be heard. "Come in."

She smiles at Pippa as she carries in a tray of food, then sets it down in front of her. The King's seer's gaze shifts to Deryn, darkening at him and the shackles he is carrying. Pippa kneels down with him, lifting the seer's skirts in a manner that ensures no more leg shows than is necessary when he places the fetters on. Seeing that the pair is distracted, the seer brings her eyes to her breakfast; an ever so slight purple glow encases it momentarily. Once she feels the shackles click into place, her eyes narrow coldly on Deryn. "Now. Get out!"

Deryn runs for the door and closes it behind him, muttering under his breath to the other guards that they will be the ones to restrain her next time.

The King's seer eats her breakfast while Pippa fusses over her hair, setting a jeweled crown upon her head and pinning it in place with two matching hairpins. Pippa separates out a few strands of hair from either side of her face, twists twin braids down her back, and ties them off with a dark purple ribbon. Once Pippa is done, she returns to the dresser, sifting through the necklaces before deciding on a thin chain with a single teardrop lavender gem. She fastens it around the seer's neck, then lifts her hair so it flows down her back. Pippa moves to the armoire and pulls out a dark pair of slippers, sighing at the shackles as she places them on the seer's feet. "Are you ready, Miss?"

"As ready as always." She pushes her plate aside and rises from the chair, moving to the mirror and straightening her skirts as she inspects her appearance. Her overdress is royal purple and black, with light amethyst gems sewn onto it. Delicate chains drape around her shoulders to her back, where beads and gems dangling from the center. A wide waistband enhances her slender waist, from which matching chains and beads loop across and dangle down. The seer lifts her gaze to her hair, smiling at the dark purple gems glittering in the morning light. She reaches up to touch the chains that dangled on either side of her face. She gives a nod, knowing her appearance will meet the approval of the king.

Pippa moves to the door and knocks lightly; the locks snap out of place, and the door opens. The King's seer nods to Pippa and enters the hallway. She eyes the four guards that stand waiting. "Only four today? I thought it was market day."

"It is, King's seer; the others wait downstairs."

The seer rolls her eyes, muttering under her breath. "Of course they are."

She heads through the hallways to the main doors, seeing her other five guards awaiting her arrival in the courtyard. She catches the sympathetic look in Xyl's eyes before clearly avoiding his gaze, as the nine step into formation around her. She lowers her gaze to Alvero's feet, keeping them pinned on his sabatons as they enter the city proper, doing her best not to draw any of their attention. Feet scurry as people run from the entourage, while others stop and stare, hoping to meet the violet eyes of the seer.

Near the end of main street, she feels the power nearby that she has been searching for, causing her to stumble as she looks up. Violet eyes meet red, visions flood her mind as she staggers back into Xyl. She quickly averts her eyes, hoping the guards missed her reaction but knows they have never missed any interactions before. The procession comes to a stop as Cedrik steps in closer to the seer while Drue and Krim approach the man who caught her gaze. "You there, we need to speak with you."

Zalgren

Zalgren's red eyes look over the two guards before they return to the seer standing before him. His tone is dismissive as he addresses them. "Of course, you may speak, though I might not choose to listen."

The seer's shoulders slump as she sighs inwardly, lifting her gaze to meet him again. Her face pales slightly as she studies him. He is a good head taller than her. His long black hair has red streaks and is pulled back in braids. He wears a woven metal crown of sorts, the tips of it like wings that reach skyward. His black and red robes are studded with diamonds and rubies, while silver and gold threads are woven into a pattern of flames that lines the edges of his cloak; each garment giving a clear indication of his wealth.

"The King's seer has looked your way. The King will want to see you. We suggest you come willingly, Mister...?"

Zalgren surveys the guards standing protectively around the seer; a slight smile crosses his lips at the arrogance of them. "You may address me as Zalgren. And, of course, I would be honored to meet *your* King." His eyes return to the seer's, intrigued by the violet eyes staring back at him. He bows and steps in behind the seer as her entourage shuffles to keep guards surrounding them both, making their way back to the castle.

Zalgren's gaze shifts downward when he hears the quiet chink of metal on metal as she steps. He suspects her paces are bound and notices that she has once again returned her gaze to the ground. He can feel a slight probing in his mind, recognizing it from six months earlier. This time he allows her access to his thoughts. Here is the power that he seeks, having mistakenly assumed the source was living within the city limits, not locked away in the castle. The corners of his lips tip up slightly at the soft whisper in his thoughts.

You are either incredibly brave or foolish to be stepping into the court of the King, who kills dragons like you.'

Zalgren smiles, answering with thoughts of his own, *'I will leave that for you to decide, King's seer, but I will state this, I am not worried about your precious King killing me. I came for two reasons: to seek the power I felt in this city and to see how his seer is tracking us dragons down so easily. You have already answered one of them with the power I can feel rolling off you. But, it does bear the questions, why not turn me in, and does the King know the true power you hold?'*

She stiffens at his words, cutting off the mind link, hearing his chuckle.

Zalgren's thoughts reach into hers anyhow. *'I take it the answer is no. How interesting. Now, I want to know more, King's seer and I always get what I want.'*

The entourage returns to the castle courtyard quickly. Alvero moves ahead to let Kivu know they bring forth a citizen.

He smiles at the seer's silence as his eyes glance around the courtyard and the display of wealth as he enters the castle. He allows the guards to lead him into the grand hall, watching the seer make her way behind the king to stand silently. He catches the slight bow she offers him before she shifts her gaze to some point in space behind him, which intrigues him even more. He bows to the king, though his focus remains on the seer. "Greetings, Your Majesty. To what do I owe this escort into your halls when I was simply exploring the wares at the marketplace?"

Zane follows Zalgren's gaze to his seer, noting her paler-than-normal continence and how her eyes avoid the man in the center of the room. Zane narrows his own eyes before addressing the question asked. "I believe my seer saw some vision involving you. She usually does if she makes eye contact with someone in the marketplace, although you do have the most unusual color of eyes."

"They are inherited from my Great Grandmother, Your Majesty. There is a rumor in my family that she had an affair with a Jinni, but it was never proven."

"Fascinating. King's seer, did you see something?"

"No, Your Majesty." The seer keeps her eyes pinned on the drapes in the back of the hall.

"Alvero stated that you clearly made eye contact with him and that you even stumbled a step."

She frowns ever so slightly before schooling her expression once more. "No, Sire, I was looking at the mulberry bush behind him. I thought perhaps I saw a faerie."

"Is that so? A faerie in my kingdom? Well, now that he's here, look at him and tell him a story."

"Yes, Your Majesty." Her hands tighten on her skirts to stop their shake within it as she turns her attention to the dragon in the room.

She stares at the man, who is to be her escape and her undoing. She keeps her sight on him for a moment too long, catching the king's throat clearing, lowering her gaze again. "I am sorry, Your Majesty. There are a lot of merchant stories to sort through, but there is one that he will need to be concerned about. Someone small in stature will approach him, carrying a black quartz bull with a purple heart in its center, and ask him to inspect its value for trade. Do not touch it. Any who does will be forced to accept the object. The figurine is cursed and seeks a new home. It will remain with the occupant until their wealth runs dry. Thereafter the curse forces the owner to find the figurine a new home, just as it is doing to the short one bringing it to you."

Zane nods. "Now that is the type of story I am looking for, King's seer."

"Yes, Your Majesty." She offers a slight bow, feeling a wave of dizziness strike her, reaching out to the throne to steady herself and earning a frown from Zane. Her eyes glow ever so softly as she sinks to the ground, her thoughts reaching the dragons moments before darkness takes her. *What I said is true, but I also have a message for you dragon. You will find the cleric you seek north of Omens Lake. I cannot say what it means, but I will see you one week from today, and you will understand more.*

Zalgren watches the seer drop to the ground, a single arch of his brow the only indication of any emotion. He spots the manacles on her ankles, which further entices him to learn more about this seer. "Is she alright, Your Majesty? She looks a touch pale."

Zane rises in shock at the collapse of the seer on the ground next to him. "She's fine. Randolph, escort the merchant out and collect his gold for the vision."

"Yes, Your Majesty. Right this way, M'lord."

Zalgren turns, pausing long enough to catch the conversation as the seer is carried from the hall. He moves to follow Randolph after dropping some gold coins in the basket.

Zane lifts the seer into his arms, quietly addressing one of her guards. "Did she eat this morning?"

"Yes, Sire."

"All of it?"

"Yes, Sire"

"And you are certain the antidote was in her food."

"Pretty certain, Sire. Kenworth prepared her food."

"Well, get her some now. And find me Kenworth."

"Yes, Sire. Right away, Sire." Her guard turns and races off.

Zane carries the seer to her room, waiting for Jesper to open the door, noticing just how shallow her breathing is. "Damn it, where is her maid? And why isn't she here?"

"It's washing day, Sire. She's likely down scrubbing the seer's clothes and bedding, which she normally does while the seer is at court."

"Fetch her."

Jesper nods, pivots, and runs off to the washing stations.

Zane crosses the room and places the seer carefully on the bed, feeling her wrist for a pulse and barely finds it. He growls in frustration that somehow she managed to skip eating her breakfast this morning. He picks up a nearby chair, smashing it into the wall and watching pieces skittering across the room. He turns upon hearing Jesper speak, noting the guard eyeing the broken chair. "She's on her way, Sire. She is just hanging the sheets in her arms."

"Good. Where is Drue?"

"Also on his way, Sire."

Drue runs into the room with a small vial in his hand; he moves to the King's seer. Drue removes the cap, blanching slightly at the smell that comes out. He lifts the seer's head and pours the liquid gently into her mouth, rubbing her throat to force her to swallow. He lays her back down, recaps the vial, and slips it into his pocket. Kenworth enters the room, his eyes landing on the still form of the seer. "She was given the stuff this morning, Your Majesty. And she ate all her breakfast. However, she's been given the poison so long that her body could be weakened from its effects, and now it's affecting her sooner. We might need to consider cutting back the doses or risk losing her."

Zane kicks a broken chair leg. "Dammit! I will think about it. I do not want her to escape. Get the healer in here. I want the seer checked out to see how long it will take before she wakes."

"Yes, Sire." Drue bows and rushes from the room as Pippa enters. She bows to the king. Her face pales at seeing her mistress lying on the bed. Pippa moves to the seer's side, taking her hand. "Miss?"

"She's ill, Pippa. She collapsed in court. A healer has been called. Watch over her."

"Yes, Sire."

Zane gives a final glance at the seer. He strides from the room, rage in his step, as he descends to the dungeons to vent some of his frustrations.

Within the hour, Drue leads a healer into the room. "Healer Irma has been called away to Pleta, so Master Roger is here to help."

Master Roger moves to the bed and looks over the seer with concern in his eyes. He places his bag down as he tests her temperature and feels for a pulse. "What happened?"

"She collapsed in court, Master Roger."

"She is very weak. How has this not been noticed before now?" His eyes land on Pippa.

"She was fine this morning, sir. I don't know how this happened."

"Has she eaten anything out of the ordinary?"

"Nothing but her standard fare of bacon and eggs for breakfast."

Master Roger turns to Drue, "Is anyone else sick?"

"No, she is the only one."

The healer nods, his fingers rubbing his chin as he ponders her condition. He reaches into his bag, pulls out some few herbs, and rolls one around in his fingers, tucking some in her mouth on her tongue. He pulls out a mortar and pestle, grinding up a few more herbs, then rubs the paste onto her wrists and behind her ears. "Near as I can tell, she's been poisoned. I do not have the same power as Healer Irma, but I can help in other ways. These herbs should hopefully slow down its progress and draw the poison out, but tonight will be crucial as to whether she survives. I will need a bowl or dish of some kind."

Pippa rises, moves to the dresser, dumps jewelry from a tray, and hands it to him. Master Roger scoops the poultice onto the tray and hands it back to Pippa. "She will need this applied every hour on her wrists and neck. I suggest her meals are checked from this day forward. Someone meant to take the seer out and might still succeed, especially if no one else is ill. If she makes it through the night, apply the poultice three times a day for the next three days. She needs at least a week of bed rest, or she may relapse, and I cannot be certain

I can save her if she does. I will return tomorrow to check on her progress."

Drue and Pippa watch Master Roger pack up his belongings. Drue leads him from the castle while Pippa closes the door behind them and places the poultice on the nightstand nearby. She takes the seer's hand in hers. "Oh, Miss, you need to fight this."

Pippa drags the remaining chair over to the side of the bed, leaving only to take Spider out. The afternoon passes slowly, with Martha checking in regularly and Pippa diligently applies the poultice. Pippa remains quiet when the king checks in; each time, he leaves in a rage that his seer hasn't woken up yet. At the dinner hour, Pippa rises stiffly, feeling an ache in her bones from the long hours of sitting on a hard chair. She moves to the door just as it opens. Martha comes in bearing food for her and broth for the seer. Another maid carries in the bedding Pippa had washed earlier. "Place it over there, Elo, and return to your duties."

"Yes, Ma'am." She places the bedding on the table before exiting the room and closing the door behind her.

"How is she, Pippa?"

"The same, Miss Martha. She barely breathes and is so still and cold. It's almost as if she's already…"

"DON'T you say it. She will pull through this."

Pippa nods, moving to the tray of food on the table. "I'm sorry, I'm just so scared. Thank you for the food."

"Me too, Pippa, she's strong and has endured much. We won't lose her. Now, eat your food. It's gonna be a long night." Martha moves over to the bed with her bowl of broth. She slides an extra pillow under the seer's head, then gingerly spoons broth into her mouth, watching for the reflexive swallows. Twenty minutes later, Martha returns the bowl to the tray. "I will spell you off at midnight, so you can get a few hours of sleep, as I doubt the King will check on her at that time. He likes his sleep too much."

"What about the guards at her door?"

"What about them? You don't think they stay awake all night, do you?"

"Well, yes, I thought they did."

Martha laughs at the thought. "NO, half the time they sleep through the night, and I wake them before the King does his morning patrol past her door. The only one I have ever found who stays awake is Xyl. He seems to be more dedicated to the seer than the King, and he's on tonight."

"Thank you, Miss Martha."

The night passes. Martha slips into the room at midnight, giving a nod to Xyl as Tai sleeps. She covers a few hours as Pippa curls up in a corner on the bedding brought in earlier, slipping out of the room an hour before sunrise. Pippa moves to sit in silence beside the seer, feeling pain in her heart, praying she will just wake up as if the previous day had not happened. Her eyes lift to the sunrise shining through the balcony doors, tears slipping from them as she places her head on the bed and cries next to her best friend.

The King's seer opens her eyes, blinking at the blurriness of the room and struggling to focus her vision. She hears crying beside her, feeling a dizziness within her as she tries to face Pippa. The seer reaches out and squeezes Pippa's hand gently. "There is no need to cry, Pippa."

Pippa snaps her head up and launches herself on her mistress, hugging her tightly. "Miss! You made it!"

"What happened, Pippa?"

"You collapsed in court. The King brought in a healer to look you over."

"Yes, that's right. I was feeling unwell as I was standing there, and the room started to spin. That's the last thing I remember."

Pippa returns to sitting beside the seer, taking her hand again. "The healer figured you were poisoned, Miss."

"I suspect I was, Pippa. I should get up for the King's court."

"No, Miss, healer's orders. One week of bed rest."

The seer struggles to sit up before lying back down in bed, knowing she isn't going anywhere today, even if she wants to. "And the King approved this?"

"I don't think Master Roger gave the King much choice, Miss. He said if you didn't, you might still die."

"Right, and we can't have that, can we? Thank you, Pippa." Her voice fades away as the exhaustion in her body pulls her away from the room and back into darkness.

Pippa watches her slip back into sleep, noticing that her breathing is more stable. She rises and moves to the door, knocking on it and waiting for the locks to click, glancing at Tai and Xyl in surprise as the door just opens. "Please tell the King that the seer woke up for a minute before falling back asleep."

Xyl watches Tai run off, smiling at Pippa and breathing a sigh of relief. "Thank you, Pippa, for looking after her."

Pippa nods, moving back to the chair beside the bed, and sits in it just as the king enters. His guards follow, standing just inside the door to wait. Pippa rises and bows to the king. "Your Majesty."

He moves to the side of the bed, looking over the seer, who hasn't moved from where he placed her. "You said she woke up?"

"Yes, Your Majesty, for a minute. But if you look, her breathing is more stable, and she has a bit of color in her face now. The poultice the medic gave her seems to be working."

"Good, keep applying it. I want to know when she wakes up again."

"Yes, Sire. I will let you know."

Zane lingers there a moment before turning, leaving the room, and closing the door behind him. "Randolph, please announce that there will be no court for the next week."

"You're giving her a week of bed rest, Sire?"

"It seems that way."

Shadows of Abduction

One Week later.

THE KING'S SEER wakes, knowing that today her week of rest is over and that her time at the castle is over. She closes her eyes, preparing herself mentally for the impending chaos she is about to unleash, well aware that her actions will inevitably lead the castle and its inhabitants to self-destruct later in the afternoon. She knows the aftermath will include some deaths and many punishments, but she also knows there is no other way if she wants to live. She pushes herself up and slides from the bed, feeling a slight unsteadiness within as the room spins for a few seconds.

She pads slowly to the bathing chamber, freshens herself, and returns to the bedroom. She pulls a dress from her armoire, a rich purple with green layers of silk hidden in the folds. She selects a lavender underdress before placing slippers on the floor. Once done, she moves to the dresser to pull out a satchel she tucked in the back of a drawer. She runs her hands over its soft leather, pulling out four dragon necklaces and laying them with her other jewelry. She stares at them for a moment, feeling a measure of regret flicker through her before pushing it aside, knowing this must be done. Her hands glow softly as she motions a few runes in the air, watching as a purple glow settles into three of the four necklaces. Pippa's knock comes as she tucks the three magical pieces back in the satchel, covering the remaining one with her jewelry that is visible on the dresser tray. "Come in, Pippa."

The locks outside click, and the door opens for Pippa to step through before it closes behind her again. Pippa moves to place her breakfast tray on the table. "Good morning, Miss. It is good to see you up and about. I have been worried about you."

"I know you were, Pippa." The King's seer studies her maid of the past nine years. "You know I love you, right, Pippa?"

"Of course, Miss. I love you too. You are the daughter I never had, even if I am barely enough to be your mother."

The King's seer laughs softly. "More like sisters, I suppose." She takes Pippa's hand in hers. "You will have your daughter, Pippa, twins, actually, and a son. The girls, of course, will be a handful, but I have no doubt you and Dunivan can handle it."

Pippas gasps softly. "How do you know?"

The seer smiles gently at her maid, bringing a hand up to caress her cheek. "Pippa, I am the King's seer. I see things all the time, most of which I keep silent about. Now, I need you to do me a favor."

"Of course, Miss. Anything."

"I need you to leave. I need you to take Dunivan and run. Head to the town of Kork in Sibath and take the boat to the Isle of Lockyae. Raise your family there. It is protected by druids, and the King's reach can't find you there."

Pippa shakes her head, panic flooding her eyes at the thought of leaving. "I can't leave you, Miss."

"I won't be here, Pippa. Not after today, and all that are tied with me, will die if they are still here. Please, you need to make me this promise, the second I am led from this room, you will run."

"I will try to, Miss, but the King's guards are everywhere."

"Yes, they are." The King's seer nods and moves to the dresser to pick up the satchel. She turns and places it in Pippa's hands.

"Inside are three necklaces, charms as you may call them. They will disguise you and Dunivan for six hours. There is also one for Xyl. Please take him. His true love is on the Isle, but he doesn't know it yet, for he thinks he loves me. I am sorry, this is all the time I can offer in my weakened state, and you need to make use of it. Do not take the time to pack, take only what's necessary, for if you delay, he will find you. There are gems to start a new life for all three of you, as well as three of Runestone's anti-scrying gems so you cannot be found magically. Keep one on each of you at all times. There is enough gold in the pouch to buy horses in town, for if you take from the royal stables, the guards will recognize them. Lead the horses out as if you are farmers buying livestock, and do not draw attention to yourselves. Once outside the gates and out of sight of the guards, urge the horses into a gallop and get as far away as fast as you can. Do not stop until evening, and even then, walk until the wee hours of dawn. Sleep for two hours and ride again until nightfall. It will be a long day for you three but even longer for those left in the castle when the King goes on his rampage. I will do my best to detain the King in court, and perhaps lunch, to give you more time, but I cannot guarantee you any longer than court."

Pippa shakes her head, tears running down her eyes. "I don't want to leave you, Miss."

"You must, Pippa. Please. I can't have your death on my hands." She steps in to hug her best friend and maid. "I need to know you are safe."

Pippa hugs her tightly, steps back, and tucks the pouch into her pockets. "I will. Now, let's get you dressed one last time."

The King's seer smiles. "Yes, I picked one out already."

Pippa moves over to the dress. "It seems a bit warm for this time of year, Miss."

"Yes. That's intentional, Pippa."

"Do I want to know?"

"No, but you will likely find out before you hit Vline. That is why I need you to run as fast as you can."

"Yes, Miss." Pippa sets about dressing her in the gown of her choosing, tying the ribbons and placing the beaded sash around her waist, then guiding her to sit. Pippa gathers some hairpins and fixes the seer's hair up in several braids. She skillfully inserts the pins to secure her hair, ensuring the optimal arrangement of the beads and chains that sway gracefully from them. Pippa weaves green and lavender ribbons through the braids and chains to hang down the seer's back. Finally, Pippa leans down to slide on her slippers. She steps back as the seer rises, smiling at how truly beautiful this woman is. "I am going to miss you, King's seer."

"I will miss you, too, Pippa. I hope that one day we may see each other again."

Tears fall from Pippa's eyes. "We aren't, are we?"

"No, Pippa, we are not. But you will have a happy life and see a grandchild or two in your future if you do as I say." The King's seer rests a hand on her cheek, sending a flickering of images through her touch to her maid. She watches as Pippa's eyes widen in shock at what she sees.

"You can show visions?"

"I always could, Pippa; I just never told anyone. I was careful not to pass any on until the night of the ball when I somehow let one slip to the King. I have granted you the power with that touch to pass what you saw over to Dunivan and Xyl, should you need to encourage them to leave with you."

"I will, Miss. I love you, King's seer." Pippa hugs her a final time before using her sleeve to dry her eyes and giving her a nod.

"I love you, too, Pippa."

Pippa smiles and heads to the door, knocking lightly on it. "The King's seer is ready for court."

Deryn and Tai watch the seer move through the doorway and step into the hallway. She and Pippa lift her skirts for the shackles to be placed on. "I will see you after court, Pippa."

"Of course, Miss. Are you having lunch with His Majesty?"

"I am not certain. I will send a guard for you when I return to my room."

"Yes, Miss. It's laundry day, so I will be out washing."

"Of course. Thank you, Pippa, for everything."

"You are most welcome, Miss. See you later." Pippa gives her a bow, turns, and heads to her room. She grabs only the essentials and stuffs them into her pockets. She waits until the guards lead the seer away before going to find the other two as requested.

The King's seer turns to her guards after Pippa enters her rooms, her eyes cool as she addresses them, showing no remorse for those that held her down during the king's torture sessions. "Ready when you are."

They nod, one in front leading her, the other following behind as she walks gracefully despite the shackles, ensuring the metal didn't clink. She enters the court moments later, bows to the king, and moves to stand silently behind him.

Zane studies her pale complexion, her cool eyes, and the stiffness of her back as she approaches. He listens for the rattle of chains but hears nothing that will allow him to take his rage out on her today. "King's seer."

"King Zane, I trust you are well."

"Of course, and you?"

"Well enough. I apologize for being unable to attend court the past week. It will not happen again."

He sneers. "See that it doesn't."

She smiles an ever so slight smile. "Indeed, I will."

Zane's eyes flash in anger. "What does that mean?"

"Exactly what it means, King Zane. I do believe Randolph is seeking your attention." She offers him a slight bow before she adjusts her eyes forward and dismisses him, feeling his rage emanate through the air at her actions.

His eyes snap to Randolph, his fury growing at the seer's behavior before plastering a smile on his face. "Let them in, Randolph. The sooner we start, the sooner we get this done and over with."

Randolph nods, moving to let the people in, each seeking their moment of time before the king and his seer, hoping that they will have their desires met. The seer remains silent, catching Zane's angry looks directed her way. He pauses the session halfway through. "King's seer. Have you seen anything?"

"Of course, King Zane. I see things all the time, just nothing that would benefit *you*." Her voice drips with disdain as she addresses him.

"Why do I get the feeling you are lying to me, King's seer?"

Her eyes narrow on him, the violet crystalizing to a light lavender for a brief second, which causes him to shift back in his seat. "I wouldn't know, King Zane. Perhaps as the old adage says, *it takes one to know one.*"

Zane's rage intensifies, reaching a tipping point. He stands up from his throne to confront her, lifting his hand with the intention of striking, noticing the subtle stiffening of her back in response to the threat.

She lifts her chin in defiance, knowing if he does follow through, it will be the second time he has left marks that others can see. "DO it Zane, place a lovely bruise on my cheek and give me a black eye. Then explain to your masses why your seer is missing for yet another week or why she is bruised. I will ensure they learn what the King is really like and the darkness that lies within him, for I will not lie *to them.*"

Zane clenches his fist and lowers it down to his side as he stares at his seer.

"That's *a good* King. Now sit down and behave. Your people are waiting."

He grits his teeth, hissing in rage. "Are you provoking me, King's seer?"

"Is it working, Zane? Will I get another beating tonight? Or a whipping with salt poured in the wounds afterward when I haven't cried out in pain? At least this way, I will have a reason for it."

He glares at her coldly. "There is always a reason."

"There is not. You just make one up to appease your inner demon."

He grabs her throat and steps in close. He studies her eyes intently, seeing that she is not backing down, nor reaching for the hands that choked her, evening daring him to challenge her, knowing something is up. He releases her, watching her stagger a bit as her breath returns, only to meet her glare as she straightens to face him. He spins, moves back to his throne, and growls at Randolph. "Send the rest in."

"Yes, Your Majesty."

The rest of the morning passes before the court closes at noon. The seer remains standing and waits to see if the king is inviting her to lunch, knowing he isn't. Her eyes follow him as he stops in front of her to glare into her eyes, then heads off in the direction of the dungeons. She smiles slightly, knowing he will be busy downstairs torturing his prisoners, something she deliberately drove him to, thereby giving her and the others more time. She waits until the king leaves the hall before turning and heading back to her room. Her guards follow diligently behind her, stopping at her door to have her shackles removed.

Tai's hands fumble nervously with the locks, having never seen such a power struggle between the king and the seer before. He falls back a step in fear at the new behavior the seer is displaying.

She kicks the shackles to the side as she pushes her door open, then slams it behind her. She leans against it, closing her eyes a moment, hearing the locks click into place. She feels the poison's effects calling her to sleep but knows today is not the day to answer that call.

She moves to the balcony, catching a red shadow within the clouds looming across the landscape. A faint smile crosses her lips as she moves to the basket and places it on the chair. She picks up one of her books and drops it in the bottom, along with two of Runestone's anti-scrying gems. She tucks a small pillow on top of it and moves to her bed to collect Spider. She carries him to the basket and places him gently inside. "We are going for a ride, little one; you need to stay there." Her gaze drifts to the bear he was curled up in and she returns to it. She picks it up and squishes it lightly, memories of when she first got it flooding her mind. She hugs it close; a few tears escape as she kisses the top of the bear's head, bringing it back and placing it in with Spider. She knows it is risky taking the bear and the book, but is willing to place bets the king will not remember she has them to scry on, assuming he can find someone to bypass Runestone's magic. She places the lid carefully on the basket and ties bands tightly around it so it cannot open during her escape from the castle.

She glances around the room as she moves to the dresser, knowing this is going to be the last time she sees this room and everything in it. She smiles at the wealth of jewelry sitting there, matching the wealth in dresses that still hang in her wardrobe, understanding most of it is meant to buy her silence and her visions. She picks up the necklace she hid this morning, caressing it gently before her fingers tighten on the dragon emblem, smiling at the irony of it. Hurriedly, she moves to the desk and sits, pulling a sheet of parchment forward. Her fingers glow softly as she scribes a letter to the king using magic. The words fade away before she writes over top of it a letter to Martha. Soft purple writing fills the page. She folds the necklace and a gem inside the letter and places them all in a pouch. Finally, she moves to her door to knock upon it. The locks click, and the door opens as she addresses the guards. "Deryn, Tai, I have two things. First, I need a pouch delivered to Martha, and second, Pippa hasn't come around with my lunch. Would you fetch her for me?"

"Of course."

"Thank you." She hands the pouch over to Deryn as she steps back into the room. After hearing the locks click in place, her hands glow dimly, and a weakness suffuses her body upon using her powers. A palms-up gesture floats her dresser above the floor and gently slides it to block the door and delay anyone that tries to get in. She twists her hands a little, and purple motes of light form as a kingdom banner appears in her hands. She moves to the bed and lays it across it before calling forth her blade. She inspects for a moment, recalling the first day she received it, placing it carefully upon the banner. She strides back to the basket, picks it up, and ties the straps securely over her shoulders so it won't slip off.

She opens the garden door, hikes up her skirts, and runs down to the open area, knowing she has very little time. Screams of people sound over the wall as the Red Phantom razes the city. She moves to stand on the stump of her beloved arbutus tree, its fall another punishment from the king since her attempted escape. Her eyes lift skyward, and she turns to the dragon heading her way; red eyes meet violet as he swoops down to claim her. She closes her eyes a moment, feeling the claws strike her, her breath taken away upon impact as the dragon lifts her high into the sky.

The cold wind cuts through her thin silks. Mentally she berates herself for not grabbing a cloak as she sails away from the castle in the clutches of a dragon. She glances back towards the king's balcony, seeing the fury and rage in his expression and knowing he saw her run through the gardens to the tree. She smiles and lifts a hand to wave goodbye.

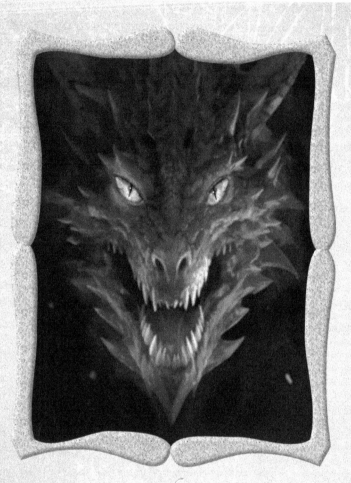

Rendgren
The Red Phantom

In the meantime, Deryn heads down to the kitchen as requested. He finds Martha in her usual spot at the table and places the pouch down in front of her. "From the King's seer." He turns and leaves, returning to his post at the seer's door.

Martha looks at the pouch, feeling a sudden measure of dread as she opens it. She pulls the letter out as the necklace and gem fall into her lap. She lifts the gem, recognizing it as an anti-scrying gem, and tucks it in her bodice. She looks at the necklace, recalling the King's seer purchasing them on her very first shopping trip when she was twelve, wondering what happened to them. While she reads the letter, her face pales, and she feels her heart still inside her, clutching the dragon pendant tight enough for it to cut her hand in places.

My Dearest Martha.

I write you this letter to help you understand my decision today. As you read this, you will see the words fade with each line read so that Zane cannot punish you for letting me escape or knowing that I have foreseen what is about to happen. I cannot stay here any longer for one of these days; I will not survive his beatings, for I have seen it. While I have the ability to deflect his whip, I did not want him to know what powers I possess and have kept hidden since I arrived here at nine years old. I have seen it all within the castle walls and felt the evil taint the castle holds. I could see the darkness within Zane, even though he did try to hide it for many years, but it can only be suppressed for so long.

You see, I made my first mistake when I was thirteen. I decided that with Zane struggling to be good for me, I would help him. But I found I was not strong enough to tangle with both a witch who had stolen a soul and a demon not willing to relinquish a body. I should have looked at all the consequences of my actions, but I didn't. And for that, I will have to live with the deaths I caused of the four guards patrolling the walls outside my room. I understand you have restrictions on what you can do, being bound by your oath, as you call it, but it is not an oath. It is a curse placed upon you by the witch doctor Zolvinta and the old king Wallace on his deathbed. It was made with the hope that you could keep the demon inside Zane tamed, but you cannot. A demon is a demon, and nothing can change that.

I know you are wondering why I am stating this, but I need you to know a few things as you will have a decision to make at the end of this letter. Zane's soul was stolen from within the womb of Rimorhia by the witch Lavinia. She replaced it with a demonic one because Wallace rejected her, and he knew it. He sought Zolvinta to break the curse when the child was born, but the demon clung to the body he was granted. Not that he had Zane's true soul to put back, as the witch still had it. I found the soul that was removed, but I was not strong enough to remove the demon from within. So I stole it and placed it within Pippa instead so that it might find a home in one of her children.

The witch was quite angry with me for stealing her soul and sent assassins in to kill me. I suspect because she could not find the soul, she assumed I had succeeded in replacing the demon within the king, but I had not. He was born of evil and will remain so despite my interference. Because of my actions, I drove him back to the dark side, for the room downstairs opened the next day. I did not say anything to him, for I knew it was my mistake, and in that, the timelines shifted for many. It is something I will need to accept and live with, especially knowing I am leaving the castle with the rage of a demon unbound. But I did shackle the witch. When the mage Antimagic was here, dispelling the witches' objects, it weakened her enough that I was able to place a mind block within her. She has forgotten who I am, but should she ever see me again, that block will fade, and there will be a battle between us. I can only hope I am strong enough at that point to face her.

Zane will punish many for my escape and kill those he feels betrayed him. My guards. My parents, and while I know I should feel sadness for my parent's death, I feel nothing. For they are the ones that sold me to the evil in this castle. His wrath will continue until I am found, but no matter who he brings in to search, he will not find me. And for this, I am truly sorry for the innocents that will suffer at his hand. Now, I know it is not any more than normal, for I am aware that no servant can leave this castle alive, and none of them ever have. When their term ends, their life ends, but not until he satisfies the demon that resides within him downstairs in the room. I cannot save them all, but I can choose to save those that I care about, and so have set things in motion to do so.

Pippa, Dunivan, and Xyl should already be five hours away from the castle on their way to Lochyae by the time you read this. So that leaves you. Within this pouch, there is an enchanted necklace and an anti-scrying stone. Once it is placed around your neck, it has the power, my power, to break the curse that was placed upon you. But beware, for in that curse; the king cannot kill you as you are bound together. With this necklace on, he can, but he will not know it, so use it wisely. It also has a charm placed within the gems to change your appearance should you decide to run. And while I could only grant the three six hours of disguise, you get a full day and night. I am truly sorry for what this afternoon will bring; but I want you to know that I appreciate all that you have done for me, Martha. In the years I have been here, you and Pippa were the family I never had and gave me the love I needed to survive. I hope you break free from this place that has held you captive for so long and that you find peace and happiness elsewhere. I love you Miss Martha.

Sincerely and with love.
The King's Seer.

Martha stands up quickly. The blank parchment flutters to the table as the chair crashes to the ground behind her, causing others in the kitchen to stop and stare. "No, please, No." Martha turns upon hearing the horns of war blow and runs to the seer's room. She sees two pale guards standing at her door. "Where is she?"

"She's in her room, but her maid is missing."

"Open the door."

They nod, unlocking the door, but find the door won't open. "What the hell?"

"OPEN IT NOW!"

The three of them push on the door, hearing the grinding of the dresser against the floor. They open up enough space to allow them to slip inside. Martha looks around the room, noticing that everything remains untouched, and runs down the stairs to the garden. She sees the red dragon flying away from the castle, the seer's skirts in his clutches, and the rage of the king as he grasps his balcony. Martha sinks to the ground in fear at the destruction that is about to happen, tucking the necklace in her pocket. "Oh, King's seer. What have you done?"

The Unbound Demon

ZANE RETURNS TO his room. His rage still brewing since the torture session below ended with a dead prisoner before he was sated. He moves to his balcony just as he hears the city folk scream, followed by the roar of a dragon. His eyes drop to the garden below, seeing his seer running through it, her skirts pulled up as she clambers up onto the tree stump. He frowns, realizing too late just what is happening as a shadow hovers over the garden seconds before a red dragon appears. He watches in horror as it collects his seer in its claws and flies past his balcony, catching the smile upon her lips as she lifts a hand to wave goodbye.

"NOOOOO!" He slams his fists down on the railing. "GUARDS! Get the catapults! BRING that Dragon down NOW!" He hears the guard at his door run away as he watches Martha enter the garden and sink to the ground. He narrows his eyes on her, suspecting she knows something. Zane leaves his chamber with Randolph falling into step behind him. He arrives at the seer's partially open door, realizing that her provoking him today in court was part of her plan to keep him distracted, and he had fallen for it. He steps through the door, glaring at the two guards standing there. Zane sees the sword on the banner and pauses to stare at it, understanding in that gesture the war she has declared upon him. "How the hell did she get access to her blade and a banner?"

"We don't know, Sire. The blade has been in the barracks since she was confined to her room and we are not certain where the banner came from."

151

Zane growls and strides to the garden door, watching Martha walk up the stairs towards him. "DID you know?"

She shakes her head; her shoulders slumped in defeat. "I did not."

"Then why are you here?"

"I just received her letter."

Deryn pales. "The King's seer asked us to deliver a pouch to Martha, Your Majesty, as well as finding her maid because she had not received lunch yet. We did not think anything of it."

"And where is her maid?"

Tai and Deryn glance at each other. "Missing. She's not in her room nor at the washing station as she said she would be this morning."

"Find her!" He turns to Martha. "Where is the letter?"

"In the kitchen, but…"

"Let's go!" He grabs her wrist and drags her to the kitchens, not caring that she stumbles behind him nor that her skirts are in the way as he pushes her through the door. The maids gasp and bow, feeling the rage emanating off the king as he enters the kitchen, backing away to hide in the corners. Martha moves to the table and collects the parchment, handing it over to him.

"This is blank, Martha. Where's the actual letter?" Zane starts to crumple it as a purple glow surrounds it, causing him to pause and stare at the small motes of light forming words upon the paper.

King Zane.

> *I know at this point, you will have watched me being taken away and seen Martha in the gardens below, arriving moments too late to stop me. You will have stormed to my rooms, finding and confronting her on the stairs. Deryn will mention that I sent a satchel to her, thus dragging her to the kitchens where you are standing now. As you are reading this, you will discover some of the power I have concealed from you, for the letter Martha read has faded, and this one is writing itself. You were right in that I was holding back my powers, but you never did discover to what extent, and you never truly will. I have bound within its writing,*

magic that has forbidden Martha from speaking of what she has read. So do not waste your time trying to retrieve that information.

Flickers of purple lights appear as the letter splits apart in his hand, swirls around, and creates an illusion of the seer standing before him. She is nine years old again, looking up into his eyes, the wonder portrayed there fades to a hardness that should not be seen in a child. The child speaks, not with the childlike innocence she had upon arrival but the cold cunning seer she has become.

"I knew at nine years old when my parents sold me to you that you were evil, Zane, and I made the decision at that moment you would not see all I had to offer." The image reaches towards Martha, stopping short of touching her, retracting her hand back slowly. *"Martha is right. I am a Mystic. She even warned you my powers would grow as my eyes shifted from lavender to violet, and they did. But I gave you just enough to ensure you didn't question it. One might even say I played you, Zane, keeping my cards close at hand, encouraging you to play yours. All the while growing up faster than a nine-year-old should."*

The image smiles, shifting to when she is twelve years old. *"I set things in motion six years ago to escape the evil this castle has, and the abuse I knew was coming. Abuse I had hoped to avoid, but I couldn't find the threads to weave it out completely. I just needed to keep you happy and delay it for as long as I could, and I did. Unlike your past seer who died at your hands. I saw the darkness within you growing. I saw what you did in secret, hoping it was beyond the scope of my sight. It was not."*

The illusion ages four years; the night of the ball, diamonds glittering all around her as a small dog appears momentarily in her hands. *"But I did make a mistake on the night of my sixteenth birthday by giving you a hint of a power I've had since I was nine years old. And that is granting my sight to others. With but an uncontrolled touch, you received a glimpse of your death in the breath of a gold dragon."* The diamonds fade as she stands there, images of the vision appearing behind her, showing Zane what he has tortured and beat her to see again. A gold dragon drawing in and breathing out a wave of flame upon him and his throne. The heat of the vision fills the room as everyone flinches before fading away in golden motes of light.

The seer's eyes grow frosty as she narrows them on Zane. *"I suffered in silence at your hands, Zane, knowing I could have lessened the punishment if I just gave what you wanted. But I was not willing to grant you access to that power, and so I didn't. I knew it was never going to be enough. So I drew boundaries and kept them no matter what I had to endure to make it happen. The sad thing is, you never did figure out what caused my slip-up. It wasn't control; it wasn't fear; it certainly wasn't the torture you bestowed upon me often, but happiness, Zane. I was truly happy at the ball that day, and that was what caused my mistake. Had you recognized that, you could have had so much more of the power I wield, and I would have given it to you. We all have a point at which we convert, where the sides become blurred, and one can be beckoned to walk the other path."*

The image takes his face gently in her hands, rising on her tiptoes, and kisses his lips softly. *"I would have helped you rule the realm and move your troops into the right places to make that happen. If you had just seen... For that was my turning point."* She returns to standing, her fingers running lightly over his lips as her eyes meet his. *"It would have taken but a kiss on that dance floor to own me completely. I would have changed everything for you and made the gold dragon disappear... Everything... It was, in fact, my point of trusting and following you blindly, without the hand of force, until it was too late for me to turn back. You played your game well, my King and you almost had me... but not well enough because you didn't see."* She pulls her hand back as sadness crosses her features. *"But I did see my mistake in your anger. I did see the demon arise and realized what I had done. So I shut it down, for the threads changed even as we stood there. It was an emotion I never dared to feel again, until today, that is, as I flew away from your demon...One that even I could not tame."*

She shifts to become another illusion, dressed in Pippa's cloak, hiding her features. Soft laughter echoes in the kitchen, causing the maids to shiver slightly. *"The thing with a mystic Zane, is unlike a seer, we can rewrite storylines. Or twist them to our desires as we see many endings to get the one we want. We have the power to create and destroy, to conjure and dismiss. To see, feel and speak into people's thoughts and minds, among many other talents I won't get into. Whereas a seer only sees what is and cannot change what they see. It was the day before the ball that I first sensed the power, but in my distraction, I did not recognize it for what it was. It was not until a year later, while I was on my balcony, that I truly felt the power of the dragon within the city in his mortal form. One that was to be my way out of this castle. I tried to reach out telepathically but received nothing but silence back. I suspect he was curious, though, for he returned to the city several times after that. I knew, as I was sneaking out to meet him that you would catch me. But it was a thread that I needed woven to ensure you played a card I knew you had and one I needed... poison."*

She pushes the hood off, her gaze landing on Martha a moment before it shifts to the pantry behind her. The doors open, and from deep within its darkness, small vials float forward into the seer's hand. She turns the vials over, watching the liquid move within them. *"I knew when each meal was poisoned by your guard's hands, for I could see the darkness in it, even though you kept that particular guard out of my sight. It was a dangerous game I played, but I ate it anyway because I did not want you to know that I had the power to see things as they truly are. Although I did give that away the day I arrived when I commented on the magical flames within the castle and how they were different in the secret room. It was something that was overlooked, and for that, I was grateful."* She smiles his way, a cunning look entering her eyes as the lids slowly twist off by themselves. The poison lifts from the vials, floating in the air above the hand that held them. *"Just as I knew which meals I needed to eat to get the antidote, but what happens when you can magically lift the antidote from the food."*

A soft gasp escapes Martha at her words, her eyes narrow on the king, understanding immediately why some days the guards collected her food from the kitchen. "YOU were the one that poisoned her?"

"Now you ask, why would I lift the antidote out of the food? Why would I even eat the poisoned food when I could have removed it as well. The reason is fear. I wanted you to feel fear before I left, Zane. Fear that you might actually lose something you value. Something that is worth more than all the gold in this castle to you. I wanted you to feel it so that you

would recognize it within you as you stand before this image. And as much as I have had the power to leave you for many years, there is a reason for everything, and it's all tied together to the threads I have woven." Her gaze moves to the liquid, watching it flow through her fingers before it splatters on the floor. The vials follow shortly, glass shattering and spreading at their feet.

Zane glares at the image, picks up a chair, and throws it through her. He watches as the motes of light scatter only to reform before him. She offers him a bow, a knowing smile crossing her lips as the image shifts to that of this morning. *"I can feel your rage, Zane, even from where I am, free from your clutches. I did warn you next time you would not catch me, and you didn't. I am aware you will search for me, but do you have the power to find me? I know what cards you hold and can bring to the war room table. For I have played them all, but you have only had a glimpse of mine. Right now, you are looking to pick a fight, Zane, and I am willing to grant it, but not in the way you want. It is not my destiny to end you. It is another's. I will just set the playing board up, with all the pieces to counter yours, to ensure that happens."*

The image reaches out again to caress Zane's cheek lightly. *"Did you ever wonder why there was never a gold dragon brought to you? That's because they had advance warning any time someone hunted them, even from within the confines of the castle. I saved them all, Zane, just for you. But there is one thing that surprises even me. I cannot see which of the six gold dragons currently in existence will kill you, but one will. And so now, I will become the Red Phantom's seer. It will be most interesting being a seer for a legend, the strongest and most feared dragon in all the lands."* The image fades, the soft laughter of the seer echoing throughout the castle. *"Oh, one last thing. You have approximately two years, Zane before the vision comes true, and I have that time to keep the gold dragons safe. The war has been called, and may the best player win."*

Zane roars, uncontrolled fury racing through him, and places his hands under the table to heave it across the room before he storms out of the kitchen.

Martha stands there in shock with the maids, silence filling the kitchen as they all stare at the overturned table. Each of them going over what they had just seen and what it all means. Martha collects herself, giving a nod to the others, and strides from the kitchen, heading to her chambers.

Zane stalks to the war room, cursing his seer and the plans she made with the power she kept hidden. He stops at a vase, picks it up, and throws it against the wall, watching the porcelain shatter, knowing if he ever gets his hands on his seer, he is going to break her the same way. "DAMN YOU, SEER!" He turns to Randolph, who has followed safely along behind him. "She's DEAD if I ever see her again."

"Yes, Your Majesty."

"FIND me Dunivan."

He bows, "Yes, Your Majesty."

"AND I want all Nine of her guards to be presented to me immediately."

"Yes, Your Majesty." Randolph runs from the hall, attempting to compose himself after what he had just seen in the kitchen. Within ten minutes, he has eight of the nine guards standing before the king. "Dunivan and Xyl are missing, Sire."

Zane glares at Randolph. "What do you mean they are missing?"

"I can't find them, Sire, and others have not seen them either. Not since this morning. It's like they vanished with the seer's maid."

Zane narrows his eyes, knowing the seer had something to do with it. "Put posters out for the return of them. Five hundred gold dead, double that if they are brought in alive. Ten thousand gold to whoever finds my seer and brings her back." He turns back to the guards that stand nervously before him. "Alvero, who was patrolling outside?"

"Cedrik, Jesper and Krim, Sire."

"Were Tai and Deryn at her door since dawn?"

"Yes, Your Majesty."

"So, five guards and the seer still managed to outmaneuver them all and escape."

Alvero cringes at the anger in the king's voice. "She was stolen, Sire. We were not expecting the Phantom to take her."

"She did, though. She even planned it! And for that, those five guards are to be taken to the dungeons... Now." He snaps his fingers, and his guards rush in to fulfill his orders. He ignores the protests of the five guards as they struggle against the king's force, eventually being dragged away from the war room. "Now, the remaining three have ONE month to find my Seer, or you will be joining them. If you defect, your family will die. Everyone you love will die. Do you understand me?"

They all bow, fear creeping into their soul, knowing their lives are ending. "Yes, Sire."

"Now, GO find her!"

"Yes, Sire."

The Dragon's Domain

THE DRAGON SAILS through the air with ease, smiling at his victory today, stealing the most precious thing that pompous king had right from beneath his nose. He lifts himself up into the clouds to avoid being tracked, his grip tightening around his prize as he returns to his lair.

She feels the claws tighten around her as she struggles against the weakness in her body, finding exhaustion winning as she slips into darkness. She wakes suddenly at the unexpected jarring of her body as the dragon lands in front of a cave entrance, feeling a warmth in the air surrounding her, and wonders just how far they have flown. He carries her into the cave and drops her unceremoniously on the floor near a table and chairs before shifting back to his human form.

She groans while she struggles to her feet, unstrapping the basket she carries and placing it on the ground beside her. She rubs her arms, trying to return some circulation and warmth to them, feeling chilled from the flight here. "What do you want, Dragon?"

"You, of course."

She sighs softly, straightening her skirts, before meeting his gaze. "I gathered that. Now that you have me, I ask again. What do you want?"

"Shouldn't a true seer be able to see what I desire?"

"Oh, yes, I can see it, but I want to hear it from you."

He steps in close, doing his best to intimidate her. His eyes flare with fire as he looks down at the seer standing before him. "You are not scared of me, Seer?"

"Should I be?"

"Yes. I would think you should be. I am the Red Phantom, and I just stole you from your king. I can kill you here and now."

"You stole me because I let myself be stolen. And you won't kill me because I have value to you." Her violet eyes glow slightly as she lifts her chin to stare defiantly into his gaze. "That and I don't foresee myself dying by your hand, Dragon. Are you going to prove my vision wrong?"

"Have you seen your death then?"

"I have."

"How interesting. When is it?"

"You do not need to know, Dragon."

"Is it soon, or do I have time to get value out of my theft?"

"Again, you do not need to know."

"Can it be changed, your sights?"

"They can."

"Then why not change it."

"Because it is out of my hands. You still haven't answered what you want."

He takes her chin in his hand and studies her violet eyes, noticing the defiance written within them along with the stiffness in her stance. He ponders her for a moment, having lived long enough to recognize by her look that he should not push the issue just yet. "You might be right; a seer in my pocket could prove useful."

"Of course it will, but before I become your seer, you will swear an oath to me."

"I don't make oaths or promises to mortals."

She smiles, reaching up to pull his hand away from her. "You will to me, and you will be magically bound to keep it. In exchange for this oath, I will be your seer and guide you to all the dragon treasures I did not guide the King to."

"Cunning little seer, aren't you."

"I learned a lot in the court of King Zane."

"If I am to consider your proposal, not saying that I am, what would this oath be?"

"That you find a good home for Spider should something happen to me."

"And Spider is?"

She leans down, untying the straps on the basket at her feet, lifting the lid off carefully. She smiles at her best friend as she pulls him out of the basket and into her arms. She holds the little dog out for the dragon to see, catching the growl from both of them.

"A mutt! You want a home for the mutt?"

"Yes, I do. A good one even."

"What makes you so certain I won't eat that thing right now."

"Dragon treasure, and a lot of it."

"You are willing to risk both yours and a dog's life for gold."

"I am."

"How do you know where this treasure is?"

"I am the King's seer."

"Why did you not tell the king?"

"He had enough."

"And I do not?"

"You are a dragon. You can never have enough treasure, and I needed leverage."

His eyes flare red as he looks at the pair standing before him. A smile spreads across his lips at the audacity of the seer. "You have yourself a deal, Seer. I swear, should something happen to you, I will find a good home for the mutt."

"Good. Now I will need a map and a round amethyst. Then I can show you where the first hoard is." Her shoulders relax at his oath.

"How many hordes are there?"

"Close to a hundred."

"A hundred, you say?" Rendgren arches his brow and smiles. He creates a portal behind him and steps through it, disappearing from her sight.

The King's seer picks up the basket and moves to sit at the table nearby, placing Spider in her lap. She pats him gently as she waits for the requested items. "Well, little one, at least I know you will be safe when the time comes."

Ten minutes later, Rendgren returns with a large map of the realm. He rolls it out before her on the table and places the gem upon it. "Alright, *King's* seer, prove to me you can find the treasures."

She places Spider on the ground as she rises to stand next to him. She picks up the amethyst and fills it with a soft purple glow. She watches as it spins gently with power, moving her other hand to the map. Motes of purple light fall from her fingertips, fading into the map. She places the gem down in the center, where it rotates for a moment before it rolls across the map and stops at a location in the Grim Tundra. "There is your first unattended horde, Dragon."

"This is how you found the dragons for the king?"

The seer watches the gem for a moment as the glow fades ever so slightly. "No. I was required to find him one dragon per month and simply placed a purple marker out where their hunting grounds were by searching with my mind. He did not see this gift, though I will admit, this is easier only because I already know where the dragons were killed."

"And yet, you show me this power?"

"Yes, I have a contract with you. Dragon treasure for Spider's safety. I did not have one with the King. I was owned by him."

"Owned?"

"He bought me off my parents when I was nine. He owned me and reminded me of it often. But just because one is owned, does not mean one needs to play all the cards they have."

"And are you playing all your cards with me, Seer?"

"What do you think, Dragon?"

"That you are not."

"And he's a clever dragon to boot."

"I could make you."

"You could try, but you won't succeed." She smiles as she catches his eyes narrow on her, then gestures to the map. "Your treasures are waiting, Dragon; perhaps you should see if I can do what I promise before you think about killing me, as you are right now."

Shock fills his eyes. Rendgren spins, his robes flowing about him as he creates a red ring of fire and steps through it in search of what she promises.

She watches him leave and smiles when he portals back a few minutes later to grab some bags and disappears again without a word.

"Come, Spider, let's go explore our new home." The dog bounces after her as she heads back through the passage she was carried in and steps into the sunlight. She glances up at the high canyon walls that surround her, noticing immediately that the only way out is to fly. She wonders momentarily if she can ever be free of people's desire for her power but knows it is just a dream, never to come true.

Once she is certain Spider's curiosity is satisfied, she pads back into the cave, looking more closely at the room they came from with three other passages off it. She pauses at the gemstone on the table, twists her fingers around as the stone rolls to a new location, then turns and heads through the first doorway. She glances around, seeing a few alcoves in the stone wall, much like shelves, which hold a few plates, bowls, glasses, and what appears to be a washing station. Off to the side sits a simple table and chairs, similar to the one in the main room. She frowns as she notes an absence of food or any pantry that might store any. At that moment, her stomach growls, being accustomed to eating on schedule for the past nine years and knowing she missed lunch. She pushes the hunger aside as she returns to the map room.

She wanders through to the next passage, stopping to stare at the room before her. While the past two rooms were bare, this room is well-furnished. A large, four-post bed sits in the middle, exquisitely carved posts reach the ceiling of the cave. The bed looks soft, with high-quality red and black bedding and a multitude of pillows propped up at the headboard. She shifts her eyes to the armoire and dressers, a rich red wood that she has never seen. Each piece is intricately carved with the captivating design of dragons. A large overstuffed chair sits next to a small bookcase with a scattering of books upon it. Art is somehow hung on the stone walls, none of them as striking as the one that hangs above the head of the bed. The large painting features a dragon breathing fire down up an army, suspecting the dragon in the picture is him or an ancestor of his. She turns her attention to the hair adornments lying scattered on the dresser tops, wanting to go over and inspect them, but does not dare to step into his domain. She looks down at Spider, hearing his soft growl, and pats his head lightly. "Spider, you can't growl at his room, or him for that matter."

The seer turns and heads back, working her way into the third passage. She follows it as it winds downward; soft torches light the walls as the passage descends deeper into the mountain. Partway down the curving tunnel, she sees a vast underground lake, where a light mist floats over its surface. She approaches the edge and reaches into the water, feeling its warmth. She smiles at the thought of being able to soak in this lake, noticing a table nearby with a stack of towels. She spots a narrow hallway off to the left of the lake and peeks into it, seeing it houses the privy. She smiles down at Spider, drinking from the lake. "Well, it's not the castle, but it has what we need, Spider."

She continues down to the end of the spiraling passageway and gasps in shock as she steps into a dimly lit cavern, its floor space doubling that of the castle she lived in. Heaps of treasure spread across the floor, rising in height well above her head in places. Valuables from art and jewelry to coins and gems litter the floor, mixed in with adventuring bags, suits of armor, and weapons. She feels the coins shift under her feet as she walks through the treasury, wondering just how many adventurers this dragon has dispatched. She observes the wealth in the room, knowing she is only going to add to it as visions filter through her mind.

She pauses at a pack nearby, rummages through it, finds some chalk, and tucks it into her pocket. She unfastens a bedroll and looks it over, determining it will be acceptable for her needs. She picks up five copper and five silver coins, carrying her plunder back to the main room with the map. She retrieves her basket and finds a nook to lay the bedroll in. She lifts out the pillow and sets it near the bedroll, watching as Spider curls up on it and patting him lightly as she sits down next to him. She pulls out the chalk, setting it and the coins nearby. She tips the basket on its side, then removes her well-worn teddy and book but leaves the gems inside. She carefully lifts the pillow with Spider on it and slides them back into the basket, creating a small den for her pup. She draws a pattern of crossed lines on the floor and sets the coins inside. She hunkers down to read but finds her body has other plans as she drifts off to sleep.

In the meantime, Rendgren stares at the treasure in the well-hidden cave. He smiles at the thought of having a seer in his pocket and begins to fill the bags that he brought. He fills the second sack when he hears the mental alarm in his head that his treasure is being disturbed, feeling rage within at the thought of anyone touching it. He stares at the treasure that remains, instinct to return to his lair warring within, but he decides to stay and finish filling the bags. If the seer is stealing, then he will deal with her when he returns, as there is no way out of that cavern for her. He packs quickly, calling upon his portal home, and steps into the main room, a soft growl drawing his attention to his right.

He narrows his eyes on the dog in the basket, placing his bags down as he steps gracefully over to the still seer, her arms wrapped around a stuffed bear.

He watches her sleep in a bedroll she clearly filched from his pile, along with the coins in a pattern beside her. He picks up the book near her, not recognizing it, and flips it open. He reads the inscription on the inside *To the King's seer, may the faeries watch over you, Martha.* He places the book down beside her sleeping form on the floor, feeling a slight twinge of guilt as he stares at her and the dog. He mutters softly under his breath as he strides to his room, digs into one of the dressers, and pulls out a blanket. He moves to the bed and yanks a pillow off it, then heads back to where she sleeps. He drops the blanket over her and kneels, lifting her head gently as he tucks a pillow under her head, disturbing her enough to wake her up, her violet eyes meeting his red ones.

She whispers ever so softly, her eyes narrowing at his closeness. "What are you doing, Dragon?"

Rendgren pauses, wondering himself what the hell he is doing, rises, and stands back up. "Since you stole a bedroll, I thought perhaps you might want a pillow too."

"It's not stealing if you know where it is, Dragon."

"It was taken from my treasure pile. It's stealing if I do not grant permission."

She pushes herself up to sit against the wall, eyeing the well-made blanket that slips off her. "It's not like it left your cave." Her eyes move to the sacks behind him. "And I think you can spare a bedroll and a few coins with what I have offered you."

He follows her gaze, then returns them to hers. "What were you doing down there?"

"I was exploring. If this is going to be my new home, then I wanted to see what it is like. On that note, you have no food in your kitchen."

"Of course not; why would I keep food there?"

"Well, some of us have to eat to survive."

"Are you saying I don't need to eat to survive, because I assure you, I do. You would be nothing but a snack to me."

"What do you do then? Eat farmers' cattle?"

He glares at her, the red in his eyes flaring as fires form around his fingertips. "Please, I would expect a seer to see that I am more refined than that."

She narrows her eyes at him. "Indeed, but you did just say I was nothing more than a snack to you. I don't see everything; that's not how it works."

"You said it yourself, Seer, that you did not foresee your death at my hands. Has that vision changed?"

"No, Dragon, it hasn't."

He studies her a moment before he moves to his bags and lifts them with ease. "The kitchen has food if you are hungry." He heads down the passage to the lower chamber, finding himself frustrated with the woman he can sense rising and moving above him. He empties the treasure out, adding the new loot to his piles, feeling delight spread to his heart as he caresses his newly acquired gold. Soon, if he is not already, he will be the richest dragon in the realm. He grabs a few extra bags and heads back upstairs. His eyes catch the gem on the map, which glows in a new location. He strides into the kitchen, where he knows the seer stands. "Seer, the gem is glowing on the map."

She turns his way as he approaches, "Yes, it's your next location once you have cleared out the first one. The gem will continue to move as you enter each lair. I suggest you clear out one before entering the second, as the gem will not return to its last location."

"Are you saying if I go to this new location, it will move to another?"

"Yes, and if you go to the third, it will move again, but it will never go back, so if you forget or misread where the gem was, that treasure is lost. Is that understood?"

"Understood." His gaze drifts over to where she stands in the kitchen, the dog growling at her feet, noticing she has not moved from where he sensed her from down below. "Now, sit." He points to the table in the room, watching as she nods and walks with grace to sit at the table. He moves over to the plates and pulls two off the shelf, as well as a bowl and a glass. He stacks them and returns to the table, setting a plate and glass before her. "Think of what you want to eat, and it will appear." He takes the bowl and places it on the ground, where it fills with water; the second plate produces meat for the dog.

Her eyes snap to him as her plate fills with bacon and eggs while the glass fills with orange juice.

He chuckles, "What, Seer, you didn't see that coming?"

A blush crosses her cheeks. "Not at all. Thank you for the food."

"Now you understand why I need no food in the kitchen."

"Yes, Dragon, I do."

"I do have a name, Seer. It's Rendgren."

"Yes, but until you grant me permission to use your name, it's Dragon. It's safer that way."

"You may use my name, Seer. Now, enjoy your lunch; I have more treasure to take."

"Thank you, Rendgren." Her eyes follow him through the portal, the gleam of treasure behind him as he steps out of the kitchen into the lair he is looting. She eats silently, the hunger pains in her stomach diminishing as she finishes, smiling as Spider clears his plate. She collects the dishes and takes them to the bin, watching as it fills with hot water, setting about washing them and setting them out to dry. She picks up the water bowl, heading back to the main room and places it next to the basket and her bedroll. She curls up to read, pulling the blanket around her as Spider nestles in her arms.

Unveiling Fate's Bond

TWO DAYS PASS with the same routine; the gem moves along the map to new locations, as Rendgren clears out each treasure. The seer remains quiet in the corner, either playing her criss cross game with her dog or reading to him. She feels her body weakening from the poison in her system, knowing she is placing her life in the hands of the Red Phantom and praying he follows the threads she had woven. She kisses Spider on the head, hugs him tight against her, then places him in his den. "Be good for the dragon, Spider, and try not to bite him." She lies down on her bedroll, feeling the need to sleep, pulling the blanket up over her and closes her eyes, embracing the darkness.

Rendgren returns from the forests around Aezogh, the sixth treasure over the past two days the stone has given him; his room downstairs is full to the point that he used magic to expand his chamber. He glances at the bedroll, expecting to see the seer in her usual position, reading or moving coins around. He immediately observes that her pale skin is whiter than it should be, and the pesky mutt is whining and licking her hand. He frowns slightly, dropping the sacks of gold as it scatters around him, approaching her still form, noticing the slight glisten on her skin. He places a hand on her forehead, suspecting that she shouldn't be this warm and that sleeping on the floor probably isn't helping. He lifts her up as her body slumps against him, feeling the heat radiating off her, and carries her back to his bed.

He places her down gently in the softness, pulling the covers over her, and tucks her in, scowling at the dog circling at his feet. "Fine, you bite me, Mutt, and I will eat you." He picks up the dog and places it on the bed, watching as it curls up next to her and whimpers. He lifts her hand, feeling for a pulse, as images suddenly flash through his mind. Pain ricochets in his body, bringing him to his knees. He takes deep breaths, feeling the whip marks as if they were on him, the sting of salt in the wounds afterward. He closes his eyes as the branding iron burns through his skin, something he should never feel, being a dragon immune to fire. A weakness takes over his body, the inability to even lift his arms as chains rattle in his mind before it is all suddenly over, and he is lying on his floor.

Rendgren takes a few moments, processing what he saw, and rises unsteadily to his feet, seeing the dog watch him carefully as he looks over the seer. He rolls the seer over onto her side, fingers shifting into claws, and slices through the back of her gown, earning a deep growl from Spider. "I am just looking, Mutt." He pales, his eyes darkening in fury as he sees the wounds and scars on her back. Some that are just over a week old, others indicating years of torture. He stumbles back a step as words echo softly in his mind. *You will find the priestess you seek, north of Omens Lake... Can you change your death?... No, because it is out of my hands.'*

"Oh, Bloody hell! You are NOT dying on me, Seer! Watch her Mutt."

He creates a portal to Sibeth, taking to the air in his dragon form, knowing he is inciting a dragon hunt by the wretched king of Oblait, but somehow doesn't care. He has a healer to find; the faster, the better, and flying gives him the advantage of speed and vision. He circles around the north end of the lake, spotting a group moving towards the city of Yark, swooping in close to see the white robes of a priestess. Rendgren hovers over them a minute to determine who the threat is before descending down and landing before them, expecting a fight but finding them looking at the priestess.

Gwynevere lifts her hand up to the others, watching as the red dragon lands before them and shifts into his mortal form. She studies him carefully, noting the red streaks in his braided hair and set into a crown, the red eyes, the black and red hanfu, embroidered and inset with rubies and diamonds. "A dragon, daring to present himself before Honors Light, renowned dragon killers. You are either very brave or foolish."

His eyes flare, recalling the seer stating the same words as he stepped into King Zane's halls. "Yes, I have heard that before and of your exploits in killing dragons. Your group does not have the power to take me on, Priestess, and I suspect you know that by the fact that you haven't dared to attack me yet."

Gwynevere smiles. "You are correct to some extent. It seemed we were guided not to attack the red at Omens Lake, but I must ask, what color flag do you come bearing?"

"What do you mean what color flag? I have no flag."

"Exactly as I ask, red for war, or white for peace?"

"White Priestess. I have need of your healing skills."

"You do not look injured to me, dragon; why would you need my skills?"

"It's for another. We must go; she is dying as we speak."

Solilque steps forward to stand next to Gwynevere protectively. "As her guardian, I am not letting you just take her without me."

The dwarf steps forward, his voice gruff and irritable, "Me either."

"Fine, you may all come with her, but we need to go." He turns behind him, his hands glowing red as he moves them in a circle, a fiery ring opening behind him. He turns to Gwynevere. "After you, Priestess."

Solilque narrows her eyes on the dragon before her. "I will go first, then Gwyn; the others can follow if they like."

Rendgren growls impatiently at the group, never understanding how groups like this manage to get anything done. "Bloody hell! Get through the Damn portal already."

He watches as they step through before following them, catching the rogue's eyes alighting on the bags of gold still sitting in the center of the room. "Touch that, and I WILL end you. You may sit at that table. Do not touch the stone or the map either. In fact, TOUCH Nothing! Priestess, this way." He leads Gwynevere to the bedroom, Solilque following closely behind, hearing them both gasp at the seer lying pale in the bed.

"You have the King's seer?"

"Thanks for stating the obvious."

Gwynevere hurries forward, resting a hand on her forehead, "What have you done with her?"

Rendgren arches a brow, disdain clear in his expression at her accusations. "I have done nothing to her; this is entirely that precious King you are working for."

Solilque moves up next to her, "What's wrong with her, Gwyn?"

"I am not sure, Sol, but the dragon is right; she's in bad shape. I need some cold cloths to get her temperature down to start."

Solilque turns to Rendgren. "I need water and cloth strips."

"I heard the priestess; I am not deaf." He growls under his breath as he moves to his wardrobe, pulls out a black silk shirt, and tosses it her way. "That will have to do. Tear it up; I will return with water." He strides out of the room, into the main hall, catching the rest of the group eying the glowing stone and map. "It's a marker for me; leave it alone." He heads into the kitchen, retrieves a bowl, carries it back to the bedroom, and hands it to the purple-haired elf.

"It's empty."

"Yes, it is. Think of water, and it will appear. You mortals have no idea what kind of magic exists in this world. Make it cold water."

Solilque looks at the bowl and watches as it fills, her eyes opening in shock, causing the dragon to laugh. "The seer had that exact same expression. Now make her better. As you saw, I am not short on gold and will make it worth your while. Oh, and try not to touch her too much." He turns to head out of the room, not trusting that rogue in the least not to steal his gold.

Solilque pulls out a knife, cutting the expensive shirt into strips she can dip in the water. She turns to Gwynevere. "I wonder what that means." She dips a cloth into the water and lays it over the seer's forehead.

"I'm not certain, Sol." Gwynevere shakes her head, placing a couple of fingers at her neck, before noticing the sliced clothing and rolling her over, gasping at the wounds and scars on her back. She staggers back, slamming into the dresser, and sinks to the ground as both she and Sol are flooded with visions of the abuse the seer endured. Sol drops the bowl with a clatter and sinks to her knees, placing her hands on her temple, having never felt anything quite like it.

"Oh bloody hell." Rendgren grimaces at the crash, knowing exactly what they were going through, as the dwarf rushes past him into the chamber. The other three turn to look at him as if this is his fault, a ball of fire appearing in the hands of the mages. "Put that away, Mage; fire doesn't hurt me as it will you." He glares at the three remaining before turning and following the dwarf back into the bedroom. The rest followed closely, causing him to growl in irritation at all those that just invaded HIS bedchamber.

Ridgestalker looks over at his friends prone on the floor before moving to Gwyn's side to help her up. "Gwyn, Sol, What happened?"

Rendgren enters the room, eying the two of them. "My guess is they touched her too long and shared the vision of the King's abuse."

Solilque looks up at the dragon. "You knew about this?"

"Yes, about an hour before I found you, as I experienced the same thing. Hence my warning."

"I'm fine, Love." Gwynevere takes Ridgestalker's hand, rising to her feet with his assistance. She weaves her hands, placing a golden dome over the seer, with white lights filtering over her body like soft rain. "She's been poisoned by the King; that is why she is unwell. I cannot cleanse her until tomorrow, but I can slow its progress with my magic until the morning. Was she like this when she arrived?"

"Poisoned? I cannot say for certain, but I suspect so. I can guarantee she hasn't eaten poisoned food since I stole her two days ago after having seen her the week before in the King's court."

"You dared to step into his court?"

"Well, yes, they politely dragged me in. Seems she was out walking around the city with her entourage of guards and looked at me, so the guards escorted us all back to the main hall. She gave me a vision, but just afterwards, she collapsed in the hall. I saw the chains around her ankles and heard the King ask if she had eaten before I was removed from the hall. So I suspect the poison was laced in the food. It was a good week later before the King reopened his court with her in it. And she did say, *'I will see you in a week.'* I took that as an invitation and caused enough mayhem in the city to swoop in and steal her out from under the King's nose."

"And how did she react to this?"

"She was rather feisty, believe it or not, on the day we arrived. Even challenging me and swearing me to an oath that if something happened to her, I would save her mutt as she had foreseen her death. Otherwise, she has been quiet and withdrawn in that corner she chose to set up camp in, playing her game and reading her book. Been doing a lot of sleeping, actually. All I know is that I will not let her die on me, and you will fix her."

Gwynevere nods. "No…I'm sorry I didn't catch your name."

"I didn't give it, but you may call me Rendgren or, as others call me, The Red Phantom."

"No Rendgren, she will not die. But she will be weak for about a month. The poison has damaged her, and she will need the time to heal, so I would advise not pressing her into any strenuous activity."

"And what do you think is going on around here?"

"I wouldn't know; that is why the warning."

His eyes flash at what the tone of her voice implied. "It's been two days priestess; that sort of strenuous activity does not happen in my books in two days. Besides that, everyone knows a seer is off limits in that department, or they will lose their gift, and she is far more valuable with it than without it." He leaves the chamber, muttering at the audacity of adventuring parties, moving to collect his sacks of gold and carrying them deeper into the cave; He pours the treasure out before backing up, chanting a few words, and placing a magical wall up to protect his hoard in case the group explored more than they should. He returns back to the main floor. "I am going out; I will return in an hour. The kitchen has food, the privy is down the other hall, and that is as far as you are allowed to go. Feel free to camp in the main room or, better yet, outside."

Rendgren creates a portal and steps through it, heading to the forests outside of Teshem, deciding that while the group is there, he is not about to go treasure hunting. He suspects that the group might just be smart enough to figure out what the stone indicates if he did arrive back at his lair with sacks of gold. So he is opting for the next best thing, getting away from them and determining what the king is up to now that he has lost his seer. He magically alters his appearance, knowing the guards will recognize his main form. He wanders through the gate and keeps to the crowds, observing the flurry of activity from the guards. Posters are nailed to walls, featuring a painting of his draconic form and the seer, along with quadruple the reward the king paid for other dragons. Rendgren watches a troupe of sixteen mounted soldiers leave the city at a gallop, turning to a nearby citizen. "Could you please help me? I just got to town, and it seems more chaotic than the last time I was here. What's happening?"

The lady glances around, lowering her voice. "The King's seer was stolen by a dragon two days ago, and the King wants her back. By the Red Phantom himself, they say! Apparently, someone reported that the dragon was flying around Omens Lake in Sibath, so the King is sending troops out to find him."

Rendgren widens his eyes. "Stolen? Was she not guarded then? How did this happen?"

"The dragon swooped in, burning houses, and took her right out of her private garden. They say the King is just as mad at her because he is certain she saw it and let herself be stolen."

"Wait, why would she let herself get captured by a dragon? I hear they eat us for lunch."

"That's the question everyone wants to know, but no one does. Rumor has it, the seer's maid is missing, along with the King's head housekeeper and the captain of his guard." She straightens as a few guards pass by and gives a nod to them. "I've said too much; if you want more info, go to the King. Although I hear he's quite surly right now."

"I understand. Thank you, miss."

Rendgren wanders around the city, catching snippets of what is happening and that the king is bringing in a mage this afternoon to try and scry on the seer's whereabouts. Rendgren frowns slightly as he picks up a few bars of soap at the stall he is standing at, knowing he will need to put more of a protective shield over his cave. He certainly doesn't need bounty hunters tracking him down trying to rescue his prize. He wanders for an hour and collects some supplies for the seer. He heads out of the city with a group of people, then slips into the woods and creates a portal back to his lair.

He arrives in his cave, seeing a few of the group straighten at his presence, their hands moving to their blade, "Oh please if I wanted you dead, you would be." He moves to the room and sees Solilque sitting on the floor while Gwynevere watches over the seer. He places the packages on the dresser and moves to the seer's side, "I bought her a new dress as I cut the last one to see her back. I will leave it up to you whether you dare to dress her or wait till she wakes up. I would suggest waiting; who knows what other torment you might see."

Rendgrens gaze lands on the mutt curled up against her shoulder, his lips twitching at the dragon as if wanting to bite him. His eyes flash red a moment as he narrows them on the dog. "Don't even think about it, Mutt. I got FAR bigger teeth than you do." He moves to the chair on the far side of the room and slumps into it. "And here I wondered how she could freely give up details on dragons and what she had against us. That was why I was there initially, to gather knowledge and to meet this magical seer that could find us no matter where we hid. In the vision she granted me, it seems like she was whipped or tortured for information, specifically about a gold one. I completely understand now. Not many can withstand what she did without breaking."

Solilque mutters under her breath. "I can't believe we worked for a King like that, but all the dragons she did give us were ones that were deliberately harming innocents."

"Interesting. Are you certain?"

Gwynevere shifts her gaze to the dragon. "Yes, we researched them all before hunting them. We are, after all, Honors Light. The name speaks for itself."

He offers her a half smile. "Names hold little weight when it comes to hunters, my dear Priestess. I have heard of groups with light and holy in their name but carried the darkest souls one could meet. But the seer saw something in you because she guided me on where to find you, knowing you were needed."

"She told us approximately three years ago not to attack the red at Omens Lake. We assumed it would be within the next few months, but time passed, and here we are."

Rendgrens eyes snap to the seer. "Are you saying she knew I was going to kidnap her THREE years ago?"

Gwynevere nods, "My best guess? Yes."

"And through all that torture, she never gave me up. Nor the gold dragon, for that matter, since I didn't see one on display with the other heads unless it's inside somewhere."

"She never sent us after a gold one, but I believe he had several groups hunting them, so I can't say for certain what the others were hunting."

Rendgren nods, growing thoughtful at just how powerful this seer is when the sound of ringing bells fills the cave system. "What the hell is that?"

Gwynevere and Solilque shake their heads. "It's not your alarm?"

"No, it's not mine." Rendgren narrows his eyes slightly, rises from his seat, and moves quickly back into the main room. His temper rises as he catches the three of them staring at the rogue, her hands on the gem that was sitting on the map. Anger dances in his eyes as flames lick his fingertips, shooting a stream of fire at the rogue's hands, watching as she drops the gem and jumps back. "I told you NOT to touch it. Touch it again, as I WILL banish the four of you from my cave."

Gwynevere moves up beside Rendgren. "Aleandi, you know better than that."

"I was just curious, Gwyn. It's glowing purple, and even when the table was bumped by Ridge, it didn't move. It's round; it should have rolled a bit."

Myrlani points to the map as the bells around them die down. "It's moving now, back to where it was."

"You're lucky it did rogue, damn lucky."

"What's it marking?"

"None of your bloody business!" Rendgren turns and strides back into his bed-chamber, seeing Solilque standing protectively over the seer.

Gwynevere joins him, glancing at the dragon sinking into the chair before turning to Solilque. "It's alright, Sol. It is just Aleandi getting into mischief."

Rendgren glares at the pair of them, opting to remain silent on the matter as the three of them stand watch over the seer. Several hours pass in silence before Rendgren rises. "It's dinner. I will take the Mutt outside. Then you can get food and set up your camp. You need to sleep; I will watch for the night."

Gwynevere nods, "That sounds agreeable."

Rendgren moves to the bedside, seeing the mutt baring his teeth and growling at him. "Come on, Mutt; you need to go out; you've been here all day." He growls back and picks up the dog, and storms out of the room with Spider tucked under his arms. "Can't believe she stuck me with a bloody Mutt." He carries the dog outside to the canyon, places it on the ground, and watches it run off to sniff the area. Rendgren turns as he feels the dwarf approach behind him, the cat prowling at his side, eyeing it carefully. "If your cat eats the Mutt, you will answer to the seer, not me. Understood?"

"Loque will not eat the dog."

"Good."

Ridgestalker moves to stand beside the dragon; his gaze follows his cat moving around. "What are you going to do with her?"

"None of your damn business."

"According to Gwyn, she's been through a lot. Red dragons are not known for their, shall we say, good temperament, let alone the stories I have heard about the Red Phantom."

Rendgrens eyes blaze, wisps of flame coalescing around him as he turns to glare down upon the dwarf. "What are you implying, Dwarf, that I am as bad as the King? Because I can assure you, I can be MUCH worse if I wanted to. Push me and find out just who I am and who you are questioning."

Ridgestalker narrows his eyes. "You know what I am asking, Dragon."

Rendgren returns his gaze to the dog. "Yes, and I have no intentions of harming her. She is powerful and valuable, alive and happy. Something that the idiotic King didn't realize. I am not entirely certain he fully understands what he lost other than she belonged to him."

Ridgestalker nods. "That's what I wanted to hear, Dragon."

"And what would you do if I said I was going to do the same, Dwarf? It's not like your group can stop me."

"Not right now, but in time, we would find a way."

Rendgren rolls his eyes. "Ah yes, that whole Honor part of your name. You don't have to worry about her. What your group does need to discuss is how you are going to deal with that king. Near as I can tell, summons are going out for dragon hunters, and if you are one of his mercenary groups, one will come to you. He is already sending his troops into other kingdoms to hunt me. Actually, rather damn fast come to think of it. Too fast."

"Yes, the four of us have already been talking about it."

"Good."

"Aren't you going to ask what we discussed?"

"Not my business, and nor do I care, Dwarf. My concern is the seer, and when she is well, I will portal you back to Omens Lake, and we will part ways for good."

Ridgestalker smiles, calling Loque back to his side. "You should; we were talking about dethroning the King."

Rendgrens eyes snap back to Ridgestalker in surprise, the corners of his lips lifting ever so slightly as the mutt races past them into the cave. "In that case, perhaps our paths might cross again." He gives a small nod to Ridgestalker, turns, and follows the mutt back into the cave. Rendgren makes his way to the bedroom, seeing the mutt already curled up on the bed, thinking for such a small thing, it certainly can run when it wants to. He glances at the two females. "You may go now. If you need food, I can provide it, but I have a limited amount of dishes, so you will need to share. If you prefer to camp in the fresh air, the dwarf can take you there."

Gwynevere nods. "I will be back after dinner to check on her before retiring for the night. Sol, let's go."

Solilque nods and gives a final look at both the dragon and the seer before following her priestess out of the room.

Rendgren moves to the seer's side, noticing that even hours later, she still hasn't improved. A rage fills him at what the king has done to her. Everyone knows, even those of his nature, that true seers are precious and should be treated with respect, but clearly, the king didn't. Rendgren turns to his chair, weaving a slight pattern with his hands as motes of red light encase it, calling it forth magically to sit beside the bed. He checks the cloths, soaks them in cold water, and lays them on her forehead, then settles in the chair. His fingers drum the arm of the chair lightly as he ponders how to make the king pay for what he has done, jumping a bit at her light whisper.

"Don't do it, not yet. He will be ready for you."

"Seer, you're awake?"

"Clearly."

"I knew you weren't going to die this day."

"Today is not my day, though I still need the priestesses' magic in the morning, or it will be a very real possibility. I mean it, Rendgren. Leave it be for now."

"I don't know what you are talking about."

She smiles and closes her eyes, lifting a hand slightly in the air as small motes of purple lights flicker above her, creating an image of his thoughts. "I am the King's seer Rendgren. I see almost everything..." The image fades as she drifts off to sleep once more.

"Damn you, Seer."

Gwynevere steps into the room and arches a brow at the dragon. "It's not the Seer's fault she's in this position, Rendgren. It's the King's. You cannot fault her for being ill."

Rendgren rolls his eyes. "I wasn't, priestess."

"And yet, I clearly heard you cursing her. I should wash your mouth out with the soap you bought her."

Rendgren growls under his breath, sending a dark look her way. "Shouldn't you be resting?"

Gwynevere smiles, moving to the seer's side and checking her temperature, before feeling her pulse. "I will be. I did state I would check in after dinner."

"Right, how could I forget."

"Now, now, Rendgren, we are here to help."

"Well *you* are. The others are in my space, and I don't like it."

"We will be gone before you know it."

"Not soon enough if you ask me."

"Shall I ask the others to camp outside?"

He sighs, leaning forward to change the cloth on the seer's forehead. "Go sleep, Priestess."

She nods, turning to head back to the group.

A New Dawn

THE HOURS PASS as Rendgren keeps placing cool wraps on her. He watches the golden lights shift and move, seeping into her skin, wondering exactly what it is doing because he feels nothing when he reaches through it. He looks up, sensing movement in the other part of his cave, knowing by the footsteps the priestess is returning, and leans back in his chair. "Priestess, I trust you slept well."

"I did. I am not certain the others trusted you enough to sleep."

He chuckles. "Wise of them to think so. It will keep them alive longer."

"We are already alive because of the seer. She saved two of our group a couple of years back when we came face to face with a hydra."

"A hydra, you say?"

"Yes. I was tempted to heal Sol, but she said not to, that it would cost the lives of others. We will never know, but I suspect she was right, for we all survived."

"It seems she's pretty damn accurate in her visions, more so than a normal seer."

She laughs softly. "For a dragon that's been around as long as you have Rendgren, you sure can be blind to what's in front of you."

Rendgren's eyes flash. "What's that supposed to mean, Priestess?"

She gestures to the seer before them. "Look at her, Rendgren, really look at her. What do you see?"

"A seer."

"Wrong answer, Rendgren; try again."

"A woman?"

Gwynevere smiles as she weaves magic into the spell over the seer. Strands of gold creep into the shield and down around the seer, blending with the magenta lights that reach for the gold. "And yet the shroud is still over your eyes. Remove what you think you see and truly look at what is lying here. Do you see it now, Rendgren?"

"Power. And a lot of it between the pair of you."

"Getting closer, but that's not it." The lights twist as if in their own battle, gold fighting with magenta. Streams of red are pulled out and trapped within the gold magic as a purple aura returns, the color matching the seer's eyes.

"I don't know, Priestess; what am I looking at?" Exasperation enters his voice at the annoying questions.

The King's seer opens her violet eyes, which glow softly as she lies in a mixture of gold and purple lights. Her eyes move from the priestess to the dragon. "A Mystic, my dear Dragon, is what she's getting at."

Rendgren rises to his feet suddenly. "Are you bloody well saying you're a *Mystic*?"

Gwynevere laughs softly as the lights fade from the bed. "Glad to see you back in the land of the living, King's seer. How are you feeling?"

The King's seer smiles at Rendgren. "I don't have to say it, Dragon; you just need to see it." She shifts her gaze to the priestess. "Better, weak, very weak, but the pain and darkness within are gone."

"I'm going out." Rendgren narrows his eyes on the pair; firefly lights appear beside him as he steps through the portal and disappears from view.

Gwynevere watches him leave. "Where do you suppose he's going?"

The King's seer laughs. "To the library in Krine to learn about mystics. Thank you for healing me."

Gwynevere places a hand on her forehead, feeling her temperature drop. "You should be fine in a few weeks, but I told the dragon a month. Now, let's get you dressed in the dress he bought you before he comes back."

She nods and pushes herself up into a sitting position as her dress falls forward, sighing softly as it was one of her favorites. She slides from the bed, standing unsteadily on her feet as she slips the gown down to pool at her feet.

Gwynevere collects the dress, carries it back to the seer, and hands it to her. "Here, let me help; you seem to be a bit shaky still."

"Yes, a bit." She pulls the dress on with one hand, holding onto the bedpost with the other as Gwynevere works on the lacings before assisting her back to sitting on the bed. The seer laughs softly. "And here I used to drive my maid crazy because I would dress myself. But now that I do not have her, I need help."

Gwynevere smiles. "You weren't as weak then, my dear. Soon you will be dressing yourself again."

"Yes, soon, perhaps not in black and red." She fingers the dress lightly, noticing it is high quality. Perhaps not the same as what the king had made for her, but still worth a gold or two.

"Yes, not really your colors. At least he bought you a dress after destroying yours, and apparently some scented soap."

She pulls Spider into her lap. "He bought me soap? I can honestly say I didn't see that coming."

"Well, it's possible he bought it for himself, but berry-scent doesn't seem his type."

The King's seer laughs. "No, he is definitely not the berry type."

Gwynevere moves to sit on the bed, taking one of the seer's hands in hers. "He doesn't own you, King's seer. If you want to leave, Cecil can portal us out of here right now. We can keep you safe from both the King and the dragon."

The seer smiles, lifting her hand from Gwynevere's to touch her cheek. She sends a scattering of images into Gwynevere's mind, bringing a blush to her cheeks. "Unfortunately, that is not my path. My path is here, beside the dragon. It is what I am destined to do, just as you were destined to be here at this moment, but I do appreciate your concern."

Gwynevere leans in and hugs her. "Good, you take care of that dragon; he needs it. I mean, look at this place."

She looks around the bedroom. "Well, this room is fine, but the rest is a bit sparse. It's certainly different from the castle I lived in." Her eyes return to Gwynevere's, feeling her thoughts and where they went, and places a hand on hers. "It happened; I suffered so others did not. The scars will always be there as a reminder, but it's behind me now. Please don't feel guilty that you didn't see the King for what he is."

She looks up, tears welling in her eyes. "But to have years of it? How did you endure it?"

She smiles gently. "Anyone in my position would Gwyn, but I had the added advantage. I knew it was coming, so I had Pippa bring me the flowers of spilanthes mixed with feverfew to dull the pain of the lash. I knew that with each strike he bestowed upon me, it was not upon her, Martha, or any other servant that got in his way."

"But you are not there to stop him now."

"No, I am not, but Pippa left before I did. And I gave Martha the magic to leave, so that's on her now. I will need a favor regarding Pippa as a thread has slipped into the timeline I missed before." She closes her eyes, feeling the drowsiness kicking in.

"You should sleep, King's seer."

"Yes, I am feeling a touch tired. Thank you." She places Spider on the pillow and slides down in the bed, drawing the covers up over her, drifting off to sleep quickly.

Hours later, Rendgren returns to his room. His eyes landing on the seer, now dressed in the black and red gown he purchased, his eyes flare with approval at her wearing his colors. He moves to her side, sitting on the bed next to her. Her eyes open when the bed shifts under his weight. "So, Seer. The power I felt is just a taste of what you have to offer. Did he know you were a mystic?"

"He did."

"And he still treated you like he did. Why not kill him yourself? You clearly have the magic behind you."

"I am a mystic Dragon. I see what's ahead of me, and it is not my destiny." She slips a hand out from beneath the covers, a glimmer of purple lights forming an image of the castle hall above her. Shadows of people enter before they transform to a clear picture of a gold dragon breathing fire on him and his throne.

Rendgren watches the image with awe, feeling a measure of satisfaction at seeing the king burn. "Did he see this?"

"He did. I accidentally shared a part of this vision with him on my sixteenth birthday. He wanted more, and I wouldn't give it to him."

"That would be why you got tortured."

"Yes, but I never slipped again, and nor did I give him a gold dragon. Only those that hunted townsfolk or killed the innocents."

"What exactly did the King know of your skills?"

"Just that I could see some visions within people and objects."

"So a tenth of the power of what is written that mystics have."

"Less, I would imagine, but he knows more now; I made sure of it when I left."

"If you are a true mystic, you are one of the few people that has the power to defeat me."

She reaches up to touch his cheek gently, running the back of her fingers along his jaw. She turns her hand over to hold his chin as she meets his gaze, her eyes glowing with power. "Yes, likely I do, but perhaps not right now."

His eyes flash at her daring to touch him. "And yet, you haven't. You know who captured you, and you still let it happen. Why? What have you seen of me?"

She pulls her hand away, closing her eyes, "I can't say."

"I could put you through worse than what the King put you through."

"You could, but you won't. You know it didn't work for the King, and as much as you are the Red Phantom, you respect seers too much."

"You have the power to leave and conceal yourself from any that search for you. I am sure even Honors Light and their virtuous hides have offered to take you away. Why stay here?"

"Yes, they have, but that is not my path at the moment."

He ponders the information for a moment, studying her carefully. "If your path is here, why eat the food with poison? I am certain you could see it. Why risk yourself?"

She smiles, having known this question was coming since he left to research her. "I didn't want the king to know my power. The threads of fate needed me to be here, right now, and for you to have gotten Gwynevere and her group."

"Why?"

"Again, I can't say Rendgren; you just need to be patient."

"You are expecting ME to be patient when I know you see something?" He rises from the bed to pace, knowing there is more to the story and understanding completely how easy it would be to torture her.

"Yes. And don't even think about it, Dragon; I won't let you."

He narrows his eyes on her, the fires appearing at his fingertips in anger. "Mystics certainly are a pain in the ass with their stubbornness."

She laughs softly, lifting her hands as purple motes of light encase his fires, extinguishing them. "You haven't seen anything yet, Rendgren; just you wait."

Rendgren growls softly at her, spins, and leaves the room. He pauses to glare at the adventuring group still in his main room, not wanting to interact with them either. He heads down the passage, walks through the magical wall, and shifts into his dragon form, curling up on the gold he loves. His thoughts drift back to meeting her on the streets, knowing the second their eyes met that he was coming for her, and by her expression, she knew it too. He wonders just how much she can see. Based on what he has read, mystics can rewrite people's life threads and change everything that once was, to a new path without them even knowing it.

She clearly left the castle in chaos by taking both the captain of the guards and head housekeeper out of play. He ponders what she told the king about her powers or even how he was on the balcony while she was in the garden at that moment. Telepathy perhaps, and yet, she connected with him, even though no words were spoken. His tail shifts the gold around, feeling frustrated at the mystic and her secrets, knowing she is planning something and playing with his threads; otherwise, she would have left already.

Rendgren senses the group moving around upstairs; the priestess heads back to her room, correction, HIS room. The seer is just borrowing it until she gets better, and then she is back on that bedroll. He shifts his thoughts to the priestess, wondering what she has to do with him and why they all need to be together right now. The priestess being a beacon of goodness and light, while he is on the opposite end of the spectrum, happily within darkness and destruction. Did the seer think her goodness would rub off on him? If that is the case, she is a delusional mystic. He is the Red Phantom. He is a legend, despite retiring for a life of solitude. He can easily return to destroying cities, towns, and villages with no warning, as that is who he is, and no mystic or priestess is going to change it. Rendgren closes his eyes and growls in dismay. He knows that as long as that mystic is upstairs, his simple life of solitude has ended, and he needs to decide what to do with her.

Gwynevere moves quietly into the bedroom, seeing the seer sitting with her pup curled in her arms. "King's seer. You are awake. I saw the dragon was in here."

"Yes, he's downstairs stewing right now at how stubborn I am since I won't tell him his future."

"But you showed me a glimpse of it."

"Yes, but you can accept it; he is not ready yet."

"I see. We have received the summons to the King. It seems he needs our dragon-hunting skills. I am not certain how we are going to face him after this."

"Have you answered him?"

"Not yet. I wanted to see how long we were here for."

The King's seer reaches out to take her hand. "You will be leaving within the hour. As for the King, you will face him as you face others, with honor and respect. You don't know what happened to me or where I am, but you will keep your eyes open in your travels. If he questions your nervousness, state that you have heard the tales of the Red Phantom and his exploits. Tell him you request more than the standard fare for such a dragon, as he is stronger than any you have faced and does intimidate you. The King is blind and will see your uneasiness as fear of a legend and will pay whatever you ask despite his coffers depleting."

"I will let the others know."

She turns Gwynevere's hand over in hers and traces a rune upon her palm, motes of purple light following its path. "Now, I do have a favor to ask of Honors Light, particularly Cecil. When Rendgren was in here, I saw he was in Teshem. The King sent sixteen warriors on his swiftest horses to Sibath. It is a thread I clearly missed in my weaving for Pippa, Dunivan, and Xyl. They are riding away from Oblait on stable horses, and my magic is no longer protecting them. They will be entering Vline at the same time as the warriors and will be recognized." She places images of who they were looking for in all of their minds, hearing the shocked gasps from the others in the main room. "What the HELL? Gwyn!"

Gwynevere looks at her hand, watching as the purple moves around the rune before it fades, smiling at Cecil's curse, knowing they will be in the room shortly.

"They cannot be caught as the King will kill all three of them. Since I already helped them escape, I do not want this to happen." Her eyes shift to the others as they file into the room. "So I ask that when you message the King, you say you are on an escort mission and will return to him as soon as you can. Please find them beforehand and portal them and their horses to Sowood. Tell them to go south around Omens Lake to Kork and not through Yark. That rune I placed upon you is to show Pippa that you are with me and not the King, for she will not trust any that work for him."

Solilque looks between the two, "I gather it was you, King's seer, that placed those images in our minds."

She looks up at the guardian. "Yes, and you need to go. Please, find them and keep them safe."

"Let's pack up camp and make haste then." Solilque leads the others into the main room.

The King's seer looks at Gwynevere, touching her cheek gently. "Thank you for all that you have done. I will owe you when this is all over."

Gwynevere shakes her head, hugging her tightly. "No, you won't. You take care of yourself. Try not to eat any more poison."

The Seer laughs quietly. "I don't intend to. Now go, be safe."

Gwynevere rises and heads back to the main room as the others wait, already packed. She gives a nod as Cecil chants a few words; a shimmering blue portal appears before them. Solilque looks at Gwynevere, her eyes moving to the bedroom. "Are we leaving the seer?"

"We are."

"Will she be safe?"

Ridgestalker places an arm on Solilque, "She will. Let's go."

Solilque nods and steps through the portal first, the others following, with Cecil last and closing it behind them.

The silence in the cavern is tangible. The seer slips from the bed and feels the room spin a little, holding onto the bedpost, waiting for the world to steady itself. Once it does, she picks Spider up and places him on the floor, walking quietly down to the privy. "Right, Spider, me first, then you." After finishing in the privy, she dips her hands in the water to wash up afterwards. She glances at the wall further down, knowing Rendgren is behind it stewing. She heads back up the slope to the main room, pausing to sit for a moment to rest. "Apparently, I am still a bit weak, Spider." She struggles to her feet and pads outside, sinking to the ground in exhaustion against the rock wall as Spider bounces around in the fresh air.

Rendgren snaps his eyes open, realizing rather suddenly that his cave is empty. He searches the upper level with his senses, finding the seer and her mutt outside. He rises, shifts back to his human form, and heads up the cavern to where he feels her. He finds her resting against the wall with her eyes closed and her skin a touch too pale. "Seer! What the hell are you doing?"

She opens her eyes a moment and looks his way before she closes them again. "Spider needed out."

"You got out of bed for that Mutt?"

"Yes, well, we both needed out…"

He growls slightly, moves over, and lifts her into his arms, feeling the weakness in her body as she sinks against him. "I can let the Mutt out. YOU are required to stay in bed. Where is the priestess?"

"They had to go, and you were downstairs, Rendgren."

"You have telepathy, don't pull that independence shit on me."

Her voice is quiet as she rests her head against his shoulder. "Yes, but you don't always answer…"

Rendgren narrows his eyes on her as he strides back to the bedroom, "I don't just let anyone into my mind, Seer."

"No, you don't… I got nothing but silence the first time I tried."

"How can you know it was me?"

"I could feel you, Gren…"

He feels her slip off to sleep as he places her carefully in the bed, pulling the covers over her. He returns to the main room to get the dog, spotting the teddy and book still on the floor. He moves to pick both up, muttering a short curse under his breath as he brings them back to his room. He tucks the bear next to her, and places the book on the table. He catches the quiet snarl at his feet. "You're pushing your luck, Mutt, if you want up." He watches the dog lower his head as he reaches down to pick it up and place it on the bed. Rendgren growls under his breath as he vacates the bedroom to inspect his cave and ensure all his belongings are still in their place.

The Dragon's Seer

A WEEK PASSES, AND Rendgren remains in the cave, watching over the seer as she rests, ensuring that she is capable of moving around freely. He is not entirely certain as to what he is going to do with a mystic. A seer is one thing, but a Mystic? The power she possesses is enough to make him question his sanity in having her here in his domain. His fingers drum the table lightly, staring at the spinning crystal, magic that held for over a week. Even mages and sorcerers couldn't hold spells that long, let alone being near death or sleeping as she is right now... Or so he thought. He shifts in his chair, sensing the movement in his room, his eyes drifting to the entrance and seeing her wander out, her dress slightly rumpled from sleeping in it. "Seer. How are you feeling?"

"I'm fine, Rendgren. You may continue collecting your treasure."

"That is not..."

She smiles as she sits in the other chair. "It is, and the magic on that stone will never run out. Go, you probably are tired of me anyhow. I can manage."

"The priestess said a month of care."

"Yes. she did. But it's not like I am traveling or doing anything really. I am here, moving between three rooms in a cave. I will get the rest I need, I promise."

"If you are certain?"

She laughs softly. "I am certain, Go, get your gold."

Rendgren stands, gives her a nod, and strides back down to his treasure room. He smiles at the wealth that sits there, having removed the wall now that the annoying group has left. He collects his bags and portals out, heading to the last den he was at, hoping no one else had found the wealth that should be his.

The seer rises and pads outside with Spider, waiting until he is done with his business before moving back inside. She makes her way back into the bedroom and lifts her torn dress off the dresser, She stares at it in dismay, knowing it is the only other thing she has. She moves to the armoire, opens it, and inspects all of Rendgren's robes, muttering under her breath that they are all black and red. She pulls out a black underrobe, holding it up against her, knowing it would be too large but would have to do. She collects the scented soap that still sits on the dresser and moves down to the lake. She pulls a towel off and makes a bed for Spider to curl up in, then sets the robe on the remaining towels. She strips her gown off and drops it next to the lake with the soap. She steps into the water and hisses softly at the heat, feeling it wrap around her in comfort.

She sits near the edge, seeing the small motes of fire dancing against the ceiling, much like faeries moving through the darkness. Knowing her time is limited, she grabs the soap and pulls her dress into the water, washing it carefully before she dumps it back on the stone. She sets about scrubbing and rinsing herself, sighing in delight at feeling clean again. She rises from the water, slips one out from towels out from beneath the robe, and dries herself off before wrapping it around her hair. She lifts Rendgren's robe, and pulls it on, feeling his scent overwhelm her as she places a hand on the wall to steady herself. She closes her eyes a moment, pushing the visions aside, forcing her mind to focus as she collects her dress and wraps it in a towel. She places her soap in the bowl, lifting his to smell it; a smile crosses her lips as she places it back and heads outside, her pup on her heels.

She pulls the towel off her hair and lays it down on the stone in the sunlight, followed by the gown and the towel it was wrapped in. She returns to the kitchen, pulls out a few plates, and places one down for her pup, absent-mindedly running her fingers through her damp hair as she eats. After she finishes, she cleans the dishes and drifts back to his bedroom, stopping as she feels his presence, his scent overwhelming her again as she trembles somewhat. She turns, reaching out to steady herself with the bedpost, feeling a weakening in her legs as her gaze lands on him. "Rendgren, you're back early."

The moment Rendgren steps into his cave, his nostrils flare, taking in the scent that wafts from the lake, luring him up the hallway. He sees the towel on the ground, folded to make a bed, and picks it up, moving to the soap trays, noticing the bar he purchased is beside his. He lifts his gaze, his draconic senses telling him she is moving back to the bedroom, knowing in her state, she should have been there long before now. He follows her in, the towel in his hand slipping to the ground as she turns. Desire darkens his eyes at the sight of her being dressed in his robe. His gaze roams over her, seeing the fabric cling to her body in all the right places where her damp hair softened it. He frowns as the priestesses' words filter into his thoughts. "Seer, what are you doing?"

"I was just going to bed."

"In my robes?"

"Well yes. I only have one dress, and I've been in it for over a week. We both needed cleaning."

"And where is your dress now?"

"Outside in the sun drying, with the towels."

He nods, not really paying attention to her words as he studies her, seeing that she is still unsteady on her feet as she clutches the bedpost. He can not understand how he can feel desire for this mortal that keeps stealing his belongings. "And so you just thought you would steal one of mine."

She smiles, her violet eyes growing dark. "It's not stealing if you know where it is, Gren, and you are welcome to take it off me."

He growls, turns, and storms from the room. He creates a portal, and steps through it, leaving her alone in the cave.

She laughs softly, picks up Spider, and places him on the bed before she crawls in with him. "Well, that went well. What do you think, Spider?" She pulls her book off the small table beside the bed, propping herself up with pillows, reading softly to her dog for an hour before curling up and drifting off to sleep.

Rendgren mutters under his breath at the audacity of mystics as he strides into the city of Yark, which earns some strange looks from people walking past him. He glares at a few of them, watching as they back away before turning to run, realizing that he is drawing attention to himself when he shouldn't be. He stalks to the clothing district and wanders through the stalls, looking at the variety of dresses on display, frowning at some of the prices compared to quality. He stops at one booth, fingering the light silks as a woman approaches. "Can I assist you, M'lord?"

"Yes Miss…?"

"Gayle M'lord."

"Yes, Gayle. I need dresses for a lady."

"I can do that, M'lord. Will she be here for a fitting? Or are you buying stock?"

"Stock and no fitting."

"Very well. Do you have her measurements, M'lord?"

Rendgren frowns slightly. "No, I don't."

"That will make it hard to fit her then, M'lord."

"I need to ponder this. How many stock dresses do you have and if they need adjusting, and what time frame do you need?"

"I have ten fully done, M'lord, and another six partially done. As for time, it depends on the adjustments needed."

Rendgren nods, "Hold them all. I will return."

Gayle bows. "Yes, M'lord."

Rendgren strides away, moving through the crowds with a purpose, studying all the people wandering around before smiling in delight. He approaches a couple standing at the bread vendor, dressed in worn clothing, knowing a few extra coins would help them out. He waits until they complete their purchace and face his way, offering them a bow. "Greetings. I am Zalgren, but most call me Zal. I have need of your wife."

"Excuse me!" The man's eyes widen with indignation, his hand tightens on his wife as he pulls her away from the well-dressed stranger. "I don't think so. Come Hoype, Let's go."

Rendgren chuckles. "I do not need her that way, my good sir. I may cross boundaries, but never the one of matrimony. I have a lady I am courting, and I wish to buy her dresses but have no measurements as I am hoping for this to be a surprise. My lady is the same size as your lovely wife, and I am prepared to pay if she would go to a dress fitting for me. You are more than welcome to join us to ensure that it is just a dress fitting."

The man studies Rendgren for a moment, catching his wife's eyes wandering over the well-dressed man, wondering if he will lose her to someone who clearly had money. His wife turns to him, smiling up at him. "What harm could it do, Kevyn. This nice gentleman is needing our help and is willing to pay us. We could use the extra silver." She turns back to Rendgren. "How much are you willing to pay Zal?"

"Three gold per dress, and there are ten dresses, perhaps sixteen to try on." He watches them exchange glances at each other before nodding in agreement. "Good, then follow me." Rendgren leads them back to the dressmaker, seeing the surprise in her features at his return. He gestures to the couple. "This man's wife is the same size as the lady I aim to fit. She will be the model you need."

"Yes, M'lord, right this way, Miss." Gayle guides Hoype into a tent before turning. "Are there any particular colors you prefer, M'lord?"

"Red and black, though she is partial to purple, it seems."

"Both royal colors, M'lord. Shall you see them on the model?"

Kevyn glances at Zal before nodding, "Yes, I would like to, if it's alright with you, Zal."

Rendgren chuckles. "Of course. I am borrowing your wife. The least I can do is let you see her in all the dresses she tries on. If there is a dress you wish, you may add it to my tab, unless of course it's in purple or red."

"Truly?"

"As I said, you are helping me, and thus I will return the favor."

"Thank you, kind sir; you have no idea what this means to us."

Rendgren reaches out and touches the fabric on his shirt; his gaze moving to the boots on his feet. "I have an idea."

Kevyn blushes somewhat. "Yes, we have hit some hard times on the farm, but this… this will help us get back on our feet."

"Happy to help." Rendgren shifts his eyes to the tent flap and watches Hoype step out. Her eyes seek her husband as a blush crosses her cheeks. Rendgren gives a quick glance over the pale blue and lavender dress, ribbons dangling down into the skirts, wide waistband, and long sleeves hiding her hands that she twists before her. He steps forward, taking her hand gently in his and lifts it, noting the way the sleeves flowed, before spinning her in place, studying the flare and movement of the skirts. "It's lovely. I approve of the style of this dress, but it's not what I want. Too soft in color. My lady has black hair and pale skin; this would wash her out too much. I want everyone to notice her when she enters a room."

Gayle nods, "Yes, M'lord, come Miss."

He hands three gold coins to Kevyn, who stares at them in disbelief before tucking them into his pouch. "Thank you, sir."

"Alright." Rendgren lifts a hand to stop him. "Enough with the thanks. Just enjoy the dresses."

"Yes sir."

An hour later, and sixteen dresses tried on, Rendgren decides on seven of them, purchasing the undergarments as well, while Kevyn takes the first one Hoype tried on. Gayle happily packages them up, bowing to Rendgren as she hands them over. "Thank you, M'lord. Come back anytime."

"Thank you, Mistress Gayle. Keep making this quality, and you will do well. I am certain my lady will approve as she comes from wealth." He takes both packages and hands the thinner one over to Kevyn, seeing Hoype's look of surprise. "Enjoy. Thank you for your services, Kevyn and Hoype. Best of luck on your farm. Should you ever need help, my dwellings in Mindrift. Ask for Zalgren." He gives them a bow before striding further into the marketplace, feeling their eyes on him as he blends into the crowds.

Hoype looks at the package, glancing over at the merchant smiling her way. "A dress?"

Kevyn smiles, handing the package over to her. "Yes, M'love, and fifty gold. I think the gods finally listened to our prayers."

She kisses his cheek. "Yes, let's go home and celebrate."

Rendgren travels through the market, buying some jewelry and hair pins, before moving to the gaming merchant, searching for the game she plays so that he can take his coins back. However, not seeing it, he approaches the cloth maker, explaining what he needs and informing him that he will return after finding some tokens. He searches the marketplace for items that would work, pausing at a book vendor, recalling the book on faeries she had. He scans through the titles, picking out a few before he returns back to the cloth maker, nodding in approval at what he produces.

Several hours later, Rendgren returns to his cave, immediately sensing that the seer is in his room with her mutt. He enters the room, seeing her curled up in the pillows, and places his packages on the nearby dresser. He moves to the bed, earning a soft growl from her dog as he takes the book from her hands and sets it on the bedside table. He pulls the covers up over her and sits on the bed next to her, wondering what she is doing to him, feeling a draw to her, even as she sleeps. He brushes a stray strand of hair off her face, noticing the corners of her lips lifting into a smile as she shifts slightly closer to his touch. "What am I going to do with you, Seer?"

He rises and leaves the bedroom, his eyes landing on the remainder of her camp, knowing she is not leaving his bedroom now. He picks the basket up, placing it on the chair nearby, before he collects the things she swiped from his treasure and returns them downstairs. He empties the bags he retrieved earlier, all the while his thoughts circle around to what it is about her that intrigues and appeals to him. He has met women of power and other dragons in his lifetime, but none hold a candle to her and in only a few days. He growls softly, forcing himself to focus on the task at hand, and that is retrieving treasure, for he has certainly spent enough of it today.

After another few trips and another empty den, he smiles, suspecting he is going to need to expand the cavern down here again to accommodate all the extra gold. Since he spent most of the day out and knows it is nearing dinner, he turns and makes his way back upstairs to check on the seer. He slips quietly into the bedroom and sits on the edge of the bed. "Seer, you should eat."

She mumbles under her breath, the fuzziness of sleep hanging on to her. "I just ate."

"Did you, when?"

"After my bath."

Rendgren chuckles. "That was hours ago. Get up."

She opens her eyes, sending a slight scowl his way. "Seriously?"

"Yes. Now, there are dresses in the packages on the dresser; put one on and give me back my robe." He rises and leaves the room, giving her the space to get changed.

"Yes sir." The seer mutters under her breath as she stretches. She rolls over in the bed and slips out of it, moving to collect the packages before dumping them out on the bed. She sorts through her treasure, finding dresses, undergarments, a couple of books about the fey, jewelry, hairpins, and a strange tan satchel tied with a ribbon. She picks the satchel, hearing a soft clatter within it, knowing it isn't the right sound for jewelry. She unties the ribbon, seeing black and white wooden markers and an embroidered grid on a square piece of fabric.

She smiles at what he has done as she sorts through the dresses and decides on a dark green and purple gown. She holds it against her, sifting through the undergarments and finding one that would go with it. She strips out of his robe, dressing quickly, her hands lingering at her waist, missing the jangles but knowing that is something of her past. She lifts the skirts, feeling the soft silks under her hands, and twists moderately, watching how the dress flows. She picks up a gold hairpin with purple gems, twists her loose hair up into a roll and drives the pin through it then ties the braids that haven't fallen apart around the pin.

She collects Spider and the game, leaving the rest on the bed to meet him in the kitchens, noticing her camp was missing on the way through. She studies Rendgren sitting at the table, stirring the food in his bowl absently, staring at something that is unseen on the table. "Thank you, Rendgren, but you didn't need to do this."

He lifts his gaze, his eyes flashing in approval at just how well the dress fits. "Yes, I did. I want my belongings back."

"Your belongings never left."

"Yes, they did; the coins and bedroll were from MY treasure."

She smiles and gently places the game bag on the table before him. "And what did that cost Gren? Even without my sight, I know that it cost more than the coins, bedroll, and chalk I liberated from your pile."

He scowls as his eyes darken. "And my robe."

"Oh yes. Your robe." She rolls her eyes.

"That's not the point, Seer. Those were mine." He picks up the game and plants it over where she will be sitting. "These I bought for you. There is a difference."

"Is there?"

"Yes, there is."

"It's still gold out of your treasure."

"It's from the new hoards. I'm calling it a finder's fee."

She laughs, placing Spider down as she sits across from him at the table, pulling the plate towards her as food appears on it. "Speaking of treasure. You are going to need to spend more."

"I spent enough today. Thank you."

"The King is looking for the merchant Zalgren. He has emissaries already on the way to your mansion. It seems he thinks that with your travel, you would be a good source of information."

"I don't travel."

"As a merchant, you do."

Rendgren narrows his eyes on the seer. "You bloody well made me a merchant with your vision in court."

"You came dressed like a wealthy merchant or noble, Rendgren; what did you want me to do? Tell him you were a dragon?"

"Not exactly…. Wait, Why didn't you tell him I was a dragon?"

"Not just any dragon Rendgren. I didn't tell him that you are the Red Phantom himself. The dragon that glides in silently, destroying entire villages and towns in a single breath, leaving no survivors. The one who everyone suspects is the most powerful and oldest dragon alive, though no one seems to be able to catch him. Also, the one with the largest bounty on his head of any known creature across the realm." She offers him a hint of a smile. "Now, it's Zalgren's turn. He too will become famous selling his exotic wares, and this will be the in that we will need later."

His eyes darken dangerously on her. "Your King was never a concern of mine. The power coming from the city was. Your power, apparently. Did you play me in that court by making me a merchant?"

"Yes, because there are things that need to happen, and exposing you as a dragon was not one of them."

"Right, another of those things I need to have patience for."

She reaches out to rest her hand on his. "You will learn patience; this I have seen Gren."

He snatches his hand out from under hers. "I doubt it."

A Merchant Created

SHE SMILES AT his resistance but respects the space he demands and pulls her hand back, turning to the task at hand. "You will need to buy two horses, Clydesdales perhaps, and a wagon big enough to carry your wares. Oh, and the wares you will be selling, of course. Good quality as that is how you make your money: scented oils, gems, and jewelry. Buy them in Krine, then drive them home to Mindrift, where the King's men will be waiting when you arrive. You will also need to buy a mansion near Teshem, but that can come later."

"Dammit Seer, you are making me spend my gold. You know what a dragon's treasure is worth."

"Yes, I am aware, and I have given you more than enough to spend a few hundred on a wagon, two horses, and supplies."

"And a mansion apparently, those are not cheap, you know. But that's beside the point; I am not a bloody merchant!"

"You are now, and you will play the part."

Rendgren rises, feeling his tempers rise at the seer as he rises. "You are pushing it, Seer. I Can still end you here and now."

"You could, but if you want your thoughts of defeating the King to come true, you will do as I ask."

"And when does this need to happen?"

She lifts her gaze to where he stands, her eyes glowing softly. "The supplies must be bought no later than tomorrow afternoon in order to make a profit, and you are to leave Krine the following morning."

Rendgren stares at her, fighting an internal war over what she is asking of him. He pivots and strides from the kitchen, pausing at the entrance of his bedroom, and glares at his robe. He snatches it off the bed and storms downstairs, shifting to his draconic form before he settles on his gold. He lowers his head and rests it on the robe he clutches in his claws, the seer's soft scent emanating from the silk, bringing a growl to his throat. He closes his eyes, feeling her essence wrapping around him, soothing the fires within as he rests. He cracks an eye open at her movement upstairs, his senses following her steps as she takes her mutt out, before she returns to the bedroom and puts her belongings away. Once she settles into his bed and is still, he closes his eyes, annoyance flaring within as he dozes, thinking of a variety of ways he can dispose of an annoying mystic.

Her voice filters into his mind, touching it gently. *"I can hear those thoughts, Gren."*

"Bloody Hell, Seer. Get out of my mind!"

"I was already in your mind, Gren."

"You can't prove that."

"I don't have to, Gren; I know what I see. And that's you becoming a well-established merchant. Traveling through the kingdoms and trading your wares, making more gold than you can possibly imagine."

"Are you trying to tempt me, Seer?"

"Is it working, Gren?"

"You should be sleeping, Seer."

"Nice dodge, Gren and I will be soon."

Rendgren growls and shuts the link off as he hears her laughter upstairs. An hour later, he rises, shifts back to his human form, and heads upstairs to the bedroom. He hears the low rumble of the mutt's growl and growls back at it, causing it to shrink away from him. He approaches the bed, watching the rise and fall of her chest, watching the peaceful sleep she drifts in, finding himself curious as to where her dreams were.

He returns to the main room with his treasure marker, deciding if she is going to make him spend money, he might as well get as much as he could to compensate for it. He spends the rest of the evening collecting gold, using his magics to expand the room downstairs again as the gold slides into the new space. He glances up, sensing her moving upstairs, knowing she should still be sleeping. He places his bags to the side, then heads to the kitchens where he can feel that she has stopped.

She lifts her gaze as he enters, offering him a smile. "Gren, have you cleared the cave out yet?"

"Almost, Seer, perhaps one more run."

"Are you ready for tomorrow?"

He narrows his eyes as he sits next to her. "How do you know I will do this?"

"I have seen it. Your desire to overthrow Zane is stronger than your desire to strangle me for making you a merchant."

Rendgren chuckles. "Indeed, you certainly do have the gift of sight."

She arches her brow. "Was there any doubt?"

"No, Seer, there never was. Now, what do I have to do?"

She smiles and holds her hand out to his, watching as he hesitates before placing it in hers. She turns his hand over and sends images into his mind, showing him the path he needs to travel, who he needs to see, and what needs to be done.

"Damn it, you do know I retired from the world, Seer? Why are you doing this to me?"

"Because the King will find me if I leave your domain, and you are the best choice."

"Bloody Seer. I could just sell you back to the King, make a quick ten thousand gold, and return to my retirement."

She laughs softly. "But you won't because I have power, and you want it. Everyone does. And I will grant it to you freely if you do the small tasks I ask."

"This is NOT a small task. It is months of work, perhaps even a year's worth!"

"A year for an immortal is nothing, Rendgren, you know that."

He narrows his eyes slightly at her words. "It's still a year that I am not here, relaxing in my domain. It's a year out there, dealing with idiots that I am certain would taste delightful!"

"It will be worth it." She traces the palm of his hand, purple lights coalescing into a large pearl, hints of a purple glow deep within its core. "When you face the kingdom rulers, you will give them this pearl. It will show them what's needed. Do the same with the other dragons you will meet."

"You do know that us dragons don't get along well, let alone with me." He lifts the pearl in his fingers to study it.

"You will, Gren. All of you will be working together by the end of this."

"That will be a bloody miracle."

She smiles, hints of sadness cross her eyes as she pulls her hand away, placing it in her lap. "That's my job, Gren. To weave miracles and not have any backlash from it."

Rendgren lifts his free hand, placing it under her chin, and forcing her to face him. He studies her gaze carefully. "And have you had backlash, Seer, other than what the King put you through?"

She guides his hand away from her chin and she looks down at it, tracing her fingers along his. "I have. Four lost their lives because of it."

"You cannot fault yourself for the King's actions."

She tilts her head to the side as she meets his gaze again, lifting her hand to caress his cheek. "It was not the King's actions that cost those men their lives. It was mine and only mine."

"You can't know that, Seer."

"I can, and I accept the responsibility for what I have done. I cannot bring them back, but I did help their families after the fact. She rises from the table and gives him a bow. "Now, you have more treasure to collect, and I need sleep. Thank you, Gren, for becoming a merchant for me." She leaves the room, her shoulders slump as a few tears escape her, knowing if she even wove one thread wrong, many lives would be lost.

Rendgren watches her go, not liking this side of the seer at all, for she always seemed so certain of herself in the few weeks he has known her. He narrows his eyes as he contemplates her uncharacteristic mood and makes a mental note to find out who the four are and what happened to make them lose their lives. He rises, looking down to the mutt still sitting at his feet, staring at him. "She's in the bedroom, Mutt!" He scowls when the dog doesn't move, muttering under his breath as he picks it up and carries it to the bedroom. His eyes land on the seer, curled into a ball, a teddy clutched in her arms, silent tears slipping from her eyes. "Oh Bloody Hell!" He moves to the side of the bed and drops the dog on it, debating internally whether to run or stay.

"Go away Rendgren."

"Dammit Seer, I hate tears."

"And you won't see them if you leave."

"It's too late. The damage is done."

She rolls over on the bed, her eyes glisten with unshed tears as she studies him, a nearly imperceptible glow appears in her eyes for a second. "And what are you going to do about it then? I didn't make any sound, so I shouldn't get extra lashings because the guards complained. Or a whipping because I dare to cry at all when *I am* the King's seer and living the life everyone dreams about. How about one lash every time my chains chinked or I was a minute late to court? I mean, What could I possibly be upset about, after all?" Her eyes grow dark as images float around her: of men in racks getting tortured, their screams filling the room, of people dying at the king's hands.

Her voice turns bitter. "Yes, the dream life to see this every time I saw the King. Of feeling what they went through day in and day out until death took them. Or how about feeling my own torture twice, once in the vision and once again each time the whip struck, or the salt sank into the wounds afterward. And through all that, keeping a straight face, not daring to cry or speak out, and smiling as if I had not seen it at all. Having to hide it all behind a mask, for if you showed emotion that he did not approve of, you were punished for it. Yes, it is a dream life alright, and so I learned to suffer in silence. Now go away."

"I can't do that, Seer." Rendgren sits on the edge of the bed and brushes her hair aside. His eyes narrow as she flinches at his touch. "Were these the men you feel you killed?"

She catches his reaction; a fragile smile crosses her lips as she reaches out to take his hand; her fingers caress the palm gently as her eyes follow her touch. "No, these were some of the ones the King killed. Just like I see all those you killed Rendgren, the Red Phantom. I see your past like everyone else's when they cross my path, but I also see your future or part of it. This is my curse to live with and no one else's. Nor can I expect anyone to understand unless they go through it themselves."

Her eyes cloud momentarily, images of the attempted assassination pass on to Rendgren, the pain of the dagger as it sinks into her, the fight for her life until her guards save her. The vision shifts to her balcony and then down the wall to the four dead at the base of the castle. Her voice fills with misery at what she has done. "As for those I killed, I was responsible. You see, the king's soul was taken from him and replaced with a demonic one by a witch who felt slighted. I thought I was strong enough to tangle with the witch and the demon but found I was not, and because of that, the witch sent assassins and four men lost their lives."

Rendgren takes her hand and pulls her into his arms. "Seer, not every seer can see everything. Did you know she was going to retaliate like that?"

"No. I did not see those threads because she blocked that sight with her magic. I should have seen them though; I should have looked at all the threads."

"Then it is not your fault."

"But it is my fault and only mine... I should have seen better." She closes her eyes, accepting his comforting embrace around her, as her tears soak through his hanfu, eventually drifting off to sleep in his arms.

Rendgren strokes her hair lightly as he studies her. He tightens his hold on her when he realizes suddenly that she is only in her late teens, despite her acting as if she has been around for centuries. He feels her warmth radiating to him as he holds her, her soft alluring scent draws him nearer. Something wakes in him at the soft shake in her body. He suspects that life with the king, paired with her visions, has forced her to grow up far too fast. He makes a mental note to give her some measure of happiness. Rendgren sighs softly and glances at the mutt that is now curled up next to him. Bit by bit and getting more difficult to deny, a softness edges in that he is unaccustomed to. He shifts her more fully onto the bed and lies down next to her. He draws her back into his arms, allowing himself to doze for a few hours.

Rendgren wakes, struggling to recall the last time he slept so well. His gaze moves to the still form of the seer, watching the soft pattern of her breath, torn between staying and leaving her but knowing dawn is on the horizon. He rolls out of bed gently and pulls the covers over her, watching her shift into the warm spot he just vacated. He pads quietly over to his wardrobe, pulls out a new outfit, and sets off to the lake where he strips down and dives in. He spends some of his pent-up energy while swimming, the physical exercise allowing him to sort through his thoughts and all that she has shown him in the past twelve hours. After an hour, he leaves the lake and dries himself off. He dresses in a red hanfu with a black over-cloak, red and gold stitching along the edges with an accent of green emeralds. He senses her movement upstairs as he makes his way back to the bed chamber, pausing at the entrance as she turns around to face him.

She offers a half smile, looking down at her hands as they twist in front of her. "I'm sorry, it won't happen again."

He moves forward to stand before her, places a hand gently under her chin, and lifts her gaze to his. "Seer. I am not going to beat you, whip you, or torture you simply because you had a rough night. The King was wrong in all that he did in regards to you. He should have respected the fact that you are a seer and that visions can be stressful. I have seen other seers lock themselves away in their rooms for weeks at a time because of what they have seen. The fact that you were in court, six days a week, for what, nine years? It is too much to ask, and I won't ask it. If you need to lock yourself away in this room, do it. I might be the Red Phantom, but at least I have some sense in my head, unlike those around that castle, it seems. Just some advance warning would be nice so I can avoid the tears in the future."

"Thank you, Gren." She nods, reaching up to touch his cheek gently, a teasing smile crossing her lips. "And yes, I suppose you do have *some* sense."

He cups her hand gently on his cheek, flickers of desire creeping in. "You're welcome, Seer. Now, you need to remember all the good you did in the years you were at court, the people you helped and saved. Inside you is a good person, and it's not like you deliberately set out to kill those men. You were still trying to help the King even if they were stronger than you."

She nods, a slight sadness enters her eyes. "Not all that good, Gren. I made sure the first guards punished were the first guards that held me down. Though, I did save Martha, Pippa, Dunivan, and Xyl before I let myself get captured. Now you need to go."

He chuckles, lifting her hand to kiss the back of it. "Now, that's my type of seer. I do believe they deserved it. I would have ended them myself had I known sooner." He arches a brow, a mischievous grin crossing his lips. "Let yourself? You keep telling yourself that, Seer. I stole you fair and square. Oh, I'll have you know; *Some* is better than none." He lifts his hand as a ring of fire appears behind him and steps back through it to just outside of Krine, watching as she fades with the portal.

He moves through the city, heading to the stables first, looking over the horses there, before deciding on two Friesians, damned if he is going to abide entirely by her vision. He purchases the tack for them and leads them to the wagon wright, purchasing a wagon to suit them and fastening them in. He leads them through the market slowly throughout the day, deciding on wares, and loads them into the wagon. He studies the wagon a moment, turns, and seeks out a tailor, requesting red and black banners for both the wagon and the horse tack. He figures if he is gonna be a merchant, he damn well is going to look good doing it. He waits at the tailor, chatting with him casually as he works on the banners, knowing he has all day to spend here before retiring at the inn. A few hours later, the banners and flags adorn his wagon, finding himself smiling at them before immediately scowling at the thought that he is smiling at being a merchant. "Bloody hell!"

The tailor looks up. "Is there something wrong with them, Zalgren?"

"No, Jymkynair, they are perfect. I was cursing at the woman who made me a merchant."

He chuckles. "Ah, she wants you to make gold to keep her in style, huh. All those fancy new dresses out there."

Rendgren laughs at the thought of the seer demanding dresses, knowing that is the exact opposite of who she is. "It's more to keep her out of my wardrobe! I came home, and she was dressed in MY robes! So here I am, merchanting to make sure she has enough clothes to stay out of my closet."

Jynkynair laughs. "Well, good luck with that one, M'lord. Women are fickle, to be certain."

Rendgren rolls his eyes. "I'm beginning to learn that." He gives a nod to the tailor and leads his wagon back to the inn district, finding one that has paddocks and wagon storage for the night. He stables the horses and locks the wagon up, placing a magical alarm on his wares. He heads into the inn, books a room for the night, and settles into a corner to watch the tavern folk, his thoughts drifting to the woman in his cave. He leans back in the chair and sips his whiskey, his fingers drumming lightly on the table, watching the servers move around, some of them even daring to flirt with him, only to back off at his dark look.

He growls slightly, wondering how this seer dug her hooks into him so fast, knowing it will do him good to be away from her as she is clearly turning him soft. Getting him to bring others into his lair to rescue her, a mortal, then not tearing her to shreds when she stole from his treasure. Wearing HIS clothes and sleeping in HIS bed, to actually sharing that bed and not taking advantage of it. He grumbles under his breath, seeing the server jump as she places the food before him. "Not you, another woman. Damn, bloody woman."

The server nods, backs away with a bow, and returns to tend the happier tables.

After dinner, he retires to his room and paces upstairs before he moves to the window and watches the moon rise in the sky. After a few hours, he creates a portal into his cave and shrouds himself with invisibility. He walks silently to the bedroom and moves to the side of the bed, watching her sleep. He can feel her scent wrap around him, struggling within to resist the urge to crawl in and hold her as he did the night before. He stands silently for an hour before portaling back to the inn, thinking perhaps this merchant thing is a good idea. It would keep him away from the temptation that she is.

The next morning, he fastens the horses up and leads the wagon out of the city gates, setting off on the adventure the seer has shown him. Days pass as he makes his way down to Talic, entering the mountain pass that takes him to Mindriff and the mansion he owns but rarely stays in. Three weeks later, he arrives at his front gates, immediately noticing the king's men waiting, their horses grazing nearby. He narrows his eyes as he pulls the wagon through the gates and up to the barn, guiding them inside. He dismounts, watching as they follow him in, feeling the desire to incinerate them where they stand. "To what do I owe the honor of Zane's men being in Sibath and at my door?"

They glance at each other, hearing the irritation in his voice. "M'lord, the King has requested your presence in his court."

Zalgren gently passes his hands over the horses, ensuring their well-being following the long journey. He unhitches the first one and releases it into the paddock to graze. "And if I say no? Am I to be escorted like I was when I was in Teshem?"

"No, M'lord, but he is willing to pay you a thousand gold to get you into his court."

Rendgrens eyes light up, and he arches a brow their way as a smile graces his lips. "Now, why didn't you lead with that?"

"We were only to offer it if you objected, and you seemed like you would."

"Smart guards even. You are correct. He is Not my King. In fact, I don't have a King. I have a Queen. Queen Naanci and her four poodles, Keola, Aphta, Tara, and Sunny. Remarkable dogs, perfectly trained and beautifully groomed. She is who I report to and ONLY her."

"Yes, M'lord. The King just requests a favor as you clearly travel. He is not asking you to switch allegiances."

"Indeed. Merchants do tend to travel everywhere. And I suppose that depends on what he is asking, but I will see him. I was heading to Ewhela anyhow. You may tell your King that I will leave in the morning. I just got home and would like a night of rest."

"We are to escort you if you accept."

"Of course you are." He rolls his eyes slightly, leading the second horse to the paddock. "Right then, find an inn and return at dawn."

"Yes M'lord"

Rendgren escorts them off his property, closing the gates after them, gates he normally left open. He watches them ride away before he heads around the back of the mansion to the small cottage that sits there. He knocks softly, hearing the mutterings of his groundskeeper about who would be knocking on her door.

The door opens, and an older lady glares out before she drops her gaze, bowing immediately. "M'lord! You are back!"

"Yes, Eve. It seems I will be spending more time here over the next year." He studies his caretaker, noticing she has aged since he last saw her, wrinkles around her green eyes and a slight graying at the temples of her blonde hair.

"Yes, M'lord. Sorry M'lord. I am certain you heard my mutterings."

"I did, but it's quite alright. I did not send advance warning. I will expect you to hire some staff, minimal, just enough to make it look like I live here part-time. Find those that need work. Is there a room ready?"

"Of course. I always keep the master's chamber ready, as well as your den."

"Thank you, Eve. I will only be here for the night and will be leaving at dawn."

"Yes, M'lord."

"Thank you for looking after this place all these years."

She looks up at him in surprise. "You're welcome, M'lord."

Rendgren turns and heads into the mansion, making his way upstairs to the master bedroom, his eyes taking in the dark interior adorned in reds and blacks, much like his cave. He moves to the balcony and opens the doors to let some air in as he settles in a chair, thinking so far, things are going according to plan. His fingers tap the chair, wondering how his seer is doing as it has been a few weeks since he has returned to the cave, feeling the desire to check.

He cloaks himself with invisibility and arrives in his treasure room, immediately sensing she is in the kitchen. He moves quietly up the hallway, stopping at the entrance to watch her. He could see her game, the dog sitting on the table, picking up tokens and dropping them on the board. Her laughter at her pups' antics teased him, wanting to be a part of that laughter, wanting to see the joy in her eyes right now, directed at him. His hands clench beside him as he watches her for as long as his spell will last.

He backs away, not wanting to disturb her happiness, and makes his way back to the treasure room. He creates a portal and steps through, glancing back as it closes, knowing he is doing the right thing in leaving her to heal.

Wings of Deception

ZALGREN RISES THE next morning, changes his outfit, and heads outside to hook the Friesians up to the wagon. He is securing the final bits of tack in place when he hears the horses gallop down the road. He leads the wagon out of the barn and through his gate, closing it behind him. He steps up onto the buckboard just as the four guards arrive, wondering how he is going to survive three weeks without killing them.

As miracles would have it, they arrive at Teshem's gates three weeks later, all four guards intact, moving nervously around the merchant, who grows more and more aggravated as the days pass. Once they enter the city, another six guards join them, leading him to the castle.

Zalgren can see the people of the city scatter, reading the fear in their eyes at the guards. His gaze shifts to the wanted posters for dragons in general, the Seer, the Red Phantom, and the four missing from the castle. He smiles, his good mood returning at the chaos she created, knowing that if it makes the king unhappy, it pleases him greatly. He follows the guards as they escort him straight through the courtyard gates. He dismounts and hands the reins to a guard there. "Don't lose them."

The original four guards lead him up to the chamberlain. "Kivu, the merchant Zalgren is here to see the King."

Kivu looks up, giving a slight nod. "Right this way, he's been waiting for you."

Zalgren follows him into the hall, recalling the last time he was here. His eyes on the back of the seer, his seer now, her shoulder stiff and her thoughts closed down to him, bringing a smile to his lips. His gaze drifts to where she stood as he enters, seeing another in her spot, not nearly as striking as his seer is but pretty enough, he supposes. He turns his gaze back to the king, arching a brow a bit as he approaches. "Sire, to what do I owe the honor of being requested and escorted here?"

"Merchant Zalgren, is it?"

"You know it is Sire. You sent guards to my house."

"Yes. I see you noticed my seer is missing."

"Indeed, I saw the wanted posters for her outside, among many others. Ten thousand gold is a lot for a woman."

"She's worth it, trust me."

His eyes drift to the woman standing behind him, giving her a once over again now that he is closer. "How long has she been missing?"

"Just over six weeks. I was certain you would have heard."

"Actually, sire, I tend not to listen to gossip. It seems like a waste of time to me. I simply wish to sell my wares for a profit so that I can retire comfortably."

"As I understand, you have a decent-sized mansion in Mindrift already."

"I do, but servants and maintaining the place costs gold. I see you have found another seer."

Zane scowls at the merchant. "Not a seer, simply a mage."

Zalgren nods, his eyes returning to the king. "So what do you want, Sire? Time is money, and I have wares to sell."

"You clearly remember my seer. If you saw her again, would you recognize her?"

"Of course, there are not many out there quite as exquisite as she is, with her pale skin, black hair, and violet eyes that seemed to glow. I would think very few would forget her after meeting her."

"Right, well, I want you to watch for her. If you see her, I want her captured."

Zalgren lifts his hands, shaking them slightly. "Oh no, Sire. I don't fight or capture people. I am simply a merchant selling wares."

"Then report her to the local guards. I have sent missives to all the kingdoms asking for her return if she is found."

Zalgren smiles inwardly, knowing he is about to change all that over the next few months, but keeping his face passive as he nods. "Indeed, that I can do. What's in it for me?"

"If you report her and the guards succeed in capturing her, I will present you with the reward. As a merchant, I expect you know the ins and outs of most of the cities you frequent. Places she could be hiding. Places the Red Phantom could be hiding."

Zalgren backs up a step. "Oh, wait. Are you asking me to tangle with the Phantom himself? Because if that's the case, then my answer is a solid No. I have heard tales of him, the destruction he causes. The rage he carries within and the fact that he's a damn Legend. As I stated, I am simply a merchant and have no wish to see my demise over a seer I met once whose vision hasn't even proven itself true. I value my life, thank you very much."

"Fine. Just keep your eyes open. I will pay you one hundred gold a month to report back here with what you see. I am also missing the captain of my guards, one of her guards, her maid, and my head housekeeper. Any one of those will do as well."

"Does the Phantom have them as well, Sire?"

"No, they all disappeared the same day the seer was taken. I suspect she played her hand in helping them evade us and probably still does."

"Assuming she's still alive, Sire. I would not want to get captured by the Phantom. I have heard the stories. He has NO tolerance for us. She was probably simply his dinner."

"No. This was planned somehow. She's cunning, my seer, she will find a way to survive this."

He bows a little. "Well, I wish you luck in getting her back. I will keep my eyes open for the other four. That's more my speed. No dragons to tangle with. But to be clear, I only sell my wares about the main continent. Catching the boats to Hontby and Lochyae is not worth my time."

Zane nods. "I have people at the docks in Westshore and Oxfrost, as well as in Kork and Khotin, watching to see if they get on any ships. If they do, I will have them."

Zalgren nods. "Good call, Sire. Now, I do believe I will stay at the inn for the night and head to Ewhela in the morning. The Dwarves were expecting me."

"Thank you, merchant Zalgren. Please see Kivu out front for your gold."

"Thank you, Your Majesty." Zalgren bows and heads out of the main hall and stops at Kivu to collect his gold. A smile crosses his lips, both at the weight of it in his hands and the fact he is taking it from the king. He tucks it into his wagon and leads it out of the courtyard and back into the city, seeking storage and stables. He books a room and heads upstairs, retiring early for the night. Once he is secure in his room, he scans to see if any of the guards have followed him, more specifically, that mage, knowing she could poke holes in what they were doing.

Once he is certain they are not watching, he portals back to his cave, sensing his seer and finding her outside. He heads her way, and stops in the shadows. He observes as she throws a well-chewed belt pouch, probably filched from his treasure, trying to beat her dog to it and failing each time. He remains there for ten minutes, seeing her collapse in the late afternoon sun, gasping for breath as the dog curls up in her arms. He steps out of the shadows, "Seer, you are not overdoing it, are you?"

She sits up, her violet eyes glowing as he approaches. "I've had over a month of rest, Rendgren."

He arches a brow. "Indeed, and yet, you seem a bit out of breath."

"Yes, well, running with a dog for an hour will do that. I am out of shape, that is all."

"Out of shape? Are you saying you were in shape?"

She rises to her feet and brushes off her skirts. "As a matter of fact, before I was locked in my room for attempting to sneak out to find you, I trained with a sword for three hours a day."

"YOU can sword fight?"

"Of course."

"One day, I will see that Seer."

"You bring the swords, and I will duel you, though I suspect you are a touch more skilled than my guards were. That being said, I have the advantage of foresight and knowing where the strike is coming from."

He chuckles. "I better be a *touch* more skilled."

"I see it went well."

"Yes, he bought it all, offering me one hundred gold to feed him stories monthly."

"Good, next up, the royals and the dragons."

"Understood. I will seek King Ludy first as I will portal there from Pleta to make it look like I am heading to Ewhela, as I stated. Then I will seek King Hallihan before moving to Lamadow. Queen Diadradey and King Robertts could be an issue as elves don't tend to like red dragons."

"They will accept you with the pearl, Gren."

"Know that if they don't, I will be taking it out of your hide!"

She laughs softly. "Really? And here I recall you saying my hide is safe."

"I can change my mind, Seer."

"Indeed you can, but you won't."

He rolls his eyes. "Damn Mystics."

She smiles. "Well, rumor has it, we *are* a pain in the ass."

"More than a pain in the ass. I was retired! You forget that. I am old, MUCH older than you."

"But young at heart."

He narrows his eyes slightly, shaking his head at her, muttering under his breath. "Yes, that's right, young at heart, that's exactly what I would call it… Then, I will head back up to Spokane. King Gordyn and Queen Bobbye will be a breeze. I just have to buy or sell some of her weaving. As will Queen Naanci due to us already having a history. The Council of Lochyae, on the other hand, could prove a challenge as they are protected by two dragons of their own."

"Gren, I know you can do it."

"Yes, because YOU put me on this path. Again, I state, I was retired, and now I am out there, sleeping on bed rolls in the dirt!"

"They are not so bad, I slept in one here."

"For TWO days, Seer, then you took over MY bed!"

"You are welcome to join me in that bed, Gren." Her eyes soften as she lifts her gaze to his, recalling the night he did.

His eyes darken as the fires fill them, fighting the desire to pull her into his arms, backing up a step. "It's your bed now. I have my gold pile."

"Are you staying then or returning to the inn?"

"I should return. I just thought I would touch base, as it's been six weeks. The bloody guards always had someone watching the camp."

"Yes, and he will have a spy watching you as well, so be careful. He wants information but trusts no one."

"Good to know. You stay well, and DON'T overdo it."

"I won't, Gren."

He nods, portaling back to the inn in Teshem, settling himself on the bed, his mind drifting back to the night he held her in his arms, wanting to return to that time and place.

Days pass, and Rendgren leads his wagon into Pleta, setting it up to sell his wares for the day before parking it at the inn and portaling into Hontby just outside of Slario. He walks into the city, stopping at the nearest guard. "What is the quickest way to the castle? I wish to speak with your King."

"He won't be seeing anyone till morning, Sir. I suggest you secure a room at the inn."

"Perhaps, castle?"

The guard rolls his eyes slightly. "Straight down the road, left at the fountain, follow that road to the gardens. Then turn right, and straight up to the gates where you will be turned back."

"Thank you."

Rendgren wanders the streets, seeing the city shutting down for the night, the sun setting, as shadows loomed from the buildings. He continued his stride, arriving at the gate an hour later, the two guards there stopping him. "M'lord. The King is no longer taking visitors."

"He will see me."

"No, he won't."

"Yes, he will. Give him this." He hands the pearl over, the guard looking at it suspiciously. "Haste, Haste. He needs to see it now."

"Yes sir."

Rendgren leans against the wall, waiting, mentally counting the minutes as they pass, feeling the footfalls of several people nearing the gate. He lifts his gaze, catching the remaining guard narrowing his eyes on him as two others approach him. A tall man, dressed in dark colors, with a cloak covering his features, and a woman with white hair, dressed in a pale blue gown. Her ice blue eyes study him carefully as the man speaks. "Greetings, I am Niceacilla, and this is Runestone. The King will see you immediately."

"My thanks, Zalgren, the Merchant."

Niceacilla nods. "Right this way, Zalgren."

Rendgren smiles at the guard, giving him a wink before following the pair up to the castle, entering a smaller room where the king sat at a table. "Zalgren the Merchant, Sire."

King Ludy gestures to the other chairs. "Please, be seated. Thank you, Nice."

Niceacilla bows and leaves the room as Rendgren moves to settle into a chair. Runestone remains in the room nearby. "Tell me more about this plan, Zalgren."

"Wait. I don't have to convince you?"

"No, we have already been doing our own investigation into King Zane. It seems a number of years back; he hired my mages to disenchant some wards. In searching the castle for power, Rune found a very terrified seer there, who asked her not to tell them it was her. Instead, Rune pretended it was one of her toys, though she is not certain they believed her. Both due to the fact it was not magical, and Myke wasn't thrown across the room like he was with the other five. Now, I did meet her at her sixteenth ball and danced with her several times. She seemed happy and content at that time, but people are good at putting faces on and hiding behind a mask, so to speak. I still have my scout Chainz lurking about and gathering information, due to the fact that she went missing a few months ago." He lifts the pearl up, rolling it between his fingers. "Now I see *you* have the child."

"Well, I wouldn't exactly call her a child, but yes, I was the one that stole her."

"So that would mean you are the elusive Red Phantom."

"That is correct." Rendgren shifts his gaze to the mage, whose eyes still glow softly, giving a slight nod to her king.

"You do know there are thousands of wanted posters for your head, and here you brazenly sit before me."

"Yes, yes. And if it wasn't for that bloody Mystic, I would be retired, and no one would find me. As for the reward, your mage is not strong enough to hold me; neither are you, for that matter... Paladin protector.

And if you did, you would have one pissed-off mystic coming for you, and I wouldn't wish that on anyone."

King Ludy chuckles. "She is a woman. One never wants a woman pissed off at them. It's not a hole I desire to dig my way out of." He hands the pearl back to Rendgren. "I am assuming you will need this back."

"Yes, she enchanted it for all the royals to see. What they see, I have no idea."

"It is enough to convince me to sign your charter. You have our support. I will talk to the dragons that reside in Hontby and convince them to stand with her as well. Perhaps not you, as they likely will balk at standing with the Red Phantom."

Rendgren chuckles, pulling out the charter for the king to sign. "I completely understand. I am just the messenger and don't entirely know what she is planning, but I will keep you updated as I learn more. My mansion is in Mindrift. If you need to reach me, leave a message there."

Ludy pulls the charter forward as Runestone calls forth a quill and ink, sliding them towards him, who signs the bottom, waiting for the ink to dry before handing it back. "It's been a pleasure, Zalgren."

Rendgren rises, offering a bow, "Thank you very much."

The King rises, shaking his hand. "I am always happy to help dethrone Evil. Rune was very concerned about the child, and while I am not certain she is happy you have her, the girl has clearly made her choice to work with you, and we will respect that."

Rendgren nods. "She will appreciate that. Now I must go. I do believe Zane has spies watching my movements, just as he has some watching you. You might want to find them."

Ludy chuckles. "Oh yes, I know exactly where they are. Your mystic pointed them out. Safe journeys, Zalgren."

Rendgren smiles, impressed at how clever his seer is, before calling forth a portal and stepping through it. "We will meet again, you and I."

Ludy watches him fade before turning to Runestone. "So what do you think?"

"He is being honest, my King. He has the child, but I sense that he actually respects her despite his reputation."

"Good, now we rest for the night and take out spies in the morning."

Rendgren returns to the inn, moving to sit at the table and look out the window. He catches the shadow of movement in the streets before it fades into the darkness, bringing a slight smile to his lips. He rises, making sure to pause for effect, before turning and heading to the bed, knowing he will be on the road in the morning. He wakes up with the sun, setting out to travel; as days turn into months, Rendgren works his way around the continent, ensuring the royals sign her charter in secret.

He returns to the cave as often as he dares, sometimes just to watch her, shrouded with invisibility, other times, to sit and talk with her while playing her game as he updates her on his progress. Each time, seeing her healing emotionally, physically, and mentally without having to be fearful of when the next strike will be. And in her healing, discovering that he loves the teasing side of her, the playful side of her, and the one that torments him to no end. Finding it more and more difficult to return to the road and task she set before him as he watches her blossom.

Nearing the end of the year on the road, he leads his horses into Mindrift, grateful to be arriving at some semblance of a home. As he dismounts, the stablehand Rich races out for the horses, taking the reins off him. "Put them in the paddocks. I think we are going to stay home for a month or two."

"Yes, M'lord."

"Have George and Oz load the supplies into a spare room; I don't want bandits thinking they can make off with my wares if it sits in the barn."

"Yes, M'lord."

Rendgren reaches into the corner of the wagon, pulls out satchels of gold, and carries them into the mansion, then goes straight upstairs. He heads to the bathing chamber, needing a long soak, knowing that tomorrow he will be at the worst one of them all, the Isle of Lochyae and its Council. Where reds are banned from even stepping foot on the land. He relaxes in the water while his thoughts drift to his seer, a place they seem to linger these days. He recalls the way her eyes light up as she reads to that mutt, the way her hand caresses him, and the love she clearly has for that thing and finding he wants it directed his way. He growls softly, wondering what the hell is wrong with him. He can feel his urge to destroy being squashed down by her, so clearly, she is making him soft. After this is done, he is going to kick her out and return to who he is, The Red Phantom. After an hour, he rises from the cooling water and pulls on a light robe. He resists the urge to go see her, instead he crawls into the soft bed and dozes for the night, dreaming of her.

The next morning, he creates a portal just outside Sloit, arriving on the shores of Lake Shella. "One breath, two breath, three breath, four. Your town would be gone and so much more." He starts walking towards the town when he feels their presence, one on either side of him.

"What are you doing here, Red?"

"Impressive. They said you were quick, and so you are, but not quick enough. I would have had your town razed by now if that was my intention. You can show yourselves whelps, for I can sense where you are."

Vynloren appears just before him, moving towards the left to stop his path forward. "Well, the Red Phantom is patrolling our lands when he knows well enough that Reds are banned."

"I am simply here to speak to the council."

Jeodina appears a slight way off, closer to the woods. "I highly doubt you just seek to speak, Red. You have a reputation, and this place is protected. You've been around; you know the rules."

"Correct, on most of those accounts. But trust me, I have power backing me. If I wanted to destroy your precious isle, I would. And don't even try the time tricks with me whelp; you and your mate do not have the power to defeat me. Not many do. In fact, the only one that can stop me happens to be on my side. I have done my research and came prepared. Council. NOW."

"We can't just summon them, Red."

"You can and you will. I know you are their diplomats. As I have said, I've done the legwork. Getting impatient now."

At this point, five bears stepped out of the woods in a semi-circle around the threesome. Each bear is different in its own way, but all are clearly guardians like the one the priestess, Gwyn, had protecting her.

"Ah, there's the council I seek. Auggie, Keandre, Kittymoo, Treefeared, and Yuui."

A light tan bear steps forward, standing on two legs much like a human would, a totem upon his back. "You know we don't allow Reds on the Isle of Lochyae, especially the Red Phantom."

Rendgren lifts his hands in surrender. "Look, it's not like you can defeat me... Perhaps Treefeared might stand a chance, or if you all worked in unison, but I won't go down without a fight. And it would be a fight. Some, if not most of you, will lose your lives, and that's NOT what I am here for. I am on different mission, one which does not involve fighting the Druids of Lochyae and their two whelps."

"What is this mission that you speak of Red."

"It's Zalgren, and it involves the mystic."

"Mystics became extinct over a hundred years ago, Red."

Rendgren chuckles, noting the continuous, deliberate use of the name Red. "Apparently not." He pulls out the pearl and tosses it to Treefeared who catches it. The others start to move forward but pause as an illusion appears above them in the sky. His seer standing there, dressed in his colors of red and black, rubies adorning the hairpins, her violet eyes glow vibrantly as she meets all of their gazes.

"Druids of Lochyae, I am the mystic in which he speaks. We met on my sixteenth birthday, but I was presented simply as the King's seer. Zalgren is my emissary to keep me off the mages' sights since they are currently scrying to find my whereabouts. Just know that I am safe, which is more than I can say I ever was while I was under the King's care. Now, I know he sent a missive, requesting my safe return, but I am asking that you ignore it and work with me instead." The image flickers to her room in the castle, her guards holding her down, the whip cutting into her back, over and over. The king behind her holding the whip in his hand, demanding a dragon's location, before drifting down to the room downstairs, showing the tortures he bestowed there.

"You see, the King is evil. His soul was stolen from him while he was still in the womb of his mother, replaced by a demon's soul. I did not have the power to defeat him while I was at the castle, but together we can. We can dethrone him and end his tyranny. You are the last to sign the charter that Zalgren carries. You may think about it and do your own research, of course, as that's to be expected. But I ask that you accept my messenger back after you have made your decision. Zalgren is also seeking dragons, for they will have a part to play in the final battle. That includes you, Jeo, and Vyn, ones not of this realm. I just request that you have an open mind and see this as what it is, a land of unity and peace everywhere, not just on Lochyae." The image flickers away as the pearl fades from Treefeared's hands, returning to Rendgrens, leaving nothing but silence in the clearing.

"And that would be my mission. My mansion is in Mindrift. If you have need of me, send a bird, and I shall return. Now, I do have one other task within your lands, but it's personal and a surprise for the mystic. Once I have completed both missions, you will not see me on the Isle of Lochyae again." He gives them a bow as a portal appears behind him, stepping back and fading from their sight as it closes.

Rendgren walks through the lush woods further north, hearing the birds chirping and the wind blowing through the leaves as he stops at the edge of the small glen he is seeking. He picks up a long stick, and steps into the clearing. He pulls a white flag out of his robes, ties it on the makeshift pole and stakes into the ground beside him."

Meanwhile, the council watches as Rendgren fades from the lakes shores. Keandre turns to Jeo and Vyn, "Find where he went and watch him; stay out of his range. I want to know what he wants on our island. Report back to us. It seems we have a decision to make."

Jeo and Vyn nod, slipping into the woods as they set about tracking him.

Kittymoo moves forward as they fade away. "There were three humans that arrived here some time ago seeking sanctuary from the same King. I suggest we go talk to them."

Treefeared nods, growing thoughtful. "Yes, we need more information, especially since it's the Red Phantom we would be making a deal with."

Enchanted Beginnings

ENDGREN STANDS JUST inside the grove, a white flag flapping in the breeze as he waits patiently. He can sense them watching, but none of them are brave enough to approach the red dragon standing there. He knows it will take time, and he is willing to wait, so he stands. Hours pass, understanding they are testing his patience, and normally, he would have lost it by now, but he has a purpose and is intent on fulfilling it. His eyes watch the movement in the woods before hearing the light chatter of the fey as one appears before him.

She is taller than the rest, regal, a crown upon her head. Her long silver hair reaches the middle of her back, blending in with the blue and silver dress she wore. Iridescent wings glitter in the sunlight, matching the color shift of her eyes as she studies the red dragon standing at the doors to her realm. She offers her hand to him, the scent of lilacs surrounding him. "A red dragon knocking at my door, the dreaded Red Phantom even. To what do we owe the honor of you standing here for hours."

"Queen Thistle of the Fey. I appreciate the audience despite being kept waiting." He takes her hand and kisses the back of it, his red eyes never leaving hers.

"Faeries are tricksters themselves, and one can never be too cautious with Reds and what their intentions are, even if that Red bears a white flag."

"Indeed. We are known for raiding the faerie realm, but that is not my intention here today."

"And what is your intention, Red?"

"I wish to bring a mortal here to meet and dance with the fey."

"You know that mortals cannot just enter our realms without consequence."

"They can if the Queen grants it."

"And will you be joining this mortal?"

"Yes. And likely a mutt as she takes that thing everywhere."

"Interesting. Why would the Red Phantom wish to bring a mortal to our realm? What is your motive?"

He studies her a moment before replying softly. "She is in love with the fey, and I wish for her to meet some."

"And why do you care that she meets us?"

"Because she has suffered much in her life, and I want her to have a moment of happiness that she can cherish."

Queen Thistle arches her brow. "Are you saying the notorious Red Phantom is placing another before him? That he just spent hours standing here as my guards watched him, trying to determine his motive, simply because he wants a mortal happy?"

"I am."

"You will swear on your honor, that you will not attack my people on this visit."

Rendgren narrows his eyes as flames lick his fingertips. "Why the bloody hell is everyone expecting me to swear oaths these days. It's not in my nature."

"You will if you want into my realm, Red."

He glares at the queen, warring within at incinerating her where she stands verses wanting to see his seer smile. "Fine. On my honor, what little of it I have, I will NOT consume any fey in your realm on *this* visit."

She smiles, her eyes glowing ever so softly. "Then your request is granted. Bring her tomorrow at dawn."

A faerie behind her gasps. "My Queen! You can't."

She lifts a hand to silence her. "I can and I will. Tomorrow at dawn. You miss it, Red, and you miss the opportunity."

"Understood."

She steps back into her realm, disappearing from his view.

The faerie follows her back. "My Queen. He's *THE* Red Phantom! If you bring him here, he will wipe us all out."

"He will be here, and we will give him what he desires."

"What will King Shamrock say when he returns?"

"He will understand."

"But why are we catering to one of his kind, my Queen? He is evil!"

"Because of a prophecy. I will explain more tomorrow." Her smile widens at the thoughts in her mind. She calls the other faeries of her realm forward to court. She explains that the Red Phantom and his mortal will be entering the realm, and they are spending the day with them, earning a range of emotions as they all wonder if their queen has gone mad.

Rendgren stands in the grove, fighting the rage within at another oath being made. His eyes drift to the faeries that remain in the trees before he shape-shifts and flies away. He takes to the sky, stretching muscles that are sore from standing for so long and seeking to calm his anger. The only sign of his presence is the hint of red amongst the white clouds, a sight that has earned him his name.

Down on the ground in the area surrounding the grove, two figures discuss what they saw. "This is intriguing. The Red Phantom swore an oath for the mystic. The council will be most interested in hearing this." Jeo and Vyn look at each other, fading from the clearing and returning to the seat of the council, relaying what they heard and saw.

Rendgren returns to the mansion later that evening, before opting to spend the night at his lair instead, bringing his earnings with him and laying it on his pile. He wanders upstairs, stopping at the side of his bed, seeing the peace in his seer's expression as she sleeps. His mind drifts to her eyes and the way they look at him, feeling it beckoning him. He sighs inwardly, resisting the urge to crawl into the bed and draw her into his arms, fighting his desire as he knows seers are off-limits. He leaves the bedchamber and heads down to where he sleeps on his gold, if one could call it sleep, as his thoughts take him to forbidden places they shouldn't.

The evening passes, and Rendgren arises, knowing he needs to wake her if his surprise was going to work; assuming you can even surprise a mystic. He pulls on a red under-robe with black trim before adorning the black hanfu, the shoulders moderately flared, crossing the sides in a v-neck line, with rubies lining the neckline and cuffs.

He ties a wide waistband over it, holding it all in place and looping the red rope so that it dangled down into the skirts. He strides upstairs, sensing movement in the room. "Seer, please get yourself dressed. I have someplace to take you today."

"As you wish, Gren."

He closes his eyes at her nickname, clenching his fists at his side and moving to sit at the table, watching the gem spin. He lifts his gaze as he feels her approach, the mutt in her arms, dressed in all black, with hints of royal purple peeking out as the skirt shifts. A dark purple waistband, small diamonds, and amethysts sewn into it sparkle as she moves, matching the hairpins in her hair, holding most of it away from her face. He rises, offering her a hand, "Are you ready?"

"Of course." She places her hand in his and steps in close.

"Good." He places some distance between them as he creates a portal, guiding her through into the woods, leading her into a nearby clearing. The white flag on the stake still sits there, fluttering lightly in the wind.

She arches a brow his way. "A white flag, Gren?"

Rendgren chuckles. "Not for you, for them."

"Them?"

He smiles, glancing at the clearing as a few faeries appear before them. They surround a taller one, who this time is dressed in layers of sheer fabric, dancing lights within the folds, with iridescent wings, and a crown of silver and gold upon her head. "Queen Thistle. I would like you to meet the mortal, my Seer."

The King's seer snaps her eyes to the queen, bowing to her. "It truly is an honor to meet you, Queen Thistle." Her thoughts touch Rendgrens quietly. *Nicely played, Gren; I will figure out how you managed to get this past my sights.*

"The pleasure is all mine, my dear." The queen's eyes drift over her before locking onto Rendgrens. "You did not say she is a Mystic, my dear Phantom. This is all that much more interesting."

"What's that supposed to mean, my Queen?"

She smiles, offering her hands to both her guests. "Come. We shall spend the day enjoying the delights of the faerie realm. Food, drink, dance, whatever you wish it to be."

The King's seer shakes her head and steps back a step; her hold tightens on Spider. "But I have read that one never steps into the realm and eats the food, or you become lost forever there."

"Indeed, that is true for all those that do not have the blessing of the Queen. And you do, my dear. Time will pass the same as here, and you will return to this spot at dusk tonight. You have my word."

The King's seer shifts her gaze to Rendgren, who gives her a nod and takes the queen's hand, placing trust in her word. She smiles, her eagerness to frolic with the fey overriding any good sense as she takes the queen's other hand, all of them fading from the grove into a magical place.

The King's seer glances around in delight. Dancing lights in a rainbow of hues flicker through the woods. Strange trees with colored leaves reach skyward, glowing under the sunlight streaming down upon them. Flowers of all kinds sway in the breeze; petals lift into the air and float in the wind, swirling around as a soft floral fragrance surrounds them. Mushrooms in purple and red line what looks like a grassy glade, where faeries dance to the music that wafts their way. She spins around in awe, seeing the thrones above them, overlooking them all. Tables of food to the left and right, before meeting the queen's eyes. "It is more beautiful than I could have imagined. Thank you for bringing me here."

"You are welcome, my dear. Now, go meet the faeries and frolic with them. That is why you are here."

"Yes, Your Majesty." She places Spider down and skips to what she figures is the dance floor, recalling her ball and how much fun she had. She listens to the music and dances with the fey, and watches as the lights sparkle around her. She reaches out to run her fingers through them, seeing them break apart into a multitude of motes.

The queen glides up the stairs, sitting on the throne, gesturing to the one beside her for Rendgren to sit on.

He shakes his head. "Thank you, but that is not for me; I will sit on the other side."

"King Shamrock will not mind if you borrow his chair for the day. I will not have a guest such as you sitting on the floor."

"A guest such as me?"

"Yes, The Red Phantom, of course. Now sit."

"Where is your King, my Queen?"

"Oh, he's doing diplomatic stuff with the elves of Lamadow."

Rendgren nods and sits on the throne next to her, turning his gaze to his seer in the gardens below. He watches for hours as he enjoys light conversation with the queen, who, in turn, sits and watches them both carefully. Lunch is called and the seer returns to sit with them and eat. Rendgren rises and offers her the throne as he stands slightly behind it.

Faeries bring plates of food and drink, each of them eating in silence as they savor the rich flavors, tantalizing them into consuming more than they expected. The drink is sweet but refreshing, quenching her thirst. She feels the slight effects of alcohol within it, only heightening the joy that she feels at this moment. Her eyes drift to Rendgren, a faint glow flickering within. "Are you having fun, Gren?"

"Of course. The Queen and I are catching up."

"That's good. Thank you again, Your Majesty, for bringing me here."

"You are welcome, my dear. The question is, are you having fun?"

"Oh, yes. It's truly amazing. Your people are so sweet and fun. They have been telling me stories of all the tricks they play on us mortals."

The queen laughs. "Yes. Faeries are known for their tricks."

"I could stay here for days."

Her eyes grow serious for a moment. "Not for days, because dusk is when the time shifts for mortals and there are no guarantees after that."

"I understand. I shall treasure this always."

Queen Thistle places a hand on hers. "Now, enough serious talk. Go, spend more time out there."

"Yes, Your Majesty, Thank you." She hands her plates to the faerie that hovers nearby, hikes her skirts, and runs down to the patch to dance again.

The queen watches her, seeing happiness alight in her eyes and laughter spilling from her. Her pup chases faeries around her feet while she dances. After an hour of watching them both, the queen turns her gaze to Rendgren, who sits once more next to her. "Go to her, Red. Look at how she watches you."

"I can't. I am immortal while she is mortal."

"Yes, and time is short for her and not for you. But that does not mean you can't enjoy the moment."

He grits his teeth, feeling her words strike a cord within, something he is already struggling with. "I am a dragon, and she is off limits."

The queen laughs softly. "We know you are a dragon, Red, but that doesn't mean you can't dance with her."

"I don't dance."

"You could. I don't think she would mind if you missed a few steps."

His eyes flash with fire. He pushes his power back down, a slight edge of irritation lacing his voice. "Do you have any idea how old I am versus how old she is? I have been dancing longer than she's been alive, fifty times over at least."

"Yes, and why should that matter? Her body might be young of age, but her eyes have seen much, and she is far older than you could imagine. Think about it: every person she sees as a mystic, she gets their story as well, and that would age anyone. Now, go, dance with her, what's one dance?"

He mutters under his breath, his eyes alighting with flame as he moves his gaze from his seer to the queen. "You know, if you were the mystic, I would wonder what game you were playing, my Queen."

"Red, I am not playing at anything. You brought her here to be happy. I am simply pointing out that she wants to dance with you. Look, I mean, truly look at how she keeps glancing this way despite being surrounded by the faeries you said she loves so. Her attention is on you, just as your attention is on her."

"I am just making sure she is safe." His eyes drift back to his seer, watching her hold her hands out as faeries land upon them while she spins.

The queen laughs, a soft ringing of bells echoing around them. "Unless you decide to eat us, you know perfectly well she is safe here. That is simply an excuse and a poor one at that."

"I might eat you anyhow if you keep pestering me."

She places a hand on his arm. "I will stop pestering you if you go dance with her, just once."

"Fine, after this song."

"Now, Red. Go dance with her now."

Rendgren growls under his breath, muttering about annoying faerie queens but rises, moving gracefully towards his seer. His eyes follow her movement through the flowers; the wind lifts the fragrance to surround them as the petals float around her, a few of them clinging to her hair.

The King's seer stills as she sees him approaching her, noting the slight stiffness in his stance despite his grace, feeling a measure of sadness that their time is already up. "Is it that time already?"

Rendgren brushes a few of the petals out of her hair, before taking her hand and lifting it to his lips as he bows. "No, my dear Seer. I am here to ask for a dance."

"You wish to dance with me?"

He hesitates a moment, feeling the queen's eyes bearing down on him. "Yes, I do. Will you grant me the honor of a dance?"

She studies him a moment before smiling. "I would love to dance with you, Gren."

"Thank you." He takes her into his arms and moves through a few of the more formal steps before the music slows suddenly. He mentally curses the queen as they are drawn together, closing his eyes and stifling a groan. He feels the closeness of her body against his as she rests her head on his shoulder, wrapping her arms around him, swaying to the music. As the song continues, he finds his resistance drops, and he tightens his arms around her. He feels the music within, her scent, her being wafting over him, everything combined calling to him in ways he has never felt before.

When the song ends, he takes a small step back. He lifts a hand to her chin and raises it, his eyes seeking hers, reading hers, asking hers, before leaning in to kiss her lips softly, feeling the instant connection the moment they touch. His arm snakes around her waist as he deepens the kiss, pulling her close as a wave of power spreads from them throughout the realm of the fey, echoing into the mortal realm, leaving both of them breathless. He whispers huskily in her ear, his red eyes glowing with desire. "If you do not stop me, my dear Seer, I will take this to the next step."

She blushes softly, her hands moving along his chest as she follows the pattern of the cloth up to his neck, her eyes meeting his again. "I will not stop you, Gren."

He groans slightly, pulls her close and lifts her into his arms, a portal appearing behind them into the bedroom. "Mutt, get in here now!" He steps through as the dog does, closing it behind him. He turns and places her gently on the bed, a hand caressing her cheek delicately. "Are you certain, Seer?"

"Yes, Gren, I am more than certain."

He lowers himself to lie partially on top of her, propping himself up on an elbow, his fingers drifting along her neck as he kisses her lightly. "You will lose your seer's sight; I need you to know that."

She reaches up, cups her hands around his face as she draws him in, feeling the fires inside as she whispers against his lips. "I will not, for I am a mystic."

"Dammit, Seer, I was trying to give you a way out." He pulls her close as he kisses her deeply, his hands roaming over her body, finding the ties on her dress as his fingers undo them.

"I don't want a way out, Gren." Her voice soft and breathless as her head spins, her body craving his touch, becoming rapidly lost to his expertise.

In the meantime, the queen thinks back on the kiss they all witnessed and the power that emanated from it; the shift in the very nature of the dragon himself was palpable. The queen lifts a glass of wine to her lips, wondering when the rest of the prophecy will come true. One of the faeries approaches her. "My Queen, now can you tell us why you let a mortal and a dragon into our realm?"

She places her glass down as the faeries gather around. "There is a legend, a prophecy if you will, of a dragon falling in love with a mortal. Now, dragons can fall in love with mortals at any time, but this dragon, he is known as the scourge of the skies and killed many for no reason other than he could. It is said his heart is pure evil, with a tolerance for none, let alone mortal races. The mortal with whom he falls in love with, will change his very nature, stripping evil from his soul and turning him on the path of good. Together, they will unite races that others cannot and bear the symbol of Raya upon his chest, becoming a champion of the goddess herself."

"How can you know it is him?"

"When have you ever known a red dragon, let alone the Red Phantom himself, to stand for hours just so that a mortal would be happy? No, the prophecy has started. You all felt the power when their lips touched. That wave was a part of him leaving, opening him up to be molded by the love of a mystic. I cannot wait to see what that pair will become. Dragons and faeries might live in harmony after all."

The next morning, Rendgren wakes, feeling a measure of surprise that he actually slept. He takes in his seer sleeping peacefully beside him, smiling at the memory of yesterday. He runs his fingers lightly along her cheek, pushing a few strands of hair to the side before moving them down along her neck, amazed at how she has integrated her way into his life.

Her voice is light as his touch stirs her, violet eyes opening to meet his red ones. "Gren, if you keep doing that, we will never get out of this bed."

He leans in, kissing her lips gently, before moving along her jawline, his one hand pulling her body close, his fingers caressing along her waistline into the small of her back. "Do we have to?"

She smiles, feeling a warmth rising along the path of his touch, desire flaring within. "No Gren. Not for three days when the merchant is once more needed."

He smiles, a wicked glint to his eyes and a slight arch lifts his brow, bringing his hands up to cup her face. "Three days, you say."

A blush crosses her cheeks at his look, her voice light as she responds to his touch. "Yes, that's what's been seen."

"Good." He kisses her forehead gently before moving back to her lips, tasting softly at first, before deepening the kiss, demanding more from her as she responds, becoming lost to each other swiftly.

Three days pass, and Rendgren rises begrudgingly from the bed where his seer sleeps peacefully, padding down to the lake to go for a swim. His thoughts drift to the pleasure he had in learning her, tempting her, teasing her, and completing her. Warmth fills him as he lay floating in the water, just thinking of the delight in her eyes and the smile on her lips. She gave herself to him and no one else, causing him to groan softly, wanting more but knowing that duty calls for Zalgren. He leaves the water and dries himself off, hanging the towel up, before heading to his room and his wardrobe as he ponders what to wear.

Her voice is soft, a slight pout on her lips. "Gren, you went for a swim without me?"

"Yes, my dear." He turns to look her over, lying in the rumbled bed, the sheets barely covering her naked body, feeling desire creeping back in. He moves over to her, cupping her cheek lightly as he kisses her pouting lips. "You know I have duties, but I will return... Soon." He brushes a hand along the side of her face gently before turning back to the wardrobe, knowing that if he stays next to her, he is not leaving this chamber.

He pulls on a red undergown before drawing a black hanfu overtop, gold and green threading weaving through a pattern of flames. He fastens the dangling chains to loop across his chest, then ties a wide waistband on, looping matching chains across. He pulls strands of his hair aside, braiding it into three, pinning them up and into a metal crown, driving a hairpin through it. He turns, seeing the seer watching him intently. "Do you see something I should know about, my dear?"

"No, Gren, stay safe."

"I always do." He moves to the bed and kisses her forehead gently before stepping back through a portal. He strides through the woods, stopping at where the white flag remains, pulling it out of the ground, and looks it over. A smile graces his lips as he feels the queen arriving behind him, lifting his gaze to hers. "My Queen, that was quick. You don't feel like testing my patience today?"

She laughs as she approaches him. "I don't have to test your patience, Red. I can see it written all over you. You look happy, sated even. Did you enjoy your evening with the mortal... or should I say, three days?"

His eyes darken slightly as thoughts of the past three days enter his mind. "Indeed I did. Did you plan it?"

"No, Red, I just gave you the nudge you needed. Even if I hadn't, you could feel the attraction between you. It was just a matter of time before you gave in to her." The queen's eyes move to the white flag in his hand. "Are you ending the truce between us then, Red?"

He smiles, giving her a slight bow before moving over and offering the flag to the queen. "No, my Queen. I am forever in your debt for what you have granted me. Even if I wanted to consume you for the pestering you bestowed upon me."

She accepts the flag, bowing back. "You're most welcome, Red. Do come visit again. You and your mortal are welcome anytime, and we won't make you wait."

He chuckles. "Appreciate that, but I will wait for her if it means she is happy."

She fades back into her realm, her voice echoing around him. "I know you would, Red. Until we meet again."

Rendgren looks up at the trees, knowing the fey are hiding in them, giving them a bow before creating a portal to his manor in Mindrift. An hour later, he is back on the shores of Lake Shella, answering the message requesting his presence from the council. He gazes out over the lake, the sun casting its reflections upon the water, the peacefulness of the land surrounding him. He feels their presence before he sees them, offering a bow as he turns to face the five bears that surround him. "Council."

"Red. We have discussed it at length and will sign your contract. It helped in your favor that we met with three others who came to our shores, in need of respite from the King in question."

"Ah yes, that would be the ones she helped escape before I stole her."

"All three spoke of the same story as what was seen in the images she showed us. Xyl, as he called himself, has scars on his back for interfering one night."

"I would imagine so. I know who I am, and I have killed many. I admit that, but they were quick deaths, and I am retired now. Have been for some time... Or WAS retired until she came into my life. The King punishes for pleasure and enjoyment of seeing another suffer or die at his hands. He craves that power of control. I already have that power, and so it is never something I did or took joy in."

"Yes, we know of your exploits and the legends tied to you."

"Most do." Rendgren nods, pulling out the charter, watching as they shift back to their mortal form, each moving forward to place their signature on the charter. "We do appreciate your acceptance of this."

"From this day forward, Red, unless you prove otherwise, you and your mystic are welcome on our isle."

"Thank you, Council. I will take my leave and report back to her." Rendgren bows, stepping back through the portal into his mansion.

He glances around his room, wanting to head back straight to his seer. However, he needs to make his appearance for those that watch, having missed three days of walking around his land. A smile graces his lips as he thinks back on the reasons why, and an instant desire surfaces within him at having his seer under his control. He sits on the paddock rails, watching the Friesians wander for an hour, allowing his senses to reach outwards until he finds the scout hiding in the woods nearby.

He slides from the fence, knowing he has lingered long enough to ensure the spy reports back to the king that he is still at the mansion. He heads back inside, straight to his room, where he steps through his portal to his lair. The corners of his lips lift as he senses his seer. He strides for the lake and watches her float, the flames from above reflecting in the water and across her pale skin. "Seer, mind if I join you?"

She stands upright in shock, a blush creeping across her cheeks. "Gren! I was not expecting you back so soon."

His voice grows husky as desire fills him. "And here I thought you were waiting for me."

Her blush deepens, images of his thoughts filtering into her mind. "I will always wait for you, Gren."

"You still haven't answered my question, Seer."

"You know I can't deny you, Gren. The water's warm, come on in."

His eyes darken as a devilish grin crosses his lips. He strips hurriedly out of his clothing and steps into the water, pulling her close and kissing her gently, moving to nibble on her ear. "Council signed the charter, so that's everyone."

She closes her eyes, relishing his touch within as she whispers softly. "And the spy?"

"Still there, even after spending three days here." He kisses down along her neck to her shoulder.

She sways a bit in the water, feeling a weakening in her legs, grateful his arm is around her waist. "Mmm, he will follow you when you start vending again."

He moves his lips to the hollow of her throat, lifting her up onto his hips. "Do I have to? Can't I just stay here?"

She closes her eyes, the likelihood of getting anything done fading swiftly from her mind. "Gren, you are so bad."

"You already knew that, my Seer." He whispers softly as he carries her out of the lake and back to the bedroom, placing her gently on the bed. "We can discuss this more in the morning."

She nods, her thoughts becoming jumbled, feeling his hands roaming over her, and becoming rapidly lost to his touch as the two of them spend the afternoon together in exploration and bliss.

In the morning, Rendgren rolls over and watches her sleep. He brushes her hair aside, wondering how he managed to find someone quite like her, smiling at her as she opens her eyes at his touch. He kisses her softly. "Good morning, Seer."

"Morning Gren"

"We should discuss plans now."

"We were supposed to discuss them yesterday."

"Do you regret it?"

She blushes softly. "Not at all, Gren."

"Good. Now, what do I need to do? I did state to my staff that I was staying at the mansion for at least a month or two, but I will admit, they haven't seen me much as I have been here. I suppose I should make my presence known a bit more around there."

"Yes. You probably should be there during the day, but we will have evenings during that time. In a couple of weeks, you will need to travel again. Some of the royals have already sought out the dragons they are friendly with, but there are about fifteen to twenty that are unaccounted for. You will need to be in contact with all of them, for we will need them in the final fight."

"I can do that. Tracking dragons might take time, though. I might not be here as often as I would like, especially if I have a tail. I just can't portal here on the road, and nor can I lead my tail to the dragons."

"I know, Gren. I will be waiting when you do make it back. You will also want to buy the manor on the outskirts of Nantou to give the dragons a safe place to gather, especially as it's not that far to Teshem when we make our advance. The Royals will invite you to their court via their messengers under the pretense of requesting to see your wares. These will ideally be jewelry from the elves and perfumes, as they are expensive, and the spy will see you packing them. The courts will be closed to the spy, of course, and it is here you will meet their dragons and set the plan in motion."

He caresses her cheek gently. "It sounds like I am going to be gone for quite some time with this endeavor, my dear."

Sadness flickers across her face as she averts her gaze slightly. "Yes, it will be about four months before you return here, Gren."

"FOUR months! What the Hell, Seer? I just found you. I don't want to spend that time away from you."

"You have to, Gren, but I will be here when you return."

He pulls her close, burying his face in her neck and holding her tightly. "Once this is all done, I AM never leaving your side, you hear me? We will retire here, forever."

"I can agree with that, Gren." She whispers softly, seeing the vision flickering through her mind. She closes her eyes and pushes it away as her hand slides down to rest on her stomach.

Rendgren holds her for another ten minutes before rolling out of bed with a grumble. He pulls on a black underrobe, drawing a black and red hanfu overtop, and tying it on, fastening a red waistband on. He turns, his eyes landing on his seer, moving to sit on the bed as he caresses her cheek. "Four months, huh? Damn."

"Yes, Gren."

"Then I will see you then."

"I will be waiting."

He kisses her lips softly before rising and stepping through a portal back to his manor, wondering how he is going to make it through four months of being on the road without seeing her. He closes his eyes, and grounds himself, knowing he's going to make the next two weeks count as he leaves his chambers, heading into the mansion to make his presence known.

Two weeks later, he is back on the road, a spy traveling behind him, buying the manor in Nantou and selling his wares to the royals.

An Oath is Made

RENDGREN FROWNS SLIGHTLY, giving a glance around the court as he feels a chill within, returning his attention back to the matters at hand. He listens as Queen Naanci goes over her ideas and introduces him to her dragons as a wave of pain floods him. He stands up so suddenly that it causes the chair to scrape across the floor as it is pushed back, drawing the attention of all those at the table. "Zalgren? Are you alright?"

Rendgren shakes his head, his eyes landing on his queen, her silver hair reflecting the blue from the room around her. She is dressed impeccably as always in royal blue, sapphires glinting around her neck and in her crown with her four beautiful poodles laying around them. He holds a hand up to stop the chatter in the room as the soft whisper of his seer filters into his mind. *"Gren, please remember your promise to me in your anger that is to come. I am sorry, there is no other way."*

"My Queen, I must go. Something is wrong at the mansion." He pales suddenly and his hands tighten into balls. He bows low before striding quickly from the room, catching the gasps that he just dismissed the queen and left the court without her permission.

Once out of the grand hall, he breaks into a run, finding a secure location as he draws the circle of flame, sprinting through the portal into the main room. Rage fills him as his eyes land on the massacure, his seer lying on the ground in a pool of her own blood, her eyes closed and her breathing shallow. One of her hands grasps her stomach trying in vain to stop the bleeding; her other hand glows purple with a single strand of purple light snaking up to a floating orb, Spider rolling around within it near the ceiling.

He kneels down next to her, noticing burns amongst the claw and bite marks, narrowing his eyes on her as flames lick at his fingertips. "I will kill whoever did this to you."

She tries to speak, finding no voice within as her thoughts barely touch his, offering him a slight smile. Her hand leaves her belly, gently taking his hand in hers as she meets his gaze. *"I cannot douse your flames today; I am too weak. But you will not kill him. Please promise me you won't."*

"I cannot make that promise to you, Seer."

"You can and you will." She struggles to keep the mind-link up, needing him to understand. *"Gren, I chose these threads, and this is where it ends for me. I am a mortal; you are immortal. I am not meant to live a life like you have, but I can give you something to remind you of me, always, and this is it. The past year and a half have been the happiest I've ever had, even when you were sorting out your feelings and watching me within the cloak of invisibility."*

He clutched her hand in his. "You saw that?"

She laughs, dropping into a spasm of coughing. *"Of course, I am a Mystic, Gren, I see it all...Well, almost all..."* She closes her eyes, doing her best to stabilize her breathing. *"See that you complete what we have started, the pieces are all there."*

"I am not ready to let you go."

"You must, Gren. My body is not going to survive this, and my life is fading even as we speak. Please, raise him right."

"Raise who right?"

"Junior."

"What?"

Just then a small red dragon rounds the corner, breathing fire at the pair. His violet eyes focus on Rendgren as he charges him.

Rendgren covers the seer from the blaze, then grabs the scruff of the small dragon's neck, lifting it off the ground as it tries to claw and bite him. "How the hell did this happen?"

"Do you really need me to explain it, Gren?" She slips into darkness as her life ebbs away from her.

Rendgren feels the link break, turning his gaze on the little monster still trying to attack him. Spider drifts from the ceiling to the floor as the seer's magic is no longer able to hold aloft. "Oh No, You can't see everything, my dear. I proved that with the Faeries." He strides to the kitchen, dropping the wyrmling in there and calling forth a magical wall, blocking him in.

Junior charges the wall, striking the invisible barrier and bouncing off it, releasing his breath upon it.

Rendgren watches him for a second before turning to catch Spider in mid-air. He tucks the mutt under the arm, heads to the bedroom, and dumps him on the bed. "Stay there, Mutt." He calls forth another wall, just in case Junior makes it through the kitchen, being uncertain what powers the wyrmling has.

He runs downstairs, finds his scrying crystal, and places it on a stack of gold. He chants quietly, watching as images filter through the sphere till he finds the one he wants, the Priestess Gwynevere. He creates a portal, steps through, and gives a bow to the others present. "Pardon me, but I need her." He picks Gwynevere up, throws her over his shoulder before anyone can react, and steps back through the portal, closing it behind him.

Gwynevere gasps in shock, both at the suddenness of being pulled through the portal and also the wealth in gold that they stand in. Rendgren doesn't give her any time to register more as he carries her back upstairs to where his seer lies, placing her on her feet. "Do your magic and heal her! I will give you as much gold as you want to bring her back."

She kneels down at seer's side, testing for a pulse, tears welling in her eyes as she studies the seer's still form. She looks over the damage that is upon her, the blood that is still spreading, before shaking her head. "I can't bring back the dead, Rendgren."

"Yes, you can! You are powerful. She is powerful. Combine that magic and fix her as you did before. There is a reason the seer put us together. NOW bring her back!"

Gwynevere rises, her heart tightens as the tears slip from her eyes, knowing how hard the seer fought to free herself from the king. "I'm sorry."

Rendgren growls, the blind rage sweeping through him at a rapid rate. His power escalates as flames creep up his arms, claws lengthening on his hands, horns rising from his skull as he stalks towards her. He stops less than a foot before her as glimmers of the Red Phantom appear, his hand wrapping around her throat, lifting her off the ground. "YOU WILL fix her NOW. DO you understand me? I will do ANYTHING to get her back! YOU Name it, I WILL do it! SO whatever needs to happen to make that work, DO IT!"

Gwynevere grabs the hands at her throat, the fires burning her skin as he holds her, understanding completely how the Phantom instills fear in the realm, for she feels it right now deep in her heart. Her eyes close and she reaches for the connection with her goddess, finding her within and asking for help. She feels the wave of peacefulness wash over her, just as a soft voice echoes around the cave.

"Zalgrenzarendaguran. PUT her down now!"

Rendgren stiffens at the command, dropping the priestess as he turns to face the one who dares to use his true name, narrowing his eyes coldly. "Where the hell did you learn that name from?"

"Now, Rendgren, as you prefer, or is it the Red Phantom right now? You asked for help, and I have come to answer that call."

He studies the woman before him, taller than he is, eyes that hold knowledge and wisdom, much like his seers, but golden rather than violet. Pale blonde locks dance around her as if a light wind is flowing through the cavern, however the air is eerily still. She wears white robes, embroidered with gold threads of a sun that match the mark in the center of her forehead, which glows as if the real sun was taken from the sky and planted there. He can feel her power billowing out around him, knowing if anyone is able to bring his seer back, she is. He shifts back to his mortal form, offering her an ever-so-slight bow. "You are the Goddess Raya. I can feel your power wrapping around me."

"I am. Now I do believe you said you would do anything to get her back, Rendgren. Did you mean that?"

His eyes blaze as he stares at the goddess, fires dancing at his fingertips. "Of course, I meant that."

"Would you give up your immortality for her?"

Rendgren narrows his eyes on the goddess; his eyes drifting to the still form of the seer and seeing all the blood. He lifts his gaze to the wyrmling behind the wall in the kitchen. Finally, he turns back to the goddess, determination in his gaze. "Yes. If it means bringing her back."

She smiles, moving forward with grace to touch his cheek, quelling the fires around him. "Will you swear an oath to me, to serve and protect me, to guide others onto the path of the sun, and bear my symbol for all to see?"

"You ask much, Goddess of the Sun."

"You said anything, Rendgren; I am simply testing your boundaries on what this mortal is worth to you."

"She is worth *Everything* to me, and if that means swearing an oath to you, then I will do it."

"Then swear it, Zalgrenzarendaguran, I need to hear it."

Rendgren levels a glare her way, feeling the Red Phantom within fighting his love for the seer; each side of himself struggling to take over and succeed. He closes his eyes, feeling his seer's touch around him, seeing the violet eyes looking up at him, with such innocence and yet such knowing. The gentle smile and the smile that indicated she knew more than she was saying and clearly planning something. He opens his eyes and moves to kneel at the seer's side. He pulls her body into his arms, his heart clenching at the sight of her dead and places his forehead to hers.

The goddess watches him carefully, knowing the war he is fighting within himself. She gives him the time he needs, drifting gracefully over to Gwyn and healing the wounds on her neck. She places a finger to her lips as Gwyn starts to talk, shaking her head that silence is needed.

Rendgren brushes the strands of hair off the seer's face. He wills her eyes to open, for her to look at him and smile, to tell him that this is all part of her plan, but he knows that she isn't going to. Tears creep from his eyes, as he hugs her tight, not willing to believe that this is even happening. "Why Seer, why weave these threads? You are a mystic, you could have woven them on another path, you could have found a way, I know it..." He kisses her forehead lightly, his body shaking. He feels pain and loss deep within his soul as the rage of anguish fills him. "Dammit Seer, I would have done anything for you. How could you make me love you, only to die on me? You should have just left me as the Phantom. Life would have been easier."

He holds her close, unaware that time is passing, sobbing against her as he wages a war within himself before placing her down gently, looking at the blood on his hands. His gaze shifts to the red pup chewing on his kitchen table leg, knowing he is not raising that hellion alone. He rises to his feet, and moves to stand in front of the transparent wall, studying the young'un, his child, her child. The wyrmlings' violet eyes focus on him as he charges the wall and bounces off it. He turns to face the Goddess and Gwynevere, his eyes glowing as his power fills the room around them.

"Sun Goddess Raya. I swear on who I am, Zalgrenzarendaguran, Rendgren, The Red Phantom, and the merchant Zalgren, that if you bring my Seer back to me, I will give up my immortality for her. That I will serve you as my goddess, guide others on your path, and will bear your symbol for all to see for the rest of my life, however long that may be."

"And so it will be done, Champion of Raya." She floats over to him, her skirts lifting in the winds that grow around her as her power blends with his in the room. A golden light surrounds her as she touches his chest lightly, burning the symbol of the sun upon his soul. She smiles, pulling her hand back and turning it palm up as a small purple ball of light appears, cradled in the cup of her hand. The seer's body shifts, her mortal form fading away from the cave, being replaced by that of a gold dragon, nearly the same size as Rendgren himself. Raya sends the precious light sphere into the body, watching as the lungs take a sudden intake of breath while the symbol of the sun is etched into her scales. The goddess shifts her hands around and two more orbs appear, one heading into the kitchen, the other to the bedroom.

Rendgren staggers back under the power, feeling the pain within him as her fires burn through into his soul. He hears the wyrmling wailing in the kitchen and knows he is marked just as he is. His eyes narrow on the gold in his cave, shifting his gaze back to the goddess as he feels his ire rise. "What have you done?"

The Goddess turns, her eyes glowing with power. "Rendgren, you said yourself, that she could have woven the threads on another path. For a mortal of such a young age, she has wisdom well beyond even some gods I know. She played the threads well and wove them correctly, even daring to touch my threads, not for the benefit of herself but for the benefit of you. It turned my attention to her and what she was doing, and I agreed with her path and have been waiting for your call."

Rendgren turns his eyes on the goddess. "Are you saying she planned this?"

Yes, that's exactly what I am saying Rendgren. But we very nearly lost her to the dark side on her sixteenth birthday. So I passed the vision of the gold dragon on to the King and forced her to play the threads she avoided. She placed you together with Gwynevere so that you would run to her to save her this day. She knew the only way she could change your path of evil was for her to grant you a child and lose her life in the process. She risked all and sacrificed herself, to see you on the path that you are destined to walk, and because of this, I am granting you both a boon if you may. Instead of stripping you of your immortality, I granted her the body to join you, so that you might live together, and rule as one, uniting this realm in peace and harmony. As a bonus, I have also protected Spider from fire and dragon attacks as I suspect your wyrmling is going to be a handful." She touches his cheek lightly. "Let go of the anger, Rendgren; your Seer's soul is in that body, and she will need help adjusting. When you think upon this further, you will understand what I have done." She fades away from the cavern, her soft laughter floating around them. "I look forward to your service, Zalgrenzarendaguran."

The King's seer opens her eyes, the room spinning as they land on Gwynevere, who watches her with concern. She feels rather disoriented with a strangeness in her body. She tries to shift but finds her body doesn't want to move the way she thought. She glances down, looking at golden claws, her eyes swiftly moving to Gren standing nearby. "Gren, what happened? I am not supposed to be here, let alone have gold claws."

Rendgren turns, watching as she struggles to move her body. "Shh, Seer. It's gonna take you time to adjust."

"Adjust to what exactly? What have you done to me?"

"I didn't do it! Her goddess did!"

Gwynevere smiles, correcting Rendgren on his words. "Our Goddess Rendgren, you pledged an oath to serve her."

The King's seer locked her eyes on Gren, "You did what!?"

Rendgren narrows his eyes on Gwyn. "Way to break the news gently, priestess."

The King's seer struggles to her feet, swaying slightly as she adjusts to the new form. "This is not something I can miss, Gren. YOU turned me into a Dragon! What exactly did you swear, and how much trouble are we in?"

"Why do you think I would get us into trouble? I've been around *a lot* longer than you and lived to talk about it. Unlike you, who up and died on me today."

"It was supposed to happen, Gren. I wasn't meant to live past this day. You and I both know that."

"No! You said it was so, but I wasn't ready to let you go nor raise that monster child on my own."

"You needed to, Gren." Her eyes glance around. "Wait, where is Junior?"

"Locked in the kitchen, and the mutts in the bedroom."

"So you didn't even find Spider a good home like you promised me."

"His home is here with us, so NO, I didn't find the mutt a home."

She arches a brow, if you could call it arching on a dragon, before planting her butt down, her tail swishing around her in annoyance. "So, Now, you accept him?"

"Of course, he's part of the family. So is the priestess, not that I will admit that to anyone outside this cave."

"Gren, I don't know how to be a dragon."

"You learn, and I will teach you. Just as we will teach the hellion in the kitchen, who's currently destroying my furniture." He steps forward, caressing her cheek lightly, seeing the slight slump of her shoulders and her wings hitting the ground. "Seer, you can do this. You who survived nine years under a tyrannical king. You who stood your ground when I kidnapped you, the notorious Red Phantom, and showed no fear, even challenging me the day you arrived. This is nothing more than another step in your life, and I know you can do it."

She nods, looking at her claws once more, knowing nothing would be the same. Her eyes shift to Rendgren, a slight glow entering them as she lifts a claw to his tunic, cutting through it at his chest, seeing the tattoo of the sun there. "What did you promise her, Gren?"

"Seer, do you realize how much this outfit cost!? You are gonna drive me to be a peasant soon." His eyes darken with desire ever so slightly as her claw touches him. "Besides, you could have just asked, and I would have happily taken it off."

"I do believe you cut through the one I was wearing when I arrived here so, now we are even. Now stop dodging the question, Gren." She traces her claw lightly over the symbol there.

He sighs, grabbing her claw in both his hands. "I promised her my immortality, among other things, like doing good and serving her for the rest of my life."

"Oh, Gren. You have no idea, do you?"

"I have every idea, Seer. You are worth more to me than any of my past. The Red Phantom will cease to exist, and I am fine with that as long as you are standing beside me."

"The Red Phantom will always exist, Gren, for he is a part of who you are. Just like Zalgren and Rendgren. All of which make up who you truly are, Zalgrenzarendaguran. You cannot remove a part of yourself, but you evolve, just like I will have to, thanks to you." She looks down at her body, noting the sun etched on her scales, arching a brow his way, seeing his shrug. "Let me guess, Junior has the same mark?"

"And… ah… the Mutt."

"WHAT!"

"Well, it just kinda happened, Seer."

She sighs. "Right, well, the first thing I want to learn is how to change back to me. The human me."

"We can do that, but after I take the Priestess back. I might have kidnapped her, so I suspect her group might not be happy with me."

"Gren, you didn't."

Gwynevere smiles. "He did, threw me over his shoulder, and portalled out before any of them could react."

"I'm sorry, Gwyn."

"Quite alright, King's seer. It might teach my group to pay more attention, though I am certain Cecil is trying to find a way to portal in here as we speak."

Rendgren chuckles. "Good luck; the only portal that can come into this place is mine, as it's magically protected."

"I wouldn't put it past them to portal on the mountains above and drop down with a feather spell."

"If they knew what mountain it is. Either way, one of you in my cave is enough, so we best be getting you back, Priestess." He moves to her side, drawing a ring of flames as a portal opens up to where he took her from. He leads her through, offers a bow to the rest of Honors Light and sends a wink to Gwyn. Without saying anything, he steps back through the portal and closes it behind him.

"Gren, you could have explained why you took her."

"Not a chance. I may serve Raya now, but they are far beyond the scope of good than I ever intend to be."

She rolls her eyes. "You are impossible. Now, what am I supposed to do?"

"Well, you learn to be a dragon, a mother of the wyrmling in the kitchen, and a wife to me."

Her eyes widen in shock at his comment. "Great, the least you could do is get down on one knee if you intended to propose. And I was asking how do I get back to mortal form, Gren, as you do."

He chuckles, kneeling down before her, holding out an empty hand. "Do you accept?"

"I will say yes when you teach me how to change back."

"Deal, although, I will admit, I can't wait to go flying with you, even if you are gold…"

"What's that supposed to mean?"

"You're the seer; you should know that reds and golds are mortal enemies."

"Oh, I will show you what mortal enemies are really like if you don't teach me how to return back to my form, now!"

"Already feeling the fire of the dragon, I see." He chuckles, kissing her cheek lightly as he strokes her neck. Now, close your eyes, feel your body, feel it right down to the tips of your claws, your tail swishing arou--" He jumps back as the tail swings his way, "Hey! Not at me! Behind you. Swish it back there." He waits for her to adjust her tail before stepping in close again, resting his hand on her neck. "Feel who you are inside as a dragon. Once you know that, seek your human form; you just need to find it hidden within your dragon. When you do, trade places with it, bring it out, and put the dragon in. Eventually, you will be able to do it with a mere thought."

The seer nods, closing her eyes. She looks within, searching for who she is and thinking it is much like finding the life threads of the people she looks at. She locates herself at the center of who she is. She feels her old life there, blending with the new. The power of the dragon and the power of the mystic combine into a new being, purple and gold lights flickering around her, as she shifts back to her mortal form. She staggers back as a wave of dizziness hits her, feeling Rendgren's hands on her waist steadying her. "It's a touch disorienting the first few times."

She looks down at her hands, leaning against him. "Thank you, Gren."

"You're welcome, my dear." Rendgren brings up a hand to brush her cheek gently, the other holds her tight against him. He breathes her scent in deeply, feeling her heartbeat against his. "Now, you will be my wife."

She looks up into his eyes. "Yes, Gren, I will be your wife."

"Good. There is a monster child in the kitchen that needs some discipline. I need to determine what other damage he did while YOU left him unattended."

"Oh, Gren. He's not a monster. He just doesn't understand, and I do believe you have a court to get back to. The Queen is waiting."

"And she can keep waiting."

She shakes her head slightly, watching as he heads downstairs, shifting her gaze to their child in the kitchen. "Well, Junior, it looks like you take after your father. Gren, could you please drop the wall?"

"Right." He pauses, mutters a few words to drop the walls, then continues along his path downstairs. He notices some towels on fire, picks them up, and drops them in the lake. "The wyrmling is already costing me gold."

The King's seer steps into the kitchen as Junior turns, his violet eyes narrowing on her and charging her way. She shakes her head, picking him up by the scruff of his neck, her other hand glowing in purple lights as she weaves them over him. She watches the rage within calm down as he hangs there, looking at her quietly. She pulls him into her arms. "Now, Junior, I am your mother, and you will NOT attack me anymore.

You will find I am stronger than you and always will be. So don't push it." She turns, heading to the bedroom, catching Gren's surprised look at the pup lying in her arms quietly when he returns from downstairs.

"How did you do that, Seer?"

"I'm his mother; he just needed to learn that." She lifts him up, weaving motes of purple lights over him. "Junior, this is your father; he is also off limits for chewing on." She places him in Rendgren's arms, watching as he settles in with hints of a purr.

"You used magic on our child?"

She laughs. "Yes, Gren. I shared a vision with him. One that shows him who his parents are. His rage is because he didn't know, and seeing that he has violet eyes, he was probably flooded with visions and did not understand how to sort them out."

"Are you bloody well saying my son is a mystic too?"

"Half mystic, half dragon, Gren. His mystic powers will not be as strong as mine, but for now, I took his visions away, which is more than I can say my parents did for me. He will get them back over time, and I will teach him how they work when he is ready."

Rendgren looked over his wyrmling, petting his head gently, a strange feeling creeping into him as he held his son in his arms. "I have a son!"

"Yes, Gren, you do."

His eyes glow ever so slightly, feeling the pup chewing on his sleeve. "When did you know?"

"A long time ago, Gren."

He steps in close to her, draping his free arm around her shoulders, pulling her close, and kissing the top of her head. "Thank you, Seer, for giving me a family."

She rests her head against his chest, reaching up to bop her son's nose, smiling as he bares his teeth at her. "You helped with it, Gren."

"Yes, perhaps, but I know where the true power lies in this creation. The goddess informed me that you wove the threads to make this work."

She laughs softly, her eyes lifting up to him. "Yes, until you went behind my back and turned me into a dragon."

Rendgren leans down to kiss her, catching the noise of disgust coming from their pup, bringing a chuckle to his lips. He places him on the ground, watching as he runs into the bedroom, before pulling his wife into his arms, caressing her cheek gently. He leans in to kiss her, feeling the instant welling of desire the second their lips touch before pausing mid-kiss, realizing rather suddenly where the hellion went. He lets her go and runs towards the bedroom after Junior, only to see Spider come racing out of the room with a tiny dragon hot on his heels.

The seer looks up in confusion as Rendgren leaves her, her eyes widening momentarily at Spider's retreat from the bedroom. She moves to step in between them and lifts her son into the air as he struggles to chase his prey. "NO, Junior. No chasing Spider either."

Rendgren glances around the room to ensure there isn't anything on fire, smiling as he hears the reprimand. He turns and heads back to the main room, laughing at the frown on the seer's face. "On that note, my dear, I have a queen to return to."

"DON'T you dare, Gren!"

"You said it yourself; I need to get back to her. We can't keep a queen waiting. I will return later." He lifts his hand, creating a portal beside him, giving her a wink as he steps through it and closes it behind him.

She growls, "Dragons!" She turns her gaze back to her pup, her thoughts reaching out to Grens, *JUST you wait until you get home, Gren!!! And clean yourself up, you're covered in Blood!"*

A Plan in Motion

THE KING'S SEER mutters under her breath as she storms outside in search of Spider, a dragon pup tucked under her arms. She finds him hiding behind an outcropping of rocks and moves to kneel beside him, feeling the wyrmling struggling in her arms. "Junior! Stop that now!" Her violet eyes flash in annoyance at her son, placing him down before Spider, who stood baring his teeth. "Now Junior, Spider is off limits. Do you understand? NO eating my dog or Mom will eat you!" Her hand lifts over her son, as small motes of purple lights soothe him, showing him what is meant to be, the two of them bonding together. She rises, watching her two pups for a moment, making sure that Junior is playing nice, knowing Spider would adapt eventually. "Good, now that we are all friends, Mom needs to go clean up a bit and eat some food while cursing your father."

She strides back to the main room, eyeing the blood all over the floor, her blood. She takes a moment for herself and looks at her hands again, at the threads she had seen in her past rewrite themselves. She smiles slightly, realizing exactly why she could not see the gold dragon that is destined to kill the king. It didn't exist, not until now. She weaves purple magic over the floor, watching as the blood fades from the room. She senses her pup returning to the cave, her child close behind it. She enters the kitchen, placing a few plates on the table and a bowl on the ground for Spider. She turns as they enter the kitchen side by side. "See, that is so much better. Now come eat."

She lifts Junior onto the table, watching as he sniffs the plate of meat. He gobbles it up while she slowly eats hers. She reaches out to pet him gently, earning a slight growl from him. "Oh, Junior, you best get used to it cause Mom's going to be doing it a lot. In fact, I suspect your father will too if he survives returning here." Once they are finished their meal, she gathers the dishes, washes them, and sets them out to dry. She then collects both Spider and Junior and heads into the bedroom to have a nap. She places them on the bed and curls up with them, feeling the exhaustion of the day sinking in as she drifts off to sleep.

Rendgren returns a few hours later, sensing all three of them in the bedroom, and strides that way. He moves up to the side of the bed, a smile on his lips at his family asleep, curled up as one in his bed. He sits on the edge and caresses his seer's face gently before slipping in behind her. He draws her into his arms and allows himself time to sleep with her as the night passes.

She wakes up in the morning, her body pinned to the bed by Rendgrens arm draped across her chest, Spider lying on her shoulder, and Junior sprawled across her stomach. She shifts slightly, feeling Rendgren's arm tighten around her, and earning a slight growl from Junior. "Morning, Gren"

Rendgren kisses her softly on the cheek. "Good Morning, my dear."

"Did you sleep well?"

"Yes, you do know that dragons don't tend to sleep the way mortals do, and yet, with you in my arms, I do. It's rather peaceful."

She caresses his arm lightly. "Took you long enough to figure it out. I've been sleeping in this bed for over a year now."

He chuckles. "I might have noticed."

"And yet, it was empty till now."

He growls gently, kissing her cheek again, "I don't just let anyone in, my dear. You had to work for it."

She laughs, "Don't I know it? I tried. I even wore your robes as enticement, and you went out and bought me dresses."

He rolls over, propping up on his arm. "I recall that day. How they hugged your body. I wanted to rip the bloody robes off you, but I wasn't willing to admit it yet."

She caresses his cheek lightly. "I know, Gren. Are you here for the day?"

"Yes. I thought perhaps we can teach you the art of being a dragon since you clearly already know how to be a mystic."

"That sounds good, but before we do, I really need to visit the privy." She lifts Junior off her bladder and hands him to Gren before sliding from the bed, and running out of the bedroom.

Rendgren laughs at her escape, pulling his wyrmling closer to him. He studies the miracle they created: the tiny claws on each of his feet, his perfectly pointy teeth as he yawned, and his violet eyes that crack open and stare at him. He pauses to think how very much alike those eyes are to his seer's. "Well Junior. What do you say we teach your mom how to fly today?"

"Rawr."

"Yes, you're right; we should probably wait till she gets the hang of walking."

"I can walk, my dear Gren, on TWO legs, the way I was supposed to until you messed with my designs."

He places Junior on the ground, picks up Spider, and places him down beside his son. He rises, drawing her into his arms and kissing her softly. "And I would do it again, my dear. In a heartbeat."

She wraps her arms around him, holding him close and resting her head on his shoulder. "Thank you, Gren."

"You're welcome; now come, I want to see the gold beneath the sun that brought you back." He takes her hand, leading her outside, as the two pups follow. He glances around the canyon, knowing there is more than enough space for the two of them. "Alright, Seer. Find your dragon." He shifts into his form instantly, towering over her and taking up nearly half the space there, his red eyes watching her intently. Spider backs into the hall growling, while Junior watches with fascination beside him.

The seer looks up, realizing that in her time here, this is only the second time she has seen his draconic form. She smiles at the red scales glinting in the sun, caressing the claws that snatched her from the castle.

"If you keep doing that, Seer, I will drag you back to the bedroom, now shift."

She rolls her eyes. "Yes, sir!" She steps back, seeking within for the box she has penned the dragon in, as small motes of purple lights surround her. She pulls her dragon essence out and boxes her human side inside, feeling her body shifting as she wobbles a bit on four legs.

Rendgren reaches out to steady her. "You picked that up faster than I expected, my dear."

She lifts her wings slightly, her tail swishing around behind her. "It's much like picking threads and weaving them to a path I want, but easier as it's a box inside, rather than hundreds of threads."

"Are you saying that each vision you change, it's you sorting through hundreds of timelines?"

"Yes, and then some, as you have to go forward in time to see the consequences of those threads, which I learned the hard way the first time I tried to tamper with them."

"I remember. That was the night you broke through my resistance with your damn tears. Wait, was that thread woven?"

She laughs. "No, Gren, that was not. It was simply me being emotional. You were supposed to go down to your gold as you always did."

"Blame the Mutt, he was whining at my feet."

"That's right, blame the dog."

"It was. Now, since you mastered shifting so fast, let's see you walk, and then we can move to flying. That's what I want, my dear, so walk fast."

She brings her tail up to swat him, laughing as he takes the hit, only to feel his body hit her hard enough to knock her off her feet. She rolls over and struggles to her feet, chasing him around the canyon, the pair of them playing like puppies in dragon form. Hours later, they collapse on the ground, curling their tails together as Rendgren drapes his wing over her, resting his head near hers. The sun beats down upon their scales as red and violet eyes watch the pups come running over to curl up with them.

Months pass, with Rendgren bouncing between being the merchant, the father, the lover, and the teacher. When he finally gets the seer out to fly, he bites back his laughter as she crashes into things when landing. He avoids her violet gaze as it narrows on him because she can see his laughter, but overall she gets the hang of it. The pair soars gracefully through the skies above the cloud line, Junior within their claws, feeling the freedom of the open air as they enjoy the calm before the storm.

One afternoon, after returning from a flight, Rendgren watches his seer carefully as she stirs her food around at the table, recognizing her expression of sorting through her visions. He places a hand on hers, caressing it lightly, his gaze meeting hers as they return to focus. "What do you see, my dear?"

Her eyes drift to Junior. "We will need a sitter for Junior, one who can handle him."

"I know a sitter who would be perfect."

"Also, we need to lure the King's catapults out of the city and destroy them before we enter it, or many dragons will get injured in the takeover."

"How do you propose we do that? He's going to keep them close, especially as the time is drawing near for a gold to attack him."

"We are going to fly together daily, for an hour, over the grasslands below Sroni. Far enough away that he will wait, but after a few weeks he will send them out with orders to kill on sight." Her eyes glowing softly as she lifts her gaze to Rendgren. "Zalgren will spread the rumor to a few key people that the Red Phantom seems to have found his mate, since there have been numerous occasions that he has been seen flying with a gold. Perhaps that is something he forced the seer to grant him."

"The seer is my mate, my dear."

She smiles, a slightly mischievous grin upon her lips, "Indeed, but the King doesn't know that, although that would anger him more if he found out you bedded me. But I don't know how Zalgren would know that."

He leans over and kisses her gently. "Let me worry about that."

She narrows her eyes. "You are going to cause trouble. I can feel it, but I can't see those threads yet."

"Indeed, I like the idea of him finding out I bedded you better."

She shakes her head, "As long as it doesn't interfere with the plans in motion, Gren."

Rendgren rises, "It won't, I promise! I will return, my dear. Prepare for war." He steps through his portal, arriving on the shores of Lockyae. He counts the time spent there before the two whelps appear. "That is a minute quicker than last time, but still not quick enough. And you do know that I am welcome here now."

Vynloren steps from the forest, Jeodina behind him. "What do you want, Red?"

"I can't believe I am asking this, but I need a favor from the two of you. A few, actually. You are the only two that I know that I would consider trusting."

Jeodina laughs. "That's funny, a Red having issues trusting us?"

Rendgren narrows his eyes at the pair, fires licking at his fingertips. "Look, you protect people. You work for the side of good. I am just learning how this all works, so this is hard for me. Don't push it."

Vynloren places a hand on Jeo's arms. "What favor are you seeking, Red?"

"I need someone to look after my wyrmling, Junior, a few hours a day for about two weeks. Perhaps longer. As well as on the day we storm Teshem."

"Wait. YOU Have a child?"

"Yes, and I will admit, he takes after his father's hellion days despite the seer trying to calm him."

"When? How? Who's the mother?"

"A few months back, and well, I should think between the two of you, you would know how that happens and the Seer is."

"And she survived?"

"No, she did not."

"You lost me, Red; how is the Seer trying to calm him then?"

Rendgren rolls his eyes, untying his hanfu and sliding it off his chest, displaying the symbol of Raya, which is burned upon his skin. He backs up, shifting to his dragon form, the same symbol burned into his scales as he looks down at it a moment, his claw tracing its outline before changing back to his mortal form. "It seems when you demand a priestess to bring a soul back, her goddess steps in, and there is a price to pay, or several for that matter. My Seer is now a gold dragon, bearing the same mark, and Junior takes after Daddy, Red, also marked."

Vynloren smiles, before laughing. He moves forward to slap Rendgren on the back. "That, my friend, is priceless. She put you with a Gold, and here you are asking a Bronze and Copper for help."

He narrows his eyes. "I could still take you out whelp."

Vynloren drapes an arm over his shoulders. "But you won't. Raya won't let you. Of course. Jeo and I would be happy to look after the little wyrmling."

Rendgren slides out from beneath Vynloren's arm, pulling his hanfu back up and tying the laces. "You could have just said yes."

"But you must admit, there is humor in this situation."

Rendgren's eyes grow dark for a moment, narrowing them on the pair before him. "Perhaps for you, whelp."

Vynloren shakes his head. "Well, I will say this, Red, it is unexpected. You must love the Seer a great deal to make such a bargain that a goddess restored her and burned her symbol upon all three of you."

Rendgren's eyes soften for a moment. "Yes, I could not imagine life without her."

"That's good, my man. Now, what's the plan that we need to watch the wyrmling?"

"We are going to fly together near Sroni to lure the catapults out of Teshem. And while Junior loves flying, it would be too dangerous should something go wrong. I need to also hide this mark temporarily because we don't want the King to know I switched sides. He still needs to believe I am the Red Phantom."

Jeodina glances at Vynloren before her gaze lands on the Red. "When you drop off Junior, I can hide it temporarily on you both, a few hours at most a day."

"Thank you. We will owe you."

Vynloren smiles. "It will be nice to be owed by the Red Phantom."

Rendgren mutters under his breath. "Yes, it seems like ever since I met that woman, I have done nothing but swear oaths and owe people."

"Women will do that to you. Get used to it."

Jeodina pushes him gently. "Hush, NOT all women are like that. The Seer is playing a dangerous game, and I am certain once this is all done, Rendgren, your favors will be paid out in full."

"I certainly hope so."

"Well, ours will, right Vyn?"

"Wait, WHAT! You can't do that, Jeo. I like him indebted to us."

"Too late, Vyn, it's done."

"Woman!"

Rendgren laughs, "Thank you. It's so good to see that I am not the only one suffering. On that note, the Red Phantom needs to tell the king he bedded his seer."

Vynloren starts to cough, Jeodina patting him gently on the back. "Now THAT'S the way to start a war."

"Well, it's better than what the seer came up with, which is the merchant telling people I found my mate."

"But you did."

"Besides the point. This will anger him more."

"Indeed it will."

"Rendgren, are you going there now?"

"That's the plan."

Jeodina nods, and moves forward, chanting a few words, and placing an illusion over the mark upon him. "He cannot see Raya's mark too soon then. I will inform the council that the war starts today."

"Thank you." Rendgren bows to them both as a portal appears behind him, disappearing through it as his words linger. "I will be in touch."

Vynloren smiles at Jeodina, sensing the council as it arrives behind them. They turn to give them the good news, seeing the shock on all their expressions at what has changed since his last visit.

Rendgren appears at the edge of the White Height mountains, his eyes scanning the landscape before him, shifting into his dragon. He takes to the air, soaring above the clouds, blending with them, recalling what it is like to be the Red Phantom. He hovers above Teshem for a moment as he scans the locations of catapults and ballistas before dipping down and tucking his wings, descending around the back side of them, using the shadows of dusk to his advantage. He maneuvers quicker than they can react, lifting up to land on the side of the tower, his claws digging into the stone as chips drop to the ground below him. He roars, watching as the city folk scatter in fear, feeling the movement of the castle beneath his feet, knowing the king is arriving on the balcony nearby.

Fires dance in his eyes as he meets the gaze of the king below him, shifting his body around to face him better, barring a toothy grin, his tail twitching in delight. "King Zane. I just wanted you to know a few things about your seer before you meet your demise. She was with me for two days, sleeping on a bedroll she filched from my treasure before I carried her to my bed with no resistance. Of course, she was a bit of a hellcat when she arrived, but I AM the Red Phantom, and one can only deny me for so long. It took but a kiss to make her cave, and when she did, I will admit, I took full advantage of it and bedded her thoroughly. She was a wonder to explore. I knew every spot that made her tick, gasp, sigh, beg, plead. You name it, I discovered it. With my touch, I commanded her body, and she responded, giving me complete power of control over her to take what I wanted. And I took it. What a delight it was to have it given so freely. The bonus was she kept her power through it all, so I guess bedding a mystic is different than bedding a seer. And when I grew tired of her, I forced her to tell me who and where my mate was, who happens to be a gold actually. Clearly, I have better ways of extracting information than you do because I got the information I sought before she died, whereas I understand you didn't."

Rendgren smiles at the rage in the king's eyes, shifting his attention to the guards pushing the ballistas around. He takes to the air, the power of his wings lifting him into the sky before even one bolt can be released, his laughter echoing throughout Teshem. He sails through the clouds, hearing the king's curses below, knowing he's done his job. The scene is set, and the battle has begun. A portal appears before him, taking him to his mountain as he swoops down to his mystic waiting for him. He shifts back, eyeing her crossed arms, her tapping foot, the frown upon her face, as his grin widens. "I found a sitter for Junior, my dear."

"That's NOT all you did, Gren."

He arches a brow as he moves over, drawing her into his arms and kissing her softly. "I don't know what you're talking about."

"Ohhh, don't you think you can get away with this. I KNOW what you did. I SAW it."

He lifts her into his arms and carries her back to the bedroom, creating an opaque wall behind them to keep Junior and Spider out. He places her on the bed, his fingers moving to her ties as he kisses her along the neck. He whispers in her ear. "I simply told the truth, in a roundabout way."

She sighs, her temper fading at his touch, feeling his fingers skimming lightly along her skin as he slides her dress off, knowing he is very much correct in the control he has over her body. "Oh, Gren, what am I going to do with you?"

"Love me, Seer, as I love you." He peppers kisses along her skin, a smile crosses his lips as he feels her resistance drop and takes full advantage of it. A few hours later he held her in his arms, breathing softly as she slept next to him. He lowers the wall, sensing the pups are wondering where they are, then allows himself to sleep with her.

Over the next few weeks, the pair collect Junior, leaving Spider in the cave for some quiet time, and drop Junior off with Jeodina and Vynloren as they take to the skies over the grasslands. They fly without a care in the world, performing a primeval dance across the sky: joining claws and barrel rolling together, entwining tails, and weaving around each other. Flying up and swooping down low along the grasses, as they chase the farmer's cattle and sheep around. Each day, the seer goes through her visions, waiting for the catapults to be on the move, and is rewarded three weeks later. She smiles at Rendgren as she eats breakfast with her family. "He took the bait. He's got them on the move; they will arrive after our flight today."

"So tomorrow then, we need to be careful, as I don't want you to get hurt."

"I am safer than you are. I will see them coming."

He chuckles. "You will let me know if one comes for me, right?"

She arches a brow and levels a look his way. "I would think you would make me. Didn't you state you have complete control over me?"

His eyes darken with desire as he leans forward, caressing her cheek, before pulling her close and kissing her gently, feeling her succumb to his touch. Junior growls in disgust and jumps off the chair to race around with Spider. "I do, my dear, but not in all aspects. Perhaps one day."

She closes her eyes as a blush crosses her cheeks, feeling his thoughts flood her mind as she pushes him away. "Never. I will never allow you that power."

He rises from the chair and lifts her into his arms, his voice a soft whisper in her ear as he carries her to the bedroom. "We'll see, my dear Seer. We'll see."

The next day, they drop Junior off, watching as he scampers into the woods towards the bears; the soft *'danger danger'* could be heard along the winds. "The catapults and ballistas have moved. Zalgren will be arriving back at his manor in Nantou tomorrow, welcoming all those needing a place to stay for the week. Our advance will be next Saturday, so we will need you to watch Junior for the day."

Jeo and Vyn nod. "Happy to watch him. The little wyrmling is adorable, even if he wants to chew on the Council. A few of them have had to pin him down several times."

The seer laughs. "He does take after his father."

Rendgren narrows his eyes, humor dancing within them. "I think he's more like his mother, a royal pain in the ass."

She smiles up at him. "I can admit to that. Now, let's go get shot at."

Jeodina moves forward, casting her spell on the pair, hiding the symbols, "Today's the last day I have to do this."

The Seer smiles, taking Jeodina's hand. "Thank you for everything. Please tell the Council I will make it up to them."

Jeodina glances back, whispering softly. "I honestly think they think he's adorable but are not willing to admit it to themselves just yet."

The seer smiles. "I won't say anything." She gives them a bow, stepping through the portal Rendgren creates, landing in their usual spot on the mountain. She shifts shape as her violet eyes glow softly, assessing the situation carefully before nodding. "Two ballistae on the left, two ahead of us and one to the right. The left will fire high, forcing us down, while they will have the ones ahead and at the right-side fire low, driving us into a box. The catapults are on each corner with the wagons that carry the rocks."

"We've practiced this seer, we can do it."

"Yes, we can." She turns her head to him, giving him a nod, launching off the side of the mountain and coasting down it, picking up speed as she hits the grasslands. She rolls over on her back and grasps Rendgren's claws as they barrel roll through the clearing. They break apart at the first round of attacks, each of them lifting at the corner straight up, swiveling around, and breathing fire on the hidden catapult. They swoop around in a circle, their wing tips touching as more bolts sail past them. Rendgren catches one in his claws and snaps it in two. He rolls over the back of his seer, breathing fire on the bolt, disintegrating it before it strikes her, as she loops around and releases her breath on a pair of ballistae. They meet again, flying with a bolt as it sails between them, following it along the grasslands before separating, reigning fire down upon the area. They swing around and join again, claws grasping as they spiral straight up into the air while rocks and bolts are released. They rise high in the sky, before falling away from each other, each of them heads for the last artillery standing, fire blazing all around them. Once all the siege weapons are destroyed, they concentrate on the wagons. Purple lights release the horses, which run away in terror seconds before the wagons burst into flame. They sweep around, ensuring they got everything, before lifting into the sky and disappearing from sight.

Close to midnight, the few guards that survived the wrath of the dragons stagger into the castle, burned, beaten, and exhausted. Trevyr greets them at the door, leading them to the war room. "The King has been waiting."

Zane looks over the condition of the few remaining guards standing before him. "I gather you did not succeed in destroying them."

"No, Sire, they destroyed us. They even spun around a bolt as it sailed through the air. I tell you, it was uncanny how they knew exactly where each bolt was going to be shot and maneuvered around them to destroy each of the weapons. It's like they had the seer still working for them or strong magic on their side. That being said, he is the Red Phantom, and it was very evident in our fight as to why no one has caught him yet."

"Did any of the siege weapons survive?"

"None, Sire, and most of the wagons went down too."

Zane slams his fist into the table. "I want that Gold taken down. He is flaunting the fact that he knows a gold dragon will destroy me, and it's probably her. Get new catapults built NOW!"

"Yes, Sire."

Trevyr watches them go, knowing they should be sleeping but not daring to argue with the king. "You will win, Sire. You have over a hundred dragons hanging around the outside walls as proof of how strong you are. Let's get the adventuring groups back here to help and find some mages. Perhaps we can borrow King Ludy's mages again for a month."

Zane scowls as he looks at the map, none of his plans have worked since the seer left. "Do it. Get them all into the bloody city, as soon as they can, and find me more gold to pay them." He strides from the room.

"Yes, Sire."

Return to the King

SATURDAY MORNING ARRIVES, Rendgren heads to the barn, guiding the horses out and fastening them to the carriage, leading them to the front of the manor. He lifts a hand as black and red banners appear on each of the corners of the open-top carriage and along the harnesses of the horses. The manes and tails braid magically, with tiny red ribbons tying the ends. At the front of the carriage, a painting rolls down. The image is a red dragon with the symbol of Raya carved on his scales, smoke curling from its nostrils, and a look of disdain in his expression. Rendgren turns, feeling his seer's footsteps behind him, hearing her soft sigh. "A little overdone, don't you think?"

"Of course not, my dear. I want him to know who's coming." He turns, his eyes darkening in desire as they roll slightly at her choice of colors in black and violet. "Red would be better."

"Purples my color, Gren, and surprisingly enough, it's not the Red Phantom he's scared of. It's me. He just doesn't know it yet."

Rendgren takes her hand and kisses the back of it. "Indeed, I can't wait. Where is Junior?"

"He's with Jeo and Vyn. They came to get him."

"Good. When is Honors Light due?"

"Should be soon."

Rendgren pulls her close, wrapping his arms around her, resting his chin on her head. His hands linger on the small of her back as they wait for their escort. "Are you ready, my love?"

"I am."

"It's not going to be easy."

"No, I don't imagine it will. Remember, our goal is only the King. Are the other dragons ready?"

"They are. What of the guards that helped torture you?"

"They are all dead, and if others get in our way, we shall deal with them too." She turns to the sound of hoofbeats coming up the road. She smiles at the sight of Gwynevere and Ridgestalker leading the way, the others trailing behind them. She remains in Rendgren's arms until they stop. "Greetings, Gwyn. Are you ready for some chaos and rage?"

Gwynevere smiles. "I think most of the rage is going to be directed your way, King's seer, but yes, we are prepared. Keep the townsfolk safe, capture the guards, and protect you upon entry."

"Right then, let's go." Rendgren lifts the seer into the wagon, stepping in behind her. He takes the reins, snapping them lightly as the horses lurch forward, setting off at a steady pace. Honors Light shifts, moving three to each side of the carriage; Gwyn and Ridge leading, Solilque and Myrlani at the sides, and Aleandi and Cecil at the end.

They journey throughout the day, eventually reaching the outskirts of Teshem in the late afternoon. Rendgren slows the wagon a moment as they both mentally prepare themselves for what is to come. He leads them through the gates into the heart of the city, hearing the call of the guards and the gasps from the populace.

"Is that the King's seer? With the Merchant? Isn't he working for the King? What are they doing together? Wait, is that a banner of the Red Phantom? Why would they have the banner of him? Why does he bear Raya's sun on his chest? Wasn't the King's seer kidnapped by a red dragon? Do you think it was the Phantom that kidnapped her? No, he would have killed her. No one survives his attacks. Didn't the Phantom say she died? What do you think is happening?"

Rendgren steps off of the carriage, picking the seer up by the waist and placing her on the ground next to him. Honors Light dismounts and ties their horses to the wagon.

The King's seer smiles at the whispers, choosing to ignore them for the moment. "Alright, Honors, you know what to do."

"Indeed we do, Aleandi, shroud us." Gwynevere nods as the group disappears from sight, earning gasps from the crowd around them.

The King's seer looks up at Rendgren, placing a hand on his arm as the pair walk slowly towards the castle. She watches as some of the people scatter, though most just clear the path and whisper among themselves about the pair casually strolling towards the castle. The seer pauses, feeling the darkness ahead, her eyes drifting over to the witch, seeing the recognition in her eyes as she hears the soft hiss. "You!"

The King's seer smiles a bit, taking in her appearance, noticing it hasn't changed much from when she saw her in the market seven years ago. "Lavinia, always a pleasure."

"What did you do to me?"

"I blocked your memory and pacified you."

"I prevented your magic from seeing me. You couldn't have."

"I did when the mages were destroying your wards in the castle. It weakened you enough to let me in."

"Where is my soul, and why are you back?"

"Your soul is gone, and I am here to destroy your demon."

"You don't have the power to defeat us both."

"Try me, Witch. I can, and I WILL end him today."

The witch lifts a hand, sending a dark green bolt at the seer, who, in turn, raises her hand; a purple shield shimmers around them, reflecting her spell back at her, knocking her off her feet, pain wracking her body.

"Leave now, witch. Before I kill you too."

"You will regret this." The witch collects herself and disappears around the building.

Rendgren watches her leave, resisting the desire to chase after her. "So, that's the witch you tangled with."

"Yes, she and I will meet again..." She turns her attention to the horses approaching, seeing the king's men form a circle around them.

Kenworth dismounts and moves towards them, studying the seer and merchant carefully, before drawing his sword and pointing it at her throat. "You're pretty foolish to come back here, King's seer. You should have stayed hidden after the threats you made. The King demands your presence immediately."

Rendgren's eyes narrow at the blade. He starts to advance, only to be stopped by his seer as she tightens her hand on his, shaking her head.

She steps forward, her voice dripping with disdain. "So Kenworth, I see you have moved up the ranks since Dunivan left." She looks him over, studying his stance, the blade in his hand directed at her, knowing he doesn't fully understand the power of a mystic. "I am sure Zane does. What is he going to do if I deny him? Whip me? Torture me? Poison me with the poisons you got for him, Kenworth." She smiles at the waver in the sword, seeing the color drain from his face. She lifts her fingers to trace the blade edge lightly, leaving a slight trail of purple lights wrapped around it. "What's the matter Captain Kenworth, you're looking a bit pale."

Her eyes flash slightly as the sword fades from his hand and lands a hundred feet behind him. "Are you thinking about running? I can see that you are." She lifts her hand, drawing his thoughts out as images flicker above them, earning a gasp from those around them as the horses prance under the tightened reins. "Ah, Kenworth, are you suddenly scared of the mystic that you helped the King poison?" Her voice grows cold as a chill surrounds them. "Because you should be. We have the city surrounded by dragons, including the six golds the king was unable to track down."

"You're Lying!"

"Am I?" She turns her palm up as a small bead of purple light rises to the sky, flashing momentarily before fading. The bell on the North tower suddenly sounds, followed shortly by the other three. Horns blow along the city walls as a runner approaches. "Captain! We are surrounded by dragons. At least fifty of them, of all colors, including gold. What should we do? We don't have siege weapons anymore. Not after..."

The King's seer turns to the runner, disdain in her eyes. "If you wish to live, you will do nothing and tell the other guards to do nothing as well. If anyone attacks those dragons, this entire city dies. Is that clear?" She turns to face Kenworth as she steps closer to Rendgren, placing her arm on his. "Of course, I would like to take credit for rounding up all the dragons, but alas, I can't. The credit belongs to the Red Phantom himself."

Kenworth steps back, fear creeping into his eyes at the Legend of Terror standing before him, the other guards shifting nervously around them. "He's the Red Phantom?"

"Indeed he is. NOW, you will take us to see the king; after all, he doesn't like to be kept waiting. It's one lash per minute, isn't it? Or have the rules changed since I left?"

Kenworth composes himself, barking the command for his men to fall into formation around them as the guards lead them towards the castle.

Rendgren smiles at his love, his thoughts reaching out to hers. *'Nicely done, my dear. I think that runner actually believed you.'*

'Let's hope he did. It should give Honors Light enough time to get all the people inside and round up guards without causing too much panic.'

They walk with their entourage through the castle walls into the courtyard, where the remaining guards dismount uneasily, moving to surround them but keeping their distance at the same time. The King's seer scans the castle as they enter, noting the slight decline in the upkeep since when she was here. She can hear Zane issuing commands to attack the dragons that were outside his city, specifically the gold ones. She smiles ever so slightly as she steps into the grand hall, seeing his green eyes narrow on her as her 'entourage' and his guards back away, none wanting to be in the path of the confrontation they know is about to take place.

"King Zane. I cannot say I am pleased to see you again, but here I am. How are things? I hear you've been struggling since you lost Martha and Dunivan. Even Pippa and Xyl seemed to have given you the slip. I'm surprised your new seer has not been able to find them. She is a seer, right?" Her eyes shift to the woman standing behind him, studying the threads around her. "No, I see she's a mage. The one brought in to scry for me, but clearly not strong enough to get past Runestone's masking gems. You do recall the ones, Zane; they were given to me after the assassination attempt. I, of course, kept extras. I gave some to those that escaped, and packed the rest the day I left. Did you tell her that she is trying to bypass both a mystic's power and one of the most powerful mages in the realm?"

Rendgren pauses. "Wait, you have anti-scrying gems."

"Yes, my love. Your cave was secure enough; this just ensured I was not found."

"So you could have traveled with me?"

"I could have if I wanted to be captured. The violet eyes kind of give me away."

Zane stands, his voice a deep growl, his eyes shifting to the merchant her arm is resting on, feeling the fury growing within him at the betrayal. "You dare to come back here and mock me, King's seer, and with the merchant?"

"Oh, Zane. I am simply stating observations. I mean, most of my time here was a mockery, was it not? Me knowing what power I had and feeding you the bare minimum to keep you happy. I have to say; I am eternally grateful my parents neglected to mention what my powers actually were at the age of nine. I suspect the whippings would have started far sooner if they had."

Zane's eyes darken, a wicked smile crossing his lips. "I killed your parents, and you didn't stop that."

"I know you did, Zane. I foresaw it. And you killed my guards as well. All but Xyl, that is. Again, foresaw that, too. Now, had they been parents to me, I would have stopped you, but they were not. Martha and Pippa showed me what family is, and both of them escaped your grasp. They are the ones who mattered to me. And, of course, Gren here; he's family now."

His eyes blaze as they turn to Rendgren. "You... You knew all along where she was and lied to me."

Rendgren smiles, taking her hand in his and kissing the back of it before draping an arm over her shoulders, pulling her close for a moment. His eyes flash in delight as they turn on the king. "Indeed, you might say I'm the one that stole her from your garden and have had her all along. Also not a merchant. It was simply the story she created when I stood before you in court a few years back while she was telepathically calling me foolish."

Zane charges forward to the pair, his gaze furious. "You knew, and you still brought a DRAGON into my court?"

"Technically, your guards escorted him in, Zane. I simply saw him in the market." The King's seer lifts her hands and twists them slightly as purple threads of light spring from her fingertips, wrapping around Zane and stopping his charge. She spins as the guards gasp and draw their weapons. She tips her hand a touch as a wave of purple

271

energy flashes forward, slamming them into the walls and snapping immobilizing bands into place on them. Once she is certain they are restrained, she turns to the double doors they entered. She forms a triangle with her hands, purple lights swirled around them as the main doors slam shut and lock. She then secures the rest of the doors in the room, hearing the pounding of the guards outside.

She turns back to Zane, seeing the mix of rage and fear in his eyes as she walks forward. She brings a hand up to his cheek, taunting him softly as she walks around him. "Do you feel the fear, Zane? Is it the same fear you felt the day you nearly killed me with poison or the day you got the letter from me, realizing just what I kept from you? Or is it a combination of both because you should feel fear. Martha warned you the day I arrived in your rooms upstairs, that you never wanted a mystic angry with you but you seemed to have forgotten that. She also warned you the day after my first whipping that you were making a mistake. That one day, I would fight back and here we are, me fighting back."

She turns, her hands weaving purple motes of light before Zane. She calls forth his war table, the map, the figures, watching as it solidifies before them, catching the guards gasping at her power. She wanders around it, looking over markers before her eyes meet his. "Do you remember the first day you let me see this Zane?" She runs her fingers lightly over the wood. "In your blindness, you only saw that I could find your dragons faster." She knocks over the three pieces in Hontby. "Instead, it allowed me to control the playing field and see where you were moving your men to counter them. And counter them I did." She picks up the five in Ewhela, dropping them on the ground at his feet, watching them bounce on the floor before sitting still. She moves to stand next to him, as she turns to face the table, purple lights glitter and sparkle around the map, removing every troop off the board that is not in Oblait. "I took them ALL out of play, Zane, every last one of them."

She smiles at the empty board, and steps away from him, twisting her hands around as her bed appears in place of the table. Her eyes turn cold as she studies it a moment, before lifting them to meet his gaze. "And if I didn't find you a dragon, Zane. What happened then? Can you take the punishment you dished out? Would you survive or die in the process?"

Zane narrows his eyes, struggling against the bonds. "You can't kill me. Even you said it is not your destiny. I saw the vision of a gold dragon killing me, and they are all outside."

"You're right; all six are outside. And it WILL be a gold dragon that kills you, Zane, but we will get there." She waves her hand, sliding the bed over and dropping Zane to his knees. Images of Deryn and Tai appear, pinning his hands as hers were the first time she was whipped. "The downside to my gift, Zane, is that I suffered twice. Once in the vision, and again as the whip struck." She moves to sit on the bed, watching as he fights against her magic before touching his forehead gently. She passes the vision over to him, smiling as he jerks and screams in pain as the first lash strikes him. She places a finger gently to his lips. "Shhhh... Now Zane. I never made a sound. I expect the same from you. Now what was it you said, yes, that's right. *Show me, King's seer, and this won't happen. Tell me what I want to know.*"

He growls. "I will kill you, Seer."

She catches his yelp as the second strike crosses his back, just as it did with her. "Zane, you have six more lashes to go. And that's just the first time. Perhaps we need to skip ahead to the salt in the wounds or the branding iron."

He glares at her, hissing in pain. "You will not get away with this."

"Oh, But I am Zane. I don't see anyone stopping me." She watches his body jerk in pain as the third lash strikes him. "Your guards are pinned as you are. Your mage is standing there dumbfounded, uncertain if she wants to rescue you or herself." She turns to the wall he faces, calling forth the vision once more, him sitting on his throne, the glint of gold scales reflecting in the light as it draws in and breaths on the throne with him in it. "It is a pretty sight, seeing you burn to death."

"I've seen that before, King's seer; what do you want? Everything you do has a reason." He grits his teeth as a fourth lash strikes him, his back feeling as if it is on fire.

She rises and reaches into her robes, pulling out a scroll, letting it roll to the ground with a list of writing before him. "You're right. I am here to end your tyrannical rule. You see, my darling dragon has been busy. He has received all the other countries' blessings to have you charged with the death of your servants, your guards, my parents, and the continual abuse of power over me the last two years I was here. Let alone buying me as if I were a slave. Your time as King has ended. You are to be stripped of your Kingship and removed from the castle, in any way possible... undefined and all."

"And how do you plan to do that? Won't that go against your morals and change your seers' sight?" An edge of confidence returns to his voice, despite the fifth lash striking his body.

The King's seer walks back to stand next to Rendgren, handing him the scroll as she takes his hand in hers, turning back to study Zane. "Well, yes, it would. But I have learned much in my time away from this castle, what with being able to play with my powers freely around Gren. Unlike here, where I had to keep them under wraps or hidden within my room. What I did not understand is why, no matter what threads I played with, I could not determine which of the six gold dragons was destined to kill you. You know, I actually had to die in order to figure it out."

She lifts her hand to the vision he faced, shifting the image to that of her lying in the cave, blood everywhere, death hanging in the air as Rendgren knelt at her side. "It seems though that my dragon wasn't ready to let me die, even though I saw the day of my death at twelve. It was the first time I had gone shopping with Martha, and one of the vendors had four dragon necklaces that I purchased. Ones that I empowered and gave to the four that escaped this castle with me. But I digress, back to the Gold. I couldn't determine who it was because they did not exist in this realm; until now, that is." She turns to face the illusion, lifting both her hands up, shifting it to a pair of dragons flying together in unison, the symbol of Raya clear on both their chests.

The mage behind gasps in shock, realizing suddenly what she is seeing, knowing just how much trouble they were in. "My King..."

"Shhhh, Kalysee, He should figure it out soon." The King's seer lifts her hand, silencing the mage's voice. She narrows her eyes on Zane, seeing the sixth lash strike him as he stiffens and grunts in pain. The bed fades as she slides him back to his throne, forcing him to sit magically.

Rendgren steps to the side, giving her the space she needs, a smile spreading across his face as he watches Zane realize what is happening before him. His eyes follow the mage as she runs for the side door, ensuring she doesn't interfere with what is about to happen.

"You see, when one calls in a Goddess to help bring a person back to life, one's body can change in order to survive. And all Dragons have a mortal form, be it human, elf or another of their choosing. It was something I neglected to mention to you, that is, until my letter on the day of my escape. In fact, there were two at my sixteenth ball that you met with in court the very next day."

The seer looks at her hands, watching her fingers elongate into golden claws as gold and purple light surround her. She maintains her gaze on Zane, her violet eyes burning with righteous fury, unveiling her true power as she shapeshifts into a formidable dragon, her tail swishing around behind her. The symbol of Raya clearly etched upon her golden scales amid the myriad of colors glinting off her from the stained-glass windows in the hall.

"King's seer, let's talk about this!" Zane could feel his reign crumbling down around him as he stares in shock at his seer, struggling against the magic that held him in place.

"There is nothing to talk about Zane. You were warned. You should have listened."

The room trembles with her power, her golden scales shimmering as the inferno grows around her. Dragon eyes flash with power as she unleashes her fiery breath upon the king and his throne, engulfing them in flame. She catches the fleeting flash of green within as the room fills with the crackling of burning wood and the scent of singed fabric

Amidst the chaos, Rendgren is filled with awe and apprehension as he witnesses the destruction; the significance of the moment is not lost on him as to just how powerful she truly is.

She glances around the room, noticing the mage is gone, before focusing on each of the guards still pinned to the walls, seeing them cower in fear under her gaze. She shifts back to mortal form and steps into Rendgren's arms, feeling a slight sadness that it had to end this way but knowing she had no other choice.

"Is it done, King's seer?"

"It is… For now."

He brushes her hair lightly, chuckling softly. "For now, huh, I guess that means it's not really done."

She leans against his chest. "Is it ever really done?"

"No, I don't suppose it is. You do know I was retired before you asked me to kidnap you."

She laughs softly, "I didn't ask, you just assumed."

Rendgren smiles. "Don't think that I don't know that you played with my threads, my dear Mystic."

She looks up at him. "Do you regret it?"

He kisses her gently, pulling her body tight against him as desire flares in his eyes. "Not in the least my love."

She pushes against him, feeling breathless at his kiss. "Good. Now, we have things to do before we can go there."

"Dammit, Seer, are you really going to make me wait?" He pulls her close again, kissing her neck, whispering into her ear. "We are Junior free. We have a castle. Let's just find a room."

She slips from his embrace, taking his hand. "After, I promise, we still have things to do, and Honors Light will come looking."

"Right, Honors." He rolls his eyes slightly at her, "Virtuous pain in the asses they are."

She smiles, kissing him on the cheek. "But you love them, admit it!"

"No my love, I don't have to admit anything of the sort."

She laughs softly, and leads him through the hallways to the balcony that overlooks the city, one she had stood on with the king a time or two. The pair step out into the sunlight, seeing the guards magically bound on the alure by the dragons, who were now back in their mortal form. She could see Honors Light rounding up the guards in the streets and leading them back to the castle.

Gwynevere approaches, seeing them on the balcony waiting. "Has the King been removed from the throne, King's seer?"

"He has. Did we lose any?"

"We lost one guard; he went down fighting. A blue dragon was injured, but Myrlani healed him, so he should be fine in a day."

"So overall, it was a success."

"Seems that way."

"Good, let's get the populace out. I will have words for them." She turns to the bells behind them; purple lights surround them as they begin to ring, her eyes finding Rendgrens. "Are you up for this, Gren? We can appoint another to stand in our place."

"No my dear, it needs to be done."

"There will be a lot to do. We need to go through all the castle staff and find out who is for or against the King. For the people the King killed, we need to inform their families of their loss, find where the King buried them, and place markers on their graves so their families can mourn them properly. Send out missives to the other kingdoms, welcoming them to meet the new rulers of Oblait. Also, reset the failing economy that's due to all the taxes the king placed upon the people to fund his dragon hunts; perhaps we could use one of the dragon treasures to assist with that. To add to all that, some of the people may not accept dragons as their rulers, so it will be a challenge."

Rendgren chuckles. "And here I thought retirement was going to be peaceful."

She places a hand on his cheek, rising on her tiptoes to kiss his lips. "I Love you, Gren."

"And I love you, Seer. I never thought it would be possible."

She smiles, turning to face the people that are gathering below, taking Gren's hands in hers as she moves a step forward.

Rendgren pulls her back a moment, his eyes searching hers. "If I am to rule with you, *King's* seer, I should at least know your true name as you seem to know mine."

"I knew yours when I was twelve, my darling, Gren. When I picked up four necklaces in the market, each one bearing one of your names. Zalgren, Rendgren, The Red Phantom all within your True name..." She reaches out to touch his cheek lightly, her thoughts mingling with his. '*Zalgrenzarendaguran.*'

"Twelve, huh, and is that how the goddess knew it?"

"I wouldn't know my love."

He arches a brow, not entirely believing her. "Now stop dodging my love. True name, now."

She rises to her toes, whispering softly in his ear. "It's Pandora, my love. Pandora Concordia Boxxe."

He chuckles, pulling her in and kissing her deeply, forgetting all about the people that stood watching their new rulers on the balcony.

Parallel Realms

IN ANOTHER REALM, time and place, a witch and a king lie in pain on the edge of a beach, the waves crashing over them. The water extinguishes the fires feeding upon them while the remaining two lashes strike the king as he slips into darkness, cursing the seer.

Echoes of Tomorrow

PANDORA WANDERS INTO the living room. She smiles at Junior, who's sitting on the couch playing video games with his friend Kip. Her son, tall like his father, has red and black hair, which unlike his father, has been kept short in the current style. His violet eyes watch the video game as his hands work the controller, competing with Kip about who is the better player. "Junior, I am going to the market. Did you need anything?"

"It's a shopping mall mom, you're going to the mall. You are so far behind the times. And I'm good, thanks."

"Right, mall. You know it will always be the market for me."

"That's because you're old."

"Watch your tongue, Junior. I am only nineteen years older than you."

He turns to look at his mother, dressed in her violet and green hanfu. Chains dangle around her waist and across her chest, amethysts are inset along the neckline and sleeves of her hanfu. "Are you wearing that? In public?"

"Yes, I am."

"Mom! It's sooo old-fashioned!"

"There is nothing wrong with this. Now, don't be too loud; your father is sleeping."

"He's always sleeping, Mom."

"Well, that's because he's old!"

Junior laughs. "Don't let Dad hear you say that."

She moves over and pats his head, "He's sleeping, he won't. I will be back in a few hours."

"Aww, Mom, don't do that." He swats her hand away.

She laughs softly. "Alright, Junior." Her eyes drift to the painting in the room above the TV, a family portrait they had done before dragons had to go into hiding. The three of them in their dragon form, with their tiny dog Spider baring his teeth, commissioned by the renowned artist and his wife, Stephyn and Glynda Stefflyrs. She drifts back, recalling the day they posed for it when they ruled a kingdom and brought peace to the realm before retiring, watching as cities grew up around them. "I will be back in a few hours."

"Alright, Mom, see you when you get back."

Pandora walks down to the town, having always hated those big metal boxes everyone rides in, even if her husband loves them. She wanders through the shopping center, picking up a few things and tucking them in her bag before stopping at the puppies in the pet store window. She watches them for a moment, recalling Spider, feeling a sadness within her when they lost him to old age. She crouches down to their level, watching as one comes forward to the glass, licking at her fingertips, while the others back away, sensing more than what appears before them. "Well, you are a brave one, aren't you, you are sure to find a home quickly." She rises and turns away but stops as she hears a howl, her violet eyes shift back to the puppy, whose tail immediately starts wagging. "Oh, little one, you are going to get me into so much trouble." She enters the pet store and looks around, her gaze landing on the teller. "How much for the puppy in the window?"

"Which one, miss?"

"The black one, with the white sun mark on his chest."

"Fifty dollars."

"Right. I will take her."

The man nods, moves to the pen and picks up the pup, returning with her and placing her into Pandora's arms. "Do you need supplies?"

"No, I am certain we have some." She hands over the money.

"Alright then, have a good day miss."

"You too." Pandora smiles, feeling the puppy squirm in her arm and lick her face, bringing a laugh to her lips. "Well, Gren is going to have my hide for this but first we need to give you a name so he can't kick us both out." She ponders it as they walk home. She pushes the gate open and closes it behind her, placing the puppy on the ground and watches as she bounds after the bugs in the grass. "Alright, Bug, you need to behave around him and Junior, though I am certain Junior will love you."

She turns and heads for the house, crossing through the main entrance as the puppy follows behind her. She heads her son's way, hearing the video games still playing. "Did your father wake up, Junior?"

"No, Mom, he...Wait, YOU bought a dog? Spider?"

"Yes, I did, and her name is Bug."

Junior drops the controller and runs to the pup, dropping to his hands and knees and holding a hand out, watching her tail wag as she jumps into his lap. "Dad's gonna kill you!"

"He can try." She places her packages on the table and sorts through them, pulling out several bunches of flowers, knowing they need tending to first.

"Flowers? Are Auntie Sol and the others coming for dinner?"

"Yes, Dear, on Saturday. Along with the Council."

"Awesome! I can't wait! Fight club with the Guardians!"

She lifts her gaze, feeling her husband moving through the mansion, hearing his voice well before she saw him. "Why do I feel a rodent in the house, my dear?"

"I don't know what you're talking about, Gren."

He rounds the corner, eyeing his wife up and down, desire flaring in his eyes, even after hundreds of years together. His gaze travels down to Junior, who sits on the floor with a dog in his lap before he shifts over to Junior's friend, who is sitting on the couch and watching the whole exchange silently, game controller hanging in his hand. "YOU bought a Mutt!?"

"Yes, Gren, I did. Her name is Bug. You will adapt, just like you did with Spider." She arranges the flowers in the vase.

"I will never admit to that."

"You don't have to. I saw the truth."

Rendgren's eyes narrow slightly, shifting to the movement of the flowers she is arranging. "OH no, Bloody Hell, You didn't invite Honors Light for dinner."

"Yes, dear, I did. And the Council."

"Some days, my dear. Somedays."

She turns and smiles his way. "Everyday Gren and you love it."

He moves over to her side, pulling her in close, running a hand lightly over her forehead, brushing her hair aside as he kisses her gently, "I love you, not it. There is a difference."

Junior picks up the pup, "Ewwww, Get a room!"

"We have a room, Junior, Get out!"

"Dad!!!! Come on, Kip, let's go outside and play ball."

Kips looks at the pair, turning to his friend. "Are you gonna let your dad talk to you like that?"

"Oh, Hell ya. Do you know how old he is? My dad is like the second most powerful person in this world. He can easily kick my ass."

Kip follows along behind. "Wait, Second? So who's the first?"

"My Mother."

Rendgren watches his son vacate the house, his eyes landing on his wife. "So, my love, you want to tell me why they are coming for dinner when they were just here."

"We are going to need them."

"Damn, he finally made it back?"

"Yes, and he's coming right for us."

People

Kingdom of Oblait

King Zane Evilian (Human, green eyes, blonde hair)
Mother of Zane - Rimorhia
Father of Zane - Wallace
Child's mother - Francine Boxxe (Human, brown eyes, black hair)
Child's father - Edmund Boxxe (Human, hazel eyes, brown hair)
King's seer (Human, violet eyes, black hair - Mystic)

Castle staff

Head housekeeper - Martha (Blue-Gray eyes, brown hair mixed with
    light gray)
Seers personal maid - Pippa (Green eyes, wild red curly hair)
Unchosen maids - Belinda, Clover, Nessa, and Lena
Chamber maids - Elo, Cyndie, Jynn, and Abye
Maids - Dianne, Denise, Liz, Dee, Cyan, Susyn, Edna, Silver, Star, Vycky
Main cooks - Ray, Gerrey
Assistants cooks - Fil, Anne

Guards

Captain of the guards - Dunivan (Human male, gray eyes, dark
    brown hair, goatee)
Kings personal guards - Randolph, Trevyr, Benson (Human males)

The Seers entourage - Alvero, Cedrik, Xyl, Tai, Deryn, Drue, Krim, Jesper, Luis (Human males)
Other guards - Iyan, Bert, Kenworth (Human males)
Chamberlain - Kivu (human male - blonde hair, gray eyes)
Diplomats - Charles and David
Scribes - Herman, Erik
Gardener - Patrycia
Tailor - Habo
Healers - Irma, Roger
Dance instructor - Miranda
Witch - Lavinia
Witch doctor - Zolvinta
Mage - Kalysee

Nobles

Beatrixe Wythymms
Crimson Warlord
Magnolia Cyrlsen and Daughter Scarlyt,
Elder Snow and his sons
Khora Aryann
Zaemar Bachstaub
Ela Shrodyner
Flavvie Henwaryer
Michaella Hayryss
KR and Kryesta Deight

Kingdom of Hontby

King Ludy - Paladin Protector (Human, blonde hair, blue eyes)
Diplomats - Chainz and Niceasilla
Mage - Runestone (Human, Ice blue eyes, white hair)
Mage - Antimagic (Myke) (Human, green eyes, bald with salt/pepper goatee.)
Healer - Gronkus (Human, brown eyes, light brown hair, mustache and beard)

Bard - Cathel Sean.
The Rug Rattens
Liaam - Human Barbarian
Aeryen - Gnome Rogue
Decklane - Human Wizard
Eastonator - Gnome Ranger

Kingdom of Spokane

Queen Bobbye and King Gordyn (Human)
Diplomats - Anume and Neico
Tailor in Krine - Jymkynair
Honors light
Gwynevere - human priestess of Raya (Blue eyes, blonde hair)
Ridgestalker - Dwarf hunter (Blue eyes, bald, white beard)
Solilque - Elven Guardian (Blue eyes, purple hair, Bear)
Myrlani - Elven of sorts Shaman (Blue eyes, white hair)
Cecil - Gnome Mage (Blue eyes, black hair)
Aleandi - Human rogue (Blue eyes, red hair)

Kingdom of Ewhela

King Hallihan (Human, brown eyes, brown hair, day old facial growth)
Diplomats - Akrinar and Vincent
The Belhain Protectors
Perry - Gnome Rogue
Shamil - Gnome Bard
Jax - Human Healer
Leeroy - Human Pally
Jyrine - Elf Ranger
Koralyck - Gütel Wizard

Kingdom of Lamadow

Elven Kingdom
Queen Diadradey and King Robertts. (Elves)

Diplomats - Dawnelda and Nelowyna (Elves)
Kingdom fortune-teller and sorcerer - Ini (elf)

Kingdom of Sibath

Queen Naanci (Human, white hair, blue eyes)
Four Poodles (Aphta, Keola, Sunny and Tara)
Diplomats - Feryn, Jeaniee, Kareyn.
Captain of the Guards - Brennte
Dressmaker in Yark - Gayle
Farmers (Yark) - Hoype and Kevyn
Painters - Glynda and Stephyn Stefflyrs
Rendgren, the Red Phantom
Merchant name, Zalgren Red
True name - Zalgrenzarendaguran
    (Zal-gren-zah-Ren-Da-guur-anne)
(Tall, black hair with red streaks, often pinned up with a crown of
    sorts, red eyes.)
(Inspiration - Tan Tai Jin from Till the End of the Moon)
Disclaimer - Rendgren the Red in this book, is based on the same
    dragon in my Chahaya Durmada series - The Five Swords of
    Power. (Upcoming) I, as the writer, fell in love with the dragon
    and felt he deserved another storyline not tied to Chahaya so this
    tale occurs in another time, place, and realm.
Mindriff mansion's caretaker - Eve
Manor servants - Rich, George, Oz

The Isle of Lochyae

No king, run by a council
Council - Auggie, Keandre, Kittymoo, Treefeared, and Yuui (Elven
    Guardians - Bears)
Diplomats - Jeodina and Vynloren (Dragons)
Faerie realm entrance here
Queen Thistle and King Shamrock (Faeries)

In loving Memory.

Clover - Naomi Frantzen
Miranda Demonitchi - Colleen Joy Mah
Dawnelda - Dawn Bell
Ini - Auntie Ini Mclachlan
Myrlani - David Emigh (Honors)
Herman - Herman Surkis
Naanci - Auntie Nancy Carrol
Cathel Sean - Bruce Schneider
Dunivan - Robert Dunivan
Hallihan - Fletcher Hallihan
Gwynevere - GM always of Honors Light - Loni Rose Jones

Life is short
A dream is long
A look from three
Worlds

About the Author

Randi lives in Victoria, BC. Canada. She is a dog groomer by day and a writer/gamer by night. She loves to read and write fantasy and has been for years, but this is the first time she has dared to get published. She hopes the book draws you away from the modern world and into a land of intrigue and fantasy where magic, dragons and kings roam the lands.

Printed in the USA
CPSIA information can be obtained
at www.ICGtesting.com
JSHW020847291023
50819JS00002B/5

9 781779 411662